Louise Bagshawe was the youngest ever contributor to *The Tablet* at the age of fourteen. Young poet of the year in 1989 and former president of the Oxford University Rock Society, her first job was as Press and Promotions officer at EMI Classics. On her twenty-second birthday she joined Sony Music Entertainment International, working with rock 'n' roll bands. She has written six bestselling novels, published in eight languages, and has adapted her books for major Hollywood film studios. She lives with her husband in New York.

# THE DEVIL YOU KNOW

Rose Fiorello has nothing — except a mane of blue-black hair, she-wolf eyes and a hatred of Rothstein Realty, the ruthless New York property developer that crushed her father's business. When she meets Jake, the sexy, arrogant Rothstein heir, revenge might be within reach . . . Poppy Allen has the perfect LA princess lifestyle, but she craves the excitement of rock 'n' roll. She doesn't want to be the star, she wants to be the star-maker . . . For overweight, under-achieving Daisy Markham, life at her English boarding school is unbearable. She devours glitzy novels, but thinks she'd be better off writing them — if only she can dare to try . . . These three women share more than burning ambition. They share a secret that's going to unite them . . .

Books by Louise Bagshawe
Published by The House of Ulverscroft:

A KEPT WOMAN

LOUISE BAGSHAWE

# THE DEVIL
# YOU KNOW

*Complete and Unabridged*

# CHARNWOOD
*Leicester*

First published in Great Britain in 2003 by
Orion Books, an imprint of
The Orion Publishing Group
London

First Charnwood Edition
published 2004
by arrangement with
Orion Books, an imprint of
The Orion Publishing Group
London

British Library CIP Data

Bagshawe, Louise
    The devil you know.—Large print ed.—
Charnwood library series
    1. Balls (Parties)—Italy—Rome—Fiction
    2. Successful people—Social life and customs
—Fiction 3. Businesswomen—Social life and
customs—Fiction 4. Large type books
    I. Title
    823.9′14 [F]

    ISBN 1–84395–275–0

Published by
F. A. Thorpe (Publishing)
Anstey, Leicestershire

Set by Words & Graphics Ltd.
Anstey, Leicestershire
Printed and bound in Great Britain by
T. J. International Ltd., Padstow, Cornwall

This book is printed on acid-free paper

This book is dedicated to Michael Sissons.

I would like to thank my editors on this book, particularly Kate Mills, who along with Kirsty Fowkes gave me invaluable advice and shaped the finished product from a very different and much worse first draft. My thanks as ever go to the wonderful team at Orion, especially Susan Lamb and Jane Wood, along with Juliet Ewers, Malcolm Edwards and the whole company.

# Prologue

The sun beat down on the hills. Count Cosimo Parigi wiped his brow as he stood looking down on the town of San Stefano in Umbria. The familiar grey stone turrets, left by the Normans, and the red terracotta-tile roofs shimmered in the haze of the baking glare. It was August, and anyone with any sense had left town. The cool water of the azure Mediterranean sea and the light breeze on the lakes to the North called the Italians to their annual *vacanze*. This year, more than ever, most people had left. The war had just ground to a halt and a defeated (or 'liberated', depending on which propaganda you bought) Italy was picking itself up from the dust. It was time to recoup, to snatch at the strands of a normal life.

For most people, that was, but not for him.

Cosimo felt no lethargy, no exhaustion. He was driven, and he had a vision. He looked out at the rolling hills and forests and he wanted to ride through them. Brand new railway tracks that would glitter under the burning sun. An engine for Italy, to bring it out from the ashes of war.

He was a second son, which meant he was an irrelevance. The faded old *palazzo* of the Parigi family, mounted on the crest of a hill overlooking San Stefano, was going to pass to his brother Giuseppe, il Principe Giuseppe Parigi. Giuseppe was the heir, and that was set in stone. He would inherit the farmland that no longer offered riches, the meagre rents of the cottages they owned, the crumbling palace. Cosimo was expected to live in a small house somewhere on the estate, to assist with the farming, and generally to keep his head down.

But he had no interest in being forgotten, like other second and third sons before him. Cosimo wanted more, and he had an idea how to get it.

His parents and brother had not approved when he told them. Here he was, dressed in the overalls of a peasant, working with his hands in the August sun. He was surveying the land, taking samples of the soil, imagining a new, better route for the railway that had been smashed into useless smithereens by the Royal Air Force. When construction of the railway was done, he, Cosimo, would turn to the roads. All across Italy people still travelled by horse, or donkey and cart.

This was unacceptable in 1946. It was a new world, and Italy had to be fit for it. Cosimo was already talking to bankers in the ravaged city of Milano. He was drawing up his plans, he was going to do his part.

His future was as glorious as the landscape before him.

★  ★  ★

Cosimo Parigi had drive and intelligence. He also had a good idea. Railway executives and state bureaucrats called him 'il typhoon' — the hurricane. He blew through meetings, objections, and regulations. By 1950, Parigi Railways had been established, and it was thriving.

His parents died in 1951. They had never approved of what their younger son was doing. Trade! For a Conte di Parigi! It was unthinkable. But their natural laziness, and their desire to enjoy *la dolce vita* in their last years, had kept them silent. The old Prince wanted only to tend to his vines and taste the first pressings from his olive trees. Young people like his son did crazy things, *Madonn'*. But he would grow up and get over it.

Cosimo wept for his mother when she died, and again for his father when, unwilling to endure life without her,

2

he followed her to the family crypt in less than a month. His sorrow was lessened, though, because of his parents' advanced years, because his company was racing ahead, and because he had a new bride on whom to bestow his sudden wealth. Donna Lucia di Parenti was the daughter of another noble family, and marrying her was the one thing Cosimo did that Giuseppe, the new Principe, approved of.

'Congratulations, my dear brother,' he said to Cosimo in the rich, plummy tones he affected when speaking as the head of the family. Archbishop Fanti had just united Cosimo with his new Contessa in the chapel of the Palazzo, beneath the gaze of the busts of his ancestors, and the angels and saints carved in glorious Renaissance marble. Cosimo actually would have preferred another venue, a church in Rome, perhaps even St Peter's — nothing was good enough for his Lucia — but Giuseppe had insisted they be married from the Palazzo, and Cosimo had given way. In a matter like this one, it did not hurt. Family tradition, and all that.

'Thank you, Giuseppe,' Cosimo said. He smiled at Maria, Giuseppe's meek little wife, who was cradling Roberto, the new heir, in her arms. 'The little one is quiet today, it must be a good omen.'

Giuseppe looked at his sleeping son. 'You also will have children.'

'We hope so.'

'And may your first child be a boy,' Giuseppe said solemnly.

'Thank you,' Cosimo acknowledged, trying to suppress the thought that Giuseppe really could sound like a pompous ass sometimes.

'When the honeymoon is over, call upon me at the Palazzo. We have much to discuss,' Giuseppe told his brother.

'I will,' Cosimo promised, although he had no

intention of keeping his word. Parigi Railways was about to become Parigi Transportation. He was taking over a cement-mixing and laying company. New *autostrade* were planned across the peninsula, and Cosimo was going to be a part of it. After the honeymoon, he would be flying to Switzerland for discussions with a consortium of investors . . .

★   ★   ★

Giuseppe sat brooding in the dusty halls of his once-spectacular home. The years rolled by pretty much as they had always done; some years the wine harvest was excellent, and he could repair a roof or two, other years it had blight or drought and he was out firing workers and raising rents. The Parigi estate was, under his stewardship, much as it had been for generations beforehand.

He resented it bitterly.

Cosimo, the little upstart, had founded a firm using *his* family name. He was making billions of lire a year. He had modern cars, an estate, an old, but beautifully restored villa outside of Rome. But was he, Giuseppe, not the elder brother? That money should be *his*.

He spoke of it incessantly to the Principessa.

'What belongs to the House of Parigi belongs to the Principe, *cara*,' Giuseppe told her. And Maria nodded her head and continued to embroider, for that was her hobby, and she had long since got out of the habit of listening to her husband.

But he had an audience. Four-year-old Roberto was playing with his toy wooden train while his father spoke, and the words sunk in. Consequently he grew up loathing his upstart uncle Cosimo. Over and over, his father would lift the boy on to his knee and tell him of his inheritance.

'You are to be Prince of the Parigi,' Giuseppe told his

4

son. 'All this is yours. You must never lose the rights of the family.'

Roberto nodded gravely. He worshipped his father. That is, until that spring day, when he was six years old . . .

*   *   *

'Is the Count prepared?' Giuseppe asked of the nanny. She bobbed a curtsey.

'*Si, Principe.*'

'Very good,' Giuseppe said, regarding his son as she placed him on the back seat of the Bugatti. The little Count Roberto was bundled up against the slight March wind; a true Italian, he was ultra-sensitive to cold. Maria was in the hospital with suspected tuberculosis, and Giuseppe had bills mounting. He did not trust his son to be alone with peasants, and he had decided to take him with him on this vital errand.

Roberto bounced up and down with pleasure as his father slid the car into gear and out of the courtyard of the Palazzo, down the ancient, windy road that led into San Stefano. From there, they would take a new road, one Parigi Enterprises, as the company was now called, had helped build, to their destination.

'Where are we going, Papa?' he asked.

'To see your uncle Cosimo,' Giuseppe said.

'Why, Papa?'

'I have very important business, Roberto. Now you will be a good boy when we arrive, won't you? You will go and play with some toys.'

'I will,' Roberto lied. He had no intention of missing this. His beloved father was about to set Uncle Cosimo straight, and Roberto couldn't wait to hear him do it.

*   *   *

Little Roberto stepped out of the car and regarded his uncle's house as his father took his hand.

'What do you think, Roberto? It is very pretty, no?' Giuseppe asked him. 'Of course, it is not as fine as the Palazzo.'

'No, Papa,' Roberto agreed solemnly, even though he was lying. He was taking in Uncle Cosimo's villa, and he thought he had never seen anything so fine. The building was old, with glorious ochre walls and sprays of climbing roses, white and yellow, but it was not crumbling like their palace; the tiled roof was new and perfect, the drive was gravelled, the stables perfect, like something out of the magazines his mother read. Roberto saw new and better cars in the garage; fountains which were working, not lined with moss; gardens which were professionally tended, lawns which were neatly clipped.

Roberto was a young boy, but he knew instinctively that the villa was worth five times as much as the wreck they lived in. How fine that his father was here to demand their family rights! His father was the elder brother. Roberto examined the house with a covetous eye. He would like to play here. One day, his father said, the whole estate would be his.

'Come along,' his father said, tugging Roberto out of his reverie.

They walked towards the door, which was opened by a butler in uniform, but before he could say anything Cosimo had run out to meet them.

'Giuseppe! *Caro.*' He kissed his brother warmly on both cheeks, hugging him. 'And Roberto. How big you have grown.' Roberto hung close to his father, but Uncle Cosimo bent down and gave him a solemn handshake, which he liked. 'Are you thirsty? Would you like a lemonade? We have Coca-Cola and chocolate biscuits.'

Roberto's mouth watered. They never had American

Coca-Cola at the Palazzo. But already he was starting to feel resentful towards his uncle. He wanted to wait until Uncle Cosimo had given his father his due as head of the family, then he would drink his Coca-Cola.

'No thank you, I am not thirsty.'

'Maybe later, then. But come in, come in.'

Cosimo led them through a wide corridor hung with artwork and lined with antique Roman busts into a large kitchen filled with modern appliances.

'We can talk here, Giuseppe. Roberto, would you like to go and play in the nursery?'

Roberto looked at Papa, who nodded.

'Yes, Uncle Cosimo.'

'I will send for the nurse,' Cosimo said. 'Our Luigi is only two, and he's napping right now, but we have many toys for bigger boys.'

'I do not want the nurse, Uncle Cosimo,' said Roberto. 'I like to play by myself without my nurse.'

Cosimo laughed and ruffled Roberto's hair. 'He's independent, Giuseppe! Very well, she will just show you to the playroom.'

A nanny in a blue pinafore materialised and whisked Roberto away. He saw his uncle Cosimo close the kitchen door behind him.

★　★　★

The nursery was splendid, Roberto thought jealously. His infant cousin Luigi, who was sleeping — good, because Roberto had no interest in seeing him — was lying in a bedroom several rooms away and the nurse told him to play freely, because he would not wake his cousin up.

'Thank you,' Roberto said gravely, 'you may go.'

The nurse stared at him but left without saying anything, closing the door. Roberto wanted to run back down the corridor and listen at the kitchen door, but he decided to wait a few minutes, to be sure the servant woman was not hovering . . .

★  ★  ★

'But, Giuseppe!' Cosimo struggled with his amazement. His brother was stuffy and pompous and stuck in the ways that had kept the Parigi fortune declining for the last two hundred years, but he loved him and did not want to hurt him. Laughing at him would be the absolute worst thing he could do. 'I have made this money, myself, and you and Father did not approve.'

The Prince shrugged. 'We were wrong, and I see that now. But the fact remains, you must cede control of the majority of the company to me, as is only right and proper. I am the — '

★  ★  ★

Outside the door, Roberto smiled fiercely. He pressed his little ear to the keyhole, keeping the other open for the nanny or other intruders. Now his papa was telling Uncle Cosimo!

★  ★  ★

' — head of the family?' Cosimo's patience snapped. '*Madonna!*' He shook his head and crossed himself, regretting the outburst. 'You have a title, dear brother, one I care nothing for and never wanted. The world is changing. I am not a feudal vassal! I owe you nothing, nothing! You amaze me. You do no stroke of work, then arrive and demand . . . demand my estate, the estate of my son? You live in the twentieth century! Are you insane?'

Giuseppe scowled. 'You refuse to do your duty, then?'

'By not finding work, selling off the dead wood,

8

revitalising the Palazzo, perhaps you have failed to do yours.' That hit home, and Cosimo saw the hurt on his big brother's face. He clasped him by the shoulder. 'Ah, come now. We must not fight. You have your way and I have mine. You need money?'

'I need nothing. I am *owed* . . . '

Cosimo cut him off. 'Let us end this now. You have no legal recourse, or you would already be in the courts.'

This was true; they both knew it, and Giuseppe's face clouded with frustration. 'I have a duty to you, of course,' Cosimo went on, 'one of love . . . tell me what you need, and I will provide you with an allowance.'

Giuseppe hesitated, surprised. 'You will?'

'I will. Do you think I would let my brother and nephew want for anything? Let us fix the Palazzo together. But I will draw up the budget,' he added hastily, 'and I will take a look at your books, and send you an allowance for your family.'

Giuseppe struggled now. He wanted that money so badly he could taste it. But his pride was still there.

'I cannot have some stranger look at the fortunes of the Parigi,' he said stiffly.

Cosimo sighed. 'I will do it myself, brother. I am a Parigi too.'

Giuseppe weakened and fell. His brother was disarming him. He had expected blackmail and shame to work; he had not expected this kindness. For all his arrogant hauteur, Giuseppe Parigi was fundamentally lazy. He wanted an independent income, preferably one he controlled . . . but he would take one somebody else controlled if need be. Unexpectedly, a blissful future arose before him; he would live as should an Italian nobleman, and he would not work, and the Palazzo would be heated, restored, warm like this place, with no more rain leaking through the rotting roof beams . . .

'Cosimo.' He moved forward and embraced his

upstart brother. 'You have a good heart, *fratello*. I accept . . .'

★ ★ ★

Roberto was already stumbling down the corridor towards the nursery, tears in his eyes. He brushed them away and gulped down air. His papa had done nothing, had let Uncle Cosimo run all over him. He hated his father, hated Uncle Cosimo . . .

He barrelled into the nursery and saw the nurse there looking for him.

'Did you get lost? Were you looking for the bathroom?'

'No,' Roberto muttered.

She was carrying a tray with a big ice-frosted glass full of black Coca-Cola, with ice cubes chinking enticingly. 'Maybe you are ready for this now, little *Conte?*'

Roberto looked at the Coca-Cola. He could not resist. He took it, but he burned with shame.

'Thank you,' he mumbled.

'You miss Papa, no? But he is coming back soon,' said the nurse.

Roberto turned to the wall so she would not see his red eyes. He drank the Coca-Cola. It was delicious.

'Leave me alone,' he said.

She withdrew, thinking he was a little brat. Roberto cared nothing for her feelings. She was just a servant maid. He wondered what he would say to his papa on the way home. Probably nothing.

Papa! He despised him . . .

★ ★ ★

Luigi never forgot the first time he saw Mozel.

She was running through the market square in

Cortona when Luigi saw her. It was difficult not to. She was clad in green, black and silver, and her full skirts trailed behind her like her black hair. She was also clutching a string of sausages, and she was hurtling towards him, screaming curses at her pursuers.

Luigi laughed and took them in: a fat butcher, waving his knife and bellowing curses of his own, followed by his assistant, a child, equally tubby, crying for his father. *Madonna*, but she was a beauty. Her cheekbones were high and haughty, her hair curly and luxuriant, and she had an incredible figure that the loose gypsy clothing did not completely hide.

Well, of course, Luigi thought, I am a fine upstanding citizen of the Republic and must do my duty. He side-stepped swiftly into the path of the oncoming female who crashed into him, spitting and squealing and trying to get away, but Luigi had her by the arms in his strong grip. He was seventeen, and brawny like his father.

'*Grazie*,' the butcher huffed. 'Thank you, my friend. You have caught the witch. Filthy gypsy witch!' he yelled at her.

The wildcat in Luigi's arms struggled and snarled in Romansh, baring her teeth.

The butcher took a wary step back.

'You hold her, my friend, and I will fetch the police. A night in the cells should cool her off. Thievery,' he said malevolently, 'is a very serious matter. As for you, I will give you a discount on a nice side of lamb. Very good with salt and rosemary.'

Luigi said seriously, 'Come now, you do not wish to have the young woman arrested?'

The butcher's face turned sour. 'You do not see those sausages? The magistrates have had enough of the gypsy filth, stealing everywhere, polluting the town . . . *basta*!'

'These sausages? Fine-looking sausages,' Luigi admitted. He took out his wallet and slowly extracted a

11

hundred-thousand-lire note. 'Does this cover them, do you think?'

The butcher made to snatch the money, greedily, but Luigi held it out of reach. 'And it also covers the entire unfortunate incident, no?'

The man hesitated, hovering between covetousness and loathing. 'Who are you, *Signore*?'

'I am Count Luigi Parigi,' Luigi said.

The butcher blinked in surprise. '*Scusi*, Don Parigi,' he said, taking the money and withdrawing, followed by his now bawling child.

Luigi looked at his prisoner. Up close she was even more sensational. As well as the cheeks and hair there were full red lips, a slender nose, and the most amazing, incredible pale-grey eyes, almost silver, like a wolf's, shaded by long, dark lashes. Mesmerised, he let his grip slacken. She instantly wrenched herself free and strode away from him, in a flounce of skirts and a jangle of her coin necklace.

'Wait,' Luigi barked.

She spun around to face him. 'You want something, *gajo*? A gypsy blessing? For saving me?'

He didn't like her tone.

'Maybe a kiss,' Luigi said.

The woman rolled her eyes. 'The *gaje* think we are all for sale. I am an honest woman.'

Luigi laughed. 'The butcher does not think so, Signorina.'

'That fat fool,' she said contemptuously.

'Tell me your name,' he said.

'I know yours.' The wolf-eyes narrowed. 'Count Luigi Parigi. It rhymes.'

'What were my parents thinking?' he responded, and for the first time she smiled. Her whole face lit up, and Count Luigi, sole son and heir of Count Cosimo Parigi and one of the richest men in Tuscany, fell hopelessly, finally, and without any

12

possibility of reprieve, in love with her.

'My name is Mozel,' she said.

'That's a strange name.'

'Not to my people,' she said confidently. 'It means 'blackcurrant'.'

'You are very beautiful,' Luigi said.

'That's true,' Mozel agreed, tossing her hair and laughing.

'Let me buy you lunch,' he said.

Mozel agreed. Her father would not like it, of course, but her father was not here. And after all, she had gotten away with the sausages.

★   ★   ★

Roberto never forgot the instant he laid eyes on Mozel.

It was the crowning moment of his humiliations. His father had died early, of a heart attack. Roberto's mourning had not been very deep. He had despised his father ever since, as a child, he had heard him crawl to accept Cosimo's handouts. Ever since that day, his father had taken the handouts from the junior branch of the family. The Principe and Principessa had lived quietly, in comfort, with every modern convenience in their restored palazzo, but as far as Roberto was concerned, they had lived as slaves.

He had vowed revenge. But he was cleverer than his father. Roberto was not going to bluster in and challenge his enemies until he was able to defeat them.

He had embraced his weeping uncle Cosimo at the funeral.

'I'm so sorry, caro.' Cosimo hugged him close. 'Nothing can ever replace the loss of your papa.'

'Nothing!' Roberto said, weeping himself. 'But at least I have you, Uncle. I want to come and work at Parigi Enterprises, to be close to the family.'

'My boy,' Cosimo had said, smiling through the tears,

astonished, 'that is wonderful. It will be wonderful to have you close.'

* * *

Close he had become. Roberto, the latest Prince of the Parigi, had set himself to learn anything and everything about the company. Not the business; he was not interested in that. Instead, Roberto noted who the smart managers and consultants were. That was the extent of success, hiring smart people. His interest was in seeing who was paid off, how the bribes worked, who was close to whom, who were the people Cosimo Parigi trusted. Roberto had a grave charm to him that rendered him a favourite in the boardroom. And he took special care to get close to his cousin Luigi.

Roberto believed that risks should only be taken when necessary. His uncle had contracted hepatitis C after an operation for a skiing accident in an unsanitary mountain hospital, and his health was shaky. Luigi was a playboy, a daredevil who enjoyed not merely skiing, but tearing through the winding hills on his *motorino*, hang-gliding like Sean Connery in James Bond — there was even one occasion when he jumped from an aeroplane with a parachute. Cosimo's wife was unable to have any more children . . . well . . . Roberto was the beloved nephew. There would be no need to rock the boat.

But then there was that day in May when everything changed, when Roberto's long-lusted-for inheritance was snatched from under his nose. Luigi came home with tales of a woman, not of a noble Italian family, not even a foreigner of good breeding . . . but a *gypsy*.

The woman was barely a person. Gypsies were lower than the lowest Italian peasant, they were witches and dirty thieves.

Roberto had enjoyed a good laugh.

'Luigi! That's funny.'

His cousin's eyes flashed with that headstrong spark. 'I am not joking, Roberto.'

'Not joking! But you must be. It would be a misalliance . . . your blood . . . '

'My blood is hot,' Luigi grinned, 'that's all that matters, don't you think? It's the Seventies, bro. She's something else, too. Smart . . . sexy . . . just wait until you see her. You'll forget all about that antiquated shit . . . '

Roberto had gritted his teeth, smiled, and said, 'Of course.'

★ ★ ★

When he was introduced to Mozel, he hated her. Hated her wild beauty. Hated her fearless spirit. She called him 'Roberto' at once, never 'Principe', not even the first time.

'I expect you found it hard to adjust?' he'd asked her pointedly, as the family sat by the fire in the drawing room of Cosimo's town house in Rome.

'No, Roberto. My people are used to adjusting,' she said. '*Bi-lacio raklo.*'

He suspected that was an insult in her barbarous tongue from the way her eyes danced.

'Will you wait to have children?'

'No. I want as many as possible,' Mozel purred. 'Luigi must have heirs.'

Her wild white eyes bored into his. Witch, Roberto thought, wretched witch. She made him want to squirm and wash himself. So now, the fortune due to him would be in the hands not just of his juniors, but of half-breed gypsies.

It would not be. He was more than a match for the wild-eyed little tramp his foolish cousin intended to marry.

15

'That sounds wonderful,' Roberto assured her. 'You bring the wedding date forward. That way you can get started right away.'

Luigi gave him a grateful wink. It was good to have his cousin change his mind. Theirs was a tight, close family; he wanted nothing to alter that.

★ ★ ★

The wedding was appalling. Roberto had to stand there in the pews of Santa Maria in Ara Coeli in Rome, the traditional and romantic church at the top of the Campidoglio, watching his cousin, a count of the Parigi, unite himself to gypsy scum. The shame of it almost made him feel faint as he stood there in his morning suit, with a crisp red rose as a boutoniere, and realised he was sharing the pew with members of her dirty unwashed tribe, her family. Contessa Mozel Parigi! It was not to be borne. And Uncle Cosimo actually approved. The man had no honour at all. Maybe my grandmother deceived my grandfather, Roberto thought, taking comfort in the idea. That would mean that Cosimo and Luigi were not Parigis at all.

The gypsy wench wore red. Red! It was their tradition, she had told him, the bride wears red to symbolise her virginity. And so she stood there in the church in a huge silken gown, as open and full and red as the poppies scattered across the Roman forum, carrying a bouquet of ivory roses, and wearing a wreath of them in her long, dark hair.

She was beautiful. She was sexy. He wanted her.

And she knew it, too, the little minx, with her laughing eyes flickering over him as he watched her hungrily when the family were together. She called him names in her strange pidgin language, and muttered to herself when he passed her by. Witch things, Roberto

16

thought. How he hated her, and hated Luigi for tainting the family name and honour.

But Roberto had a remedy. He had made his plans. It only remained to put them into effect.

★　★　★

Cosimo lived long enough to see Mozel full with child, but he died before she gave birth. Luigi was inconsolable, and Roberto managed to put on a decent show of grief for his cousin, now his boss, sole owner of the Parigi fortune. Uncle Cosimo left it all to his son, nothing to speak of to Roberto, the Principe — not even a small minority stake. Instead, his will had contained an emotional letter of love, saying that he had thought of Roberto as another son, and which Roberto had thrown into the fire.

Bullshit. Another son would have been given an inheritance.

Cosimo gave Roberto a trifling amount of money, barely enough to buy a new villa with, and some useless personal items such as paintings. So what? Roberto was not interested in them. He was interested in the Parigi fortune, but once again he had been left to be dependent on the junior branch.

★　★　★

'You must snap out of this,' Roberto said to Luigi one night, as his cousin burst into a fresh round of tears. 'It is not good for you, not what your father would want.'

'He's right, *carissimo*,' Mozel said, stroking her husband's hair. 'Cosimo would not want you to be weeping when the baby comes.'

A flicker of light crossed Luigi's face. He reached out to stroke his wife's swollen belly.

'When will he be born?'

'I told you yesterday. A month.' She laughed. 'You ask me every day! And besides, it is a girl.'

'How do you know?'

'I know. I can feel it,' she said, mysteriously.

'You should not sit in this gloomy room,' Roberto insisted. 'Besides, Rome is so dirty these days. The smoke, the pollution . . . It isn't good for babies. And the *motorini* speeding everywhere, what if they knock Mozel down?'

Luigi looked alarmed and brushed the tears away. 'That's a good point, Roberto.'

'Your child should be born in the country, in the woods.'

Mozel's face lit up. She hated and mistrusted Roberto. She knew exactly what he thought of her. But she was a daughter of the country and the woods.

'He's right, Luigi . . . '

'I have that hunting cabin in Umbria. Near the town of San Clemente, which has a wonderful hospital, very modern. An excellent maternity ward, with doctors from America.' This was true; Roberto knew that would be the first thing they would investigate. It was one of the best hospitals in Italy. 'And the cabin . . . it's actually a lodge. Very luxurious, with three bedrooms, a library, a pool room, and an indoor swimming pool, heated.' He looked at the Contessa. 'Swimming is excellent exercise for the heavily pregnant, dear Mozel; you know what your doctor said.'

She looked down, she truly was as fat as a cow; Mozel longed to move, safely, of course. Roberto knew it. In fact his workmen had only finished with the pool last month.

'If you want my advice, Luigi, you will take three months off. A month with Mozel, to be in the countryside, and finish your mourning, and then a little time with your child once he is born.'

'She,' Mozel said.

'He, she. What does it matter as long as the baby arrives safely, and in good clean air, too?'

They both nodded their agreement. Fools.

'But who will run the company?' Luigi protested. 'We have contracts to fulfil, mergers on the way, acquisitions . . .'

'You're no good to Parigi in this state,' Roberto said reasonably. 'And your first-born will only arrive once. Are you going to miss the first months for *work*?'

'He's absolutely right,' Mozel said.

'I can take care of the Dulon merger. We have very capable men running the company, Luigi. Between us we'll manage for a few months without you.'

Mozel looked at her husband longingly, and Luigi agreed at once. He could never resist any plea from those intense, pale eyes.

★   ★   ★

Roberto was cunning. He knew Mozel was suspicious, and he made sure her fears were allayed. He invited their friends to stay in the lodge, and he remained in Milan while the couple enjoyed the country air, and while Luigi went hunting wild boar, his favourite pastime.

Luigi was intensely grateful, but Roberto brushed his thanks aside.

'It is the least I can do for my dear cousin,' Roberto said. 'After all, we are family.'

Mozel was surprised to find the hospital was just as Roberto had promised. It had American doctors and British nurses, and catered mostly to wealthy foreigners who did not care for Italy's friendly, broken-down state care. Her husband's arrogant cousin had also arranged for specialists to visit her weekly at the lodge, so she could be examined in comfort and privacy. Soon she relaxed, and did not worry when he came to visit, even when he disappeared with Luigi in the woods. Each night they came home again, and her friends came and went, and she felt safe.

The American doctors gave her another cause for joy, too, something that distracted her from her instinctual caution.

She was not about to have one child. She was going to have three.

★ ★ ★

Roberto rejoiced loudly and publicly. He threw a party in company headquarters the day his cousin's babies were born — three girls, ha! Three children and not a boy amongst them. He shut the entire corporation for a day, giving every employee a long weekend. He filled Mozel's bright new hospital room with flowers; he had a magnum of champagne delivered to his brother along with a box of Cuban cigars; and he offered the use of the Palazzo for the christening.

'But when are you coming to see the babies?' Luigi asked him on the end of the phone.

'I must just finish up some business, then I will come to the lodge. I can't wait to hold them,' Roberto said. 'How adorable.'

'They *are* adorable,' said his sappy cousin, voice full of foolish doting pride. 'They are the most beautiful children ever born!'

'I bet they are,' Roberto said. 'And the mother?'

'Mozel is doing wonderfully.'

'I will arrange the christening, Luigi. Let me take care of everything.'

'I can't thank you enough for all you've done for us, I feel like a new man,' Luigi said gratefully.

'Don't be silly,' Roberto said softly. 'I'm family.'

★ ★ ★

Roberto took a few days to return to San Stefano and start some very public preparations for a grand christening. The cake was ordered, balloons and banners were bought, the Archbishop was booked; Roberto showed himself around town, passing out cigars, receiving congratulations, and ordering from as many suppliers as he could. The town took note of the unusual good humour of the Principe di Parigi. As he had intended.

And then, finally, all was ready.

★  ★  ★

When Roberto arrived at the lodge, he was all smiles. Mozel, already back to her normal size three weeks after the birth, greeted him warmly, as if he were truly Luigi's brother. She was wearing a blue dress that picked out the glossy raven hue of her hair, and he thought how delicious she looked, and how much he would enjoy finally having her.

Mozel was wasted on a limp noodle like Luigi, Roberto decided. Of course, he would never have married her, but she would be good to fuck. He imagined all that wild passion squirming underneath him. Before he wiped out the stain of herself and her gypsy brats for good.

Roberto cuddled the babies. They were ugly little pink morsels with blue eyes and scraps of dark fluff on their heads. He felt no compunction at the thought of what he was going to do to them. They would never know a thing. At this age, they were hardly people. Magnanimously, he decided to smother them with a pillow before the flames took them.

'Aren't they amazing,' he cooed, and Mozel leaned over to retrieve them, smiling at him. Her heavy breasts brushed against his forearm in her thin silky blue dress, and Roberto stiffened pleasurably, and

21

thought that she wanted him.

That night, after the happy parents had retired to sleep, Roberto poured the gasoline and accelerant he had kept in an outhouse into all the channels he had dug for them. A pity to waste such a magnificent little holiday villa, yes, but he was insured to the hilt; he could always plan another . . .

★   ★   ★

In the morning, Roberto ensured that he would not be interrupted. He waited for the postman to come, and the maid to leave, tipping her handsomely. Then, accommodatingly, Luigi himself suggested they head into the woods to shoot a few boar, maybe even a stag or two . . .

It was like — what did the Americans say? — taking candy from a baby, Roberto decided, as he stood twelve metres behind Luigi, taking careful aim at his cousin and firing.

Luigi crumpled to the ground in a slither of clothes and flesh. His own gun dropped harmlessly from his hand, and blood gushed from his head as he collapsed on the forest floor, branches and twigs cracking under the weight of his body.

Roberto walked off, not even looking back. This forest was full of animals, wild boar in particular, which would take care of his cousin's remains. He had hunted in it many times by himself, and many times with Luigi; the Count never suspected for an instant that Roberto was a danger. When death came, Roberto told himself smugly as he headed back to the house, Luigi had not known a thing. He was now in heaven. Or hell. Roberto didn't care much either way.

His crotch hardened as he emerged from the thick, green dark of the forest and walked into the house. What would Mozel feel, that treacherous gypsy slut, whose sex had stolen his cousin's wits and let all the world see a Parigi united with a gypsy woman? She would be afraid, and he was looking forward to that. But would she be wet and hot when she was taken by a real man? Despite herself? That tramp . . . of course she would . . . she would love it . . .

Roberto's anger and hatred mixed with his lust. He strode past the patio, through the open doors of the living room. He was hard as a diamond now. Through into the kitchen, and then to the family room, where Mozel would be sitting with her brats . . .

There she was. She had a child at the breast. The sight of them, usually large but now even more swollen with milk, turned him on so much it hurt. For a second, Roberto just stood over her, staring, his shotgun in his hand.

She knew immediately.

Of course, he thought triumphantly; she is a witch, after all.

Mozel said nothing but snatched at the phone and started to dial for help.

'There is no tone,' Roberto said. 'The line has been cut.'

'Why?' she screamed. 'Why?'

He shrugged and moved towards her. 'I am a prince of the Parigi, *befana* slut. Put the child down.'

'No!' she shrieked, and started to run. But Roberto raised his shotgun and pointed it at the other babies.

'Unless you want me to blow their brains out, you will do exactly as I say.'

She stopped dead. 'Yes,' she said numbly. 'Yes. Yes.' She laid her baby gently down on the couch, where it started to squall with fury, because its lunch had been interrupted. Roberto found the sound annoying.

'Walk into the bedroom,' he said, 'and strip your clothes off, slut.'

Mozel obeyed him, trembling, and went into the

23

bedroom. She would fight. Maybe she could get away. Her mind was thinking only of one thing, to save her children, Luigi's children. She would mourn him later . . .

Roberto stood before her, shotgun pointed at her breasts. She was a slight, skinny little thing; he had ninety pounds on her. He was lean and muscled, his body reflecting the discipline of his life.

'Slowly,' he said, enjoying himself. She obeyed him. She slowly removed her clothing, letting the dress slither to the floor, her tits already out of the bra, they were magnificent, the tiny white silk panties peeled off and she was absolutely nude. Roberto, his hard-on full to bursting, shoved her roughly back on to the bed, tugged his pants half-down, and mounted her.

Mozel shrieked and tried to struggle, but he had her fast. Roberto raped her savagely, thrusting deep. She scratched at his face and tore it with her nails, so he slapped her, hard, on the head.

That was a mistake. He was stronger than her, and she blacked out, which stopped her struggling, and shrieking, and now he was fucking a limp body. No fun. He cursed and shook her awake.

'My children,' she groaned, 'spare my babies!'

'Of course I'm not going to,' Roberto said, grinning and thrusting. 'Let some gypsy take what is mine, inherit what is mine? You and your filthy line die tonight, witch.'

She looked up at him, with those grey wolf eyes. She stopped struggling, and started to move with his rhythm. Roberto was shocked, then he smirked. She *was* enjoying it. He knew she would. She could not resist . . .

And then, looking directly into his eyes, Mozel loudly and clearly pronounced a curse on him, a curse that seemed to go on and on, speaking the words in her barbaric language, until he wanted to throttle her.

Roberto felt his belly crisp with fear. Inside the witch, his hard-on shrivelled and died. He felt himself become limp and small, and slip out of her. Enraged and red-faced, he lifted his hand to strike her again, to beat all the life out of her . . .

'Wait!'

Her voice was strangely calm. Despite himself, Roberto Parigi hesitated.

'You can break the curse,' Mozel said calmly, 'if you spare my infants, Roberto. Then it will not come upon you.'

He hesitated. The spell . . . the spell . . . he did not like it.

'It is impossible,' he said, reaching for her throat.

Mozel spoke fast, the words tumbling out of her. 'No! Not impossible. Give them to churches, leave them on doorsteps, who will know? Separate them. Nobody will know, they are Italian girls . . . '

'They have your eyes, witch,' he snarled. 'All would know them!'

'Their eyes are blue,' she pleaded, 'blue!'

Roberto felt his limpness flop against his clothes. His rage and frustration burst, and he screamed 'Silence!' and moved forwards, choking her until she stopped breathing and lay dead and quiet on the bed, unable to torment him with more of her words and spells.

He sat there for a few minutes, panting. Now both Luigi and Mozel were dead. Calm, calm, Roberto, he told himself. Relax . . . don't let the slut get to you.

But she had, he knew she had.

When he said 'witch' Roberto Parigi believed it. Modern times did not mean modern attitudes, not in this land of long memories, where superstition was a way of life. The look in the gypsy slut's eyes as she spoke that curse . . .

Dimly, he heard the sound of crying from the other room. He stumbled back in there, zipping himself up.

There were the two in their cots and the third on the couch.

Curiously, Roberto gazed into the small eyes of the squalling one. Yes, the slut had spoken the truth. They looked like ordinary Italian brats, with dark hair, blue eyes, olive skins . . .

He picked up a cushion from the couch and stood over the screaming one. But then he hesitated.

Fuck it, Roberto thought. Nobody will ever know, and I will break my curse . . .

He scooped the three children up and carried them out to his Rolls-Royce, laying them in the back seat.

Then he walked back to the start of the first trough he had laid and filled with gasoline, struck a match, then tossed it in.

Within a few seconds the entire building was ablaze. Channels of fuel were laid all through the house, and it was a wooden structure. Within an hour, nothing would be left but that brand new pool.

Prince Roberto Parigi turned the key in his ignition and started to drive up the winding road that led into the hills, with the three little contessas screaming annoyingly in the back of his car.

*   *   *

Roberto thought he had arranged things perfectly. He had cultivated some connections in the Cosa Nostra, low-level men with no morals and a fierce love of money. He had also made sure he kept his own band of thugs on the Parigi payroll; 'security', of course, but not for the company, for himself.

His connections already had a racket going in the sale of children. Infants were highly sought after in Europe and America, and parents were prepared to pay for them. Roberto was cautious; he instructed that each child should go to a different orphanage, and that no fee

26

should be charged to adopt them. He didn't want anything getting in the way, he wanted the gypsy brats dispersed around the globe, far from each other, and far from himself.

It was done smoothly and with a minimum of fuss. A place was found in England for one girl, and, in America, Brooklyn for a second and LA for a third. Fly-by-night operations that charged heavy 'expenses' for the most part, washed a little money, and closed down when the Feds came looking.

The Prince expected reports on who chose the brats, and he got them. He was expecting there to be a delay; they were only females, after all, and who would want one of those, given a choice? But the girls went fast, and pleasingly so, to the kinds of families he had hand-selected; boring, ordinary people with enough to raise a child, who were neither especially poor nor exceptionally rich. An Italian worker from New York, a middle-class English couple, and a lawyer from Los Angeles.

After that, he forgot about his tiny cousins. They were gone from the picture, removed from being a threat, from taking the inheritance that was so rightfully his.

And he had done right by them, he thought self-righteously. They were alive, which was more than the children of a witch deserved to be.

Prince Roberto Parigi busied himself with a very public funeral, mourning the tragic loss of the new family he had been so close to. He had a service in the Cathedral in San Stefano, and the Archbishop remarked in his sermon how he had been looking forward to performing a baptism, and instead here he was, presiding over a funeral . . .

Roberto, last of the Parigis, wept bitterly, and was inconsolable. He mourned all that year, never removing his black suit, and refusing to dine out. He even wept as his cousin Luigi's will was read, making him the default heir of the entire Parigi fortune: the houses, the apartments, the villas, the cars, the private jet, and, of course, all the stock of Parigi Enterprises.

His first act as Chief Executive was to rename the company. It was now to be known as Venda Incorporated. He did not wish the ancient name of Parigi to be tainted with trade. Roberto was happy to take charge of all the money, but he regarded the means of obtaining it as beneath him. Murder was acceptable; working for a living was not.

People wondered about the name. 'I just like the way it sounds,' Roberto told them.

In fact, it stood for vendetta. His private joke.

Roberto moved back to the Palazzo after installing some very competent men to run his business affairs. He poached the brightest talent from America, even some executives from Japan, where an incredible revolution was taking place in business. Venda was known for paying huge salaries and bonuses; Roberto knew that the *Capos* made the organisation.

His judgement was sound. He grew richer and more powerful as the years rolled by, and he did not have to lift a finger for it. As a prince, his job was to be social, to attend the masked balls of Venice, to play in the casinos of Monte Carlo, to restore the glamour and lustre of the House of Parigi that his uncle and cousin had tarnished.

The gypsy brats were no longer a danger, and they faded from his mind.

# 1

'Are you hungry?'

Rose Fiorello smoothed down the pleats of her skirt and glanced over at her mom. Mrs Fiorello was standing there with that worried look on her face, the one that used only to be there when Rose left to walk to school, and now was there almost every night. 'You have to be. Look at you, you're so skinny, it's dreadful.'

'I'm not skinny, Mom.' She really wasn't hungry, but anything to make her mother feel better. 'But I could eat, I guess.'

'Good. We need to use up these cold cuts,' Daniella Fiorello replied, turning back to their tiny kitchen countertop. 'I'll make you a nice sandwich.'

'Sounds great.'

Rose eased her heavy, threadbare knapsack off her back and perched her slender frame on one of the whitewashed chairs in the cramped room. There was never any space in their Hell's Kitchen apartment, but as her father kept reminding her, it *was* Manhattan. Plus, it was rent-controlled. Even if the area wasn't of the best, there were plenty of people who would kill for this space. You only got into trouble around here if you looked lost or frightened. And Rose never did. Even when she was dressed in the cute little uniform of Our Lady of Angels — navy pleated skirt that hovered just above the knee, white socks and shirt, which most of the girls wore unbuttoned to try to look like Madonna — nobody wanted to mess with Rose. She was fifteen, tough, and pissed off. And she was beautiful.

The Fiorellos had always gotten by, up until now. But it had been at a cost. Surviving was expensive, and it meant somebody had to go without. That somebody was usually Rose, and she didn't mind that, at least not much. Sometimes she wanted stuff: new Nike sneakers, a VCR, Whitney Houston CDs, movie tickets; it was hard not to, right now, in the booming Eighties, when the Wall Street flyboys paid three hundred dollars a month just to park their Corvette convertibles, and it seemed that everybody else was getting rich. Rose told herself she was content to bide her time. She was doing great at school, even if she hated it. School was a necessary evil. She would ace her SATs, get a scholarship to Columbia or NYU, and get a high-paying job as a lawyer or an investment banker. Then she would be able to move her parents out of their shitty little apartment, and buy all the cool make-up and CDs she wanted.

Rose spent so much time being mad, she didn't really understand just how gorgeous she was. She was coltish, with long legs, dark glossy hair which looked like it came out of a comic book — so black it was almost blue — an oval-shaped face, and full, sensual lips with a natural pout. She was five feet seven, she weighed one twenty, had a cinched-in waist, firm, full breasts, and had just bought her first C-cup bra. Her nose was aquiline and arrogant, her skin was a rich olive, and her eyes — her incredible eyes — were a startling ultra-pale blue, almost white, even wolfish.

Her parents didn't have those eyes, but no wonder; Rose was adopted.

Men cat-called when she passed in the street, but usually didn't accost her. They didn't dare. That stride of hers was pure Bronx, pure menace. Rose Fiorello was permanently mad: at her mom's disease, at her father's long hours, at their filthy streets, at the Mayor, at her birth mom, at the world.

But today she had a focus. And the hatred she felt burned as strongly as the first love felt by most other girls her age.

Rose tossed her head, sending a waterfall of sleek, raven-black hair flying through the air.

'Sounds good.' She tried to temper her tone. 'More cold cuts from the deli? Did they turn off the power again?'

Daniella nodded sadly. 'Your dad's called ConEd already. But it's another day's worth of stuff ruined.'

'I could eat Dad's stuff all day long,' Rose said loyally. They both knew she already did. Today would just be one more day of it, before the choice Italian meats and cheeses and fish turned bad and had to be thrown out. Before her father lost even more money.

Paul Fiorello was fifty, and had run Paul's Famous Deli for twenty-five years. Despite the optimistic name, the Deli wasn't famous: it was in the wrong neighbourhood and too small ever to attract the new foodie crowd that would pay twenty dollars for a thin bottle of organic olive oil. But it was good, and the food was fresh and the tastiest for ten square blocks. Her father had a regular clientele, and he'd kept his head above water all these years. The Deli paid for the medications for Mom's arthritis, and Rose's Catholic school. It was cheap, but it wasn't free. Plus, there were costs; the uniform, for one thing. The Deli took care of all that, plus their rent.

Up until last month.

Manhattan property prices were going through the roof. Even the worst areas which they said would never gentrify were already being bought up; the East Village and Hell's Kitchen to name but two. Some people said Alphabet City and even Harlem would be next. Whatever. Rose didn't give a damn about the demographics.

She cared about Paul's Famous Deli.

They were located in a big building, a tall, decrepit old skyscraper on Ninth Avenue and Fiftieth. Next to them were a pizza joint and a fabric merchant which sold buttons and sequins and lengths of dingy netting; above them were offices. But somebody had sold the entire building to Rothstein Realty.

Rothstein were a big, giant, mega-bucks real estate company. They bought and sold in the tens of millions of dollars. They had plans for the building, and those plans did not include the local salami merchant.

Already Paul's neighbours had taken the hand-out offered by Rothstein and given up their rent-controlled leases. But Paul Fiorello had refused. What would he do with a lousy fifty thousand bucks? He knew nothing but the Deli, and where would he find another cheap lease? If the store moved more than five blocks away, it would lose all the regulars, and it would be competing with the smarter, bigger, cheaper delis, the ones with rows of shiny waxed fruit racked up on stands outside the store. Fifty Gs would only last them for one year. And then it would be welfare time.

'You don't have to move, Dad.'

Rose recalled talking fiercely to her dad about it as he sat in the kitchen, reading the latest letter from Rothstein. It was full of veiled menace. Nothing they could sue over, but which could be read between the lines.

'They can't force you out. You got ten more years on that lease.'

'They can do stuff, baby.'

'What, send the heavies round?' Rose glared fiercely at her father's slumping shoulders and greying hair. 'If they try any of that shit I'll go to the police. *And* the press.'

'Don't use language like that in this house,' Paul Fiorello growled.

'Sorry.' She rubbed her father's aching shoulders.

'It's not about leg-breakers. All they need to do is mess with the water, the electrics . . . '

'You pay for that, how can they shut it off?'

'Accidents. Interruptions. There are ways. Not to mention the construction noise next door. They've already started to gut the other two stores, and they start drilling the floors during lunchtime . . . crowd's thinner already.'

'They can't do that to you.'

'They can and they will, kid.' Paul sighed. 'Only question is, can I ride them out? If I could persuade Mr Rothstein that he could, you know, build around me. Maybe his fancy lawyers and architects would need a good sandwich at lunchtime? I could write him a letter.'

He looked hopefully at his daughter, the straight-A student, the one who wrote all the letters in this house.

'Sure, Dad. I'll give it a try,' Rose had said.

They had crafted the letter together and sent it off. It was a masterpiece. Firm, but amiable, respectful, and accommodating. Rose walked it down to the mail herself and sent it return-receipt.

The receipt came back. Nothing else did.

That had been two weeks ago.

Today she was going to eat more spoiled cold cuts. More stuff that would have to be thrown out when they couldn't get through it, which was exactly like tossing a handful of twenties into the fire. Rose was sick to death of cold cuts, but the whole family ate them like champs, for breakfast, lunch and dinner.

'When is Dad coming home?' she asked, as Daniella sliced the foccacia and put ham and chicken and ricotta on it.

'He's gonna be late. He has to try and get access to the mains, get the police to make him turn the electric back on. Otherwise it's two days' worth of food chucked right out.' Daniella swallowed hard, and Rose saw the tears glittering in her mother's eyes, tears she would not let herself shed in front of her baby.

God, how she hated Rothstein Realty.

How she hated them!

33

# 2

Poppy Allen sat in her room and stared longingly at her posters.

Uhh. John Bon Jovi. Joe Elliott. Def Leppard were just so *hot*. And Metallica, too. Lars was a real cutie. She liked the hard stuff and the soft stuff about the same; all her favourite bands featured gorgeous guys with long hair, black leather, studs, and plenty of rebel attitude . . . in short, the kind of babes her mom and dad would *never* let her date.

But Poppy had ways around that.

There was a knock on her door.

'Come in,' Poppy said.

Her mom, Marcia Allen, appeared in the doorway, bedecked for another gala night on the town. Poppy's parents, Jerry and Marcia, were social butterflies, which was good because so was Poppy. Unbeknownst to them.

Marcia was a lawyer's wife, a rich lawyer's wife, and didn't she look the part, in a shoulder-padded red suit from Karl Lagerfeld and a string of pearls as big as marbles.

'You look great, Mom,' Poppy lied dutifully. 'What is it tonight?'

'Opera. *Rigoletto*.'

'You hate opera.'

'I know, but the Goldfarbs had some extra tickets.' Marcia shrugged. 'Daddy says it should be a fun night out.'

'How late will you be back?'

'Late,' Marcia said reassuringly, and Poppy pouted to show she was disappointed. 'Don't worry, we've set the burglar alarm. I don't want any TV after eleven.'

'No ma'am,' Poppy said. 'I've done all my homework

34

for tonight. I was actually wondering if I could go out for a little while.'

Marcia frowned. 'While we're not here?'

She had to be careful of her little Poppy. The girl was blooming before her parents' eyes — she had dyed blonde hair, she was slim, with natural curves which meant there was no need for that sweet-sixteenth trip to the plastic surgeon all her friends were buying their daughters. And then, of course, there was that stunning face and those wild, wolf-like eyes. Poppy certainly hadn't got her looks from Jerry or Marcia, people said, and Marcia smiled brightly and told them maybe it was her grandma. Of whom, conveniently, she didn't have any pictures.

Poppy was adopted, and Marcia and Jerry saw no reason to tell her so, nor to tell anybody else. Marcia was very keen her little girl should marry a nice Jewish boy, and she was sure *his* mother would have the same standards, so why rock the boat?

The trouble with her sexy teenager was that all men were attracted to her. That was Marcia's concern.

'Well, it's with someone you know. Brian Pascal was gonna take me out for a burger and fries. But not if it's not OK,' Poppy said sweetly.

Her mother crumpled. 'Brian's a good boy . . .'

Poppy just waited her out. Mom was *always* trying to throw her together with Brian Pascal. His parents were a dentist and an orthodontist, they had tons of money, and his sister was in Hollywood, which was what Marcia wanted for Poppy. She was always on at her to take acting lessons.

Poppy had no intention of being a soap-opera star or whatever. *As the World Turns* was not her destiny.

No way. She was going into heavy metal.

'I thought I'd wear this, if you say I can go, Mom,' Poppy said, jumping off her bed and running

35

to her closet. She showed her mother a frilly blue number with a long skirt and puffy sleeves that made her look about twelve. Her mom loved it, and Poppy never wore it. 'I just know he'll flip when he sees me in this.'

'Well . . . OK.' Marcia gave in. 'As long as you're back by ten.'

'Cross my heart,' Poppy lied brightly. 'I guess I'd better get changed now, huh?'

'Is Brian coming over to pick you up?' demanded Marcia, suddenly suspicious.

'Oh yeah,' Poppy said. Damn. 'I just have to call him and let him know you said it's OK.'

Jerry Allen's head appeared with his wife's. 'What's going on?'

'Poppy wants to go out with Brian.'

'As long as you're back by nine,' Jerry said, disappearing.

Poppy pouted. 'Mom — '

'Ten,' her mother hissed, 'but don't tell Daddy.'

She waited in the doorway. 'Aren't you going to call Brian? I want to speak to him.'

Poppy's heart went into her mouth. She dialled her friend's number. Brian was never going to be interested in Poppy, blue horror of a dress or not. He was strictly a player for the other team, but neither set of parents knew that, and she and Brian covered for each other on occasion. Poppy mentally crossed all her fingers and toes and hoped Brian would get it, this time. Dark Angel, the hottest band on the Strip, were playing tonight and no way did she want to miss them.

'Hi, Mrs Pascal, can I speak to Brian? It's Poppy Allen. Hey, baby,' she added after a pause, 'my mom said you can pick me up tonight whenever.'

'Dark Angel?' Brian asked.

'You got it,' said Poppy brightly, 'and Mom wants to speak to you . . . '

'I was going to have a quiet night in. I don't feel like driving.'

'Thanks,' Poppy said, injecting an urgent note of pleading into her voice. 'Here's Mom, OK?'

She passed the receiver to her mother. 'Brian? Now you'll get my little Poppy back by ten? Yes, I'm sorry I'm not going to be here too, but I think we're leaving now. Yes, I know I can trust you with my little angel . . . '

Poppy winced. She loved her mom, but Marcia had obviously had a cool by-pass at birth.

Marcia hung up, satisfied.

'Be a good girl, Poppy,' she admonished. Poppy smiled her patented non-threatening Shirley Temple smile and agreed that she would be.

Which was another lie. But at this stage, who was counting?

★   ★   ★

Poppy covered her tracks professionally. She actually got changed into the blue horror and came downstairs to hang out with her parents until they left. The second their Ferrari pulled out past the wrought-iron gates that hissed back electronically, she raced upstairs, pulled it off, undid her long, dyed-blonde hair from its neat little-girl braids, and slipped into a black miniskirt, a low-cut top, and high-heeled boots.

Mmh! She looked just about good enough to eat right now.

Brian called to tell her he couldn't make it. Never mind; she had her own ride. He'd served his purpose. Poppy slipped downstairs and unhooked the keys to her mother's Porsche 911 from their spot above the sub-zero refrigerator. Their housekeeper, Conchita, lived in Daddy's guesthouse in the Hollywood Hills. She could park there and then walk down to Sunset.

Poppy caught a glimpse of her lithe, sexy reflection in the full-length mirrors by the door and blew it a kiss. The poor little rich girl who had to play nice was about to be let loose on LA. She just hoped they were ready for her!

# 3

'Daisy!'

Daisy stopped staring out of the window and jumped out of her skin. Her plump cheeks bore a red imprint from where her fingers had been pressed against them. The Surrey countryside was so gorgeous, all rolling hills dotted with woods and grazing cows and fat white sheep. Like something out of one of her favourite Jilly Cooper novels.

Her heart sank.

'Yes, Miss Crawford?'

'Can you give us the benefit of *your* opinion on this matter?'

Miss Crawford was staring at Daisy as though she was something unpleasant she had just scraped off the bottom of one of her stout brown brogues. Daisy heard Victoria Campbell snigger.

'Um, about this?' Daisy temporised desperately.

Miss Crawford's mono-brow rose.

'Yes, about this. *The Merchant's Tale*. One of the most gripping, funny stories in the entire cycle, which some critics take to be a proto-feminist piece only slightly less important than *The Wife of Bath's Tale*. Perhaps you feel you have nothing in common with Chaucer, Miss Markham?'

Daisy glanced down at her page. 'The slakke skin about his nekke shaketh . . . '

'He spells like me,' she joked feebly.

'Very funny. But with your *stellar* academic record, you can afford to ignore our lessons, can't you?'

Daisy flushed at the sarcasm. She hated Miss Crawford and Victoria and most of the bloody girls here. Just because she didn't do very well at school. It

39

wasn't as if she didn't already know she was thick.

Tears prickled in the back of her throat, and Daisy forced herself to see a mental picture of Mummy opening her last report, which was full of Cs and Ds, and saying it didn't matter a bit, because Daisy had tried her best.

'Miss Markham. This is one of your only O level classes. Maybe you should have been streamed in the CSE class after all.'

'No I shouldn't,' Daisy said.

Where did that come from? She was terrified of Miss Crawford. But it had popped out, defiant, mutinous.

'And why not?'

'Because I'm good at writing and I like books,' Daisy stammered.

'Good at writing!' The scorn dripped from her teacher's narrow, red-painted mouth. 'You're no Chaucer. That's a detention tonight and one demerit to Sackville House.'

Victoria was a Sackville prefect. She stopped giggling and scowled at Daisy.

'I could ask you to read the next ten lines, Daisy, but why put the class through it?' Miss Crawford sighed theatrically. 'Miss Garnett, can you continue?'

'Yes, Miss Crawford.'

Arabella Garnett tossed her sleek mane of auburn hair over her slender shoulders and began to read, pronouncing each word perfectly.

Daisy sat there mercifully dry-eyed. She had been going to cry, but luckily Miss Crawford and Victoria had been their usual hateful selves, and that gave her the resolve to keep the tears back. They could wait until she got upstairs at break.

There were a couple of good things you could say about St Mary's, Withambury. It was nestled in a picture-perfect setting in the Surrey countryside, and Daisy liked going for walks outside the school grounds.

Now she was a fourth year, she was allowed to. She also liked the fact that finally she had got her own miniature cubicle. It had space for a bed, a sink with a mirror, and a cork board for sticking pictures up on. Sharing a room with Isobel Soames hadn't been *that* bad, because Isobel was quite nice, not a bully like those prefect bitches and the snobby girls in the Oxbridge Preparation set who thought you should curtsy to them just because they were clever. But still, she hadn't enjoyed it. Isobel was pretty, very pretty — honey-blonde hair, pale green eyes, small perky breasts, and a cute dusting of freckles.

And Daisy wasn't.

It was tough, getting changed in front of Isobel. Daisy used to keep a towel around her ample thighs and try to struggle into her cream school shirt as quickly as possible, so her dimpled bottom and podgy upper arms were hidden. And it was worse because her friend tried to be so nice about it.

'You've got such a pretty face, Daisy.' She'd be almost pleading. 'If you just lost a bit of weight.'

'I know,' Daisy would say, and then she would change the subject.

Like she hadn't tried. Daisy longed to be slim and beautiful and toss her long, gleaming hair over her shoulders in what the girls all called 'The St Mary's Flick'. But she had her hair cut in a bob, because long hair made her face look even fatter, and when she tried to stop eating, she just couldn't. Her diets were secret; Victoria and Mercedes and Camilla would all be so mean if they found out. Daisy tried eating fruit and skipping pudding and sometimes she even lasted a week. But she got so hungry she could cry, and then one day it would be fresh-baked chocolate chip cookies for tea, and she'd crack — and a week later, she'd weigh more than she'd started out at.

Nothing worked. Diets only made her fatter. PE

lessons were a nightmare; she couldn't run, she couldn't shoot netball — she could hit a rounders ball, but she couldn't get to the bag in time. Besides, the bitchier girls always used to give her wobbly bottom and chunky thighs contemptuous glances which made Daisy feel about three inches high. Next year things would be even worse. Fifth form girls got to take PE lessons in the health club at the local town. This was meant to be a big treat; for Daisy, it simply meant random townies would get a good look at her cellulite and her embarrassingly large boobs that barely fitted into a D-cup.

Daisy had given up on her body. She ate what she liked, and she ate for comfort. When she failed her mock CSE in maths, she ate a whole bag of fun-sized Marathons. (Why did they call miniscule, unsatisfying morsels fun-sized? Fun-sized was a full bar with 20 per cent extra free.) Getting her own cubicle had been an immense relief. She sat next to Isobel at lunchtimes, but mostly she kept to herself. After all, on her own, she could do her favourite thing short of driving out of St Mary's gates at the end of term: reading.

Daisy loved books. Not Chaucer and Dickens and Evelyn Waugh, or whatever other boring set text they had to do in O level English; she loved Jeffrey Archer and Judith Krantz, Jilly Cooper and Shirley Conran. Her copy of *Lace* was falling apart at the seams. In her books, the women were all slender and beautiful, the men were dashing rakes, or determined power-players. Daisy was scared of flying, but with her trashy novels she could move seamlessly from the sun-drenched French Riviera to the snowy romance of the Russian Steppes. She yearned to be ravished by Rupert Campbell-Black, to work her way up to a vast empire like Abel Rosnovski; she wanted to be beautiful-yet-feisty like Maxime and Pagan, to shop at Scruples, and generally to be anything other than Daisy Markham at St Mary's, Withambury.

Daisy had the best collection of trashy novels in school, and gradually her classmates wised up to it. Soon after she'd set them all out on the shelves in her little cubicle, Lucy Gresham had sauntered in.

'Hey, Daisy.'

'Hey, Lucy,' Daisy said, pretending she hadn't heard Lucy hiss 'fat cow' under her breath when she'd sneaked an extra cream cake at tea that day.

Lucy stood there, doing The Flick with her long, expensively highlighted blonde hair. Everyone knew Lucy went to London on the train every exeat weekend and had her hair done at Vidal Sassoon. Her parents were very rich. Daisy's parents were struggling to keep up their middle-class lifestyle, even though she was an only child, and she was at St Mary's on a bursary, because her mother had been Head Girl there thirty years ago.

'I see you've got the new Jilly Cooper,' Lucy said casually.

'Haven't you?'

'Mummy doesn't want to have it in the house, because it's got s — e — x in it,' Lucy admitted.

Daisy paused. 'Would you like to borrow it?'

Lucy obviously would. 'Have you finished it?'

'The day I bought it, of course,' Daisy said sternly. As though you could put down a Jilly Cooper! She had strained her eyes finishing it under the bedclothes with a torch, but it had been worth it. 'Here.' She picked up the thick white paperback with its embossed gold letters and passed it over.

'Thanks, Daisy,' Lucy said, sweeping out.

Soon she was acting as a mini-library. The girls considered Daisy an expert and asked her opinion on which one to borrow next. There was a queue, so nobody returned the books late. Apart from Victoria and Arabella, most of the fourth form stopped teasing Daisy.

They still didn't like her much, she could tell, but it was bad manners to pick on someone you owed a favour to.

Victoria got mad and bought more than one copy of every new trashy novel worth reading, but her ploy backfired. Daisy was established as the pulp fiction queen. The girls liked gathering in her cubicle, talking to each other about the books they'd just read.

'You know,' Emma Wilkins told her one day, 'you should write one of these, Daisy.'

Daisy flicked through *Kane and Abel*. 'Don't be daft, it'd take me ten years.'

'I bet it wouldn't.' Lucy agreed with Emma. 'You know all about this stuff. You should write one. You could let us read the chapters.'

'You'd be great at that,' Emma said. 'You could put me in it.'

Daisy smiled, her fat face dimpling. This was the first compliment anyone had ever paid her at school. She'd love to be a writer. Maybe she should try it.

# 4

Rose stopped in front of the windows of Saks Fifth Avenue. The display was opulent; quietly expensive suits and summer dresses by the top designers of the day, with matching shoes, and handbags that started at a thousand dollars. But she wasn't checking out the merchandise; it was a little out of her price range.

She was staring at her own reflection.

She looked beautiful. Rose wasn't a particularly boastful girl, but facts were facts. She knew that the long, coltish legs, the aristocratic cheekbones, the dusky skin with the ice-blue eyes set under arching, elegantly shaped brows were lovely. How could she not know it? The boys stared on the street. Grown men whistled and cat-called, as though she would somehow find it endearing. And she wouldn't even be of legal age for another year. Not that that bothered them.

Rose looked good in anything. A white T-shirt and faded pair of blue jeans merely showed off her figure and contrasted with her skin. Her sheeny dark hair looked dramatic against anything, even the cheap K-Mart dresses that were all her mom could afford.

Today she needed to look a little more than beautiful. Today she needed to look adult.

She had picked the suit out of a thrift store and got it dry-cleaned. It was navy and nondescript, too slim to sell in the store, and the skirt sat on her knee, modestly. It had everything Rose fondly imagined a modern power suit should have: shoulder pads, gold buttons, the whole lot. She had put her hair up in a severe bun, and got a girlfriend to do her make-up — red mouth and nails, two coats of mascara, and blusher. She'd skipped the foundation, because she could never find a good match for her skin tone, and drawn the line at the blue eyeshadow Elise Carboni wanted to slap on her. But she thought she looked older, at any rate.

Maybe twenty-five? Rose took in her reflection. OK, that was being a bit optimistic. But she could carry herself as though she were twenty, at least. A college girl.

She turned from the window and marched a little further down the street, psyching herself up. Elise thought she was crazy to try a stunt like this, but Elise didn't know the half of it.

I'm not crazy, Rose thought, I'm desperate.

There was nothing else she *could* do. Last night had been the final straw. Rose had lain there in her tiny cupboard of a bedroom, pretending to be asleep, listening to her father sobbing his heart out in the kitchen next door. His business was as good as ruined. Even his best customers were going elsewhere now. The food was spoiled, their vegetables weren't fresh, and the construction noise was deafening. Only in the mornings, lunchtime, and at 5 p.m., of course — Rothstein timed the decibels to the peak traffic times.

The cops ignored Paul's complaints, or issued half-hearted warnings. They had all but asked for a bribe, but he had nothing to bribe them with. No way could he compete with Rothstein Realty on that front.

Or, indeed, on any front.

Her father hadn't wanted to take the money. No selling out for him. He was too proud.

Yesterday, when he got back from work, there was a letter. Gold-embossed, thick, costly paper, the hated insignia of Rothstein Realty on the front cover.

Rose had wanted to open it immediately, but her mother told her to wait till her father got home.

'It's his mail, after all,' she said flatly.

Rose did her homework in front of the letter, unable

to concentrate. It sat there, staring at her, taunting her. She had butterflies in her stomach. Finally, Rothstein had responded to her letter.

She'd known it would have results, eventually. Rose was a realist. She didn't hold out much hope that they were going to go away, she just hoped that they would let her father keep his place. But maybe they were going to up the money. In exchange for his livelihood, a hundred grand would barely last two years, and the store space was worth so much more to them. If they offered two hundred, her dad could get a nice long lease on a space nearby, somewhere else. And the dark cloud would move away from his head.

She felt almost sick with nerves by the time he got home.

'You got a letter,' her mother said, picking it up gingerly by her nails and handing it to him.

Paul glanced at his daughter. 'It can wait. I'll open it later.'

Rose swallowed hard, to force down the protest that wanted to burst from her lips. Obviously he didn't want her to see it. She knew, deep down, that she was smarter than both her parents, but she was also fifteen years old. She could have helped them to deal with it, but they still saw her as a child. And now was not the time to challenge her father on anything.

'You know what, I'm tired,' she said. 'I need an early night. I'm gonna take a shower and see you guys in the morning.'

Half an hour later, she got into bed and pretended to be asleep. The door creaked fifteen minutes later — her parents checking to see if she was out. Rose kept her eyes closed, her breathing nice and regular. She heard the door click shut. Then her father sobbing.

After a sleepless night, Rose woke up as soon as the first red streaks of dawn filtered through their tiny windows, lighting the grey air-conditioning vents of the industrial building which their apartment overlooked. She swung her feet out of bed and padded barefoot into the kitchen. The letter lay open on the side. Rose snatched it up, dry-mouthed:

Dear Mr Fiorello,
This letter is notification that the time allotted to you to take advantage of the offer of fifty thousand dollars for early vacation of your lease has expired. Rothstein Realty does not wish to renew this offer nor to offer any other compensation should you voluntarily choose to vacate the premises you have leased. The terms of your lease guaranteed by law will be honoured by Rothstein Realty in accordance with law. Rent must be paid in full and on time as specified in the lease. Eviction proceedings will begin with the first missed payment, as specified in the terms of the lease.
We remain very truly yours,
*J. Mandel, B. Wilson, H. Saperstein*
Mandel, Wilson, Saperstein & Thomas, representing Rothstein Realty, Inc.

Her heart raced, and she slid into a chair, dizzy with fear. But Rose didn't have time to be afraid. She stood up again and slipped into the bathroom, running a quick, quiet shower. Then she turned to her closet and selected her best suit, purchased for that summer job as a receptionist at an accountant's she'd landed last summer. Then she'd rushed to Elise's for help with her make-up, wound her hair into a bun, and set out for mid-town.
She was going to Rothstein Realty.
Screw the lawyers. There was no other way. Rose believed that over at Rothstein they didn't know what their lawyers were doing. After all, this was just one tiny wriggle in their vast operations. The main company

couldn't possibly be keeping track of everything. Rose would go in to see them, explain the situation, and offer a compromise. Two hundred grand, and they would just walk away. Her dad could set up nearby, Rothstein would get their vacant building — everybody would win.

The Rothstein offices were located right by Rockefeller Center, in a sleek, high skyscraper covered in gleaming polished granite. Rose was almost there now, and she suddenly realised she had no idea what she was doing.

She had no appointment . . . no one to speak to. She had been a receptionist. Would she have let a person in without an appointment? Rose paused and ducked down a side street, looking for a phone. She found one in a couple of minutes — amazingly unbroken. She got the number for Rothstein Realty from 411 and crossed her fingers. It was only eight-twenty in the morning. Yesss . . . a computerised voice was clicking in.

'If you know the name of your party's extension, press it now.' This was so modern, Rose thought bitterly. Trust Rothstein to have one of these automatic systems. She waited. 'If you do not know the extension, press star for a company directory by surname, or zero to leave a message in the general — '

Quickly Rose punched the star key.

She typed in 7 6 8 . . . R O T.

'To select . . . Giovanni Rotando, press 1 now. To select . . . Fred Rothstein, press 1 now.'

Fred Rothstein was the CEO. Rose didn't think she'd have much luck with him. She continued to listen.

'Seth Rothstein . . . ' suggested the voice. 'Tom Rothstein . . . William Rothstein.'

It was a lottery. Rose punched one.

'You have reached the mailbox for William Rothstein in public relations,' the soothing voice said. 'Please leave a message after the tone. This is extension 1156.'

Rose swallowed hard and strained to keep her tone level. 'William, this is Rose Fiorello confirming our appointment for nine. Your assistant hasn't got back to my office, so I'm assuming everything is OK. See you at nine.'

She hung up, a fine bead of sweat over her forehead. Her wristwatch said it was eight-twenty-two. There was a cheap-looking coffee and bagel joint just across the street, and she headed towards it.

She would get there in twenty minutes. She just hoped to God this would work.

★　★　★

Rose tried not to look impressed when she stepped through the glass revolving doors. Rothstein's lobby was sumptuous. The walls and floor were of perfectly matched marble, pink veins swirling through a silky-smooth, gleaming surface that screamed of money. There were three huge oil canvases hung in ornate gold-leaf frames; she didn't notice what they were of; that hardly seemed the point. The receptionist's desk was carved of mahogany. Two women sat behind it, dealing with ringing phones and a bevy of suited supplicants that buzzed in front of them with military precision. The desk rested on an Oriental rug in cream and pale blue. Rose had seen ones like it in the Metropolitan Museum. She thought it was ten thousand bucks' worth of rug, maybe more. And yes, both the receptionists were wearing ultra-smart navy Chanel suits.

Perspiration dewed the palms of her hands. She surreptitiously wiped them on the suit. It wouldn't do to look nervous. Rose breathed in deeply through her red-slicked lips, pausing before breathing out. Nature's valium.

She marched up to the receptionists' desk,

shouldering her way through the crowd of male executives.

'Yes, ma'am?' the polished girl said, not raising her eyes.

Rose prayed hard. 'Rose Fiorello, to see William Rothstein,' she said confidently.

The receptionist consulted a vellum-bound book. 'I don't see anything in there for nine, ma'am. What was the name again?'

'Ms Fiorello,' Rose said, impatiently. 'Don't tell me that stupid girl of his messed this up again? This is the second time — '

'Let me call up to his office — '

'Extension 1156,' Rose said, with just the right touch of condescension.

The receptionist bent her head apologetically and talked into the phone in a low voice.

'His assistant isn't in yet — '

'She didn't pass on the message on the machine confirming our appointment?' Rose demanded.

The girl muttered something else into the phone. There was a brief pause, and Rose tried not to hold her breath.

'Mr Rothstein says to go right up. It's the eighth floor — '

'Thank you, I've been there before,' Rose lied smoothly.

She half ran to the elevator bank before the women could inspect her and start asking questions about her age. Thank God nobody paid attention to other people any more.

Men crowded into the elevator with her, some of them looking her up and down lasciviously, but Rose stared straight ahead, ignoring everybody. She'd got this far. It was a miracle.

Maybe it was all going to work out . . .

The elevator glided to a stop at the eighth floor, and

Rose stepped out on to soft carpet and another oasis of dark woods and oil paintings. She was directed to William Rothstein's office and kept walking, just kept going, looking to neither right nor left, expecting to be challenged at any minute. There it was, with the empty assistant's desk in front of it; a heavy, imposing door made of solid oak, with a discreet brass nameplate on it.

Rose knocked.

'Come in.'

She opened it and stood in the doorway, feeling awkward. A large, thick-set man, bald and wearing a well-cut suit, sat behind his desk, flicking through a file of papers.

'Can I help you?'

He glanced up and looked her over.

'I'm Rose Fiorello,' Rose said, closing the door.

'Yes. My assistant didn't tell me about any meeting for this morning.'

'I'm here to talk to you about Paul's Famous Deli. Located in the building you've bought on Ninth Avenue. You're forcing the tenant out of his lease, and now you've withdrawn your offer of compensation.'

His eyes narrowed.

'Who the hell are you?'

'That's really not important,' Rose said, the wash of adrenaline carrying her through. Her heart was pounding now, and she had beads of sweat on her forehead. 'You run the publicity department here, don't you? It won't make very good publicity when I go to the papers and tell them that you're running a twenty-year institution out of his lease . . . '

William Rothstein was smiling now, and it wasn't a pleasant smile.

'Now I get it,' he said, and his words were soft and vicious. 'Fiorello. You're his kid. This whole thing is a stunt. You're here to blackmail me.'

'You can't talk about blackmail, cutting off our electricity — '

'Let me save you some time before I get security to throw you out,' Rothstein said silkily. 'You aren't going anywhere with this story. Do you know how many apartment ads we run in the *Post* and the *News* and the *Village Voice*? We get hundreds of people like your father every day, thinking it's open season on developers, that they can trade in their shitty leases for hundreds of thousands more than they're worth. If anybody *did* pay any attention to you — which I highly doubt — we would simply use your presence here today as evidence of your blackmail.'

'We aren't extorting you. You are driving us out. What about my father's livelihood?'

Rothstein shrugged. 'Your father was offered fifty thousand dollars to settle with us. Instead, he chose to go to the police, to make trouble. If you take on this firm, you face the consequences.' He leaned forward in his chair, casting dark eyes up and down her slim body. 'You're a very attractive girl. Is that why he sent you to me?'

Rose flushed scarlet, rage and shame bringing the blood to the surface of her cheeks. She took a step forwards, her hand shaking, intending to slap him in the face.

'Oh-ho, a regular wildcat.' She couldn't believe it; he was actually laughing at her. 'I don't think so, Missy. You're a little out of your depth here.'

There was a knock on the door. 'Mr Rothstein? It's Melissa. Shall I call security?'

Rose's ice-blue eyes flashed. 'You'll regret this, Mr Rothstein.'

'Um. Yeah. I'm sure I will.'

He leaned back, chuckling. Rose wrenched the door open, facing a pneumatic blonde in her twenties who glared at her.

'You didn't have any appointment — '

'I'll show myself out,' Rose said, ignoring her. She walked down the hall, cheeks burning, as the girl screamed, 'I'm calling security!'

There was a fire exit next to the elevator. Rose took it, jogged down three floors, then stepped out to get on a different down elevator. Nobody was going to throw her out. Fiercely, she blinked back the tears prickling in her eyes.

This was unbelievable. They were ruined. And there was absolutely nothing she could do about it.

★ ★ ★

Rose helped her parents get through the next two weeks. She contacted their landlord and got him to waive the notice period. She found a cheap two-bedroom in the Bronx, and ringed ads in the Help Wanted section. Her father closed the store, sold off what equipment he could, and donated the food to a homeless shelter. She tried not to let him reflect too much on the loss of his place.

'It's really an opportunity,' she told her father. 'You know, starting over. You have five thousand bucks and no stress. And anyway, Mom needs you to be strong.'

She told her mother the same thing, and watched each of her parents force a calm exterior for the other.

Paul Fiorello found himself a job. He got a Deli Manager position at a Pathmark store on Third Avenue, a decent job. It paid less money, and it was taxable, and it wasn't his own business. Rose knew that every day he put the uniform on, he felt humiliated. But her father never complained, and the job carried health benefits. Her mother got to go to the doctor's more often, and did her best to make the new apartment feel like home.

But her father was a man with a broken spirit, and

Rose became obsessed with putting it back together again.

Her grades went to pot. All the subjects she'd loved at school suddenly seemed like a big waste of time. English — who cared? History was the past. Geography . . . even Math . . . Rose just did not care. She was never likely to travel abroad, and as for Math, today there were calculators and computers. None of this rubbish mattered.

What mattered was money.

William Rothstein had taught her that.

Rose thought about him every day. And not just him; about the soft carpets, the rich woods, the blonde, twenty-something secretary. The toys that money bought him and his firm. And the power. The ability to take twenty years of someone's hard work, expertise in their field, and a loyal customer-base, and just throw it away.

Money had paid for that lawyers' letter. Money had bought off the NYPD. Money greased the wheels at City Hall and got the press off your back. When Rothstein had said that to her, she had believed it.

Fuck school, Rose thought bitterly, using language in her head her father would have belted her for if she'd ever said it aloud. What she needed was money. She wanted a place her father could not be thrown out of, and a home they owned themselves. A place with a garden in the back, where her father could grow his tomatoes.

Well, she was going to get it. And she was going to get it from real estate.

If that snivelling little shit Rothstein could do it, so could she.

# 5

Poppy turned into the guesthouse's drive and parked the car. She thanked all the rock 'n' roll gods her parents owned this place, near Sunset, keeping it for their maid, somewhere she could stash her ride and not worry it would get stolen. Nobody was home except the housekeeper; she could see Conchita's Mercedes station wagon in the garage, the one she sometimes got picked up from school in. Quickly she got out, before she could be seen, and ducked out into the base of the Hollywood Hills. Conchita probably wouldn't rat her out, but why take the chance?

The guest house was a spacious bungalow without much of a view, but with a fantastic little garden instead — Daddy had installed a small fountain, imported from Italy, to go with the bougainvillea and thick climbing roses over the fence. The scent of flowers was so intense there that it almost muffled the smell of gasoline fuel and smog. Of course, the best thing about the guesthouse from Poppy's point of view was that it was close enough to the Strip to walk.

Poppy clip-clipped her way two blocks south to where the Hyatt stood, tall and boringly functional. There were always cabs parked out front. She got into one and told him to take her down to the Rainbow.

'But that's only — '

Poppy flung ten bucks at him. 'I know, but I don't wanna walk.'

'You got it,' the guy said, pulling out.

Poppy grinned. Like they said in *Spinal Tap*, money talked and bullshit walked.

Excitement crackled through her. She'd made it. The

late summer sun was sinking behind the glossy towers of Sunset Strip, and she could see a few hookers right over there, too close to the chichi hotels for the doormen to feel comfortable — the cops would be along in a second — and over there, the first knot of metal-heads, dudes in jeans and black leather jackets with mullets, or long straight hair down to their asses, and a few Motley Crue-style glamsters — the guys with lipstick had to travel in packs, or they'd get beaten up. The girls kicked ass, too. You had punk chicks and biker chicks and then you had the L.A. babes — dudettes, as KNAC called them — girls with sprayed-on black pants, low-slung studded belts, fingerless lace gloves, and platinum-blonde hair teased up to the sky. The ones who couldn't get implants got padded, push-up bras. Every chick had lip-liner, red talons, and tons of attitude.

Poppy loved it. She couldn't wait. She wondered who was playing tonight. Even the shittiest gig offered possibility; getting drunk, hanging out, flirting with the boys. Even better, flirting with the band. Poppy's wet dreams all involved Jon Bon Jovi and Rick Savage, and sometimes even Ad Rock from the Beastie Boys. It was cooler to like Slayer, but Poppy didn't care. Really hard metal made her ears bleed. But it was still cool to go to those gigs, too; you were part of the heavy metal brotherhood, and you got to piss off Debbie Gibson fans. Which had to be a good thing in anybody's book.

The cab screeched to a halt outside the club. Poppy stepped out and shook her long, carefully highlighted honey-blonde hair.

'Hey, baby.'

'What's up, sugar?'

'Lookin' fine . . . '

Poppy pretended not to hear the calls of appreciation as she walked into the crowd, but she bit back a tiny smile. Somebody saw it, and a storm of wolf-whistles followed her up the queue to get in.

The bouncer on the door saw it and beckoned to her.

Poppy raised one delicately arched brow and put her manicured nails over her boobs, which were looking even bigger in the push-up bra she had crammed them in to, her low-cut top revealing generous amounts of cleavage. She pressed her hand to them, as if to say, Me?

'Yeah, you, sweetcakes.'

The bouncer looked her up and down, taking in the glorious tits, the pale eyes and tanned skin, the expensive highlights, the black miniskirt, the high-heeled ankle boots and fishnet stockings. Together with that pretty face and soft teenage skin, she was a little slice of metal heaven. She looked like she belonged in a Cinderella video.

The girl walked towards him in a confident way. Usually girls would come up deferentially, desperate for a pass or a ticket or just to avoid being thrown out. Not this kid. He didn't have respect for her, of course; wasn't his way with girls; he just liked the looks of her.

'You're on the list,' he said.

Poppy rewarded him with a stunning smile, displaying perfectly white, straight teeth that were the result of eighteen months with the best orthodontist in Bel Air.

'Hey, thanks,' she said.

'Hey, fuck that, man.' One of the Hell's Angel biker dudes at the front of the queue growled with fury. 'You didn't even check her name. You don't even *know* her name.'

The bouncer stared him down. He worked out on Muscle Beach and he could take any drunk-ass biker.

'Her name's Baby,' he said.

Poppy started to pull out her fake ID.

'You don't need that.' He winked at her, and Poppy smiled back. This was what made her feel sexy and alive, little tributes to her beauty like this. One of the dirty, unmade-up biker chicks started to call her a bitch. Poppy tossed her hair and walked into the club.

Some people — her parents included — would call it crazy and dangerous for a girl to be out on the Sunset Strip alone. Especially a Bel Air Jewish princess like Poppy. But they were wrong, Poppy thought. It was all about the care and feeding of men's egos. Once, Poppy had been in the front row at a Bad Brains gig and the mosh pit was so intense she thought she might get crushed. She'd turned a sweet smile on the guys behind her, and they had put their arms either side of her on the stage lip, creating a little pocket of protected space for her.

The club was packed. Condensation literally dripped off the walls; kids packed in together, sweat on foreheads, jackets consigned to the cloakroom. The girls did better than the dudes; they could peel off layers of clothing. Maybe it was designed to have just that effect. Poppy's eyes flickered over tonight's crowd, seeing all the girls in just their lacy bras, some of them with marker pen marks across the creamy flesh. The adrenaline crackling through her kicked up a notch. Roadies were scurrying across the club stage, pulling away equipment, setting up other stuff. Plastic cups and other trash were scattered across the floor. Obviously one band had already left the stage, and another was coming on. That was OK — support bands usually sucked. Poppy walked up to the bar.

'Hey, cutie,' the barman said.

He recognised Poppy. She was in here often enough, busting the legal drinking age, but hey, it was the Eighties, who didn't? Anyway, girls like her should be drunk. It gave you a better shot with them. Although a fox like this one had to have some big-ass metal-head boyfriend hanging around.

'Jack and Diet Coke,' she said, with not quite enough bravado to pull it off.

'Coming right up,' he agreed anyway.

Poppy took a seat at the bar and sipped at her icy drink. Oh, man, this was heaven. All the sexy dudes with their long hair and muscles . . . not that she ever wanted to *do* anything with them. She was way too young. She was saving herself for something other than a one-night stand, even if they were cool and rock 'n' roll.

These boys were strictly eye-candy.

But this was *her* scene. Her crowd, her people, her brotherhood. It might not have been the Sixties, but there was a vibe here that her parents and Tipper Gore and the PMRC, the suburban moms' pressure group that agitated to ban metal stars and their R-rated lyrics, would never understand. To Poppy's shame, her own mom had actually joined the PMRC. But it wasn't all about Satan, it was all about *fun*. Sex, drugs, and rock 'n' roll. What the hell was wrong with that?

She thought music beat the shit out of the film business. Poppy took another slug of the fiery spirit, cool to her mouth, but burning her throat. Mom would freak when she told her she wanted to quit her acting lessons. When would they get it? She wanted to be a rock star, not some boring old actress. Going to auditions and whining at an agent, no thanks. Poppy wanted to found an all-girl rock band and get out there, banging her blonde hair all over the place and toting her axe around. Or maybe she'd be a bassist. Bassists were cool, because they had a lot less to play, so they could move all over the stage. Ideally, Poppy wanted to be a lead singer, but despite Mrs Teischbaum's singing lessons, she unfortunately had a voice only marginally better than a frog with a particularly hoarse croak.

'And now . . . '

The lights dimmed. A huge roar went up from the

crowd, who were punching the air at the MC and making 'devil' sounds.

'Please welcome — Dark Angel!'

★   ★   ★

Dark Angel started to play.

They had charged on to rapturous cheering, fists thrust skywards, a surge in the club to the lip of the stage, girls pressing forwards, arms outstretched in supplication. The lights played on them, red and blue and gold, and the band blasted into the first tune.

Poppy was enraptured. She gulped at her drink, mesmerised. She was too late to get a good position in the crowd, so she stayed where she was, where she had a good view. Oh, man. They were all gorgeous, and they rocked. They sounded nothing like the average hair band, but they weren't hardcore thrash metal.

They were new, and different, and . . . incredible.

And they knew it, too. Look at the way the lead singer strutted over his tiny space as though he were headlining Madison Square Gardens. The guitarists were flirting with the squealing chicks in the front row, and the bassist . . .

He was tall and skinny and had flash rock-star pants with glitter on them, and a bandanna, and he stroked that bass suggestively, lovingly. He had almond eyes and flowing black hair, he was smooth-chested and Byronic and she *wanted* him. Most of the other girls were creaming themselves over the singer, some over one of the guitarists. But Poppy liked that dark, mysterious look. She sat up on her stool and manoeuvred herself under one of the small round lights over the bar, and over the heads of the crowd she looked right at him.

And he saw her.

His eyes flickered her way, up and across the blonde hair, the push-up bra, the hand-span waist, the rock-chick outfit. Poppy felt a wave of heat pulse through her, centring in her belly. She was always being checked out by men, but never by men she fancied. The way the guy was assessing her felt as though his eyes were peeling off her clothes. She felt exposed, and it was hot.

She couldn't help it. She dropped her gaze.

When she looked back up, the bassist was still staring at her. Like he'd been waiting for her to look at him again. He'd totally caught her.

Poppy flushed crimson, not that anyone could see it in the club. Her lips parted.

He grinned, and gave her a slow, deliberate wink.

Poppy's hand shot up to her mouth. The heat in her belly spread little tendrils all over her skin. Her nipples hardened into tiny little buds. She backed her stool out of the light, she couldn't take it. He looked away, swinging his bass out over the crowd, running to the other side of the stage.

The barman behind her chuckled.

'I guess he likes you,' he said. 'Can't blame him.'

Poppy turned to him eagerly. 'What's that guy's name?'

'Ricardo Perez,' he said. 'I think they call him Rick.'

'Rick,' Poppy repeated, as though it were somehow magical and fascinating. She had to get to meet him.

She took another, deeper slug of her Jack Daniel's. The alcohol relaxed her, made her feel confident. Poppy gazed at the stage, lost in the music and the lights, staring at Rick, fantasising, hoping he'd glance her way again.

★ ★ ★

By the time Dark Angel got off stage after their second encore, and the lights went up, she had found the backstage door. It wasn't too hard . . . there was a gaggle of chicks thronging around it, pleading with a stone-faced bouncer, squealing and jumping up and down and touching up their hair and make-up.

'Are you all waiting for autographs?' Poppy asked.

A razor-thin platinum blonde with large fake boobs looked her over witheringly. 'Yeah, that's it . . . *autographs*,' she said derisively.

The other girls tittered at Poppy for being so naïve.

'Will they come out?' she asked the security guard.

He looked down at her blankly. 'Dunno.'

'Come on, baby,' one of the bleach-blondes wheedled, jiggling her tits at him. 'I was, like, totally meant to be on the list. You should let me back, it's just a mix-up . . . '

'Name?' the security guard said in a bored manner.

'Trixie Campbell,' she pouted.

He scanned a sheet of paper. 'Your name's not down, you can't come in.'

'Hey, come on . . . '

The door was opened just a crack from inside. The girls all started to scream hysterically.

'Zach! Zaaaaach! Pete! Carl! Rick! Jason! Aaaah! Aaaah!'

The singer's face poked out half an inch, grinning. The girls thrust bits of paper at him.

'Sign this!'

'Will you sign my boob?' Trixie said, pulling down her top to reveal a rock-hard pair in a black lace bra.

Poppy was shocked, but tried not to show it.

'Sure, honey,' the singer said. He was armed with a black marker pen and scrawled something on her flesh while she cooed and giggled. One of the guitarists started to do the same thing.

'Pete, can I come back? Can I come back?' a fiery redhead pleaded abjectly. She wasn't all that good looking, too much ass for the miniscule skirt she was wearing.

The guitarist shook his head. 'It's a bit crowded back there, sorry, OK?'

Poppy blushed crimson and hung back, uncertainly. She felt out of her depth. She'd never tried to go backstage before, and she didn't want to show her tits in public nor to beg for access. She hovered on the edge of the crowd, clutching her pen and the napkin she had brought for the bass player to sign. Now she knew why the girls had laughed at her — getting an autograph was just an excuse, a way to be able to speak to a rock star and say what you really meant, which was 'Can I come backstage and hang out?'

She'd wanted that too, but this was just humiliating. She wasn't a sign-my-tits type of chick. Poppy was ashamed of herself; she wasn't as rock 'n' roll as she'd thought. Maybe she was just a nice Jewish girl and she should go home.

Rick Perez stuck his head out the door. Poppy gasped; he was gorgeous, she thought, insanely gorgeous. Those slightly slanted eyes, that coal-black hair. He was wearing mascara, but that made him look more rock-star-ish, as though he were in the New York Dolls. She flushed scarlet again, and this time the house lights were up. Now he was close, she felt incredibly embarrassed. She wanted to say something, but she felt rooted to the spot. Her hand with its sad little napkin hung limply at her side.

'Rick!' the girls screamed. 'Rick!'

He signed a few cigarette packets and body parts, then his eyes skimmed the little knot of groupies and fell on Poppy.

She could hardly breathe. He was looking right at her.

Rick beckoned. Unmistakably, he was pointing straight at her and crooking his finger.

Almost as one, the girls turned round and stared at Poppy. She stumbled forwards through them, hoping her sweating palms wouldn't dampen the napkin. Poppy tried to think of something to say, along the lines of 'Could you sign this for me please,' but her tongue seemed to be stuck to the roof of her mouth.

'Bitch,' Trixie said in a low voice, designed for Poppy to hear.

She was standing right in front of him now with the whole crowd staring at her. Poppy's blush seemed to have reached the very tips of her ears. She just couldn't look up. He was tall, and she was standing right by his chest. She could feel him looking down at her.

'Charlie.' He had a rough voice that sounded as though he smoked a lot of cigarettes and drank a lot of liquor. 'This young lady's with us.'

'Sure, Rick,' the security guard said.

'Hey!' the girls chorused.

Poppy glanced up, open-mouthed. The bassist stuck something on her left shoulder. It was made of cloth-like sticky paper, square and green, and said 'Guest'.

The security guard opened the door to let Poppy through.

'Wait a minute!' the redhead squealed. 'I'm with her! I'm her friend! I know her — '

Poppy was pulled through the backstage door by Rick Perez, and it shut behind her with a clang, drowning out the sound of the desperate girls. She was in a grey-painted corridor, leading off to wide open doors that looked like regular offices. It didn't seem all that glamorous. But here she was, surrounded by the members of Dark Angel, and Rick Perez had one hand proprietorially on her shoulder.

Zach Mason, the lead singer, checked her out, then grinned at Perez.

'Nice,' he said. 'Cutest chick in the place.'

Poppy could hardly breathe.

'Look,' said Pete the guitarist, 'she's blushing. I don't

know when I last saw a chick blush.'

Rick Perez looked down at Poppy.

'Hi,' he said.

Poppy half whispered, 'Hi.'

'Would you like to get a drink?' Perez said. 'We've got a cooler of beers and shit in the dressing room.'

'Thank you, that would be lovely,' Poppy said politely.

Perez stared at her and snorted with laughter. 'You're a riot. Come on. This way.'

# 6

Poppy followed Rick into a small room, crammed with people.

The walls were covered with graffiti, every spare inch thick with marker pen; obscenities, band names, complaints about the showers, fuck-yous to the promoters of the gigs. There were a couple of ratty old black leather couches, covered with slashes, the rest of the band sprawled across them with their friends — long-haired dudes, talking loudly, drunk, chopping out lines of coke on mirrors, or whatever flat surface came to hand. There was a large plastic cooler in one corner, full of ice and cans of soda and beer. On a table there were the remains of a buffet — metal platters of cheese and fruit and bits of sandwiches. Not very rock 'n' roll. There was a more recently set up table with bottles of vodka, packets of cranberry juice, and plastic cups; it wasn't quite so wrecked. Poppy realised that someone had only put the alcohol there once the band had gone onstage. No need to risk a drunk group until after the performance. Hovering round the drinks table, primping their hair in the grimy dressing-room mirror, laughing and pretending to talk to one another, were the girls.

Poppy tried and failed not to stare.

They were the same as the chicks outside, but they had the edge on them. Dressed in exactly the same trashy style: skirts as short as belts, lace, bras, leather, heels and studs; exactly the same long blonde hair, full-on make-up, and with lots of flesh on display. But these girls were better-looking and acted a little less desperate. They carried nothing suggestive of auto-graphs; they drank the band's liquor and nibbled on their celery sticks and acted like they had a right to be there.

'What are you drinking?'

Rick was talking to her again. Poppy couldn't quite believe it. She was here and she was talking to the bassist!

Suddenly, the crowded, filthy little dressing room seemed like the coolest place on earth.

'I'll take a vodka and cranberry juice,' Poppy said, 'thanks.' She sat down on an unoccupied corner of one of the couches and looked at him expectantly.

Rick Perez grinned and went to mix her a drink. At the makeshift bar, the girls elegantly draped themselves over him, smiling right into his eyes, as though Poppy didn't exist.

Poppy was picking up the rules of the game. It was the jungle in here, survival of the fittest. Or the prettiest. They didn't give a damn about her; several of the chicks were eyeing her with disdain . . .

But Rick came back over to her and handed her her drink. Poppy took refuge in a big gulp, then spluttered.

He laughed. 'Too strong for you?'

'You could say that.'

'How old are you, anyway?'

'Seventeen,' Poppy lied.

'I'm twenty-two.'

'That's cool,' Poppy said, trying to be sophisticated.

Rick settled back on the couch and casually draped one arm across her back. His fingers rested lightly on her shoulder, and the touch was electric. Poppy saw the other girls gazing at her, their mascaraed eyes narrowing in loathing. She felt an instant thrill of triumph. He preferred her, he'd taken her right out of the crowd.

*This rocks*, Poppy thought.

'I saw you out there,' he said.

'I know,' Poppy said confidently. She grinned. 'I saw you too.'

'Did you like the band?'

This question she felt comfortable with. She un-tensed slightly. 'I think you guys really have something.'

'They 'have something',' said one of the blondes at the bar. 'Well, that's nice.'

The guitarist glanced Poppy's way.

'Dark Angel are, like, totally the best band ever,' cooed the chick with whom he was intertwined.

Poppy rolled her eyes. 'No they're not. Come on.'

Rick Perez laughed again, this time in disbelief. Poppy realised a second too late that the entire room was now staring at her. It also dawned on her that backstage girls weren't meant to venture opinions, unless they were along the lines of: 'You guys are God.'

'Did she even *like* us?'

Zach Mason was asking the question of Rick. As though Poppy was his property and he was responsible for her big mouth. Mason had two long-limbed beauties, both redheads, draped against him, one in each arm. One of the chicks was resting her head drunkenly against his chest, the other had her shirt halfway unbuttoned, with a white lace bra peeking out.

'No, I did. I mean, I thought you guys put on an excellent show. But the PA was too loud for the melodies and you look like you need a bigger stage to run around in, and the lighting guy was messing up in that fast number — '

'Fighting fire,' Jason, the drummer, said.

'Yeah, like you know about stage shows,' said the redhead with her buttons undone. She pouted at the singer. 'Why is she even here?'

The singer ignored her and tilted his full glass slightly towards Poppy. 'He did mess it up.'

'He didn't light me during my fucking solo,' said Carl, the guitarist, sullenly.

'OK, Sharon Osbourne,' said Rick Perez, 'and what did you like about it?'

'All the songs and the way you work the crowd,' Poppy said simply.

Mason smiled broadly. 'She's cool. Not to mention the hottest chick in the place.'

'I know,' said Perez, with the air of a connoisseur.

The girls at the bar scowled and headed for the other members of the band, like mosquitoes homing in on a patch of bare flesh.

Poppy looked into her drink, taking another slug. She had sounded really stupid, she thought. Why couldn't she just shut up and be cool? After all, he was sooo gorgeous . . .

Her watch caught her eye. It said eleven-thirty.

'Shit. Fuck. I have to go,' she said.

'Already? You just got here.'

'I know. I'm sorry, I really gotta leave.' She jumped up from the couch.

'I don't even have your phone number,' Perez said, blinking. He couldn't believe it. She was blowing him off?

'Here.' Poppy wrote it down for him, feeling miserable. Zach Mason and the others were staring at her again. She felt like a little girl.

'Goodbye, Cinderella,' said the blonde bitchily. She waggled just the tips of her blood-red fingernails in a snide farewell. 'Better get going, before you turn into a pumpkin.'

Poppy blushed again and hastily let herself out of the dressing room. She barrelled through the corridors and out into the club. It was empty now; the girls had dispersed, giving up hope of getting backstage. The club lights were up; the place which had seemed so magical and rock 'n' roll was now dirty, squalid and messy, with crushed plastic cups and other debris all over the floor. A side door was slightly ajar, and she pushed against the heavy metal bar and walked out on to the sidewalk.

It wasn't even midnight, and Sunset wasn't done. The metal-heads and bikers and whores were out in full force now, the street lights washed over the scene, the clubs glittered neon under the movie-poster bill-boards . . .

But Poppy was done. She was hella late, as Metallica would put it. She got lucky and grabbed a cab, which drove her back to the Hollywood hills. Conchita's lights were on, but she didn't have time to worry about that now. Poppy threw ten bucks at the cabbie and jumped out, grabbing the door of the Porsche and putting it into gear. The front door opened and Conchita came out in a pink housecoat, lace flapping, fat arms waving.

'Signora Poppy, what you doin'?'

Poppy wound down the window. 'I'm OK, Conchita, don't say anything, OK? Please?'

Before the housekeeper could answer, Poppy screeched forwards out of the gate, blasting off down the hill and on to Sunset. Oh, shit. At least there wasn't traffic, not to speak of, this late at night. At the lights she peeled off her jacket; at the next lights, her lace hose. If she made it back before Mom and Dad, she'd have, like, three seconds to change. She breathed into her hands — that wasn't too bad, vodka didn't smell, and she hadn't had that much Jack Daniel's. Maybe, just maybe, she'd get away with it —

She finally turned in through the wrought-iron gates and —

Busted.

Oh, shit. Her parents' car was parked right there in the driveway. The lights were on, and she could see her mother pacing up and down in the living room, talking into a hands-free phone and gesticulating wildly. The front door was wrenched open and her father came charging out. Poppy hastily stuffed the fishnets into her jacket pocket.

71

'Poppy!'

Her mother dropped the phone and came racing out after her husband. Oy, they're so melodramatic, Poppy thought. Look at them. Or not. She quailed at her dad's face.

'What — what — where the hell have you been?' He reached into the car and started shaking her shoulders. 'Damn it to hell! And what are you wearing? You look like a hooker! It's that goddamn devil music again, isn't it!'

'Poppy! Oh, Poppy!' her mom was wailing. 'Are you all right? My baby!' She looked Poppy over tearfully, ascertained she was all in one piece, then started to scream with rage. 'What are you wearing! My daughter, she should go out looking like some tramp! We trusted you! You betrayed us!'

'It's that music. Only drunks and junkies like that filthy punk music,' growled her father.

'You're grounded for ever!'

'Mom — be reasonable — '

'For ever!' her father bellowed. 'Don't even say a word to your mother, young lady! Get the hell in the house!'

'Language, honey,' said her mom, automatically.

Mr Allen turned a baleful eye on his daughter.

'Just wait till I'm through with you,' he said. 'You're in my house, you *will* abide by my rules.'

# 7

'Well, what do we have here?'

Daisy froze. Oh no, help. She had been so lost in her story she hadn't heard Miss Crawford's footsteps. The old cow was renowned for having specially soft leather soles on all her shoes, so that nobody heard her sneaking around the dorms at night. She managed to catch more girls smoking or being in each other's cubicles after lights out than any other teacher.

Plus, she hated Daisy.

I should have been paying attention, Daisy thought, her pudgy face flushing.

Too late.

Her teacher snatched up the red-covered rough book and started to read Daisy's hastily scrawled biro aloud, in a nasty sing-song voice.

'Chapter One.' She frowned, her bushy brow contracting down at Daisy. The rest of the class stared. 'My, my, how thrilling! Finding the English classics boring, Miss Markham has decided to give us all the benefit of her own creations!'

The girls were all holding their breath, watching the scene with horrified fascination.

'*Emily McCloud shivered in the cold Highland air,*' Miss Crawford read sarcastically. '*She wasn't at all sure about this. After all, she had never met any of her British cousins, and this Rory was only a distant relative. Scotland was freezing when you were used to LA sunshine. But her mother had insisted, and so, here she was. It was an honour for Emily to be invited to this ball. Mom was determined that her only daughter should make a splash at the castle.*

'*Castle. The very word gave Emily a chill. How do*

you behave at a place like that? The closest Emily had ever come to a castle was the toy one at Disneyland.'

Miss Crawford gave a sarcastic laugh. 'Honestly, Daisy. If you're going to get a detention, at least make it for something worthwhile. Not this kind of trash. Maybe if you paid more attention in my classes, you might actually learn to write something people wanted to read.'

Daisy bowed her head. Of course it was no good. What had she been thinking? Now the entire fourth form had heard her pathetic attempt at a trashy novel.

'It's so bad, it reminds me of Judith Krantz,' Miss Crawford added, in a final, stinging put-down. 'Detention for you and two more demerits for Sackville House.'

She tossed the rough book back at Daisy, who hastily put it away and opened up her copy of *As You Like It*.

She was glad she could hide the sparkle in her eyes.

Yes! Miss Crawford thought she wrote like Judith Krantz!

As the class filed dutifully out, Victoria shoving Daisy meanly because she'd got Sackville two more demerits, some of the other girls looked at her with keen interest.

'So,' said Arabella, curious despite herself, 'what happens with this Rory bloke? Does she fall in love with him?'

'Well, he's a laird,' Daisy said, 'and he meets her and he doesn't know who she is and he laughs at her because she's a tourist. Then they meet again at his castle for the ball and when she realises he was the one who made fun of her in Edinburgh she runs away.'

'Like Cinderella,' Arabella said, breathlessly.

Isobel Soames said proudly, 'Daisy read me the next bit. She's trying to get to the airport, but there's a big storm and she's stuck in Scotland.'

'I want to read it!' said Arabella.

Victoria hit her. 'No you don't. Some silly story by fat Daisy.'

'God, you're a bitch, Vicky,' Isobel said.

'I *do* want to read it,' Arabella said. She went slightly pink from defying Victoria.

'You can,' Daisy said, 'but Emma Wilkins asked me first.'

She felt a strange rush of pleasure. Even though Arabella was in her house, she wasn't mad about the demerits. She just wanted to read Daisy's story.

Daisy had to work out what happened when the airport told Emily she had to go back into town. Suddenly all she wanted was to get upstairs to her cubicle and start writing again.

'Got to go,' she said, and waddled off.

★　★　★

Winter came early that year. There was a great storm which blew down thousands of trees in the south of England, blocking the roads in and out of Withambury. The girls watched the news and ooh-ed and aah-ed over the dramatic pictures of flooded villages and stranded trains. In their dormitory, the only talk was of the Chatsford Dance — the annual dance with Chatsford School for Boys — and whether or not St Mary's would still be able to go.

Daisy prayed the answer was no. All she wanted to do was stay in her room and write her book. She enjoyed winter, watching the green hills outside her window silver over with sugary frost, and the dark clouds scud across an angry white sky. She liked the sparseness of the dark branches and twigs against the bare landscape, and her favourite thing was to be inside, preferably by a log fire, while a severe wind howled and whipped around the roofs outside. There were no fires at St Mary's, but there was a lot of warmth. It was perfect writing weather. She tried counting up the words in a line and multiplying the answer by the number of lines on a page, and then the number of the pages she had written. It was mounting up. She might even have done about twenty thousand words by now.

There was a queue to read her stuff. The teasing she'd been used to all her life had died off a little. Even Victoria just avoided her now.

Daisy didn't want it to start again.

'Hey.' Isobel walked in and dropped her satchel on the bed. 'Have you seen this?'

'What is it?' Daisy said.

Isobel fished out a ripped-up magazine page. '*Company* magazine is having a book competition. If you win, they give you dinner with an agent and a publisher and Marcia Watson.'

'Really?' Daisy snatched it up. It was true; they wanted a sample chapter, no longer than three thousand words. The top prize was five hundred pounds and the chance to give your manuscript to a real agent. Her heart thudded in her chest. What if she actually won? It could be destiny.

'It has to be typed, though.'

'I could type it. I'm learning in computer club,' Daisy said resolutely.

'You totally should. Everybody thinks it's awesome,' Isobel said.

Emma burst into their room. 'Hi, Daisy. Isobel, guess what! They've just announced the Chatsford Dance is on, after all.'

'Awesome,' Isobel said. 'I hope Tom Rhys is going to be there. He's gorgeous.'

'What are you going to wear?'

'I don't know,' Isobel said. 'Maybe the pink. It's very figure-hugging.'

'What about you, Daisy?'

'I'm not going. Those dances are so childish.'

'You have to go,' Emma said, horrified. 'Otherwise you'll just look like a total weirdo. Everybody else is going. You can't be the only girl in the year not to go.'

'I bet I can find you something that'll look really good on you,' Isobel added, not quite convincingly.

The excitement of the writing competition died away. She was trapped. Emma was right, it would be even worse not to go — so obvious that she was ashamed. Daisy thought about it. She could go, and just find someplace quiet and wait it all out.

'OK,' she said.

'Honestly.' Isobel relished a challenge. 'If you put yourself totally in my hands I can make you look really good.'

Daisy caught a glimpse of her reflection in the cracked and grimy mirror nailed above the small washbasin. She had the beginnings of a double chin and her hair was looking lanky. There was a zit on the side of her nose. Writing had proved so addictive, she'd taken even less care of herself than usual.

'I suppose I'll have to let you try,' she said.

Isobel clapped her hands. 'Don't worry, this is going to be good.'

⋆   ⋆   ⋆

As the weather got colder, Daisy did her best to forget about the Christmas ball. After all there was the end of term to look forward to. She had typed up Chapter One of her novel and mailed it off — it was only fifteen hundred words, though, was that too short? She hoped not. Anyway, having it out there gave Daisy a dream. All the girls loved her stuff. She was starting to believe she was actually talented. Isobel kept telling her she could be the next Jilly Cooper. She felt happier, and she lost a tiny bit of weight. When they got a free weekend and were allowed to go shopping in Withambury, Daisy haunted W.H. Smith and bought copies of the magazines aimed at aspiring writers. They filled her with a curious mixture of hope and despair. On the one hand, there were stories of publishers and mainstream authors and interviews with supposedly best-selling writers, even though she had not heard of any of them. But on the other hand, all the photo-opportunity pictures made it look a bit seedy, and everyone in them seemed to be grey-haired and over fifty. They attended conferences in run-down hotels in Brighton; they won competitions organised by the magazine; and mostly, it seemed, they paid money for correspondence courses to teach you how to write. Gushing praise for the results of these courses ran along the lines of 'Thanks to your course, I placed a story in *Trout Fishing Monthly* and was paid sixty pounds!'

Daisy didn't want to do that sort of thing. She wanted to write a big bestseller. Maybe she was being too ambitious, though?

No way. She was quietly confident about the *Company* competition. After all, the popular clique at St Mary's believed in her writing, and they were never wrong.

# 8

'OK.'

Isobel tossed her honey-coloured hair and regarded Daisy critically.

'I'm not sure about this,' Daisy said.

She looked at her reflection. Even though she had tried to diet, it hadn't really worked. Daisy looked at her podgy, pasty cheeks and was filled with her usual self-loathing. Trying to dress it up a little didn't work. The only thing that worked was forgetting about herself.

Her stories helped her do that. Emily, her heroine, was waifish with cheekbones like knives and perky breasts. Her blossoming romance with Rory, laird of Craithy Castle, was far more interesting than Daisy Markham suffering at the Chatsford dance.

'You said you'd put yourself in my hands. So trust me,' Isobel insisted.

Daisy tilted her head, her bob plastered to her head and covered in goop. Isobel was dying her hair with what the cardboard box promised would become 'Rich Russet Auburn'. Right now it looked like food-additive.

'I guess it's too late,' Daisy muttered.

Her tactics at the hideous dances and parties she couldn't avoid were to find a quiet corner and blend into the wallpaper. Not to be noticed.

Isobel's watch bleeped. 'Thirty minutes. OK. Let's wash you out. Head back, please.'

Daisy tilted her head back against the cracked washbasin. The rim of the sink dug into her neck and it was cold and uncomfortable. She felt Isobel running the taps on her hair, then massaging in the little packet of conditioner that came with the hair dye. She'd spent almost five whole pounds on this. She hoped it worked.

There was a creak as the door opened. Daisy tried to lift her head to see who it was.

'Don't move.' Isobel splashed more water on her from the BBC Pebble Mill toothbrush mug. 'Hi, Victoria.'

'You must report to the prefects by seven,' Victoria said officiously, 'so that we can take roll-call for the coach. What are you doing?'

'None of your business,' said Isobel stoutly.

Victoria's voice was all sweetness. 'Tarting Daisy up? How nice,' she said, in a tone that meant, 'Good luck.'

As she walked out of the room, Daisy heard her sniggering to herself.

'That's it.' She sat bolt upright. 'Isobel, this isn't working. I'm not going.'

'You have to go. Everyone will know if you don't.' Her friend's slim, pretty face stared down at Daisy. 'It'll be even worse if you don't. Now sit over there while I blow-dry you, OK?'

Daisy stared out of the window while Isobel worked on her. It was six-thirty and already dark and cold; early December chill was hanging over the air. The courtyard of St Mary's was lit up from the headlights of the giant coach parked in the forecourt; teachers were milling around it, Miss Crawford was dressed in a blood-red satin gown which emphasised her bony body. Despite the neon glare, Daisy could see stars speckled over the inky sky; it was going to be freezing later. Her nose always went bright red in the cold, like Rudolf's. She made a mental note to have Isobel slap on an extra layer of concealer.

'Now for the make-up,' Isobel said. 'A bit of blusher, not too much . . . Hold steady, will you . . . and no mascara, you don't need it, amazing lashes . . . '

'Let me see. I know you're making me look like a clown,' Daisy muttered.

'Only when I'm finished. Close your eyes, please.'

'That eyeshadow's pink,' Daisy said, horrified.

'Pale-pink works great with red hair. Now shut your eyes. *Thank* you. Finally.'

When she was done, Isobel made Daisy get into the dress she had picked out for her. It had been a horrible day when they'd gone dress-shopping. Daisy didn't even want to think about her bottom in that changing-room mirror — dimpled, orange-peel skin on her wobbly butt that rippled down her upper thighs, even gathered in a tiny pocket on her knees. Until she'd seen herself in the harsh overhead lighting of the dressing room at Top Shop she didn't know just how ugly her body was. Daisy had blinked back tears, thanking God that she was alone and Isobel had agreed to wait outside. Her reflection made her want to go and live alone on an island somewhere in the Orkneys, with no company except a puffin or two.

No wonder she never went shopping.

Isobel had taken charge and picked out a dress based on the sizes of all the other clothes Daisy rejected. It was too expensive, but she'd stumped up for it — anything to get away from the stores and their cruel mirrors. Now she struggled into it. It was tight, but it seemed to fit OK. The bodice was boned, almost like a corset, hiding her jiggly pot belly, and the skirt flared out over two petticoats, which did a creditable job of covering her wide hips and soft, rippling thighs. The colour was practical; dark burgundy, not quite black. 'To hide red wine stains,' as Isobel put it.

'Right.' Her friend zipped her up at the back and tugged the hook and eye at the top into position. 'Face the mirror. Now look.'

She took her hands away.

Daisy blinked.

She hardly recognised the girl in the mirror. Her hair was gorgeous, all shiny, brown with hints of cherry wood, the bob cut blow-dried a little choppy, half-hiding her burgeoning double chin. Isobel had done something clever with her make-up; the pink eyeshadow did bring out her blue eyes, the foundation evened her skin tone, and the blusher painted on a suggestion of cheekbones she didn't have.

The dress was stately. She looked heavy-set, but it wasn't that bad, was it? A little black lace jacket covered her plump arms, the spiderweb embroidery making them look delicate, and her figure was at least half-disguised. And of course the dress pushed up and out her one good feature, her boobs. They were spilling out of the burgundy silk like two creamy white pillows.

For the first time since she was a child, Daisy experienced a tiny bit of pleasure at the way she looked.

'Wow. Thanks.'

'You're *gorgeous*,' Isobel gushed.

'Please.' Daisy took in Isobel's long blonde hair, clear lip gloss, and above-the-knee cocktail dress in pale blue silk. 'No need to lie. But I look less awful.'

'You'll be such a hit,' Isobel exulted.

Daisy stood there grinning stupidly.

'Come on, you two.' Emma stuck her head round the door. 'Seven o'clock . . . Daisy, gosh. That looks awesome.'

'Do you really think so?' Daisy said shyly.

'You look really pretty.'

Isobel tugged at her hand. 'Let's go. I totally can't wait.'

★ ★ ★

Miss Crawford and Mr James, the maths teacher, looking uncomfortable in hired black tie that didn't quite fit, packed the girls on to the bus, ticking off all the names. Fifty teenage chicks crammed themselves against the grey and orange seats in a rustle of satin and silk and the relentless click-click of toweringly high heels. Daisy couldn't wear high heels, her ankles swelled every time. In this dress she didn't have to, though.

A few of the girls said she looked great. Victoria passed her and raised an eyebrow sarcastically.

'Quite the transformation. When do you turn back into a pumpkin?'

'The coach turned into the pumpkin,' said Arabella, in a black satin gown and real diamond stud earrings.

'Well, we *are* talking about Daisy,' Victoria stage-whispered, so Daisy could hear.

'Don't mind her,' Isobel said. 'She's just jealous. I told her you were entering the *Company* competition. She's been extra-nasty since then. She's terrified you're going to win.'

'Do you think so?' Daisy said, very pleased.

'Settle down please, girls,' said Miss Crawford. 'Remember, everybody must be back here by a quarter to eleven without fail. And no drinking except for the sixth form, on pain of suspension.'

'Wooh-hooh!' said Victoria.

The coach sped through the Surrey countryside. Daisy stared out of the window while Isobel chatted to Emma about the Chatsford boys. She loved watching the branches of the trees that overhung the little country lanes brush against the window, and the villages with their adorable red-brick cottages loom up in the sweep of the headlights. Anything to be out of St Mary's. She half wished the drive would last all night. But a small part of her was excited. She didn't look so bad; at least, she'd never looked this good. And maybe, just maybe, a boy would ask her to dance. Obviously not a good-looking boy; but that didn't matter. Maybe there was a fat boy in her year at Chatsford and he was dreading this like she was. Daisy looked at her face reflected against the coach window. She *did* have a pretty face — it was one of those things they said to overweight girls to make them feel better, but in her case, it was true. She cursed her sweet tooth. Her stomach was always betraying her. Gosh, she could go for a big packet of salt 'n' vinegar Golden Wonder right now . . .

'Here we are!' Victoria crowed.

All the girls stopped talking and pressed themselves up against the window. Chatsford was a big grey Victorian school with a gravel drive and lions and turrets; mock-gothic, standard-issue public school. But it was incredibly exotic, because it was full of boys.

Large flaming torches had been placed outside the front door, and there was a teacher and a crowd of boys gathered, dressed in black tie, waiting.

'What are they doing?' Isobel wondered. 'Why are they out there?'

'Ooh. Top totty,' Emma squealed, to gales of laughter.

'That'll do, ladies,' Miss Crawford said. 'File out of the bus in an orderly manner, please. Front seats first. Victoria Campbell, lead the way.'

'Yes, Miss Crawford,' Victoria said, like a pussycat. She stood up in her clinging, almost see-through little gold number, tossed her hair in The Flick, and walked down the coach-door steps, smiling like a movie star.

Daisy was dragged up and thrust into the aisle, in between all the other girls. She heard whoops and wolf-whistles.

'Nine! Nine! Nine!'

There was a chant of male voices. Then Emma stepped out.

'Eight!' 'Nine!' 'Eight!'

'What are they doing?' Daisy hissed to Isobel.

Isobel looked at her friend. She had gone slightly pale. 'Don't let them bother you.'

'I don't get it — ' Daisy said.

Then Isobel was shoved forwards. Daisy watched her friend descend into a torrent of wolf-whistles. The boys were yelling at her.

'Ten!' 'Ten!' 'Yeah!'

Daisy stepped out.

There was silence and a bit of laughter. She stared at the boys, confused. Somebody shouted out, 'Two!'

Somebody else said cruelly, 'You think that much?'

Isobel grabbed her as she stood there blinking and tugged her away. And then Daisy realised.

They had been grading her out of ten.

Daisy burst into tears and ran into the school, blundering her way through the crowd of grinning boys. The wave of shame and humiliation beat everything she'd ever known.

Isobel hissed, 'You bastards!' and raced after her.

Daisy lumbered through the oak-panelled hallway, decorated with large wooden plaques commemorating Rectors of the School and Captains of the Cricket Team in burnished gold letters. There were marble busts on plinths, polished granite floors, and vases of flowers. She could not see a girls' bathroom, and tears were rolling down her fat face.

'Daisy!'

Isobel caught up with her and grabbed her by the lace jacket.

'Just leave me alone, will you,' Daisy howled. 'I look like a stupid clown.'

Isobel opened the nearest door and shoved her inside. It was an empty classroom. She flicked on the light and shook her.

'For God's sake, wipe your eyes,' Isobel half shouted. 'You have to pull it together. You can't let them see you like this.'

'Bit bloody late,' Daisy said. Crying had made her eyes all bloodshot, her nose was running, and she was white as a ghost, the blusher standing out on her garishly. 'I can't believe I let you talk me into this, Isobel. I'm so fat and ugly. Of course no boy would ever want me.'

'Here.' Isobel opened her little silk purse and fished out a small cellophane-wrapped packet of tissues. 'Wipe your eyes. We're stuck here till eleven now. You have to — '

There was a creak and the wooden door pushed back against them. Daisy felt her stomach drop through the floor. Oh, God — it was getting worse, it was a Chatsford master telling her to get out of the classroom, he'd see her like this —

'What the bloody hell are you doing?'

Victoria Campbell regarded the two girls with total contempt. 'Get out of there. Only the ballroom and the loo are in bounds for St Mary's girls.'

'Here's an idea, Victoria,' Isobel said, 'fuck off. OK?'

Victoria's skinny face coloured. 'I'm a prefect, actually. You have to do what I say.'

'Arrange these two words into a well-known phrase or saying,' Isobel snapped. 'Off. Fuck.'

Victoria looked at Daisy. 'What are you crying for? They gave you a two. That's two more than you normally get.'

'They rated me higher than you,' Isobel said. 'And that's before they even knew your personality.'

'Get into the ballroom, or I'll go and get Miss Crawford,' Victoria threatened. 'And drag her with you.' She jabbed a thumb at the quivering Daisy and marched out, slamming the door.

'You don't want Miss Crawford to come,' Isobel pleaded.

'No, I don't!'

Daisy had calmed down a little. She didn't want Victoria to triumph over her any more. Fuck Victoria. Isobel was right.

'Can I borrow that tissue?' Daisy asked.

'Atta girl,' Isobel said.

Daisy looked at her loyal friend. Isobel was a bit twitchy. Daisy knew she wanted to go and hook up with that boy Tom Rhys. She was always talking about him.

Daisy dabbed at her eyes, blew her nose, and took in a few deep breaths. 'OK. Let's go to the ball. I'm going to sneak one of the sixth former's drinks, anyway.' She tossed her head in a conscious imitation of The Flick. 'I don't look that bad. If they don't want to dance with me it's their loss.'

She wrenched the door open and gave Isobel a gentle push into the corridor.

★   ★   ★

Once she had got Isobel into the 'ballroom', which was in fact the refectory with all the tables temporarily removed, and some strobe lights and a cheesy mirror ball brought in, Daisy managed to find the designated girls' bathroom. Mercifully she was the only person there. All the other St Mary's girls were off trying to find dark corners to be pawed in, or shaking loose their long hair and dancing off their firm teenage asses so some penguin-suited spotty boy would come up and attempt to paw them . . .

Daisy smiled a bit at that thought. OK, so the face staring back at her from the mirror above the stinking urinals was plump, but was that any worse than some of the buck-teeth and pizza-faces her year was drooling over out there? She'd spotted one lad in that baying crowd who had a face that was erupting like Etna on a bad day, and another with coke-bottle glasses and railway-track braces on his teeth. She took out the free sample of Estée Lauder perfume she'd ripped from a magazine and brought with her in her bag, rubbed it over her neck and wrists, and marched into the ballroom.

There was definite revenge to be had, she thought, determined to make the best of it. After all, she wasn't going to be the only person who was about to have a bad night. She was a *writer*. So she'd sit here and watch and take notes. Daisy longed for her rough book, but it was back in her room at school. She would have to do it all mentally. She swept into the room, telling herself she was a stately Spanish galleon, just like in that poem they had learned in last week's English class, and made a beeline for a stretch of wall not already covered by gaggles of boys or girls. Isobel and Emma were on the dance floor with partners already. Daisy hoped one of them was Tom Rhys. Victoria and Arabella and most of the other girls were dancing by themselves, though.

Daisy instantly saw how it was going to be. A black-tie version of all the excruciating teenage dances she'd been dragged to. For three quarters of the time, the boys would huddle together, making loud coarse comments and trying to score a cider. The girls would dance with each other, pretending they didn't want the boys to come over and approach them. When the boys finally worked up enough courage to say something, the event would be almost over. One guy usually asked one girl, then there was a flood. Dancing lasted for less than five minutes, because people needed to get their snogs in before the final curtain. Watches were checked, lads fumbled enthusiastically and clumsily at bras stuffed with tissue paper, there was some tongue wrestling, and the lights went up. Girls ran off giggling and hoping for phone calls, and boys ran off to lie to each other about how Jo Smith had let them feel under her knickers . . .

Her internal monologue made her laugh. Victoria Campbell heard it. She was twirling stiffly to 'Venus' by Bananarama at the edge of the dance floor.

'Don't laugh at me, you fat cow,' Victoria hissed, flushing.

'Hard not to,' Daisy said. 'You can't dance. You should hang out by the drinks table.'

'Excuse me,' said a voice.

Daisy turned around. There was a tall, very lanky boy

standing next to her. His suit fitted immaculately, but she could instantly see that he was as skinny as a rake.

'May I have the honour of this dance?'

Victoria tossed her hair triumphantly and made towards him, flashing her green eyes at Daisy, but he shifted, and extended one bony hand to Daisy.

Victoria drew back like a snake poked with a stick, but Daisy hesitated. How did she know this wasn't just a cruel joke?

She glanced up at the boy's face.

It was terrified.

Daisy knew that look. She wore it every day. It was the look of waiting for the humiliation to happen.

'I'd love to,' she said, smiling radiantly at him.

He beamed, a mixture of pleasure and relief. 'Shall we?'

Victoria stage-whispered, as Daisy passed her, 'Couldn't you do better than that, Markham?'

Isobel, dancing with Tom Rhys, saw to her astonishment that Daisy was on the dance floor.

'Who's that boy?' she asked.

'Edward Powers,' Rhys told her. 'Very good family. Very rich. Clever. Bit eccentric. Who's the fat girl? It's like Jack Sprat and his wife.' He laughed.

Isobel hit him. 'Lay off.' She waved frantically at Daisy. 'This is brilliant. Everyone can see her dance.'

★  ★  ★

When Daisy said goodbye to Edward at eleven, he kissed her hand. She felt overwhelmed with gratitude towards him and had to bite her lip to stop from saying so.

'I hope I shall see you again,' he said, with old-fashioned courtliness.

'Of course,' Daisy said. She wasn't remotely attracted to him, but there was no way she'd allow him to suffer

89

one second's worth of humiliation. 'Here's my phone number.'

Miss Crawford shepherded them all back on to the bus, and as Daisy climbed on, everybody went, 'Woooh.'

She thought it was one of the happiest moments of her life.

# 9

'And we want to congratulate Daisy Markham,' Sister Clare said in her booming voice at Assembly. Her wrinkled hands gripped the polished wooden podium firmly as she looked out over the rows of girls sitting quietly in their neat navy uniforms. 'Daisy has been placed third in a national writing competition and although she did not get the prize, she has won a certificate of merit. I'm sure we're all very proud of her.'

Daisy sat on her polished wooden bench between Isobel and Emma, who clapped enthusiastically. The whole school gave her some dutiful applause. Behind her, Daisy could hear Victoria going, 'Oooh' sarcastically. Miss Crawford, up on the teachers' dais, looked satisfyingly green with aggravation.

That was nice, but it really didn't make Daisy feel any better.

Third. As in, not first and not even second. Basically, not close.

'Come up here and get your certificate of merit, Daisy!' barked Sister Clare excitedly.

Daisy lumbered to her feet, putting on a fake smile. She couldn't let Sister see how disappointed she'd been. Gutted, in fact. Everybody loved their old Headmistress, with the twinkle in her eye and the stout tweed skirts she habitually wore. Sister Clare always liked to see 'her girls' do well at anything.

Clearly, Sister thought this was a pinnacle of achievement for Daisy. Her results streamed her into a university, but not Oxbridge, and not even the second rank of London, Edinburgh, Durham, and the rest. She had avoided being put in the polytechnic class, but only barely, so there were not to be any great academic laurels for Daisy.

Instead, though, there was this stupid certificate of merit, Daisy thought, as she stumped up the podium steps.

'Well done, dear!' Sister Clare said brightly, thrusting the gold-embossed piece of paper at her. 'Smile for the school magazine.'

Oh, God. Now this humiliation. Daisy blushed and twisted the scowl on her face into a rictus grin. Some impossibly tall Upper Sixth-former, eighteen with coltish legs, neat little breasts and the long, glossy trademark St Mary's hair, was standing there snapping her for the *Gazette*.

Now all the parents would know she hadn't made it, as well as the entire school.

I ought to feel grateful, Daisy told herself.

But she didn't. She couldn't.

She felt like a big loser who had blown her only chance.

'You can go back to your place again now, dear,' said Sister Clare.

'Thank you, Sister,' Daisy muttered.

★   ★   ★

'What about this one?'

Isobel threw the prospectus across at Daisy. It landed with a little thud on top of all the other glossy brochures that were strewn across her coverlet.

'Rackham University,' Daisy read. 'A small university set in the heart of the ancient City of Oxford . . . oh, come on, there's only one university in Oxford. All the other ones are secretaries' colleges and places with 'college' stuck on the end of their names so they can overcharge stupid Americans who think they have something to do with actual Oxford University.'

92

Isobel sniggered. 'Mostly true. But Rackham's not all that bad. They have an entrance requirement of a B and two Cs. You could make that easily. You'd make three Bs if you bothered to pay attention to any of your subjects.'

Daisy pouted. 'But they're so boooring.'

'You're telling me. But no pain, no gain. They specialise in the arts. History, French, English, History of Art . . . and it's near the university. Near Christ Church. Just think of all the interesting people you could meet there. In fact, I hear,' Isobel said slyly, 'that Edward Powers is going to study at Christ Church.'

Daisy sighed. 'Subtle as a brick, aren't you?'

'I had a date with Tom last weekend.'

'How did that go? I'm much more interested in your love life than in you trying to fix me up.'

'And he mentioned,' said Isobel, not to be put off, 'that Edward wanted to know where you were going to go to university.'

'Edward Powers is very nice.'

'So you said after your last dinner with him.'

'But,' Daisy said, putting her foot down, 'I don't fancy him. Not at all, not even a little bit. I don't like boys that are really skinny. I like muscles. Now, I know I am not a big catch and I should be grateful to Edward for dancing with me and being interested at all, and I *am*. But I'd rather be alone than date somebody just because I'm — I'm the desperate fat girl who should take anybody that'll look twice at me.'

Her cheeks had gone shiny pink with high spots of red right in the middle, like they did when she was more than common-or-garden embarrassed. This might be the most honest she'd ever been with Isobel. And herself, come to that.

For a second her friend was stumped.

'But you could like him as a friend,' she said.

'Of course. He *is* my friend.' Daisy smiled. 'He's so clever. And he's such a gentleman. How could anybody *not* like him?'

'Well, then. I'm trying for St Anne's. So that would make two friends. And you always said that beauty mattered to you.'

'It matters so much.' Daisy finally paid attention. 'I couldn't bear some grim, industrial town somewhere. I need trees, or at least beautiful buildings.'

'Rackham's red-brick,' Isobel admitted, 'but it's near everything beautiful. Walking around is gorgeous in Oxford. And it's full of music, lots of chamber performances, debates — you can join the Union . . . '

Daisy looked at the prospectus.

'You can read English.'

'If I have to study one more Shakespeare play, I think I'll burst. Friends, Romans, Countrymen, fuck off,' Daisy declaimed.

Isobel burst out laughing. 'You're awful. It's Miss Crawford, she can make anything seem crap.'

'Maybe History of Art. I wouldn't mind taking lots of trips to museums and galleries.'

'There you go, then.' Isobel grinned. 'Thank your lucky stars you're not me. I have to cram three hours a night for the Oxford entrance examination.'

'Yeah.' Daisy smiled at her friend, but her thoughts were sarcastic. Thank heavens she wasn't in a class like Isobel! What a stroke of luck, *Daisy* wasn't going to Oxford University, she wasn't going to distinguish herself in any way.

Close, but no cigar. It seemed to be the story of her life.

\* \* \*

Daisy spent the next six months doing some half-hearted studying. The teasing had pretty much

94

stopped since Edward Powers had called at the school to see her. Victoria Campbell and her cronies made cruel remarks about Edward being a nine-stone weakling, but not too many; they were, Daisy had realised with a delicious jolt of pleasure, jealous.

It didn't really matter to girls like Victoria if a boy wasn't all that good-looking if he had money and was the heir to a title.

When Edward's father died, he would be Sir Edward, and his wife would be Lady Powers. Daisy hadn't realised the depths of Victoria's snobbery until she watched her reaction when Isobel told her about Edward being the son of a baronet. Her enemy had gone pale around the gills. Later, Daisy had had the delicious pleasure of catching Victoria poring over a Burke's in the library, open at the Powers page.

'Hadley Park,' Victoria was muttering to Catherine Jackson, her new lieutenant. 'Eighty acres of deer park, built in the eighteenth century, with a lake and . . . '

'I wouldn't bother, Victoria. He's taken,' Daisy had said triumphantly. Then she'd felt bad, because she knew she wasn't interested in Edward, not like that. But the look on Victoria's face was enough for her.

'I wasn't looking at that. Mr Skinny-Minny, you can have him,' Victoria said, but she blushed scarlet. 'You two will make a perfect ten.'

'Yeah, yeah.' Daisy patted the ink drawing of the Powers coat of arms and grinned smugly. 'Bothers you, doesn't it?'

Then she had walked out, without getting the history textbook she'd wanted. But Daisy knew how to make an exit.

Victoria had avoided Daisy after that. Most of the crueller girls did. Daisy understood. They judged a person's worth by men's standards. A rich boy wanted Daisy, and so now she wasn't such a loser. Even though she was exactly the same plump dumpling she'd always been, with the same bad grades.

Daisy worked out her time at school with nobody paying attention to her. Even Isobel didn't bother with her quite as much, because she didn't need so much defending. And she wasn't writing any more. A sense of listlessness and lethargy overcame her. Daisy coasted through her exams, and managed two Bs and a C, which both her parents and the school were thrilled with.

She knew she could have done better, but she didn't see the point.

Rackham accepted her for History of Art, and Daisy called to confirm she was taking up her place. When her parents came to pick her up from St Mary's for the last time, Daisy felt a sense of relief. School was done with.

Now she was an adult. Oxford would be different, it had to be. Something had to change in her life.

# 10

'Stop living pay-cheque to pay-cheque!'

The beaming faces of the people in the infomercial stared back at Rose. A man in his early twenties wheeled a yellow Porsche on to the screen as he pulled up to a comfortable-looking suburban house with a landscaped garden.

'Yes!' said the booming voice. 'You too can reach for your dreams with real estate! No need to rent! Houses can be purchased for no money down! Start with no credit! Put cash in *your* pocket every month!'

Rose reached up and turned the TV off.

'Mom,' she said, 'how's your credit?'

Her mother laughed, tossing the pasta.

'What credit?' she said.

★ ★ ★

After her dinner, Rose told her mother she was going to the library.

'That's real good, honey.' Mrs Fiorello smiled proudly, glad that Rose was finally going to do some homework. Her grades had plummeted, but her parents had attributed it to stress. Rose was so responsible, they just knew she'd come around.

Rose walked to the large, uninviting brick building three streets away. Her backpack was empty of schoolbooks. She walked straight to the real estate investing section, then to the personal finance section. Ten minutes later she was back in her apartment with a full load of books.

'I'll be down later,' she told her parents. 'I'm studying for something special.'

97

'What is it, honey?' Daniella asked.

Rose thought about it. 'Just a project.'

She went into her new bedroom, shut the door, and laid the library books out on the second-hand desk Paul had found her at the consignment store. Her bedroom was plain, apart from the posters. Other kids her age had Def Leppard and Motley Crue staring back at them from the walls, maybe with a touch of Madonna or the Beastie Boys.

Rose Fiorello had pictures of skyscrapers. New York prints in black and white, tattered around the edges so she'd gotten them for a discount; fifty cents, mostly. She was in the low-rise, low-rent, dirty Bronx, but she had glittering dreams; soaring buildings, covered in wraparound granite and sparkling glass, with smooth black tinted windows, jabbing into the sky.

And now she had these books to start off with. Eagerly, Rose bent her lovely head, her glossy raven hair pooling on to the chipped wood in front of her, and started to read.

After less than an hour, it became clear to her that 'no credit' was a crock. The chapters for 'no credit' dealt with how to get yourself credit.

'Take a thousand dollars and deposit it in the bank, then ask for a secured loan and — '

And where was she supposed to get a thousand dollars?

'Borrow it from a relative,' the infomercial king suggested.

Um, yeah. So many desperate people would pay three hundred dollars for the infomercial course to find out the first great 'secret' was to borrow money from a relation. If you had a relation rich enough to loan you a thousand bucks, you wouldn't need these books, would you?

Rose refused to be put off. After all, if you could buy

real estate for free with no credit, nobody would be renting. Her parents paid their rent cheque in each month and never saw that money again. Nobody would do that unless they had to.

Still, there had to be a way.

She thought about the money she'd saved up so assiduously from her summer job at the accountant's. There was over two thousand dollars there, just sitting in a bank. Her parents' credit was worse than non-existent. Rose mulled this over, then turned back to her books.

It seemed simple enough. Get enough money together for a two-family house, rent out one unit, live in the lower one . . . that way, you would get rent to cover the mortgage, each month.

Of course, you needed to find the right property, cheap enough. And the right loan, and you'd need to join a credit union, and check tenants, and you'd need to buy in an area with great rentability and one which was improving . . .

Rose read until darkness fell, then switched on her light and read some more.

She was startled when her door opened sharply, and her father stood there, shielding his eyes in his worn-out bathrobe.

'What the . . . ? You know what time it is, Rose?'

'No.' Rose rubbed her eyes. They were aching, but she hadn't noticed.

'It's two a.m. Get to bed, now! You got school tomorrow.'

She tumbled into her bed and tried to sleep, but she was too excited. Rose tossed and turned, full of adrenaline. There had to be a way to find properties better than the crazy stuff they put in the get-rich-quick books. Rose wasn't a sucker; she knew it was all a load of crock. 'Driving for Dollars', 'Hand Out Flyers', 'Hold a Real Estate Seminar' . . . Puh-leese. And what were you supposed to do in the real world? She wasn't going to start her empire that way.

What did the professionals do?

Rose finally got to sleep a few fitful hours before dawn woke her. She never drew her curtains; natural light was the best alarm clock in the world. When she rubbed the sleep from her eyes, she felt a crackle of excitement, despite her tiredness.

All the books talked about appraisals. An independent appraiser would value the house for the bank. You could hardly buy a house without one. Mostly, the get-rich-quick books talked about ways to avoid paying for the appraisal, which could be well over a hundred dollars. But wouldn't appraisers be the best-placed people in the world to know what a house was worth, and what it cost? They might even get to know where the bargains were. At any rate, they wouldn't get ripped off. How could they, their job was to know what everything was worth.

Rose figured she had two years to learn. She'd be eighteen then. She made a vow; on her eighteenth birthday she was going to own a house.

She packed up the real-estate books in her backpack and got dressed in her school uniform, ready to take the bus into Manhattan to go back to school. Her parents had been determined not to break that last link to their old life, and Rose agreed. She wanted to be in Manhattan.

That was where the action was.

At school that day, in between paying as little attention as she could get away with, Rose studied her books at break. At lunch she went to the phone booth in the hall, which kept a copy of the *Yellow Pages* chained to the wall. Rose took a pen and her rough notebook, flipped to the Property section, and started writing down names and numbers.

'Hey!'

Mike Chastain, the King Jock, their star quarterback with aspirations to Nôtre Dame, was tapping on the windows. Rose flipped him the bird.

'Get out of there, Fiorello!'

'When I'm done,' Rose snapped. It wasn't done to cross Mike at this school; he was super-popular, the favourite of the blondes in white bobby-sox.

'Bitch,' Mike snarled, turning away. Rose had turned him down for dates twice, even though her family was way too poor — which everyone knew — and he drove a BMW. Mike and his buddies had a bet on who was going to pop that cherry. He didn't like the fact he hadn't collected yet.

Mike thought it was about time Rose got taught a lesson. She wasn't even the super-brain any more. Her grades were dreadful, and she kept getting sent up to Sister Heloise's office. The teachers wouldn't be so bothered about her now, now she wasn't a scholarship prospect.

Rose moved out of the booth, holding her notebook. Mike snatched it from her.

'Give me that back!' Rose snarled, making a grab for it.

Mike laughed and held it up out of reach.

'Pay for it,' he said. 'Give me a kiss.'

'With your dog-breath?' Rose said. 'I don't think so.'

A small crowd of kids had stopped walking through the hallway and were watching. Some of them giggled. Mike Chastain's face darkened.

'The price went up,' he said. 'Now I want to feel up your tits.'

'You asshole,' Rose said.

'Let's see what we got here.' Mike held the book up out of reach, taunting her. 'Manhattan Real Estate Appraising. Option One Appraisals, Inc. Oooh.' He read out her notes in a sing-song voice. 'Norman Hubbard Appraisals. I think I see a pattern here.

What are you having appraised, Fiorello? A house? Oh wait, you don't have one, you got evicted.'

'Fuck you,' Rose said.

'Any time, baby.' He threw the notebook back at her — a teacher was heading their way. 'Do you know how *dumb* you have to be to get evicted from a rent-controlled apartment? That was nice going by your parents there, Rose. Hey, I got fifty bucks whenever you want to supplement your father's income. I got some friends that'd be interested too.'

Rose reached across and slashed at him, her nails raking viciously across his cheek, drawing blood.

Mike gasped and put his fingers to his face. The kids scattered, and Rose felt a heavy hand descend upon her shoulder.

'Name?'

'Rose Fiorello,' Rose muttered.

The teacher was wearing a heavy tweed suit and a thunderous scowl. 'Physical violence is cause for expulsion, Ms Fiorello. Unless it was self-defence?'

'I never touched her!' Mike started whining.

'He didn't hit me,' Rose said.

'Go straight to Sister's office, Ms Fiorello. Right now.'

★   ★   ★

'You must really like this décor,' Sister Heloise said dryly. 'You can't seem to keep away from this office.'

Rose mumbled something, but Sister wasn't letting her get away with it. Her face was crinkled under the dark-blue habit and crisp white wimple, and the old eyes, green and watery, stared piercingly back at her.

'Lift your head, girl. I'm going to give you my theory.' Sister lifted the sheet of paper in front of her. 'Grade A student until eight months ago, when your father lost his business and you moved out of your apartment near here.'

'We were evicted.'

'Yes, I know,' Sister said unapologetically. 'This is a school. Word gets around. Your teachers have been wondering about the drop in your grades, your lack of discipline and attentiveness; but they heard the children talking.'

Rose smothered a small smile at hearing her classmates referred to as 'children'.

'But,' said Sister Heloise firmly, 'to use a colloquial expression, I don't buy it. You may be many things, Rose, such as stubborn and wilful. But you are not lazy. You are also not responsive to stress. I do not subscribe to the fact that you have been traumatised by your family's financial troubles. There is some other reason for your behaviour. Now, what is it?'

Rose found herself squirming a little on the burgundy leather armchair. She preferred the usual lecture and detention . . .

'The reason for me hitting Mike Chastain was that he . . . said bad things about my father — '

'You are neither stupid nor five years old,' Sister said firmly. 'He *insulted* your father. If you want to carry on pretending to be stupid that's your affair, but you will not do it in this office.'

'Yes, Sister,' Rose said, taken aback. 'He insulted him. And he then said I could make some money on the side by — by — '

She looked at the nun's habit and blushed.

'I see,' Sister Heloise said. 'Sounds as though he deserved it, but violence is not the answer.'

Rose wasn't sure she agreed with that. Violence had certainly made her feel better.

'Why have you decided to stop trying to succeed here?'

'I haven't.'

'I do assure you, young woman, *I* am not stupid.'

Rose blushed and stammered. 'I — I think school

isn't as important as — '

'As what?'

'As making money,' Rose admitted.

Sister Heloise sighed.

'First, man does not live on bread alone. Someone said that once. But I understand that the viewpoint is not as fashionable as it might be. Second, even if you are not cut out as a pure academic, staying in school, and in your case winning a scholarship to an Ivy League university, is a good plan even from a mercenary point of view.' Her eyes twinkled. 'By taking one path, you will become a salaried employee who will be lucky to work your way up to middle management. By taking the other, you become a white-collar executive.'

'There is a third path.' Rose had settled slightly in her chair, and, the old nun was relieved to see, was speaking to her as an equal.

'Enlighten me.'

'I could get a job and train in something and then become an entrepreneur when I learned the trade.'

'I assume you have something in mind?'

'Real estate,' Rose said, proudly.

Sister's eyebrows lifted a fraction more.

'You sound very certain of that.'

'I am.'

'I'll make a deal with you,' Sister Heloise said. 'You can go ahead and get a part-time job. I will see to it that your homework is reduced. But not eliminated; you may have to study on weekends. However, I expect your grades to improve, starting tomorrow. You are going to go to college. And if your work and your attitude does not improve, I will call your parents and tell them everything before I expel you. I think their sorrow will be enough of a motivation for you to avoid that eventuality.'

Rose grinned. 'Thank you, Sister. I'll be going to interviews tonight.'

'Not tonight you won't,' Sister said. 'Tonight you have detention. We do not tolerate physical violence. That will be all, Miss Fiorello.'

* * *

Rose had six interviews before finally landing a job. It was out in Brooklyn, and she was to do filing and typing for two hours a night, cleaning the offices, and acting as a receptionist on Saturdays.

She made the most of it. Small as her salary was, she banked it each week, and her work was efficient. Rose countered the mind-numbing tedium by racing to get each job done as fast as possible. After two weeks, her fingers flew over the keyboard, and she could assign a file to its proper place by merely glancing at it. This made time for what she really wanted to do, which was talk to the appraisers.

'*This* is your ambition?' they asked, and Rose would answer sincerely, 'Yes.'

It wasn't so hard to believe. The top appraisers wore fancy suits and drove nice cars. There was plenty of work; appraising values all over the Tri-State area. Many of the best guys worked nights, frantically typing up jobs, trying to free up space in the day for even more appointments. Rose even saw one thirty-year-old, keen and ambitious, sleep in his office.

But this was the go-getting Eighties. Nobody thought twice about it.

'How do you work it out, though?' Rose kept asking.

'I'll tell you when I've got some time.' Keith Harding, the thirty-year-old, laughed. 'I guess that'll be the Tuesday after never, huh?'

Eventually Rose started to pick it up. You got the address and square footage, went to the place, measured the dimensions, took photographs. Then you looked up 'comps', industry slang for comparable properties. You had to find out what properties in a similar area, of a similar type and size, had sold for over the past six months. Appraisers had contacts in the area — realtors' offices, mortgage brokers — and they gave them this information.

It didn't matter what your house was worth — what someone would be willing to pay for it — only what the appraiser could prove.

Everything came down to those comps.

Of course, mortgage brokers and realtors were always desperate for the deal to go through. They would call every day, asking for a 'juiced' number. Push the value up, say it's worth more, or lose our business.

This was illegal.

It was also 'S.O.P.', or standard practice.

If the appraiser listened, though, they took a risk with the bank. A mortgage went south based on your false value, and you could be sued. Losing your licence was the least of it. You were then liable for millions.

All for a hundred and fifty dollars.

Good appraisers did more than measure and run comps, however. They were attuned to neighbourhoods. They got a feel for housing, for rent rolls, for values, and shysters.

Rose learned quickly.

She got promoted. After a while, they let her take photos on Saturdays. She drove round houses in a banged-up second-hand Nissan belonging to her boss, snapped them, and got more money. The appraisers got used to her nagging and her questions.

On Saturday nights Rose was often in the office, reading reports by lamplight, learning, soaking everything up.

'Why don't you buy something?' she asked Keith one day, when her courage was particularly high.

He made a dismissive gesture. 'My credit's not great. Down payment is too big. And tenants are a pain. Who needs the headache?'

106

Whomever she asked gave her the same answer: who wanted that kind of hassle?

I do, Rose thought.

When she'd finished at Richmond Appraising, Rose would pore over her school books. She liked history best, and now she'd started paying attention again. She had to; Sister Heloise watched her like a hawk. Her grades shot back up to normal. When the time came for SATs, Rose aced them.

Her parents were overjoyed. They expected her to get a scholarship, and so did Our Lady of Angels. The only problem was that Rose was falling asleep on her feet.

After Sunday Mass, she used to sleep all day.

And then Keith came to her with 22 Maple Leaf Drive.

# 11

'Good morning, class.'

'Good morning, Madame LaTour,' the class chorused brightly.

'Good morning, Madame LaTour,' Poppy muttered.

She was stuck in the acting class of Madame Marie LaTour, the famous fifty-year-old French doyenne of LA acting classes. Despite her un-chic uniform of a black dress which looked like a dyed potato sack and heavy brown brogues, Madame LaTour was the hottest ticket in Hollywood for rich teenagers. Her acting classes, priced exorbitantly high, had in the past produced more than a smattering of stars. Framed headshots adorned her corridors and outer office, the bigger stars in the more prominent positions. Madame was evidently proud not only of her two Oscar winners, but also of everybody you could see on the big and small screen — the soap stars and game-show hostesses amongst them.

Poppy grimaced. Mommy and Daddy had slashed her allowance to the bone, taken away her ride, and forced her into this. It was worse because she knew Mommy had to lean hard on all her social contacts just to get her in. Producers' daughters and studio vice-presidents' sons were in this class — that didn't leave much room for the offspring of divorce lawyers.

Her parents, she knew, secretly longed to be in 'the biz'. 'The biz' was films, or TV at a pinch — TV was looked down on, but that was where all the money was. Music, apparently, didn't count. Certainly not with her parents. And the fact that Poppy was passionate about rock didn't matter in the slightest.

'Today, you 'ave great opportunity.' Madame

LaTour's voice was masculine and raspy and she had bristling white hairs sprouting from her upper lip. 'You learn your craft in the cradle of the art. Of course, acting is more than a craft. Eet ees a joy, a calling . . . noble . . . powerful . . . '

Her audience was loving it. They sighed, with rapt attention.

'Through eemagination come performance!' Madame shouted, making Poppy jump in her seat. She pounded a black stick on the ground. 'Today — you start the dream!'

The class applauded wildly.

Oy vey, Poppy thought.

'You become a cup of coffee!'

'Hey, that's brilliant,' said the pasty boy in front of her with the Rolex. 'I mean, that's, like, super-inspired.'

Poppy stuck up her hand. She knew she shouldn't, but she couldn't help it.

'Mademoiselle?'

'Yeah, Mrs LaTour,' Poppy said, in a not-deferential-enough tone of voice. Her fellow students turned round in their chairs to face the back of the room, and sent her a barrage of deadly stares. Poppy ignored them. 'How can we act a cup of coffee? A cup of coffee is an inanimate object. We're never going to be asked to act an inanimate object, I mean, not since I was a tree in the third grade — '

Madame held up an imperious hand.

'You become, you feel, the heat, the confinement . . . Are you een a paper cup, are you een a silver coffee pot?' She waved her hands expansively. 'The choice ees yours!'

The class started to hum and rock. Some of them shuddered and made perking noises. Another one flung himself headlong to the carpet.

'Breeliant!' shouted Madame. 'He ees speeling all over the floor!'

'Fuck me,' Poppy muttered. 'How long is this class?'

'Eight weeks,' whispered the pasty youth in front of her. 'Isn't it, like, awesome?'

★ ★ ★

'Daddy,' Poppy wheedled. She was wearing her best good-girl outfit, the silk shirt-dress with the small shoulder-pads, the strappy sandals, and her Gucci sunglasses perched on top of her head. 'Honestly, I swear. I'll be good at school. I got an A for my math paper last week. I'm taking those classes — '

'You're not dropping out,' her father said darkly.

'No way,' said her mom.

'I don't want to. I totally love those classes! And I'm getting on really well with Jonathan Epstein,' Poppy lied.

'He's a very nice boy,' her mother said, softening slightly.

The phone rang in the next room and the maid entered the living room.

'Call for Miss Poppy.'

'Who is it?' her father asked, suspiciously.

'He say his name is Rick Perez,' the maid informed him.

Poppy felt the flush rise instantly to her cheek. Her hands started to sweat. 'I have to take this call, Daddy.'

'Who is this Rick? How do you know him?'

'From acting class,' Poppy said. 'He's my partner for our next assignment.'

Her mother noted the blush. 'He's not Jewish, with a name like that.'

'Mo-om,' Poppy protested.

Her father waved her away. Poppy hurried out to the hallway, forcing herself not to run.

'Hello, this is Poppy,' she said.

'What's up, baby?' said the bassist's voice. It had been

110

two weeks since the gig and she had given up hope that he'd call. An indescribable thrill shot through her. Her nipples tautened under her virginal white cotton bra, and that heat curled a new fist in her belly.

'You didn't call,' she said plaintively, then wanted to kick herself very hard in the shins.

'I've been on the road. You know how it is.'

Wish I did, Poppy thought.

'We got a gig tonight at the Whiskey. Want me to put you on the guest list?'

Poppy died a million deaths.

'I can't,' she whispered miserably. 'I'm kind of grounded.'

He chuckled. 'Tell me you're sixteen, at least.'

'Oh, definitely,' Poppy lied. She was getting good at lying, she thought. Maybe she wasn't such a shitty actress after all.

'How about we meet for lunch tomorrow? You know Nathan's? About one?'

Tomorrow was a school day. 'No problem,' Poppy said decisively. 'See you then, OK?'

She went back in and faced her parents again. Now it was really important! Poppy started to plead passionately.

'You know, Daddy — '

'Give me one good reason why I should restart your allowance,' her father snapped. 'How do I know what you'll do with it after *the incident*?'

'Well — all the other kids in class have, like, the hot records and they see all the movies and there's this cafeteria and I don't have any money and . . . ' Poppy lowered her voice in horror — 'I look like the *poor* kid in class.'

Her mom blanched visibly. Yes! Score one.

'Jerry . . . '

'On sufferance, Poppy.' Her father smothered an equally horrified look, but Poppy wasn't fooled. 'And you can only have half.' He pulled out his wallet and gave her two twenties. 'That's *it*, young lady.'

'Thanks, Dad.' Poppy gave him a jaunty kiss on the cheek, and her father tried not to look pleased. 'I'll be upstairs studying my lines.'

★ ★ ★

She couldn't concentrate in school the next day. Would Rick even be there? And would they miss her? If she was caught absent . . . it didn't bear thinking about. Plus, she had no sexy clothes. She was going to have to go in her uniform. She almost didn't want to do it, but she had no way to call him back.

And besides, Poppy secretly admitted to herself, she had to get real — there was no way in hell she wasn't gonna meet that guy.

It was so exciting. Finally, a little colour in her boring, middle-class life. She had kept flashing back to the concert, the lights, the sweat, the crackle of sex . . .

She grabbed a ride and headed over to La Brea at lunchtime, casually walking out of the school grounds. Nobody stopped her — she doubted anybody cared. One less JAP to worry about. That was all she was to this school. What the fuck.

Poppy arrived at Nathan's by twelve-forty and ordered a bunch of food she was too nervous to eat. She pushed the fries and sauce around her plate and watched the clock.

One . . . he didn't come.

One-fifteen, one-twenty — nothing.

Poppy was starting to feel embarrassed. She threw some money on the table and got up to leave when she saw him; standing in the doorway in a T-shirt and jeans, dark hair tumbling down his back, rock-star shades, looking about for her.

The girls were all staring at him, too.

She jumped up and waved. 'Rick! Over here!'

He saw her and threaded his way through the crowd. Poppy was suddenly ashamed of her waving and her lack of make-up and her little pleated navy skirt and white school shirt. She wished the linoleum floor would open up and swallow her whole.

'Hey, baby.' He pushed up the sunglasses to reveal a pair of bloodshot eyes, which travelled lazily up and down her uniform. 'Dig that skirt. That's sexy.' Perez leaned forwards and kissed her lightly on the mouth.

Poppy felt her knees buckle. She was overwhelmed with desire. He was so hot. Her peripheral vision noticed the girls in the diner staring at her. All probably wondering what a cool musician was doing with a schoolgirl. She felt geeky.

'Already ate, huh?' He was glancing down at her plate.

'I didn't think you'd come.'

'Wouldn't have missed it.' He looked deep into her eyes, in a way that made her want to dissolve. Poppy felt herself slick up.

'Do you want something . . . I can get the waitress . . . '

'Nothing on this menu.' He grinned and tugged at her hand. 'Let's get out of here.'

# 12

'Get in,' Perez said. He yanked open the sliding door of a beat-up blue van and Poppy jumped up on to the passenger seat. It smelled faintly of incense and weed, and there were empty bottles rolling around in the back. He walked around the other side, got in, and pulled away from the kerb.

'Hi,' he said, looking into her eyes.

Poppy felt a rush of joy. This was awesome. She was going on an adventure. Her life was finally interesting. It felt like being released from prison. What a high!

'Hi,' she said, and she didn't even blush.

He turned a knob on the ancient-looking radio and blasted KNAC. The strains of Metallica's 'Master of Puppets' filled the van, blasting from the windows, and he gunned the accelerator. Poppy cranked her window down — it actually worked with a handle, it wasn't even electric — and hastily tugged the scrunchie out of her hair, so it tumbled loose and golden, streaming in the blast of air that rushed past them.

'Where are we going?' she asked.

'You'll see.' He drove lazily, one hand on the wheel, caressing it almost. Poppy was attracted to everything about him. She loved the cool skull rings he wore all over his fingers. This guy was a badass.

'So what's it like, being in a band?'

He chuckled. 'Lots of sex, drugs, and rock 'n' roll; no goddam money.'

Poppy hated the idea of the sex. All those bitches hanging around him. She felt her first pang of jealousy.

'Is that why you got into it?'

'No, I wanted the money, too.' He laughed loudly at his own joke, then glanced at her through those dark-fringed eyes. 'Zach Mason writes awesome songs. I wanted to be in his band. It might go places. And anyway, what else am I gonna do? Be a bank teller? I'd rather shoot myself.'

Poppy was a bit embarrassed. She hoped he didn't ask too many questions. She was little Miss Suburban Rich.

'But why don't you have any money?'

'No record deal.' He shrugged. 'Even if we got one, we'd likely get screwed. Most acts do.'

'But you sold out your gig,' Poppy persisted. There couldn't be that much of a gap between the glamorous band onstage, with the glitter and the flash and the screaming girls and the hardcore security, and his real life — could there?

Perez scowled. 'You'd think so, honey . . . wouldn't you? We have to kick back money just to be allowed to play. The house gets most of the take, what's left has to go on roadie fees, and gas to the next gig, and if there's anything left over for the band we get a pizza or something. That food in the dressing room is the best we eat all week.'

Poppy was horrified. 'How do you survive?'

He gave her a sly wink. 'Chicks, mostly. If they come over to the crib we only let them in if they bring a bag of groceries, or a six-pack. Oh, don't worry, not you, baby. You're just a schoolkid.'

Poppy didn't want to tell him she had over seven thousand dollars in her checking account and a twenty-thousand-dollar CD which would mature when she was eighteen as a graduation gift. He was heading past the Beverly Center, barrelling down Third Street.

'But what about you? What are you gonna do with your life? Besides looking hotter than hell.'

'I'm going to be a rock star, too,' Poppy said enthusiastically.

Perez grinned. 'A singer?'

115

'I can't sing. I sound like a screech owl with a sore throat.'

'You're a riot.' He shook his head. 'You play something?'

'I'm going to be learning the guitar,' Poppy told him. She'd have to speak to Daddy about getting some lessons. A glorious vision of herself flung on her knees onstage, axe lifted up to the spotlight, head thrown back, her long, teased blonde hair cascading behind her, came blazing into her head. Yeah! She could be the next Nancy Wilson from Heart.

'Sounds good. What would you play?'

'Stuff like you,' Poppy said adoringly.

He reached out and traced a callused fingertip under her chin. 'You're cute.'

The van slowed and he turned the Metallica off. Poppy glanced outside, and saw they were pulling into a motel. Cars were parked in the forecourt, and it was painted Pepto-Bismol pink.

'You stay here, OK? I'll get us a room,' Perez said. He got out of the van and walked towards the main door.

Poppy's heart thudded. *He wanted to have sex with her.*

She felt confused and naïve. What should she do? Get out and run? Wasn't that childish, though? He thought she was hot and sixteen . . . was she acting like a teenager? She wanted him to be her boyfriend.

*Guys like that don't go out with girls that don't put out.*

Oh yeah, she was a wild rebellious rock 'n' roller — who wanted to run for the hills. Don't be pathetic, Poppy! she screamed at herself. All those girls shooting you the dirty looks, they'd give their eye teeth for this!

If she wanted to go out with Rick she'd definitely need to give him a reason; after all, he had women throwing themselves at him all the time . . .

He was coming back. Poppy took deep breaths,

composing herself. OK. OK. Everything was going to be fine.

'Ready, sugar?' He dangled the keys in front of her.

'Got any liquor?' Poppy managed.

He looked impressed. 'Good thinking. I got some in the back.' He walked around the back of the van and rummaged around, emerging triumphantly with a bottle of cheap vodka. 'We can make our own Martinis. Without the olive.'

Poppy clambered out of the van. Perez locked it — 'Who'd want to steal this piece of shit anyway?' he said — and took her hand. That same squirmy feeling returned to her belly, but she was scared, too. She wasn't gonna show it, though. He led her along the ground floor to a wooden door, 5E, and unlocked it with the key, flicking the light on. Poppy stood awkwardly in the room, glancing about; there was a twin bed with a brown coverlet, ugly, but clean; linoleum on the floor; a small TV wall-mounted, screwed into the wall, with a remote on a chain; a phone; and a tiny bathroom with a shower and washbasin. The tiles in the bathroom had grout that needed attention for mildew, but apart from that, the place didn't look dirty. Small and bare, but not dirty. There was no kettle, nothing like that. There wasn't even a glass by the sink for toothbrushes. Too easy to steal, she realised. In this place, even the bedside lamp was screwed down.

Perez noticed her shrinking. 'Relax, babe — this might be the one roach-free motel in LA. It cost me forty bucks but that's for the whole day, and this place never has bedbugs.'

She realised he was speaking like an expert, but told herself that he used it for previous girlfriends.

'There's nothing to pour the drinks into,' she said.

'Who needs it?' Perez turned the radio on again, found the rock station.

'And now — a little Queen for ya. Here's 'Under Pressure',' the DJ said.

Poppy smothered a laugh. This whole thing was crazy. The bass player tossed her the bottle. 'Go ahead. Internal heating.'

She didn't want to look like a putz. She took a long swallow of the fiery liquid, gulping it down. It seared her throat, and she broke off, spluttering.

'Hey! Hey,' Perez said, laughing. 'You're wild. Easy there, slugger. I don't want to carry you out of here.'

Poppy felt an instant head rush. She flopped down on the bed and twisted up the radio volume. He was standing over her, tall and gorgeous. His smile made her feel almost as dizzy as the alcohol. She tried to relax; the booze helped.

'You know, you're really beautiful,' he said, sitting beside her. 'Your face is one you remember out of a crowd.'

Then he pressed his mouth to hers and kissed her. His tongue curled into her mouth, tracing a line on her upper lip. Poppy had never French-kissed anyone before. She tried to reciprocate. His hand came up and cupped her left breast, kneading it lightly. Poppy suppressed a rising feeling of panic.

'I'm just gonna wash up, put a rubber on. Make yourself comfortable,' he said. He got up and went into the bathroom with the dirty tiles, shutting the door.

Poppy blinked. She was gonna go through with it. She reached for the bottle and took another large swallow, then another. She started to feel light-headed. She peeled off her clothes and put them neatly on top of the dresser and breathed in through her nose to relax.

Perez came out of the bathroom nude. Poppy swallowed a nervous giggle. He was hard, and she'd never seen a man naked before. It was different from the still photos they showed you in class.

The lust in his eyes took her aback. He was gazing at

her like a dog looks at a steak, she thought. Perez rushed over to the bed, took her into his arms, and started to kiss her nipples. Poppy lay back unresisting, looking at the textured white paint on the ceiling.

'Ah!' she said. There was a stabbing pain, and she felt pierced. She froze. So did he.

'Oh shit,' Perez said, 'you're a *virgin?*'

★   ★   ★

It was about the worst afternoon of her life.

After he was done, Poppy stumbled into the bathroom and puked her guts out. At last she retched herself dry, washed her face, sluiced out her mouth with tap water, and found a sullen Rick waiting.

'Let's go, OK?' he said.

Miserably she clambered into the van. Her head ached, her eyes were throbbing, and he was avoiding looking at her. At least the pain between her legs had gone away. Poppy could still see him, frozen above her. She had said, 'Well go on — don't stop now,' and had been relieved when it was over. Except that he'd said, 'So, how do you feel?' with that expectant look, as if he was about to get a gold star, and her answer had been to rush to the tiny windowless bathroom and start chucking her guts out.

Washing that stain from her inner thigh had been almost as bad. She wasn't a virgin any more. It was supposed to have been magical and sexy and to have lived up to that hot feeling in her belly, but it hadn't been anything like that. The best Poppy could say was that it hadn't taken long.

She hoped that next time it would be a lot better. Rick Perez would be a great boyfriend. Look at him, with that long black hair, tousled from the bed, and that stubble, and the skull rings. Poppy comforted herself that it was definitely worth it to have him as a boyfriend.

'When will I see you again? You have to give me a number,' she croaked, as he made the turn towards Beverly Hills.

'Uh.' Unlike before, Perez was the model driver, keeping his eyes firmly fixed on the road. 'I dunno. We're on the road. I don't have a number, we travel.'

'But you'll call me?'

'Sure,' he said, unconvincingly.

Poppy rested her head against the window and tried to concentrate on not crying and not throwing up. She had definitely screwed up. Maybe she hadn't been sexy enough. It was a dumb move to have drunk all that vodka. Nobody wanted a chick that threw up.

'Turn left here,' she said when they got near the school. 'Drop me over there.'

'OK.' He pulled up to the kerb with an obvious expression of relief.

Poppy got out, searching for something, anything, in his face that would let her hope that he still cared about her. She knew she should be sophisticated and act like she didn't care; all the girls said you should never sound desperate. But she really couldn't help herself.

'Make sure and call me, OK?' she said, and it came out in a definite pleading whine.

Perez looked her over, the white, sickened face, her beautiful cheeks gone colourless and pasty, her eyes bloodshot, her hair messed up. In the schoolgirl's uniform she was vulnerable and needy and she couldn't handle her drink. She had a hot body, but she wasn't a rock chick, just a kid living with her parents. No doubt she'd lied about her age, too. He preferred his girls willing and slutty. No guilt trips. Besides, he wanted to gun the van right out of there, before some state trooper came along with an arrest warrant for statutory rape.

'Uh-huh,' he said. 'See ya, Polly.'

Then he drove off without looking back at the little forlorn figure standing by the roadside.

★  ★  ★

She somehow got through the rest of the day. Nobody had missed her in school, and when Conchita arrived to pick her up, Poppy buried her face under a pile of books. She told her mom she had to study, went up to her bedroom, and flung herself on her bed amidst the dolls and teddy bears, and started to cry.

At least she had an ensuite bathroom. Poppy crawled into it, grateful for the spaciousness, the stand-alone shower, the bottles of expensive Floris bath oils, and her antique-style tub. She ran the water as hot as she could stand and poured in half a bottle of gardenia oil, so the entire room was filled with the scent of flowers. Anything to make herself feel less dirty. While the bath was running, she grabbed her toothbrush and scrubbed away the feeling of sick on her teeth, rinsing over and over with Listerine. Then she clambered into the bath and submerged herself, her hair, her entire body, washing her thighs, getting the dust and the smell off her.

Poppy dumped her school uniform in the laundry basket and changed into jeans and a T-shirt. She looked in the mirror. With her hair freshly dried, and the smell of sweat and old smoke particles from the motel no longer clinging to her, she felt like a different person. Her innate optimism reared its head. Maybe it hadn't been all that bad. The drink had been a mistake, for sure, but maybe all chicks did that, maybe everyone needed help with their first time . . .

Maybe he'd call her?

It wasn't working. He would not call. She remembered with a wince that at the end he'd called her 'Polly'.

She'd just lost her virginity in a seedy motel to some impoverished rocker who didn't give a fuck about her. Then she'd crowned the experience by vomiting and pleading.

Poppy thought bitterly that her parents would be pleased. Not at what had happened — yeah, like she'd tell them — but at the fact that she wouldn't be running off to rock gigs any more. She felt another one of her trademark blushes creep up her neck. Everyone would know. She pictured a scene of those girls in the stockings and garter-belts and fingerless lace gloves whispering that she was the girl who puked up with the bassist of Dark Angel . . .

She could never show her face at a club again. Poppy looked wistfully at her pile of hard-rock CDs. Well, obviously she'd never listen to them any more. Too painful.

She tossed back her luxuriant blonde hair and the fifteen-year-old face in the mirror sighed back, wisely, at her.

That part of my life is over, Poppy thought.

★   ★   ★

'I guess we can think about it.' Marcia Allen looked at her husband.

'She has been pretty well behaved.'

'What kind of bass?' Jerry Allen said suspiciously.

'Both kinds,' Poppy said innocently.

It had been a month since the motel episode. She hadn't been out to a club even one time. But Poppy hadn't been able to stop thinking about rock 'n' roll. She listened to Ozzy and Metallica on her headphones, and even the sordid sex had acquired a patina of rebellious adventure now she'd gained some distance from it. Her period had come, thank God, so she knew there would be no permanent consequences.

122

Poppy wanted some of the magic she'd had that night at the club. The crackling excitement, the roar of the crowd . . . lights sweeping the packed bodies, teenagers and college students all packed together like sardines, hands thrust into the air, fighting for a place in the front row. She wanted it so bad it nagged at her like toothache. But she'd learned her lesson. She didn't want to be one of the girls at the backstage door any more. Even if it felt good to be the girl that was picked. Poppy wanted to be onstage, and have all the kids screaming at *her*.

Like Nancy Wilson from Heart or Lita Ford or something. 'Kiss Me Deadly' . . . yeah! She could totally do that.

And then, as she didn't acknowledge even to herself, she could date rock stars. It was OK for girl rock stars to date their male peers. That was the stuff in X magazine. If non-musician girls did it then they were groupies. Look at Patti Smith. In her day she'd dated everyone. Chrissie Hynde, too. Even Heather Locklear. She'd gone out with a bunch of rock stars, now that dude from Motley Crue, and nobody called her a groupie because she was in *Dynasty* . . .

Girl rock stars had all the perks. Poppy wanted to be one. True, she couldn't sing and she also couldn't play. But she could definitely learn to play, if Mommy and Daddy would just stump up.

'Both? Why do you need to know the electric bass?' Jerry said.

'Daddy, you're such a lawyer. Always with the interrogation,' Poppy pouted.

Her father grinned. She knew he was melting. Poppy zoomed in for the kill.

'I want to learn some flamenco and some folk tunes, maybe even a little classical, but I'd also like to play Country and Western and you know, some Everly Brothers and Buddy Holly.'

Her mother smiled proudly. Marcia Allen was a huge Everly Brothers fan.

'Bye, Bye, Love,' Poppy started to hum.

Jerry's eyes crinkled. 'So no heavy metal then?'

Poppy rolled her eyes. 'Daddy! That stuff is so over. Come on, now all the kids are learning an instrument. Josh Cohen even started a rockabilly band.'

'All right, honey.' Her father gave in. 'Sign up, if you want to.'

'Thanks, Dad.'

# 13

Daisy opened the door to her tiny flat and sighed with satisfaction.

It was located down St Aldgate's, in a modern building. She hated everything modern, being strictly a country girl whose idea of perfection was anything which looked like it belonged in a Beatrix Potter book. But once you rode up in the lift — her flat was on the sixth floor — there was an incredible view. She had windows on two sides, flooding the place with light and looking over Tom Tower in Christ Church in one direction, and the green meadows leading down to the Isis in the other. It was autumn, and there was a pleasant crispness in the air, with the trees turning gold and red, and white mist creeping up over the fields in the morning.

Daisy adored her place. It even had a tiny balcony with a wrought-iron chair and table, so she could take her morning cup of real coffee, brewed up in a Bodum's pot, and sit out there in her white towelling bathrobe and just watch the beauty of Oxford. From a height, even traffic was romantic. She loved watching the students zip around on their bicycles, like so many ants, in jeans and sweaters, occasionally wearing some delightfully clichéd college scarf. It was the start of the academic year, and that meant the new crop of Britain's brightest, attending the University, were going through a bunch of ceremonies. They whirred past her in tasselled black caps and all sorts of gowns, like something out of an Anthony Trollope novel. Even her envy couldn't dampen her delight.

Daisy was only cynical about herself. This might have an air of Disneyland-England about it if you were a

125

*Guardian* reader, she conceded. But not to her. To her it was pageantry, and she loved it.

This was her first week up and she still wasn't used to anything. Not the city, with its glorious old piles of Elizabethan beauty around every corner, not her own little college with its lectures and classes, and not this flat. Mummy and Daddy had rented it for her fully furnished. It was by far the most luxurious place she'd ever lived in. Almost all Rackham students were crammed into dingy flat-shares on the Woodstock road, or thereabouts.

'We don't have to pay those school fees any more,' Quentin Markham told his daughter, solemnly. 'Budgeting is very important. You realise that, Daisy.'

'Of course I do, Dad.'

When had it ever not been important in their house? Daisy sometimes felt guilty about her hatred for school, knowing what a stretch it was for her parents to afford it. They went without holidays and her mother often secretly bought clothes at the Oxfam shop. But her mother was a clever cook and decorator and gardener, and kept an attractive house on a minute budget.

Being a teacher just did not pay well, and her father's job brought in even less, editing a line of translations of the classics. Academia may have been fascinating, Daisy thought, but it certainly wasn't lucrative. And yet, having adopted her as a child — endometriosis having left Sally Markham infertile — her parents had been determined to bring her up as a lady, as a member of the upper classes. And that meant public school.

If only she'd been scholarship material! They barely made it even with the shameful bursary Daisy received for being her mother's daughter.

But now the school fees monkey was off the Markhams' back, and Quentin Markham wanted his daughter to have the best possible time at university. He sometimes wondered if Daisy had really enjoyed her schooldays as much as she protested she did. He himself was lanky and small-boned and had been beaten up as a boy. But Quentin Markham did not allow himself to think like that. Daisy had survived, and even made her way to university. He wanted her to have the best. Or something like it.

So no faded wallpaper or shares with drunken freshmen for Daisy Markham. He rented this tiny jewel of a studio flat, with the view and the gated development, nice and safe, at five hundred pounds a month. And if Quentin Markham had seen how happy his daughter was to be there, he'd have thought it money well spent.

Daisy loved all the furniture. Everything was from IKEA, clean Swedish lines, lots of stripped pine. She had a sofabed, which saved space, and which she pulled out at night, shoved a fitted sheet and a duvet on to it, and then was able to sleep like a queen. There was a wardrobe, a chest of drawers, and a real sheepskin rug in which she loved to rub her toes. The bathroom had brand new tiling and shiny fixtures with a stand-alone shower as well as a bath, and the kitchenette even had a microwave. Perfect for baked potatoes.

For once in her life, Daisy had just about everything she wanted. She was filled with a wild, heady optimism. Oxford was gorgeous, her flat was gorgeous, and all she had to do now was go to a few boring lectures on Titian and Rembrandt!

I can't wait for Isobel to see this, Daisy thought.

Then she remembered. Isobel hadn't made it through the rigorous Oxonian entrance procedure. She'd been 'desummonsed', a horrible way of telling candidates 'don't call us, we'll call you'. She hadn't even made it to interview stage, and Daisy for once had had to comfort her friend, letting Isobel cry all over her shoulder and passing wads of Andrex over to her.

'Wait a year and reapply,' Daisy had urged, but Isobel

wouldn't hear of it. She took a place at Edinburgh and promised she'd stay in touch.

Deep down they both knew that it was unlikely. University was where people made the friends that stayed with them for life. But they hugged and cried as though it were a certainty.

Daisy anticipated starting out with a few acquaintances. There were six others in her particular History of Art course, though she'd only seen them a couple of times. And, of course, there was Edward Powers.

Daisy walked into her neat little kitchenette and put the kettle on. She got out the Tetley and her packet of milk-chocolate Hob-Nobs and made a small pot of tea, considering Edward and what to do about him. He was so nice, and she enjoyed his company so much. But he seemed to be so into her, and she wasn't interested. Was it cruel to be friends with him? Leading him on?

Oh come on, now, she told herself. Edward's rich and sort-of titled and this is Oxford. There are hundreds of gorgeous, intelligent girls just in his own college. He'd soon forget all about her. He could do so much better. And meanwhile, he was the only person that she knew at Oxford University.

Edward could be a window into that whole glittering life. Besides, she liked him. So why not?

Daisy ate three Hob-Nobs and started on a fourth before deciding that perhaps she'd better not. She was meant to lose some weight. At St Mary's it had been too hard, but here it should be easier. She could control her own diet. What did the skinny girls eat? Fruit.

Blergh, fruit. Daisy had never seen the point of apples and oranges when God made Buttons, Flakes and Hob-Nobs. But . . .

She looked down at her soft thighs, spreading out under her ample 501s. There were plenty of amazing-looking men here, and she still wanted to meet somebody. A new Marks & Spencer had opened in Cornmarket. She could buy some peaches there, maybe. And then walk round to Merton and see Edward.

★　★　★

Daisy picked up some healthy, taste-free options for supper — diet sandwiches and masses of fruit; vegetables was going a bit too far — then walked back down the High Street towards Queen's. There was a turning off to the left that took you down an ancient, cobbled road towards Merton. It ended in a little square by a back gate to Christ Church and the unimpressive frontage of Oriel College. To her left was Merton, apparently the only college in Oxford that served edible food. It was small and well-regarded. A bit like Edward, Daisy thought.

She went nervously inside the college gates. There was a sign directing tourists to pay an entrance fee. But nobody stopped her. She looked like any other undergraduate, Daisy realised.

Inside the porter's lodge were pigeon-holes with names stencilled above them. She found Edward's in a second. Daisy didn't quite dare approach the frock-coated porter in the bowler hat to ask where Edward's rooms were. She dug a biro out of her handbag and scribbled a note to Edward on the back of a scrap of paper.

'Hey.'

Daisy jumped out of her skin. There was a tall American boy standing right behind her. He was gorgeous, with black hair, dark eyes, a tan, and muscles. A rower, Daisy thought instantly.

'Sending a note to Powers? I'll give it to him, if you like. I'm his room-mate.'

'Yeah. Sure.' He was so good-looking that it came out

129

as a high-pitched squeal, like a dying mouse. Daisy loathed herself, but giggled nervously. 'I'm a friend of his from school. Daisy Markham.'

He shook her hand warmly and gave her a little bow. 'Brad Evans,' he said.

# 14

'And of course artists' relationships with their patrons were complex. Take Lorenzo de Medici . . . '

Dr Marsh droned on in his annoyingly monotonous voice and Daisy found herself drifting off. Marsh's lectures reminded her of particularly boring sermons at St Mary's. Back then, she used to stare at the stained-glass windows. Now, she gazed at the beautiful pictures of Renaissance masters in her book.

Luckily she was also sitting by the window. The lawns outside Rackham's lecture hall led down to the river Isis, and boasted an enormous weeping willow right by the river bank. Daisy loved that tree, loved to go and sit under its shade and imagine herself picnicking there with Brad Evans.

Ooh. He was *too* gorgeous. Thick muscles, broad shoulders like an American football player, dark eyelashes, and a sexy Southern accent. Daisy knew he was out of her league, of course. But he seemed to enjoy her company, at least.

She could see her silhouette reflected in the windows. Yes . . . There was definitely a little more definition to her chin. Eating fruit and Shapers sandwiches sucked, but it seemed to be worth it.

Losing weight was all about motivation.

Now she had some.

'Thank you, class, see you on Wednesday.'

'Thank you, Professor,' they chorused.

Daisy packed up her book and notepad and hurried out of Rackham's rather suburban grounds, making a right on St Aldate's, heading up towards Christ Church. She cut through the college to Merton. It was the shortest way, and it was so incredibly beautiful. Walking through Peckwater Quad always gave her a buzz; the stately beauty of the library made Daisy feel as though she were in a Jane Austen novel, and that Mr Darcy would drive a coach and eight horses past her any second.

Merton was not quite as attractive, but it was still beautiful. She didn't particularly envy Brad and Edward their room, though. Daisy liked privacy. She didn't have to share her own place. And even if it was modern, it had a view, and you didn't have to use a communal bathroom.

There was the sound of classical music drifting out of their room. Daisy rapped on the door. Obviously Edward was in. Brad preferred country and western.

'Come in,' Edward called. 'Ah, Miss Markham. Good morning.'

'Hi, Edward.'

Brad wasn't around. Daisy suppressed her stab of disappointment. What the hell, she liked Edward. Maybe Brad would be coming later. Edward had asked to take her to a speaker meeting at the Union, and Daisy hadn't been crass enough to ask if Brad would be coming too.

'You look as lovely as ever,' Edward said, his eyes drinking her in.

Edward was wearing a well-cut dark suit and expensive-looking shoes that picked out his black eyes. He always wore the same thing anyway.

Daisy twirled, feeling a bit uncomfortable, but smiling at her friend. She was wearing a navy dress with a heavy silk lining and a forgiving A-line skirt. Navy was just as slimming as black, but kinder to her skin tones. She had kept her make-up light and neutral, and she was trying to grow her hair. It was at that awkward stage right now, but she had twisted it up in a French pleat. The dress had little chiffon sleeves that covered her plump dimpled upper arms. Since she'd met Brad,

132

she'd become so much more aware of her figure. She'd thrown out every pair of shorts she owned, all her trousers that weren't jeans, every skirt that was made of thin material.

Fat girls — Daisy was harsh with herself, why not? Everybody else was — should only wear lined skirts and dresses. She had learned how to take five pounds off her figure by dressing better. Dark colours, monochromes, coverage of tell-tale bits like the arms, push-up bras for the huge boobs that were her one asset. And, yes, waists. If she gave in to the temptation to disappear in a huge piece of fabric it just made her look bigger. She needed well-fitting stuff that came down around her ankles. With blusher she could shade away — or at least minimise — the pouch under her chin, she could paint on cheekbones.

The other fat girls Daisy saw around the place went one of two ways: they either gave up completely, and wore shorts that showed their cellulite, had dirty hair and glasses, or they pretended they didn't care and wore God-awful 'funny' outfits — sweaters with 3-D animals embroidered on them.

Why did people expect fat girls to be funny? Daisy swallowed hard. Her eyes had started to glitter. No tears right now. She wasn't into feeling sorry for herself.

'You're so elegant,' Edward said. He sounded completely sincere. 'I feel quite underdressed.'

'Who are you dragging me out to see?' Daisy asked.

'It's a surprise.'

Daisy hit him.

'Oh, very well. It's Richard Weston.'

'No!'

Her skin prickled with excitement. Now it felt less like a dutiful evening out. Richard Weston was Daisy's favourite author. Bankrupt in a share scandal as a young father, he had written his first bestseller, *The Kensington*, out of sheer desperation — wanting to try something, anything, to get his family out of debt. He had received a slender advance, but the word of mouth on the slim paperback had been incredible. Weston had *it*; he knew plot, and he knew how to sweep the reader along in a frenzy of 'and then what happened?'.

Daisy wanted to jump up and down.

'Edward, you beauty.'

He grinned. 'I rather thought you'd enjoy that.'

★ ★ ★

The small, dank alleyway that led up to the wrought-iron gates of the Oxford Union was packed. Edward effortlessly managed to thread a path through the crowd of undergraduates, a few of them in white tie, most in jeans and sweaters.

'Officers,' he whispered in Daisy's ear. 'They always have to wear penguin suits. I'm only a college rep, so I get away with this.'

Daisy was ushered through the building's doors, where a man stood checking membership cards.

'Oh.' She blushed. 'I don't have one, I'm not actually at the University — '

'Sorry, miss, members only. The event's very oversubscribed — '

'She's with me, Paul.'

'Oh.' The hefty man grunted and stepped aside. 'Very good, Mr Powers. Come in, Miss.'

Daisy was impressed. Edward took her through the building and out into a little garden, thronging with students. A gravel path led up to another large gothic-looking building.

'The Chamber. It's meant to be an exact replica of the House of Commons, but it hasn't seen a lick of paint for about twenty years.' Edward shrugged. 'Doesn't stop people coming to speak, though.'

Daisy felt a pang of envy. 'You're so lucky, getting to

see people like Richard Weston in the flesh.'

'You have me.' Edward smiled at her gently. 'You can come as my guest to anything you like.'

He was so gentlemanly. Daisy suddenly felt very happy. She was lucky that Edward was such a good friend to her. Without him, she might have felt swamped here. As it was, the bullying and teasing of her miserable schooldays were already starting to fade into a bad memory, like something that had happened to somebody else.

Maybe it was just that men were kinder than women.

Edward showed her inside the dilapidated chamber with its wooden benches and ushered her to a spot near the front. The whole room was filling up fast.

Daisy sat there breathless with excitement and squeezed Edward's hand. Her eyes were sparkling. When the President, a young woman in a burgundy ballgown, and her officers, in white tie, entered the chamber, she could hardly breathe. Richard Weston followed them in, wearing a beautifully cut dark suit, with a sober tie and expensive-looking shoes. His watch was gold, and as he passed right by her, she thought it was a Rolex.

Everything about him screamed money, far more than any designer suit could have done. He was a step up from Hugo Boss or Armani. She could tell that everything he wore was bespoke.

Imagine writing books, the best job in the world, and getting paid a fortune for them!

Daisy felt like she was a groupie at a Bon Jovi concert. Her heart was racing and there was a light mist of sweat on her palms. She *loved* Richard Weston's stuff.

'Good evening, ladies and gentlemen.' The Librarian, a stocky-looking young Yorkshireman, stood to introduce his guest. 'We are privileged to have as our guest tonight the best-selling author . . . '

Daisy watched Weston's face. His eyes twinkled and he was watching the room carefully. The way he was observing them reminded her of herself. He glanced over at her and caught her looking.

Daisy blushed scarlet.

Weston winked at her.

' . . . Richard Weston!'

Weston got to his feet and started to speak. He had an open, easygoing manner, but he was extremely charismatic. Daisy drank in every word.

'I'm open to questions,' he said, when he was done.

Sixty hands shot into the air. Daisy tentatively stuck hers up, too.

'Yes?'

Weston was looking right at her.

'How do you feel about the critics sneering at popular culture, and do you find that your work is . . . '

Daisy shut her mouth. An eager and spotty youth next to her had jumped in with his question. She'd thought Weston was looking at her, but of course she wasn't about to be that lucky.

He answered patiently. A new forest of hands surged up. Daisy didn't feel brave enough to try again. She sat and listened as the undergraduates asked Weston to deconstruct his work, to comment on royalty structures, to speak on the decline of the English novel, and, rudely, to condemn what he did as pure trash that sapped the minds of the British people.

'Good God.' He laughed at that one. 'Sometimes you want to drink Château Lafite, and sometimes you want a Diet Coke. I'm in the Diet Coke business.'

The girl who had asked the question was slender and had a severely cut dark bob. She gave Weston a sneering look. Daisy was outraged. Snobby cow. If she hated Weston's books so much, why had she come tonight?

'We'd like to thank Mr Weston very much for agreeing to address the Society,' said the President smoothly. 'I'm afraid we're out of time for questions this evening.'

'I can take one last one, Madam President,' Weston said. 'Young lady.'

Daisy stared at her soft white hands.

'In the blue dress,' Weston said.

Daisy's cheeks flamed. She looked up. 'Me?'

'Yes. You had a question, didn't you?'

'Um, yes.' Daisy felt extremely shy, but he was smiling at her. Her question seemed a bit stupid after all the complex ones the other students had asked, but she thought it was what everyone secretly wanted to know. 'Are you very rich?'

'Really,' said the President, disapprovingly.

Edward chuckled softly.

'Bloody good question,' Weston said. 'Yes. As a matter of fact I'm phenomenally rich. I don't work much, I do something I enjoy and that other people enjoy, and I've made so much money I never need to write anything else in my life. But I still do, because it's so much fun.' He gave Daisy a wink. 'You should try it.'

'Thank you,' Daisy said. 'Maybe I will.'

The President stood and ushered her guest out, and the rank and file shuffled from the Chamber. Edward escorted Daisy through the crush of young bodies into the garden. It was dark now, and the stars were clearly visible even through the ugly orange glow of the street lamps. There was a mad run for the bar, but Daisy didn't feel like drinking subsidised beer in a crowd of rowdy students.

'Did you enjoy it?'

'Yes. Gosh, thanks.' Daisy hugged herself. 'It was so exciting.'

'He liked you, obviously. He wasn't pleased when that undergraduate took your spot.'

'I thought he was looking at me. But I suppose I was a bit crass . . .'

'Bloody hell, no. Everybody was wondering the same thing, but didn't have the guts to say so. I think you amused him.'

'I'd love to be Richard Weston,' Daisy sighed.

Edward looked at her. 'I'm very glad you're not.'

There it was again. That awful feeling. Daisy stammered, 'Look, Edward — '

'Forget it. Do you feel like eating?'

'Uhm — '

'Brad's asked me to meet him at the Bird and Baby.'

'Sure.' Daisy relaxed. 'Why not?'

★ ★ ★

The Eagle and Child — known to students as everything from Bird and Baby to Fowl and Foetus — was a little walk uptown, and Edward shepherded Daisy through the crowded streets. Oxford had an incredible combination of beauty and electricity. After school, the sense of freedom was like a drug. Daisy wondered what it would be like to be here and actually be at the University. Like Edward and like Brad. There was a slight regret in the pit of her stomach. If she'd applied herself, she could have been there, too. She kind of knew it.

Maybe I've been settling, Daisy thought. Unhappiness was a great excuse to settle.

As she walked along, she could feel the first signs of her changing body. Her thighs, which usually chafed uncomfortably, weren't quite so close together. She could feel a bit more definition in her face. Small changes, yeah. But something. Brad's body was pure muscle, thick, but not fat. She'd gone down to the river once to watch him row. When the Merton eight came in first, Brad pulled his shirt off. Daisy had stood on the wet, cold bank of the Isis and felt something unfamiliar — the pull of real desire. Of course, she knew she wasn't in his league; she was going to have to stop thinking about him.

Easier said than done, though.

Edward took her into the pub and Daisy tried not to look too eager. Where was he? Oh yeah, there, sitting by the fire and nursing a Budweiser, a weak American beer. But Daisy forgave him for that, because everyone knew Americans didn't drink. Edward lifted a hand, spotting him, and went across the room.

'Hello,' he said.

'Ed. How's it going?'

Daisy laughed; she'd never seen anyone less 'Ed'-like than Edward Powers.

'Hey, pretty lady,' Brad said to her, 'How you doing tonight?'

'I'm OK,' Daisy said, blushing lightly. She lowered her head so Edward wouldn't see.

'What you guys been doing tonight?'

'We went down to the Union to see Richard Weston.' Brad looked blank.

'A famous author; and Daisy here wowed him.'

'I didn't wow him, I just asked him if he was rich.'

'Getting right to the point, huh.' Brad grinned. 'I like a chick who speaks her mind.'

He looked at her, and Daisy thought she could lose herself for ever in those dark-lashed eyes; and then his eyes slid off her.

'I was thinking about trying out for the rugby team,' he told Edward.

'You don't know the first thing about rugby,' Powers replied.

'True, but I'm built like a linebacker and I can play football.' He flexed his biceps. 'Whaddaya think, Daisy?'

She gingerly felt his arm; it was hard as a rock. 'I think you'd be a great rugby player,' she murmured.

'Piffle, rugby's an art,' Edward protested, and the two men started talking about sports, which bored Daisy

139

rigid. She just sat and nursed her half-a-cider and tried not to be too obvious as she gazed at Brad. He was just so hot. Of course, his eyes weren't on Daisy; he kept checking out other girls around the pub as he talked. But it didn't put her off. She couldn't help it, she just wanted him.

# 15

Rose qualified her tenants through an open house. She had everything ready; the place was clean and sparkling, and she put fresh flowers in each apartment. The response was encouraging. Rose was polite and friendly; she didn't tell anyone she was the owner. She selected tenants, took deposits, and ran credit checks. The ones with the best records got the apartments.

Meanwhile, Rose moved into the basement. She'd had it fitted out as cheaply as possible, getting her furniture from garage sales and deep-discount stores, and even though it was gloomy, she added lots of lamps and mirrors opposite the windows and had everything white, to make the most of the light from the small openings.

She banked her first month rent cheques and held her breath, but they all cleared.

Rose took money from the first and paid the mortgage; the rest she had to live on. It amounted to over a thousand dollars a month.

A fortune.

Her parents couldn't believe it. Rose made her father come out to Maple Leaf Drive the first Sunday she moved in.

'You own it?' her father said. 'I don't understand.'

Her mother just burst into tears again.

Neither one of them minded her moving out, or if they did, they didn't let Rose see it.

'I always knew you'd be spreading your wings, sugar,' Paul said proudly. 'My daughter, a homeowner.'

Rose didn't see them having to park the car around the corner, sobbing in each other's arms, right after they drove away.

She was tempted not to bother with Columbia. She had run the numbers on 22 Maple Leaf right after she bought it, adding in projected rents, and she thought that right off the bat she'd probably made twenty thousand. What she wanted to do was refinance, take out fifteen, and buy something else. It was risky; she had no equity cushion. But rents were going up everywhere, and one three-family in Mount Vernon wasn't the glittering skyscraper she had pictured on her walls.

But she didn't dare. It would upset her mom and dad. For all the love they'd given her, Rose thought, she owed them.

So she showered in the tiny, tiled but windowless cubicle she had down in the basement, got up at seven, and walked down to Columbus Avenue to catch the bus for the city.

★   ★   ★

'Welcome to Orientation Week,' a student said brightly, a young man with too-long curly hair and I'm-smart glasses. 'My name is Sebastian, and I'll be showing you around the campus today . . . '

Rose quietly slipped out at the back. She thought she could find her way around without this guy. All she needed to know was the location of the library and the classrooms for her various courses. For the rest of it, she was going to be the loner she'd been at high school. Student housing blocks — who cared? Community room? No thanks. She regarded her fellow students not exactly with disdain, but with total disinterest. Rich kids, bright-cheeked, with scarves trailing and neat hair and new leather ankle boots under their 501s; no scuffs, and being driven up to the door in shiny cars — Mercedes, Rolls-Royces, Porsche 911s. Rose had nothing in common with them. She

142

sighed, and tossed her long fountain of raven-black hair behind her. Four years of *this*. Maybe if she made enough on the side she could drop out, and her parents wouldn't mind.

Rose started quietly at the history faculty. She took a spot in the back of the class, listened politely to the professors, and took notes. She never bothered to ask questions. What would be the point of that? She understood what they were saying. Rose cared more about getting out and taking the bus back home, walking around her neighbourhood and looking for more properties.

★ ★ ★

'Miss Fiorello.'

Rose stopped, startled. Professor Bartlett was calling her. She paused on her way out of the lecture hall. Had she done something wrong? He'd seen her taking notes. She never talked in his class.

'Yes?'

'Come here, please.' Bartlett was in his late forties, a crisp, neat and rather effeminate man, with a manicure and a piercing stare. He was also her favourite lecturer. Rose never missed even one of his talks on the Renaissance. Reluctantly, she walked up to the front of the hall, where he was standing by the podium.

'You have an appointment? A job to go to?'

'Not exactly,' Rose said.

'I'm having a symposium tonight. Various students will be attending. It's a discussion group on Elizabeth I. I would like you to come.'

'I really — '

'It's an invitation-only group,' Bartlett said. He shrugged. 'If you are not interested, it's not compulsory. This is extra work, without credit of any kind. There's nothing in it for you except academic interest.'

'I'd love to come.' Rose smiled at him. 'Thank you, Professor.'

'We'll be meeting in my rooms at five-thirty.' He gave her the directions and turned back to gathering up his notes.

Rose walked out of the lecture hall and headed to the library. She could sit and read there without having to spend a dollar on a cup of coffee. Also, nobody could bother her. Rose didn't like to wait around for guys to hit on her. Ever since William Rothstein, and then Mike Chastain, she'd avoided boys.

All they wanted to do was fuck her, use her. She guessed that one day she'd meet a 'nice' man, whatever that was — somebody like her father, just a little smarter. Rose blushed with disloyalty at the thought, but she instinctively knew that intelligence was the single most important thing for her. She shared a culture, a faith and a childhood with her parents, but what she didn't share was genes.

She was cut from a different cloth, and it wasn't simply a matter of her dusky skin and ice-blue eyes, her slanting cheekbones and the tall, slim frame that could not have come from her mother. Her father was hard-working, but he had no dreams, no ambition. All of which, and the brains to achieve them, were millions of miles from Paul and Daniella. Not from their daughter.

But there would be time to find this nice guy after she'd got where she needed to go. When she was a millionaire and had ruined Rothstein Realty, then she could get married. Right now, Rose wasn't even looking.

She pored over her notes on the Papal States until five-twenty, then grabbed her papers and headed off to Professor Bartlett's rooms. Rose might have mistrusted the invitation, but she was pretty sure Bartlett swung

144

from the other side of the plate. Anyway, she loved his lectures.

Rose grudgingly guessed that since she was at Columbia, she might as well get a real education.

She knocked on the door.

'Who is it?' demanded Bartlett's soft, rather breathy voice.

'Rose Fiorello.'

'Come in, please.'

The door opened and Rose found herself in a room which would have been spacious were it not for the books everywhere — stacked in piles on the table, on chairs, on the floor, looking as though they multiplied themselves when people weren't watching, like Tribbles in *Star Trek*. There were two couches and two chairs ranged on a rare book-free stretch of floor, and students were already sitting perched upon them.

There were eight in total. Marion Watson was bookish and always asked Bartlett questions; Rose wasn't surprised to see her here. Apart from herself, Marion was the only woman. The others were all kids whom she regarded as 'keen' — library hounds and lecture hogs who signed up for courses they weren't even studying, just for fun: Keith Jones, Tommy Crawford, Hank Javits, Peter Blake, Brad Oliver. Two others she didn't recognise; one was small and skinny, the other taller than herself, and muscular. He had brown hair and hazel eyes fringed with dark, thick lashes, and a square, masculine jaw with a touch of five o'clock shadow. Rose noticed his confidence — his arrogance — first. Then her eyes flickered over the suit and the shoes. She had seen suits like those before — in the front windows of Saks. Her gaze darted to his wrist. Yeah, there was a Rolex there.

How predictable, Rose thought.

'Now we are all assembled, I'll make the introductions,' Professor Bartlett said. 'Everybody, this is Rose Fiorello.'

There was a chorus of greeting.

'I know everybody,' Rose said, 'apart from these two . . . gentlemen.'

'This is Stanley Young,' Bartlett said, indicating the weedy kid, 'and this is Jacob Rothstein.'

'Hi,' Stanley said. Jacob nodded at her, his dark eyes examining her in the way men usually did.

'Of Rothstein Realty?' Rose joked.

Jacob looked annoyed. 'I prefer not to talk about that, if you don't mind.'

Rose sat down sharply. A flush of shock had hit her, creeping from her neck right up to her hairline. Her heart started to race and she felt a sheen of sweat hit her skin.

The entire group caught her reaction.

'I didn't mean to embarrass you,' Jacob said.

Rose just managed to catch her breath, with a supreme effort of will. 'You didn't. It was — a — a — head-rush.'

'This week's meeting is on Elizabeth I of England,' Bartlett said. 'Last week I asked the symposium to consider how Elizabeth's childhood affected her policies as Queen.' He turned to Rose. 'You are our new member, but you'll pick it up. You can learn a good deal from these meetings.'

'I'm sure,' Rose said softly.

'Mr Rothstein,' said Bartlett. 'Why don't you start?'

146

# 16

'I feel therefore that this sense of danger, of being hunted, remained with the Queen throughout her reign and that the diplomatic skills she learned during her various confinements were put to full use in the avoidance of marriage.'

Jacob Rothstein stopped speaking, setting a sheaf of neatly typed notes to one side.

The room gave a collective sigh and leaned backwards in their seats. Rose saw that they had been spellbound by watching Rothstein talk. He had a soft, even voice, very confident, she would even say polished. He had made eye contact with each one of them, including the Professor, drawing them in to his argument, binding them to him. He was obviously quite used to public speaking. She had to force herself to keep looking away, so that nobody saw her staring at him with loathing.

Jacob Rothstein spoke like a man entitled. Entitled to their attention, to their respect, to commanding this room.

'Jacob, that was wonderful,' Marion Watson purred. Rose watched with disbelief as Marion fluttered her eyelashes at him. Marion Watson, who hardly seemed to know men were alive!

Well, Rothstein *was* good-looking, Rose conceded privately, if you liked that *obvious* sort of thing.

She didn't. Rich Columbia jocks were two a penny.

'Yes, fascinating,' Keith agreed.

'I disagree with your conclusions,' Rose snapped.

Everyone blinked and looked at her. Professor Bartlett raised a neatly plucked brow.

'Ah, Miss Fiorello; I was hoping a more informal

setting might bring you out of your shell. You have an alternative viewpoint?'

Rose nodded, holding Jacob Rothstein's gaze as he looked at her. Evidently he wasn't used to being challenged here.

'I think Mr Rothstein, and historians in general, are looking for neat little facts to fit neat little theses,' she said, coldly. 'But real life doesn't fall into such patterns; or very rarely. And not in the case of Elizabeth.'

'I believe,' Jacob said, equally coolly, 'that the facts I have presented support my conclusions.'

'So do I.' Rose gave him a polite smile that did not reach her eyes. 'But what about the facts you did not present? If Elizabeth had such a sense of fear, why did she react as she did to the preacher at Mary I's funeral, who said, 'Better a dead lion than a live dog?' If her dance around suitable princes was evidence of such incredible diplomatic tact, honed by years of sucking up to her father and brother and sister, how come she put on madrigals insulting the French and Spanish, and in her lifetime gained a reputation for sleeping around?'

Bartlett was now staring at her, fascinated. His eyes began to twinkle gleefully.

'What of the Queen being suspected of the murder of the wife of one of her favourites? When the Countess of Essex was killed by a suspicious fall down the stairs, people thought Elizabeth was behind it. This level of cavorting at Court — which, after all, endangered her crown when the Irish rebellion was raised by Essex — does not tend to your view of a frightened monarch, desperately calling on all her reserves of diplomacy.'

Rose took a deep breath and settled back in her seat. The class gazed at her, as though they were watching a train wreck. She instantly understood that Jacob was the big star of this group. Her pale blue eyes challenged him.

Rothstein squared his shoulders and regarded her.

'You cannot try to deny that Elizabeth was able to string her various suitors along in a masterly way, before they finally gave up hope. And, furthermore, this . . . tease,' he said, deliberately looking her over, slowly, his glance travelling up her legs and flickering over her breasts before rising to meet her stare, 'was applied not only to foreign courts but also to the pressure from her ministers at home, who looked for an heir.'

'I do not deny that,' Rose said.

Jacob shrugged. 'Well, then.'

'I challenge the causation you are trying to establish,' Rose went on. 'You assert that this skill was the result of the privations of her childhood, and all the loyal protestations she had to make to her father and siblings in order to keep her head on her neck. However, it seems more likely that this skill was simply innate. If she'd felt hunted and threatened all her life, she would not have been prancing around with married men — her inferiors, men who could only hurt her political aims. Nor would she have authorised pirate raids on Spain . . . '

'Very interesting.' Bartlett's measured tones cut her off. 'I see you two could engage in debate all night. Clearly we have added another valuable member to our group,' he inclined his head slightly towards Rose, 'especially as Miss Fiorello was not aware of the subject of tonight's discussion. Wouldn't you agree, Mr Rothstein?'

Jacob Rothstein examined his rival and grinned very slightly, which Rose found extremely annoying.

'Yes, I would,' he said softly.

'For next week, we will discuss Renaissance literature. Miss Watson, you will speak on Dante. I would like the rest of you to study the topic in pairs and each pair will speak briefly after Miss Watson. Mr Crawford and Mr Blake; Mr Javits and Mr Young; Mr Oliver and Mr Jones; and Miss Fiorello and Mr Rothstein.'

Rose blushed with anger, but what the hell could she do, say no?

Bartlett was looking her way, with a hint of mischief in his eyes.

'That's OK with you, Rose?'

'Certainly, Professor Bartlett,' Rose muttered.

'Wonderful. See you all next week.' And the class stood and filed out of Bartlett's room in pairs.

The students pooled out on the stairwell, and Rose found herself trapped by admirers.

'Wow, that was awesome,' Stanley Young said earnestly. 'How could you argue like that off the top of your head?'

'I've always liked Elizabeth,' Rose mumbled, desperate to get away.

Jacob Rothstein glanced at her over the top of the crowd. 'I'll make an appointment to meet you, Miss Fiorello. Where are your rooms?'

'Off-campus,' Rose said shortly.

He scribbled a note on a business card which she saw him pull from a solid gold card-case. 'These are mine. Does noon tomorrow suit?'

'Whatever,' Rose snapped.

'See you then.' Rothstein turned and walked down the stairs, leaving Rose stranded in a throng of admirers.

★   ★   ★

The next morning, Rose did a little research.

Jacob Rothstein. Star debater, pussy hound, jock — he boxed, apparently — and top of his class. He was in the year above her, and he had aced his exams. Women flung themselves at him, and, one of the girls she occasionally spoke to told her in the bathroom, giggling, 'he's just too polite to say no'.

150

He had the charm of a Southern gentleman married with the sophistication of New York. Add the fact that he was an heir to a vast fortune — 'They're in *Forbes*,' Anna told her, with a wink. 'You interested?' — and girls could not stay away.

'So he loves 'em and leaves 'em?' Rose asked.

'Yeah, but in a nice way.'

'How the hell can you do that in a nice way? Come on.'

'Look.' Anna fluffed up her blonde curls and reapplied her lipstick, with liner. 'He doesn't promise anything, you know? That's what the bullshitters do. He just promises you a real nice time. *Reeaal* nice. And when it's over, he sends you a nice piece of jewellery.' She sighed. 'He's very generous.'

Rose stared at Anna suspiciously. She was a short, luscious-looking chick, with porno lips and platinum hair and more than a handful of T & A. She was carrying a few pounds, maybe, but she was definitely attractive, in that easy sort of way.

'How do you know all this?'

'See these earrings?' Anna twirled her head. 'You should go for it, too. He'd love a chick like you. Maybe you could even date him for real, you know? It's worth a shot.'

Rose bit down on her lip. She wasn't going to say that she'd never have casual sex with any guy, much less with arrogant Jacob Rothstein. Anna didn't see the world the way she did.

'He's really not my type. I just have to study with him,' she explained.

Anna giggled again. 'Is that what they call it these days?'

Rose shut up. She couldn't convince her, and she didn't want to try.

★   ★   ★

151

When she turned up at Rothstein's rooms it was noon on the dot.

'Come in,' he called, to her smart rap on the door.

Rose opened it, but did not enter. Rothstein's room was sumptuously decorated; it looked like dorm-room via Ralph Lauren. English country house chic.

'Why don't we study in the library?' she suggested.

'Um, because we can't talk there?' Jacob Rothstein said. He looked her over again, and she bristled.

'Don't look at me like that.'

'Like what?' Rothstein said innocently. 'You're an attractive girl. What am I supposed to do, go blind?'

Rose entered his room and closed the door behind her.

'Let's get one thing straight. I don't like you.'

Jacob snapped his fingers. 'Damnation. And my first impression was that you couldn't wait to jump my bones, you were so bowled over by my devastating good looks.'

'Save that for girls like Anna Kent, OK?'

'Ah.' Jacob's eyes lit up. 'Anna. She was lots of fun.'

'She returns the compliment. Now if you would just get to work, we can complete this assignment and I can get out of here.'

'Perfect.' Jacob turned to his books. 'Just out of interest, though, enlighten me. What exactly have I done to make you dislike me quite so much?'

★   ★   ★

God, she's gorgeous, Rothstein thought. She didn't want him staring at her? Too bad; he'd already inventoried the hand-span waist, the long, lean legs in those sexy blue jeans, the tumbling waterfall of sleek, black hair that, amazingly enough, did not look as though it had been dyed, the soft, olive skin, and those incredible eyes.

Of course, the eyes were fake. They had to be coloured lenses. Nobody had palest-blue wolf-eyes like that, so intense and startling under the soft lashes. He wondered if those tits were real, too, but honestly — who cared?

She was the total package, and didn't she know it, he thought. Rothstein liked chicks. His tastes were catholic, as far as bed went. Short girls with lusciously slung hips and big tits — delicious. Tall, lean girls with that arrogant model look — great. He didn't like extremes of weight in either direction; apart from that, he really didn't care. Rothstein enjoyed sex and wasn't looking for commitment. He took pride in his lovemaking, regarding it as a form of art. When women sobbed and scratched in his arms, Jacob thought he was doing OK by them.

But Rose Fiorello would be nobody's one-night stand, even if it weren't for the fuck-you attitude and the general air of frigidity. It was as though the ice in her eyes had spread little frozen tendrils all over the girl's body. She was the polar opposite of come-hither beauty. Rose was stay-away beauty. Moral beauty. Which made her all the more appealing.

Jacob had seen her before. Most of the males that studied history had seen her before. She was always bolting out of her seat after lectures, as though an errant wasp had stung her on the ass, carrying her thick sheaf of notes with her, looking neither to the right nor left, for all the world like a Wall Street banker barrelling through the crowd on his way to work. She was pure New York, with that don't-mess-with-me attitude.

You could not miss her. She was tall and spectacular. Her clothes might be plain, but they did nothing to detract from her beauty. Her long hair was, surprisingly in this heavy-metal decade, not teased, back-combed, crimped or otherwise messed with; just sleek and glossy, like an otter darting from a stream. Her eyes were just startling. Her figure was lean, but not skinny; she had some tits and ass going, he thought approvingly. And her face, from the shockingly gorgeous eyes to the high, aristocratic cheekbones, the full lips and the long, straight Roman nose, was just . . . perfect.

She was a million miles from Malibu Barbie, but really, so what.

Other girls at Columbia — and Barnard, which was across the way — dressed more sexily. They had implants, mini-skirts, towering heels, Donna Karan, manicures, bleached-blonde hair. There were plenty of milk-fed, All-American, rosy-cheeked beauties hanging around this campus.

Not one of them was like Rose Fiorello.

But asking her out was taking your ego in your hands. He knew guys that had tried it — or at least attempted to try it. Mostly, they never got further than 'Hi', or 'Excuse me, sugar — ' before Rose cut them off, and barrelled out of the lecture hall.

She didn't mingle. She didn't socialise. She wasn't in student politics or dramatics or night-classes.

Her whole, gorgeous body threw off her lack of interest in everyone around her.

Jacob had suggested to Professor Bartlett that Rose be invited to join the symposium. He had studied her carefully. She seemed to pay the most attention in Bartlett's lectures, according to his informants. And he assumed she would appreciate a challenge.

Well, he thought dryly, I got that right.

'Let's see.' Rose shut his door and sat down on one of his chairs, perching on the edge of it as though it were contagious. 'Why don't I like you? Maybe because I hear things. Cheap Lotharios don't really do it for me.'

Jacob arched a brow. 'Honey, there's nothing cheap about me.'

'Don't call me honey.'

'And I doubt you heard anything before last night.

You may have asked afterwards. It was clear then that you didn't know who I was.' He grinned. 'I like the idea that you had me checked out later, though. Now tell me; what did I do to you last night?'

'Do? Nothing.' Rose's eyes narrowed. 'Maybe your fancy suits and watch that costs what some students here live off all year bugged me. Maybe I noticed your cocky attitude and thought you needed a little deflating.'

Jacob thought about making a joke on the topic of Rose not being that likely to *deflate* him, but decided against it.

'Maybe I don't particularly warm to little princes who come to college with Daddy's money and assume they own the place.'

'Maybe you should pull that stick out of your ass.'

'Excuse me?' Rose said, outraged.

Jacob looked at her evenly. 'Oh, get over yourself, kid. You can dish it out, but I don't have to take it. I make no apology for the success of my family. In fact, I'm very proud of it.'

'I bet you are.'

'Damn straight. And as to my being here on Daddy's money, I made 4.0 and the ninety-seventh percentile on my SATs. Don't make the mistake of thinking rich kids are all stupid, just because you won a scholarship. I deserve to be at Columbia. In fact, I deserve to be anywhere in the Ivy League. I'm in Professor Bartlett's class because I am one of his best students and aced my midterms. And if some girls like me' — he shrugged — 'you know what that is? None of your business.'

Rose stared at him and tried to think of a decent retort. Nothing sprang to mind. Shit.

'Now we've cleared the air,' Rothstein said after a second, giving her a superior smile, 'if you want to storm out of my room in a tantrum, can you please do it right away? Then you can call Professor Bartlett, and we can both get reassigned.'

'You're not as hot as you think you are,' Rose hissed.

Rothstein moved a fraction closer to her, staring her right in the eyes.

'How do you know?' he said softly. 'If you want to find out, there's a spot here for you anytime.'

He patted his bed.

'You're making a pass at me?'

'Don't look so jumpy. I'm issuing an invitation. I don't take any chick to bed unless she asks me to. And . . . '

That lazy, confident gaze trickling over her again. Rose fought an impulse to squirm.

' . . . you'd have to ask me at least twice.'

Rose deliberately settled back in her chair. He was attractive, she admitted it to herself.

But not to her.

She thought of William Rothstein. Loathsome, ugly slug; very little like the princeling in front of her, except in his arrogance. Rose tried to recall William's features, but time had blurred them; she had only an impression of revulsion, and the memory of the sound of his voice, the cutting, contemptuous words.

She smiled thinly, despising him and his clan.

'Don't hold your breath. And as for me storming out of here, I hate to break it to you, but you're really not that important. Shall we turn to the subject? I've brought some books.'

*　　*　　*

They worked through the lunch hour. Rose argued her points quietly and methodically, but she was crackling with adrenaline. She wanted to stare at Jacob Rothstein, the heir to the company she was going to destroy. Not that he would know it. Rose wanted to scream it in his ear, to hit him, to let him know without the shadow of a doubt that she was after him, that it wouldn't be long now.

But she did not. She simply debated with him, took notes and discussed the topic.

Rothstein was infuriating. After that introduction, he'd just continued to work as though nothing had happened. He was smart, too, and he knew his period. He could match her point for point. In fact, he had insight. At the end of an hour, the two of them had prepared a remarkable paper.

'It's been interesting,' he said, offering his hand when she stood up to go.

Rose let it hang there.

'We aren't friends,' she said.

Rothstein shrugged.

'Your loss,' he said. 'I was looking forward to getting to know you.'

Rose turned on her heel and walked out.

'See you tomorrow, toots,' he called after her.

Rose's heart didn't stop pounding until she'd got out of his building and two streets away from campus. Bastard, sexist, womanising bastard! Patronising jerk! She was hot with fury, almost fighting to get her breath.

It took twenty minutes of bus ride to realise she had made a mistake.

Rothstein was a scion of Rothstein Realty. If she was serious about striking back at them, she should use him — the same way he'd used all those chicks. He looked at her like a sex object, and he said he was proud of the company. She shouldn't have any hesitation about deceiving him.

When she saw him tomorrow, Rose thought, she'd be nicer to him.

The arrogant son of a bitch.

# 17

'Yeah, baby,' Fiona crooned. '*Yeah!*'

Poppy thrashed out the last chord on her bass and tossed her black mane of hair into the red spotlight trained on her. That was it; last song. She felt the sweat dripping from her body. Her leather pants looked hot, but they also felt hot. She needed $H_2O$ badly.

'Thank yew!' Fiona screeched. 'Good night!'

Poppy smiled out at the crowd who were clapping dutifully. A couple of metal-heads in the front who had been leering at the band all night stuck their fists in the air and whooped.

Make noise, make some noise, Poppy thought.

But she knew it wasn't working. Fiona grabbed one of her hands and Lianne, their rhythm guitarist, the other. Behind the drum-kit Elise stood up and did her patented Nikki-Six drumstick twirl. The band bowed and blew kisses to the audience.

'Hey man, they want an encore, let's do 'Outcast',' Fiona hissed.

Poppy could see the crowd was already drifting off to the bar.

'No they don't. Let's go.'

To forestall further debate, she waved at the club and ran into the tiny dressing room at the back. It wasn't much bigger than a bathroom stall and didn't smell much better. Graffiti from a hundred club acts covered the walls. Poppy thought about scrawling her own — *Snaggletooth was here and we sucked ass.* At least that would be honest.

The other four girls followed behind her and went straight for their pathetic rider, a bottle of cheap vodka and a carton of cranberry juice. There were also some plastic bottles of water and Poppy drained one of those instead.

'Dude! Did you hear that! We fuckin' rocked,' Fiona gloated. 'They were, like, so into it, man. And I sounded awesome, I sounded like Lita Ford.'

Hoo boy, Poppy thought.

'Yeah, we rule,' Lianne said. 'Those guys were totally staring at us.'

'I thought we sucked,' Poppy said. 'We really need some new stuff. And more practice.'

'You're so negative.'

'Shut up.'

'You don't know.'

'Ignore her, she's always like that.' Fiona scowled at her bassist. 'Maybe we need some other chick on bass.'

'She looks good, though,' Elise said.

'You're real lucky, Poppy. Lucky that not too many chicks play bass,' Fiona said again, like she always did. 'Anyway,' she added, tossing her long blonde hair and brightening, 'guess what? Fix your make-up, ladies. Guess who's waiting to see us after the set?'

Poppy had a sinking feeling.

'Joel Stein, that's who.'

'Please tell me you're joking,' Poppy said.

'Who's Joel Stein?' Lianne asked.

'He's this big-time manager. And he's here to see us!'

The other girls screamed, jumping up and down and clapping their hands.

Poppy blushed from pure embarrassment. Her band, Snaggletooth, had only just started. The girls didn't want to rehearse enough, their songs sucked, and they all thought they were about to be discovered by John Kalodner and turned into the next Guns n' Roses. Joel Stein, she knew who Joel Stein was. He ran the Dreams management company. He had a huge stable of multi-platinum bands and a handful of up-and-coming new acts.

She hoped Stein had not come to see them. They were nowhere near ready. Poppy wasn't sure if they ever would be.

'We're gonna meet him at the bar. Let's go!'

'Wait!' Elise said. She turned to the small, grimy, cracked mirror over the doorway and adjusted herself, undoing her leather zip-top to show a generous amount of cleavage. The band tarted up; lipsticks, liners, perfumes were all generously applied. Poppy reluctantly checked that her mascara had not run.

'Wooh! Yeah!' Fiona was giving that annoying screechy cheering she loved to do. 'Let's go, Snaggletooth!'

She flung open the door and raced out into the club. Poppy followed. Girls ignored them totally; a few of the guys patted their asses as they threaded their way through the packed darkness.

'Hey, babes. Great band.'

'You ladies are hot, you want a drink?'

'What's up, sugar?'

'See?' Fiona turned around and looked disdainfully at Poppy. 'They *love* us, man.'

They reached the stairs that led up to the bar area. There was a tiny, cordoned-off section in the back; the 'VIP' room, what a joke, Poppy thought. A small cubby hole that only stank less than the rest of this poorly ventilated cess pit because there were less bodies crammed into it like human sardines. Oh no . . . there *was* a guy there . . .

Fiona flashed her laminate at the security guard and he drew back the shabby red rope to let them in.

'Joel, dude, so nice of you to come,' Fiona purred. The other four swarmed around him, batting their eyelashes and jiggling their boobs. Poppy blushed some more; no matter, it was too dark in here for that to show. She looked at Joel Stein. He was tall, well-dressed; beautifully cut chinos, a pressed white

T-shirt, a Rolex, a gold pinky ring, and long hair in a pony tail, with Ray-Bans on top of his head. Typical record exec, one of those fit forty-year-olds.

He glanced at her.

'How do you do, Mr Stein,' Poppy said politely, and offered her hand.

Stein shook it, crooking an eyebrow. Fiona kicked her, none too subtly.

'So, hey, we rocked! Huh? Huh? We should talk contracts!' Fiona screeched.

Stein's face was impassive.

'I'm gonna have to pass, girls. You're a good band, but you're just not what Dreams is looking for.'

'Whaddya mean, *pass*? Didn't you see the set?' Fiona demanded.

'Shut up, Fiona. Thank you for coming to see us, Mr Stein,' Poppy said.

'You always ruin everything, Poppy!' Fiona's voice was almost a scream now. 'Keep your fucking trap shut!'

'Um, good luck with finding management,' Stein said.

'No, wait!' Fiona yelled, but he was gone.

'Oh — shit!' Lianne rounded on Poppy. 'You just blew it for us! We could have talked him into it!'

'You're fired!' Fiona yelled.

'No, man, we can't find another chick bassist,' Elise moaned.

'We'll get a guy then,' Fiona snarled.

'No, Fi — '

'Save yourselves the trouble.' Poppy's disgust overflowed. 'Joel Stein isn't stupid. He didn't think we were good, he was just being polite. We don't practise enough to be good. The songs suck and Fiona has a voice like a barn owl. It takes more than long hair and big tits to be a rock band. I quit.'

'You suck as a bassist! You're always off-beat!' Elise, the drummer, accused.

Poppy considered this. 'You're right. I do. But you know what the man said — 'If at first you don't succeed, try, try, try again. Then quit. No use being a damn fool about it.' '

Fiona reached out and pulled the laminate off Poppy's neck. 'Fuck you, bitch! You're out of Snaggletooth!'

'I'll try to get over it,' Poppy said.

'Come on, girls. Let's get the hell out of this dump.' Tossing her hair, Fiona stormed off with the others, leaving Poppy behind.

'If you don't have a laminate you can't stay in the VIP section,' the guard grunted.

Poppy looked around her at the empty four square feet of ground.

'That's fine.' She bit back a smile and went to the bar. 'Jack and diet Pepsi, please.'

'Diet?'

'Damage limitation,' Poppy said. She slid ten bucks across the bar and waited for the glass to appear. This was her drink now. The alcohol and soda and ice was cool and pleasant in the heat of the club.

Poppy needed a drink. She'd have this one, then leave. So much for her career as a rock star. And Joel Stein had actually seen that disaster . . .

Ugh.

'And now, please welcome Silver Bullet,' the PA said.

The nightclubs had opened now and the crowd was thinner, unenthused. Poppy looked at the stage with sympathy. A quartet of girls ran on, waving. They were cute; they looked a lot like Snaggletooth.

This is gonna be *bad*, Poppy thought. She wondered exactly how bad. Worse or better than her own shitty band? They couldn't be all that much worse . . .

'This one's called 'Flying',' the lead singer said. Poppy saw that she was cute and in her early twenties.

The band started to play.

Poppy blinked.

She couldn't believe it. They were awesome. They were everything Snaggletooth wasn't; put together, on-beat, punk rock with a nice dose of pop, and a singer with a rich voice. Kind of low and husky for a girl. Great rock-star voice. Kind of Janis Joplin . . .

Her drink lay untouched before her on the bar. Poppy watched the whole set. Even the thinning crowd moved to the front of the stage. People cheered and whistled.

It's a pity for Joel Stein he didn't stay to hear *them*, Poppy thought.

And then it hit her.

She tossed back her drink — it felt good — and slid off the bar stool, moving down the steps into the main body of the club, trying to get a good look.

The place was half-empty, but the electricity was still there. Tunes. They actually had tunes. What a change from her own shitty band; from just about every other half-baked act that played this dive. Excited, Poppy did an inventory in her head. Songs, check, attitude, check — the bass player was a bit overweight and was playing her instrument like she was Keith Richards, with a cigarette hanging on for dear life out of the corner of her mouth — and looks, check — no matter if the bass player was overweight and the rhythm guitarist had the jaw of a horse, the singer was hot, with long red hair, and the lead guitarist was a pretty punk; her hair was spiked up, but it was a disconcerting pastel-pink and the girl had the face of a model. Poppy couldn't see the drummer. Chops weren't so great, they weren't all that polished. But that didn't matter with a rock 'n' roll band.

They were stars.

She could see it, right away. They were everything Snaggletooth wasn't. And she had ideas for them, plenty of ideas.

Poppy wasn't interested in being a bassist any more.

She watched these chicks and she knew she had no talent. It didn't bother her, though. She had a better idea.

She wanted to be a manager.

Silver Bullet ripped into another number.

Poppy turned her attention to the small crowd. They were going mental. It was probably a shock to them to watch something that wasn't a total suck-fest.

Poppy had found her vocation. She knew something was wrong when her own band stunk the joint out and she didn't really care. Her heart hadn't been in it. But when she'd heard Joel Stein was there, *then* she'd started to give a shit. Poppy had been so impressed by him. The way he'd stood there, so calm. Such command. His eyes had swept over everything, processing data like a computer.

She had wanted to be him. Instantly.

And maybe now she could. She wasn't sure how, but she'd think of something.

'Hey.' The singer tapped the mike. 'Thanks. We're Silver Bullet.'

The whole band stood up and just walked right offstage, ignoring the baying cries for more.

Stylish.

Wait a second, Poppy thought, I know that girl —

The drummer was walking off. She had a cute haircut, very distinctive, a platinum-blonde bob. Poppy had seen her earlier that evening, up in the bar before Snaggletooth went on. She was getting her rider — the plastic bottle of four-dollar vodka — to carry it backstage, and had seen the girl then. She was tall and lean and surrounded. A group of drunk guys were homing in on her; Poppy had only noticed in the packed darkness because that blonde hair caught one of the dim club lights and reflected it.

Poppy hadn't thought twice. She'd had her band laminate on, and had strode into the men.

'Hey!'

'Ease up, sugar.' A brawny biker-type with tattoos was stroking the girl's denim-clad butt as she swore at him and tried to get away. 'Unless you wanna join the party.'

Poppy was wearing her spiked-heel boots. She ground one of them into the thug's toe and he yelped and stared at her.

'I'm with the club,' Poppy said. 'Leave the young lady alone or get the fuck out.'

Her voice had so much venom they actually backed off.

'You OK?'

'I am now. Thanks.' The girl had looked shaken and moved off. Poppy had headed backstage, feeling slightly virtuous, and then forgotten all about it.

She grinned. That was a start, no? Managers were supposed to make trouble go away. Now the band were backstage. Poppy checked out the door that led back into the club. Nobody was going to see them. She felt a tiny sense of relief. Mingled with nerves.

Was she really about to pitch these girls to let her manage them? She was younger than them. Poppy tossed her long black hair. It didn't do to think too much about it.

They emerged. She saw they'd changed outfits. They were now in jeans and T-shirts. Poppy's excitement grew. That was rad. Even this early on, they had stage clothes. She loved it.

Poppy walked up to them.

'Hey.'

'Hi. Oh, hey.' The drummer thrust out her hand. 'This is the chick I was telling you about, she saved my butt. How you doing? I'm Lisa.'

'Poppy Allen.'

'Kate,' said the singer. 'Molly.' The bassist. 'Claire.' 'Debbie.' Rhythm and lead. They were all smiling at her; that was a start.

'I watched your set,' Poppy said without preamble. 'You rocked. I'd like to manage you.'

★　★　★

She took them to Luigi's.

'I'm starving,' Kate had said.

'Let's go get a bite. I'll buy you dinner.'

'Really? That'd be great,' plump Molly said hungrily. 'I can normally only afford White Castle.'

Which explains the size, Poppy thought.

'Can we go to Denny's?' Molly said, hopefully. The other girls looked a bit embarrassed, but nobody contradicted Molly. 'We don't get paid that much,' Lisa explained.

'The diner? We can do better than that. You guys like Italian?'

They were practically drooling.

Poppy fetched her car from the parking lot and tipped the valet. It was a drop-top Chevy. They looked impressed.

'I'm afraid you're gonna have to cram in there.'

'Hey, no problem,' Kate said, looking pleased. 'I get the passenger seat.'

Her band exchanged looks, but they clambered into the two back seats, crouching on top of each other.

Poppy drove to Luigi's because it was close. Her father gave this place a ridiculous amount of business.

'Signorina Poppy, ciao, cara,' Stefano said, kissing her extravagantly on the cheek. 'Ees so good to see you.'

'These are my friends, Stefano,' Poppy said firmly. He had been looking askance at the jeans and T-shirts and beat-up leather jackets.

'Ah, si? No problem, for you no problem. This way, please.'

He led them into the restaurant and seated them in a corner banquette. Normally the place had a dress code:

166

jackets and ties only. The girls looked at the other diners in their Hugo Boss and Armani and pearls.

'This is real fancy,' Kate said approvingly.

'The food here's not bad.' A waiter handed them their menus. 'Anything you want, ladies.'

Poppy saw their mouths were watering.

'Lasagne,' Molly moaned. 'Oh, man. Hey, thanks a lot.'

Poppy ordered a carafe of house red. 'And bring some champagne cocktails to start off with.'

'Very good, madam.'

Now they were gazing at her with something close to awe. Poppy felt a bit ashamed. She was buying all this with Daddy's money, Daddy's connections. But she had nothing, herself. Fuck it. A manager couldn't afford those kinds of scruples. Let them think she was super-successful.

The cocktails arrived, Kir royals in crystal flutes. Poppy lifted hers in a toast.

'To your success.'

'Success,' they echoed.

'This is awesome,' Kate said. 'You should definitely manage us.'

'Glad to hear that,' Poppy said confidently. 'You won't regret it.'

She talked a good game over dinner. Record companies, radio stations, booking them into clubs which weren't pay-to-play. They were obviously broke and hungry. They scythed through the food when it came, relished the wine, sopped up the flavoured oils with their bread. Poppy could see a warm glow, part contentment, part alcohol, descend over the table.

But it wasn't quite that easy. The cute pink-haired punk, Debbie, tried three times to ask her who else she managed, and how she could do it so young. The other girls kicked her under the table, and Poppy just smiled and refilled her glass. But she saw that Kate, the singer, watched with keen interest.

The band knew they were hot.

She was going to need to convince them with more than a good meal. But one step at a time. Right now, she just didn't want them talking to anybody else.

'Thanks, that was awesome,' Molly said when she had settled up and they were standing on the street outside.

'I'll give you a ride home,' Poppy offered.

'That's OK,' Claire said. 'We live right around here.'

'Give me your numbers.'

They looked at each other.

'We don't have a phone,' Debbie said, 'but I got a beeper. OK?'

Poppy understood at once. They were probably squatting someplace. 'That's fine.'

'We're gonna need to talk with you some more before we sign a contract,' Kate said.

'I know. I'll buzz you, we can meet up.' The valet parker pulled up with Poppy's car and she jumped into it. 'See you girls later.'

That went well, she thought as she drove off. But she knew it wasn't going to be enough.

She needed a plan. Bad.

# 18

'This is Kate.'

'Hi, this is Poppy. Where are you?'

'At a payphone on Wilshire. Hey, I'm glad you called. We had a band meeting. You're really great, everybody likes you — '

Poppy could hear the 'but' in her voice.

'We were, you know, kinda wondering what contacts you have at the big labels and stuff.'

'I know people at college radio, people at venues, and I can get you guys great deals at — '

'Um.' Kate sounded awkward. 'That's the kind of thing we thought, but that's not really enough . . . '

'Oh, that's not all.' Poppy laughed. 'I'm gonna call you girls back tomorrow. I have a few meetings. Just wanted to touch base and see if you were OK.'

'We're fine, but — '

'Talk to you tomorrow,' Poppy said firmly. 'Bye.'

She hung up. *Damn.*

Oh well. She'd expected that. They were all older than she was. It was always going to be a rough sell.

Poppy felt in the pocket of her coat. She had the demo tape that Kate had given her last night. And now she had exactly twenty-four hours to do something with it, or give up the whole idea.

The band may have been starving musicians, but they weren't naïve. They had probably been together a few years, been around the block, just never got discovered. Poppy knew what they were looking for: a major label deal, money for recording time, a professional producer, a support slot on a big tour. The usual. The Sunset Strip dream.

She had to deliver it or she'd be out before she'd even got in.

Poppy had no contacts. Last night she'd thought about Daddy, but his roster of clients was all film and TV. Snaggletooth had never made so much as a ripple in the music scene. It was a mystery to her how Fiona had managed to get Joel Stein to come and see them. And she could hardly ask Fiona.

*Joel Stein.*

Of course. That was it. Her first instinct was always the right one. Pity Joel Stein couldn't see them, she'd thought.

Dream Management. Big offices on Wilshire Boulevard, near the Whisky and the Rainbow, right in the heart of the scene. Mercedes and Porsches always parked out front in its lot. They managed so many big stars; they'd know everybody, forget it; the promo guys, MTV, the Monsters of Rock people, and all the major labels.

I could take them to him. And go to work for him.

Poppy dialled 411. 'Dream Management, Hollywood, please.'

★ ★ ★

It was exactly what she had expected.

The office screamed money. It had polished marble floors, a giant mock-up of the cover of *Sergeant Pepper* on the walls, a kidney-shaped reception desk, a receptionist in Donna Karan, and framed gold and platinum records everywhere. There were coffee tables in front of the couch laden with *Billboard, Music Week* from the UK, *Variety*, and other trade publications.

'I don't see you in the book, Miss,' the receptionist told her.

'Check again.' Poppy was wearing her most expensive clothes, a gorgeous vintage black Dolce & Gabanna suit, with Wolford hose, Calvin Klein shoes, and the gold Patek Philippe she'd been given for her last birthday. 'I'm with Reckless Records. Poppy Allen? We made the appointment two weeks back, at least.'

She opened up her Hermes bag and handed the girl a business card.

It said: 'Poppy Allen. A & R Director, Reckless Records.' The script was embossed in black. Poppy was quite proud of it, for something she'd knocked up at Kinkos in ten minutes flat.

'Let me see what I can do,' the receptionist said, warily.

She punched a button on her phone bank and talked low into the receiver for a few minutes.

'He says you can go straight in. It's right at the end of the corridor.'

'Thanks,' Poppy said, trying not to reveal her joy. She turned and pushed open the glass doors. There was a long corridor with offices at either side; some of them had two or three people inside, shouting into phones. Fax machines were spurting, there was rock music playing in the background, the whole thing was electric.

Poppy's palms started to sweat.

This is rock 'n' roll, she told herself. Just do it.

Stein's office was at the very end of the corridor. The door, like the others, was open. He had large windows and a Persian carpet and the sun glittered off all the records which covered his office, floor-to-ceiling, like multi-platinum wallpaper. He was sitting behind a desk; antique, she recognised at once.

'Hey.' He didn't get up, but beckoned her in. 'Take a seat. Poppy, is it?'

She walked over to the Louis XIV-style chair, must be a repro, in front of his desk and sat down. Stein was looking at her curiously, with that same assessing manner he'd had last night in the club.

'I don't recall Susie booking this meeting in. She's at

lunch now. What is this about?'

Poppy made an instant decision. She wasn't going to snow him. At least, not much.

'It's about this.' She pulled out the demo tape and laid it on his desk. She was gabbling. 'This band I manage. They're young, they look good, the tunes rock. And I can't take them any further, they need to move up a step. It was a lie about me being in a record company. We had no appointment. But you don't need to call security, Mr Stein, because I'm leaving right now. I wrote my phone number on the tape. If you're interested you can call me.'

She got up.

'And why should I listen to a tape of some baby band? Do you know how many tapes this office gets in every day?' asked Stein.

He hadn't pressed any buttons or lifted his phone. Poppy hovered a second.

'Because you're impressed with my ingenuity in getting in to your office?'

He laughed. 'I guess I am impressed.' His eyes narrowed slightly. 'Do I know you, kid?'

'Not really. You met me last night. I was in that band you came to see, Snaggletooth.'

Stein's expression changed. 'This tape's your band?'

'No. Don't worry, I left the band. They absolutely sucked. And I have no chops.'

He laughed again. 'You're an interesting young woman.'

'This band is also girls, but nothing like us. They're good. Punk-pop. It won't cost you anything to listen to them.'

'You don't manage them, do you?'

'Not as such,' Poppy admitted. 'But in the sense that you don't know who they are or how to contact them, I do.'

Stein was grinning broadly.

'You know what 'chutzpah' is?'

Poppy grinned back and fished out the small gold Star of David she always wore around her neck.

'Uh-huh. I should have guessed. Well, you've got it, toots, I'll tell you that for nothing.'

'Thank you, Mr Stein.'

'I remember you,' he said suddenly. 'You're the one that wasn't shaking her tits at me.'

'Um, yes.'

'Don't worry, that never works. I'm gay.'

'Ah.' Poor Fiona, Poppy thought.

'Well, I'll listen to your band, toots. Since we're being so honest, let me tell you that they'll probably suck. Ninety per cent of everything is crap. That's rule number one.'

'OK,' Poppy said.

'Thanks for dropping by,' he said, dismissing her.

Poppy said, 'Thank you, Mr Stein,' again, and walked out. She felt slightly let down. She'd expected him to put the tape in instantly, be wowed, and offer her a job on the spot. *Ninety per cent of everything is crap.* Well, at least that was upfront. But it didn't make her feel any better. She felt down when she got home. It was a mad scheme, he was never going to go for it.

'Hi, honey.' Her mother gave her a kiss.

'Hi, Mom.'

'You're on your own for dinner tonight, your father and I are out at the opera house benefit.'

'No problem,' Poppy said.

'Conchita dropped off your dry cleaning.'

'Great.' She really felt down about it. The phone wasn't ringing. She thought she'd have a hot bath, then call Kate and tell her she couldn't do anything for her. Damn it.

'Oh, and a Mr Joel Stein called. He left a number.'

'Is that a joke?'

'Why would it be?'

'When did he call?'

'Ten minutes ago. Here's the number — '

Her mother looked at her daughter in amazement as Poppy snatched the piece of paper and rushed out to the phone. Teenagers. Oh well, she suspected it was love.

# 19

It started out as a perfectly ordinary Oxford day. Daisy came back from the library with some books on Monet, put the kettle on, and hit the red light on her blinking phone; the message didn't sound important.

'Daisy, darling, it's Mummy.'

Sally Markham's voice was distant and tinny. It usually was, as though she hadn't quite come to terms with something as newfangled as the telephone. Much less the answering machine.

'Can you call home? Daddy and I want to talk to you.'

Daisy punched in her parents' number, guiltily. She'd been having too much fun, hanging out with Brad, enjoying college. She hadn't called her parents for weeks.

'Mum, it's me.'

'Oh, hello, darling. Let me just go and take the cakes out of the oven, or they'll burn.'

She heard her mother clattering about in the kitchen and felt a sharp pang of homesickness. Mum always made cakes on Sunday afternoon. Daisy thought she could do with a little hot cake and a cup of Earl Grey with two sugars right now. Diet or no diet. Sod fruit. There were only so many Granny Smiths you could eat.

'Darling, it's Daisy . . . hold on, Daddy wants a word.'

Quentin Markham came on the other end of the line.

'Darling, I've got a bit of bad news for you.'

Daisy's heart sped up instantly. Oh God. Had Granny died? Oh God.

'It's all right, nobody's dead.' Her father read her mind. 'But we've had a bit of bad luck financially.'

'What are you talking about?'

'Lloyd's of London has crashed.'

'Hmm, yes.' Daisy thought about it. 'I saw something about it on the news. Edward Powers told me about it. All the poor Names.'

'Darling.' She could hear the strain in her father's voice. 'I was a Name. Am, still.'

The bottom dropped out of Daisy's stomach. 'Oh, Daddy. Did you lose a lot of money?'

Her parents had only started investing five years ago. It was too awful, to think that once her father had finally got a little nest-egg to invest it was wiped out.

'We lost everything.'

'Oh, *no*. Everything you invested?'

'No, darling, you don't understand.' Her father's voice was patient, almost soothing, as Daisy's heart started to pound. 'Names are partners. They have open-ended liability. We don't just lose what we invested, which was about fifteen thousand. They call us for more money. We have to give them everything we own.'

She blinked, trying to get her head around it.

'But Daddy, it's a bad investment. Why would you put more money into it? Tell them they can't have any more.'

He chuckled. 'I wish I could. They have the right to take it. They have to pay back the people they insured . . . '

'That can't be right.' She pressed a soft finger to her temple. 'No way. You invest fifteen thousand, how can you lose more than that? What can they take . . . You don't have all that much else.'

'The house, the car.'

'The *house*? But you just paid off the mortgage.'

'It's an asset, darling. They may settle, leave each Name with a little something. But I'm afraid we are

176

looking for a place to rent. And we'll have to give up your lease.'

Daisy looked around her gorgeous little flat. 'That's no problem,' she said numbly, 'that doesn't matter at all.'

Sally Markham came back on the phone. Daisy could hear the tears behind the brightness of her voice.

'Don't worry, darling. Your father and I have been fine all this time, and we'll be fine now.'

'But renting a house,' Daisy said.

'Just think of all the maintenance bills somebody else will have to pay! And anyway, I wanted a change,' she said firmly.

Mummy loved their house. Daisy remembered the celebration dinner they'd had when the mortgage had finally been paid off. Shepherd's pie and champagne.

'Well, we're all OK. And that's all that counts,' Daisy said, blinking back tears. The lump in her throat was swelling up, and she did not want to start crying in front of her parents.

'That's right, Daisy.'

'Talk to you guys soon,' Daisy said, hanging up.

She sat there and stared into space. She wanted to believe it was all a bad dream, but it wasn't. Daisy walked out to her little balcony and sat there, gazing out towards the river.

She had to do something.

Mummy and Daddy would be devastated. No matter what kind of a stiff upper lip they presented to the world right now, they had just been wiped out. Her father had always tried to do the gentlemanly thing, and he'd been proud to become a Name at Lloyd's.

*Unlimited liability*. What a fucking disaster. She would never, ever go into anything open-ended like that, Daisy thought. When she was an investor . . .

Mechanically she walked back into her room and

started to pull the sheets off the bed. It was 21 November. She could pack up and be out of here in a day. Of course, everybody else in Oxford already had rooms. Finding new accommodation would be a nightmare.

Daisy lifted the phone by her bed and punched in the landlord's number.

'Foxworth's Realty,' a woman's voice said.

'Hello, Diane. This is Daisy Markham.'

'Hi, there. Getting on OK, are we?' said her letting agent in that shrill, fake-smile voice she always used.

'Actually, I'm quitting the flat. I'm giving you a week's notice.'

The woman sucked in her breath annoyingly. Melodramatic cow, Daisy thought.

'You can't do that. Your lease is for a year — '

'Yes I can. You have to re-advertise. You can deduct the cost of the advertisement, but that's it.'

'That's not what your lease says.'

'I know the law. If you don't try to find another renter, you're breaking it. And don't think I won't take you to court, because I will.'

There was a pause at the end of the line.

'Send the keys back,' the woman said, and hung up.

Daisy got up and spent the next two hours packing up her room. The furniture had come with the place; most of her stuff fitted into the suitcases she'd arrived with. Then she went to the bank and cancelled her standing order to Foxworth's. It made her feel slightly more in control. Then she called on Brad.

He opened the door slightly.

'Can I come in?'

'Sure.' Brad let the door open a little wider. 'As it's you. Just let me go and put some clothes on, OK?'

He had just got out of the shower. There was a towel wrapped around his waist. Daisy stepped inside his

178

hallway, trying not to stare.

Damn. He could talk. Daisy felt weakened by the rush of heat to her belly. Brad's body was just incredible. Tanned, even in winter, thickly muscled, his chest and shoulders huge, his biceps . . . chiselled wasn't the word for it. And he had a dark, lush trail of hair, gathering down from his chest and matting just above the towel. Little droplets of water had been trickling all over his body. She was distracted. Daisy went into Brad's living room and sat down on the sofa, twisting her fingers.

'So.' He came back in and sat opposite her. He'd just pulled on a pair of blue jeans and a white T-shirt, and he looked incredible. 'What's up, babe?'

'I need a place to live. Can't stay in my apartment any more.'

'That's a great little space.'

'I know, but — '

She paused. She didn't want Brad to know about her parents. His family were rich, and Daisy was suddenly embarrassed.

'I had a fight with the owners. I don't really want to go into it.'

'You picked a real bad time to start looking. Accommodation's a nightmare in this town.'

Daisy looked around. Brad had a four-bedroom place just to himself, now he'd moved out of Edward's rooms.

'I guess I thought I could stay here?'

His gorgeous brow furrowed. 'I dunno. I don't think that'd be cool. You know, having a girl here. But I'll keep an eye out for you. Want a drink?'

'It's ten a.m.' And he wasn't much of a drinker, was he?

Brad got up and walked into his kitchen, returning with an opened bottle of Pouilly Fuissé.

'I know. It's great, being at college, isn't it?'

Daisy accepted a glass of wine. She felt like she

needed it. Disappointment mingled with longing in the pit of her stomach. There was plenty of room in this house. Yeah, she had to respect Brad's space, but . . .

A tiny part of her thought he should have been there for her. She suppressed it.

'Thanks.'

He sat across from her, and his eyes travelled lazily over her body. She was wearing a heavy black skirt, ankle boots, a push-up bra and a low-cut black camisole under a cardigan. She'd dressed nicely this morning, working on the assumption that she might see Brad today. Of course, that was before the phone call.

Lust had been driven out of her head.

Now it was back.

She took a large hit of the wine, which calmed her.

'You really do look great. You've lost a ton of weight.'

'Have I?' Daisy said absently. 'I suppose my clothes are a bit loose.'

'Not everywhere,' Brad said. His gaze lingered on the slopes of her cleavage, swelling up from her bra, soft and sexy. She really had great tits, he thought.

'Hey.' Daisy had wanted him to notice her in this way for so long, but now she was at a loss. 'Cut that out, dude.'

'Dude?' He grinned. 'That's cute. Very American. And why should I cut it out? You look hot.'

'Me?' Daisy said, stunned. She blushed.

'I'll show you. Get up.' When Daisy just sat there, he got up and pulled her to her feet. His strong hand was firm. She could feel all his strength. Brad shut the living room door and showed her her reflection in the full-length mirror.

'So what?' Daisy scoffed.

Brad stood behind her, his height towering over her. Her shoulder blades pressed against his chest, her hair hung loose against his neck. He put his arms around her

180

body, holding her. His grip was iron.

'You don't see it? Take a look. Almond eyes, that white-blue. Your face is so beautiful, sugar.' His voice was low, his breath hot on her neck. 'You got cheekbones. And a waist.' His left hand splayed against her ribcage, caressing it with his fingertips. Daisy started to squirm, but his arms held her locked in place. The hot feeling in her belly was starting up with a vengeance. Her breath shortened.

'Brad — '

'And these,' he said, stroking a finger across the tops of her breasts. It was like a line of fire trailing over her skin. Daisy bit down on her tongue to stop from panting.

'You're teasing me,' she said, gritting her teeth. 'Cut it out.'

'Who says?'

He spun her around and tilted up her head to face him. Daisy's eyes were moist, her lips parted. Brad thought idly that it wasn't bullshit; she was turning into a pretty girl.

He was getting turned on by her heat. She was brimming with desire. Brad lowered his head to her full lips and crushed them in a kiss.

★   ★   ★

'Man.'

Daisy lay snuggled against Brad, her soft, out-of-shape body against his unyielding muscle. He was as gorgeous now as ever. She thought, detachedly, that he should be lighting up a cigarette now. But of course Brad was a healthy American and he never smoked.

Thoughts like this helped her not to cry.

She'd wanted Brad. Longed for him. But the sex had been painful, teeth-gritting stuff, and he'd acted all shocked when he'd discovered she was a virgin, and

181

Daisy had buried her face in the pillow so that he wouldn't see that she was crying.

It was nothing like she'd read in her books. It hurt. And it felt all wrong.

But she loved Brad, didn't she?

'Wow, honey, that was great.' He looked down at her with what she could only describe as a friendly smile. Which ripped her heart out. 'I can't believe it was your first time.'

'I went to an all-girls' school,' Daisy said, shortly.

'I never popped anybody's cherry before.' He looked as proud as a rooster.

Daisy blanched. Suddenly she imagined him laughing, telling this story to the boat club. 'Look, Brad. This is between us.'

His chiselled face looked hurt. 'I wouldn't tell. You're my friend, OK?'

She was, yeah. But, she noted, not his 'girlfriend'.

All she wanted was to take a shower. 'I have to run, can I use your bathroom to freshen up?'

'Absolutely,' Brad said. He beamed at her, with his white, healthy teeth.

Daisy got up, clutching her clothes to her self-consciously. Brad regarded her still too-plump bottom with fondness. She was the perfect woman, he thought. He liked her, and she'd jumped right into bed, and now she wanted to leave ... no 'cuddling', none of that bullshit. She couldn't wait to get out of there. Daisy's just like a guy, he thought, approvingly.

She shut the bathroom door and ran the water, stepping into his shower and scrubbing the spots of blood from her leg. Daisy helped herself liberally to his shower gel, some pine-fresh manly thing. Washing the smell and the sweat of Brad from her, and trying not to feel dirty.

She wasn't a virgin any more. Daisy wanted to cry,

182

but forced it back. Years of public school came into their own.

You can't waste time with this, she thought.

She turned the water off, briskly towelled herself down, and pulled her clothes on.

'Hey.'

Brad was still lying there as she re-emerged into the bedroom. 'It'll be better next time. Won't hurt.' He winked at her. 'I'll make sure of it.'

'Yeah, sure. See you,' Daisy said, with a forced brightness.

She half ran down the stairs and back out into the street.

It was still daylight. She glanced at her watch. She hadn't been in there more than an hour and a half.

Daisy took a deep breath, and headed for Edward's rooms.

# 20

'But why would you want to move?'

Edward sat across from her in the armchair in his rooms. Now that Brad had moved out, he had the place to himself. Daisy saw evidence of his taste everywhere: oil paintings on the walls, rush matting on the floors. Even though these were cramped undergraduate quarters, he made it look like a reading room in some upper-class London club.

Daisy looked at him. Edward actually cared.

'My parents were Lloyd's Names.'

He grasped the situation instantly. 'Oh. I'm sorry.'

'I have to give up the flat,' Daisy said. 'I already broke my lease.' She twisted her hands in her lap and bit down inside her mouth, trying not to cry.

Edward sensed her mood. 'The situation,' he said gravely, 'calls for a cup of tea. Earl Grey or Lapsang?'

'Either is fine.' Daisy looked at his back gratefully as he got up and went over to his kettle, giving her time to compose herself.

'I have somewhere for you. We have a flat on Walton Street. Two bedrooms, rather nice.'

'What's the rent? I can't afford very much.'

'Two hundred,' Edward said, 'but if that's too much we can come to some arrangement.'

Two hundred a month. She knew right away that he had named a desultory sum so that she wouldn't feel it was charity. The lump in her throat rose up again.

'Thank you,' she said, and she couldn't keep her voice from breaking.

'Oh, come on, now, old bean. Everything will be fine. You just have a job to do.'

'What are you talking about?' Daisy said, miserably.

Edward passed her the tea, black, no sugar. 'We all have to look after our aged parents. Your time for doing that has just arrived a little earlier. You aren't as helpless as you like to think, Daisy. You just need to work out what your talents are, and act on that. Focus on something else. It will help.'

Daisy smiled weakly. 'Give me an illusion of control, you mean.'

She took a sip of the tea. Edward was great; he knew exactly how to settle her.

'Can I be frank?'

She laughed. 'Why the hell not. Give it to me straight.'

'You've been coasting. I know you're too intelligent to be at Rackham. And History of Art?' Edward's thin, patrician features creased in disdain. 'What on earth is that? Why not the history of pottery?'

'Philistine.'

'It's hardly a real subject, Daisy. It's what nice girls pick to read when they can't be bothered to work, and are only planning on looking for a husband. And you aren't dull enough to be one of those girls. Now,' he methodically added three level spoonfuls of sugar to his tea with a precise motion of the wrist, 'you've received something of a shock, which only means you have to stop messing about, and do something.'

She considered this.

'You can write,' Edward suggested.

'Oh.' Daisy shook her head. 'I tried that, it didn't work.'

'You failed to win one competition.' Edward was firm. 'You should try again. You told Richard Weston you would. If his kind of trash made him a millionaire, why shouldn't you do the same?'

Daisy shook her head. 'It's a pipe dream. Do you know how many people want to be writers?'

'As a matter of fact, I do. Mother belongs to a writing

circle. But, you see,' Edward leaned forward and whispered conspiratorially, 'she's no good. Most of them can't write at all.'

'And what makes you think I can?'

'The girls liked your stuff, you told me. Anyway, the point is not whether you can or can't. The point is that you should at least try. At some point, Richard Weston was an unpublished author. Jilly Cooper, too.'

'Hmm.' Daisy smiled at Edward, incredibly grateful. She almost felt excited about it. 'I suppose I could rework my old idea . . . '

'I wouldn't do that. Start with something fresh. You'll be better the second time around.'

His words chimed with Brad's, reminding her of this morning. The mood was shattered. Daisy put her bone-china cup down. 'I think I should get going.'

'Wait a second.' Edward pulled open a drawer in his walnut coffee-table and handed her the keys. '89 Walton Street, Flat 2. That's the front door, the other one opens the flat.'

'I don't have two hundred right now,' Daisy admitted. It brought a pink spot of embarrassment to her cheeks.

'That's fine. Any time before the end of the month.' Edward stood and walked her to the door. 'Let me know if there's anything else you need.'

Daisy wanted to thank him profusely, to pour her heart out, but she knew if she did she would start to cry.

'Thanks,' she muttered.

'See you soon, I trust,' Edward said.

\*   \*   \*

She didn't go home. She went straight round to Walton Street and let herself in.

Brad would have called it a perfect 'space'. It was spacious, with lead-panelled windows, antique furniture in dark oak, and red fabric on the walls. It was unbelievably sumptuous, a little weekend retreat for Edward's family. Far better than the flat she was giving up.

The very beauty of the place made Daisy wretched. She was imposing on her friend. But what choice did she have?

Writing. That was a joke. But she was going to try it. Rackham had computers with word processing software . . . Edward was right; she'd been coasting, she had to try *something*. Meanwhile, in the real world, she could look for a part-time job. That might help her afford a commercial rental, and get out of Edward's hair.

She decided she would think about that. She would think about getting on her feet, helping her parents.

Anything but Brad.

★　★　★

Daisy sat at the mahogany dining table in Edward's flat and breathed out.

There it was, laid out neatly before the lead-panelled window with its view of Walton Street and the driving rain that was lashing it. Her submission. One chapter, a synopsis, and a bunch of letters. She had printed up thirteen of them, addressed to agents whose names she had found after combing through a large yellow-covered reference book. Daisy had craftily changed a couple of sentences at the start of each letter to reflect the person to whom she was writing. She loved so-and-so's work, whom they represented. Or she knew of the agency's reputation for romance. Your basic sucking up. Apart from that, she had kept the letters very short.

This went against what she read in the thin, overpriced magazines they published for aspiring authors. You were supposed to do a tap-dance in your 'query letter'. Something boastful and snappy, something that would grab the overworked agent's attention.

187

'Don't give him a reason to say no,' they advised.

The problem was that when Daisy read those sample letters they made her cringe. Her cheeks would pink in purely empathetic embarrassment. 'Dear Sir, What if Queen Katherine Parr had kept a diary? Now you can read what it was like to have been married to Henry VIII — and survived. My novel *The Merry Widow* is a gripping tale of romance and treachery in the sixteenth century . . . '

Ugh. Ugh. Daisy didn't have a 'high concept', and she wasn't about to start writing stupid letters. She put in her age, the genre, and the fact that she'd had no experience apart from a mention in the *Company* competition. Then she asked the agents to read her material and get back to her if they were interested in seeing more of it.

Of course, it was all hopeless, and she didn't see why she should embarrass herself.

Daisy picked up her twenty-six envelopes and started to address thirteen of them to herself. She could make the ten-thirty post, then she was due at work by eleven. It was a four-hour shift at Frederico's today. She was dreading it, as always. But at least she was starting to get some real money.

Her life had changed. She'd only been living at Walton Street a month, and her papers had started to get As. Edward might have been right about History of Art, but now she was doing it, she needed to get a First. She was working constantly; either writing essays, or doing lunch and evening shifts at the Italian restaurant that had given her a job. Minimum wage, of course, but students and townies were pretty cool with the tips. Daisy had a great smile.

And she was starting to get really pretty.

Even she herself had begun to notice it. The irony was that after Brad, she'd been so down, so depressed, that she had stopped watching what she ate. But Edward

188

Powers had lit a fire under her. Daisy wanted to help her parents. So she worked, she waitressed, and she wrote. Between all three activities she'd had no time to stuff herself.

The distracted diet. It worked wonders. That, and the depression.

She saw Brad around. He kept calling, asking to hook up again, but making it clear that he wasn't interested in having her as a girlfriend.

Daisy had cracked, gone out with him one more time. He'd plied her with drink, but it wasn't necessary. She intended going to bed with him anyway, just to stop that first time from being a one-night stand.

It didn't hurt. At least, not physically.

'Hey, man, check you out.' Brad had run an approving hand over her tighter, smaller butt and thinner thighs. 'You dropped even more weight. A ton.'

'I don't think it was quite that much,' Daisy said dryly.

The irony went right over his head.

'Hey, you're really hot. I could do this every night,' he murmured, surrounding her with his strong arms.

She couldn't quite suppress the ray of hope. 'So am I your girlfriend now?'

'Sure, hon. You're my girlfriend,' Brad said expansively, 'but it's not like we're *exclusive* or anything. I mean, we're young. Right?'

'Right,' Daisy muttered.

Since that night she had avoided him completely.

She finished stuffing the envelopes and got up. Her navy coat was worn-out, she really needed a new one. But she was saving her money for more important things than that. Daisy quickly twisted her hair, which was down past her shoulders now, up against the nape of her neck. She didn't bother with make-up, apart from a quick slick of rose-tinted chap stick. Her skin needed nothing; it was soft and dewy as a child's. Anyway, she

189

thought the other girls at Frederico's made themselves look like clowns, with too-thick foundation settling into the fine lines around their eyes and mouths, and chalky-blue eyeshadow that did nothing for them.

Daisy walked down the stairs and out into the street. It was freezing. She held her umbrella against the wind, hoping it would not turn inside out. She half ran down Cornmarket towards the Post Office, her nose and the tips of her ears turning red against the cold. She hated weather like this, it made her fingertips turn white. The thought came into her mind that her natural parents couldn't be British, she just wasn't equipped to handle all this foul sleet and icy wind . . .

The Post Office felt ridiculously warm, just because it wasn't exposed to the elements. Daisy walked up to the counter and paid for her packages to be sent first-class. As she shivered, she had a tiny thrill of accomplishment. At least she'd tried.

She bundled up in preparation for another blast of cold air —

'Hey.'

Daisy glanced up. It was Brad, walking into the Post Office. She instantly registered that he was embarrassed to see her. A second later, she realised why.

There was a girl standing next to him — tall and lanky, very skinny, with a tan and a cascade of platinum-blonde hair. She was wearing a pair of expensive-looking leather trousers, matching jacket, and a Burberry scarf. Her eyebrows were plucked and her nails manicured. Obviously American.

Daisy's heart started to thud. Maybe it was a sister, or something. Come to visit for Thanksgiving.

Then her eye was drawn downwards to the stack of pretty little envelopes in the girl's hand, creamy, stiff paper, with little silver bells stuck on them.

She knew the situation before he said anything.

'Daisy, hi. Honey, this is my friend Daisy Markham.'

Brad was gabbling, tripping on his words. 'Edward's friend. Daisy, this is Elise Mariano, my fiancée.'

'Hey,' the girl said, with a disinterested stare.

'We're just mailing some invitations. Elise has picked Merton's chapel, so that's where the ceremony is . . . '

'I just luurve those old windows,' Elise said.

'You should come,' Brad mumbled.

'I'd love to,' Daisy said brightly, her eyes glittering with tears she was determined not to shed, 'but I just remembered I'm busy that day. Nice to meet you, Elise.'

As she barged past her out into St Aldate's, Daisy heard the American girl say, 'But I never said what the date was . . . '

Daisy raced up towards Cornmarket, sobbing. Oh, God. She really had been nothing to him. He was sowing his wild oats. One last fling before he married the blonde, perfect American cow with the handbag perfectly matched to her shoes. And now she was off to be a waitress. She thanked God she had never told anybody about this job. Not Brad, not even Edward.

She rested at the corner of the street and fished a tissue out of her bag, wiping her eyes and blowing her nose. No way she wanted to let that bastard Frederico know she'd been crying. He was a surly jerk who always tried to cheat his waiting staff of their tips and make them work overtime without pay. The only reason she'd been able to land a job here was because he had such high turnover. Nobody wanted to work for him. He'd accepted Daisy, without any experience, because he had to.

The clock said it was bang on eleven. Daisy rushed miserably up to the restaurant's side door and let herself into the kitchen.

'She finally arrives,' Frederico said. 'I think you are going to be late again and I will dock your pay again.'

'Right on time,' Daisy said firmly. A quick glance out front told her they were already busy; older couples taking advantage of the early-bird specials and the happy half-hour (her boss would never stretch to an hour).

'So get you uniform on. You working the front section today. Hurry up.'

Daisy felt another sob rise up in her throat, but choked it back. She needed this job. At least the work would give her something to do.

'Right away, Frederico,' she said obediently.

# 21

She was woken by the doorbell ringing.

It had an old-fashioned chime rather than an electric buzz, but it was still insistent. Daisy's eyes flicked open. She was sleeping in the gorgeous oak four-poster in the main bedroom; linen sheets and dark woods, with the scent of lavender and pot-pourri in the air. The William Morris curtains were slightly drawn back from the lead-paned windows. Enough for her to see that bright light was streaming into the room, catching motes of dust which shimmered like miniature galaxies.

Sod it. How late was it?

Daisy squinted at the grandmother clock across the room. Half past twelve?

Ding-dong, said the bell again.

Shit. Shit. She jumped out of bed, the cobwebs swept away.

'Coming, coming,' she said. Daisy grabbed her old towelling robe and raced downstairs, yanking the door open.

Edward stood there in a suit.

'Edward! Come in,' Daisy said, blushing.

He hesitated awkwardly. 'I fear I've disturbed you — '

'No! Well, yes,' Daisy admitted. 'But I overslept ... I don't know what happened, must have slept through the alarm. Come on in, I'll be two seconds.' She ushered him into the small living room and ran back into her bedroom, tugging on some underwear and a pair of jeans and a T-shirt, shoving her feet into her shoes.

She felt faintly ashamed; Edward was so disciplined and well-dressed . . . he'd never be opening the door in a shitty, greying robe. She grabbed her bottle of scent and spritzed herself.

'Hey.'

Edward looked surprisingly ill at ease. He was never uncomfortable with her; Daisy thought of him as her one true friend here. Yeah, she had other people she hung out with, Rackham students she ate lunch with, girls from the restaurant she occasionally took to the pub. But Edward she cared about.

'Is something wrong?'

'Not at all.' He smiled gingerly. 'I wondered if you'd heard Brad's news.'

She couldn't suppress a smile. He was so delicate, treading carefully around her feelings. Nobody else had ever bothered to try and prevent her from feeling pain like this. No man, at least.

'Yes.' Daisy smiled crisply. 'I'm happy for him.'

'Are you? I thought you had . . . feelings for him.'

'Brad? Not at all. I liked him,' Daisy said firmly. 'That was about it.'

'Ah. Well. That's good.' Edward twisted a bit. 'I, um, I've met someone too.'

The room seemed to spin. Daisy gripped the arm-rests of her chair. What? Edward had found someone? Rake-thin Edward?

*Her* Edward?

'That's a surprise,' she managed.

'She's at St Hilda's.'

The all-girl college.

'How nice.' Daisy could not understand why her heart had started to race. She felt almost dizzy. 'Tell me about her.'

'Oh, well.' Edward's eyes lit up. He started to talk enthusiastically, like someone who could not believe his luck. 'She's a brick. I met her in the Union bar one night, she was coming to the speaker meeting for Sir Georg Solti. She loves opera . . .'

'Perfect for you,' Daisy muttered. She herself was more Madonna and Wham. But Edward went for the classical stuff.

'She's called Edwina. Can you believe that?'

'It's obviously fate,' Daisy agreed. 'Edwina who?'

'Edwina Latham. She's Monty Latham's daughter,' Edward said.

The name rang the vaguest of bells. Oh God, yes. Some Tory frontbencher in the House of Lords. Daisy felt the pit of her stomach give way. She pictured Edwina, a horsey, upper-class girl who loved opera and was at Oxford proper and had a title. Jolly hockey-sticks, and all that.

An ideal future Lady Powers.

Daisy should have been happy for Edward, but she wasn't. She realised instantly that she was insanely jealous. How pathetic!

'How long have you been seeing her?'

'We had dinner a couple of times. Went to her parents' place last weekend.'

'How nice,' Daisy said. 'You must introduce me.'

'Oh, I shall. You'll love her.'

It was so fourth-form, for her to think her friend shouldn't have a girlfriend. After all, it wouldn't stop him being friends with her. This Edwina would never be jealous, because Edward had asked Daisy out, and she'd always turned him down. She didn't like rail-thin men, she liked muscles, and . . .

'Do you love her?' Daisy asked. Her own voice sounded tinny and far-away, as if it were coming up from the bottom of a cave.

'Bit early for that.' Edward looked all bashful again. 'But, you know, she's a peach, and we do seem to get on OK.'

A huge wave of nausea rocked through Daisy. This made what she'd gone through with Brad pale into total insignificance. Immediately, fatally, she understood her mistake.

She didn't just like Edward. She loved him. She was in love with him.

And now he was in love with somebody else.

'Isn't that wonderful,' Daisy said.

Please, she thought. Please go away.

'Oh, no.' She looked at the ornate gold mantel-piece clock. 'Edward, you're going to think me amazingly rude, but I've got a job, and I'm going to be late . . . '

'Not at all.' He stood up, and it was hard to tell which of them looked the more relieved. 'How very enterprising of you to have found a job. What is it?'

She was beyond being ashamed. 'Waitressing.'

He didn't flinch. 'Well done. Do you make decent money?'

'Yes,' Daisy lied. 'Almost enough to get a place of my own. I'll be out of your hair soon.'

'I hope never,' Edward said, with his old politeness. He gave her a slight bow. 'Perhaps you can meet us later for a drink? I'll be with Edwina at the Union tonight.'

'Sounds great. Eight suit you?'

'See you then,' Edward said. 'I'll let myself out.'

Daisy waited till he had gone, then raced to get ready. She had coped with too much in the past week to pretend to be strong. She burst into tears.

★  ★  ★

When she finished her shift, it was already 4 p.m. Daisy gathered up her tips; not much today. Eighteen quid and change. She pulled her coat on and shivered her way back to Walton Street. At least it would enable her to buy the ghastly Edwina a drink.

Daisy unlocked her door and walked into her living room. The answer machine was blinking; she'd check it later. She felt so exhausted, her weariness had seeped into her bones, along with the aching cold.

At half past four she had a lecture on the Rackham campus.

Sod it, Daisy thought. She could call her girlfriend Lucy and crib from her notes. She just could not drag herself out to do one more unpleasant thing. Daisy walked into the bathroom and peeled off her rain-drenched clothes, running a hot bath, pouring her Radox under the tap and watching the white, scented clouds of bubbles rise up the sides of the ancient tub. Fantastic. She jumped in, washing herself, making it as warm as she could bear it.

It got so cold here in the winter she sometimes thought she would never get warm. Baths were a help, and, right now, her only real pleasure most days.

She knew she should wash her hair. Not let the Edwina cow see her like this. But she was just too exhausted to spend forty minutes blow-drying it. Fuck it, she could just keep her hair twisted in this French pleat. All she needed to do was look respectable . . .

The misery of it engulfed her soul the way the warm water was lapping at her body.

God, Daisy thought, tears prickling at the back of her throat, will anything ever go right for me again?

She'd once thought that if she could lose weight, she'd be happy, and everything would be OK. What a laugh. Now, sadness and overwork had managed to do what willpower couldn't, and she was a perfectly respectable size 12.

And she didn't think she'd ever felt more worthless in her life.

But Daisy wasn't going to let it show. She owed it to Edward to turn up tonight. He'd always looked out for her; she wasn't going to ruin his happiness now.

She reached for one of the big white towels that came with the place and swaddled herself in it. Maybe she'd go out and get a bottle of wine or something; no, one of those ready-mixed gin and tonics they sold in the individual bottles. She was gonna need a drink just to get up the courage to go to the bar!

Daisy dispiritedly reached out to her answer machine and pressed play.

'You have one message,' said the electronic voice soothingly. It beeped. A woman's voice came on.

'Hi, this message is for Daisy Markham,' she said. Daisy could hear the sounds of a busy office in the background. 'This is Gemma Brown in Ted Elliott's office. Mr Elliott received your material and he'd like to talk to you about representation. Can you call us back on 01 555 5764? Thanks very much.'

# 22

'I've got something I think you should see,' George Benham told her.

Rose looked at him with her unreadable expression. She sat in front of him in a well-cut, vintage Chanel suit that belied her youth, her dark fountain of hair twisted behind her head in a sleek chignon. She kept her make-up light; startling beauty like hers needed no help, anyway.

Benham tried not to obsess over the plum lips, the endless tumbling legs, or those she-wolf eyes. It didn't matter how respectably Rose Fiorello dressed. All he thought about was pulling off that jacket, slipping those pumps off her slender ankles, reaching up to loosen that glossy waterfall of hair. He imagined her naked whenever he saw her. She made him as horny as a teenager.

He didn't dare let it show. One false move and the ice-queen would fire him. And he could not afford to lose her business. He owed his new Mercedes to it.

Benham remembered the first time he had seen Rose. She had sounded so straight-laced on the phone he'd been shocked when a student walked into his office, wearing skinny jeans and a plain white shirt.

'You're Rose Fiorello?'

'That's right,' she'd said, those pale eyes daring him to disbelieve her.

'But Rose Fiorello owns four buildings . . . '

His voice had trailed off.

'Right again.' She had laid a cardboard folder in front of him. Inside it were neatly typed-out operating statements, with rental incomes, costs and taxes laid out

199

as professionally as any spreadsheet from a real company.

'You seem very young to own so many units,' Benham mumbled.

The cold look in her eye said she didn't appreciate the comment.

'I only own fifteen. I was hoping you would work with me to find some more.' The vision had sprung to her feet, preparing to storm out.

'Wait a second — ma'am. I'm sorry. Benham Realty would love to do business with you. Won't you have a seat?'

Since that day a year ago they had worked together.

Well, he had pretty much been working *for* Rose. It meant total dedication, late nights, credit checks, hours of phone calls to lawyers and hours of negotiations. But he'd fast learned to do whatever he was told. The commissions made everything worth it.

In the first six months, he'd closed five more deals.

Rose Fiorello was a powerhouse. She now owned nine buildings, with a total of thirty-one units. She had occupancy at 100 per cent, with a waiting list, for her apartments. She raked in over fifty thousand a year in profits, and paid peanuts in taxes.

And she was still at college.

Rose discouraged talk about her personal life. Benham wondered if she really had one. But look at her — she must be fucking some lucky bastard.

'What is it?'

She had that sceptical look. He hated that look. Rose Fiorello rejected 90 per cent of the deals he brought her. But it only took one deal to get that fat commission he loved.

Even his wife was into it, nagging him less and screwing him more. He hastened to convince her.

'That last foreclosure you brought me was a real dog, George.'

'Yeah, well. This is a little different. It's not what you've been doing up to now.' He knew the one thing that would convince her. 'It's a bigger deal. The next step. You might not be ready for it . . . '

The wolf-eyes glinted. 'Let me be the judge of that.'

'Of course, Ms Fiorello. Well . . . This isn't in foreclosure yet, but it will be. It's a motel. The guy just doesn't know how to run a hotel business . . . '

Benham didn't know if Rose would, either. It was a long-shot, but he gave her all his long-shots. She turned down almost everything, so he plastered her with deals. Benham Realty specialised in foreclosures. He had tentacles everywhere. Now people were coming to him, because word had leaked out that Fiorello gave more money to owners than anybody else. If you had something worth selling, she threw you a lifeline.

'Are you interested in the hotel business, Ms Fiorello?'

The thick black lashes flickered. 'No.'

'Oh.' Disappointment. 'Well, I have some other nice properties to show you, an eight-family in Red Hook — '

'I didn't say I wasn't interested in the property.'

She extended one manicured hand.

George Benham was confused, but he handed it over. He watched, almost holding his breath, as Rose skimmed through the details. She was like a very chic hawk, hovering above her prey, waiting to pounce.

With every deal he had seen her outward appearance change. As soon as Rose had money, she had appeared in his office in new shoes, with a matching bag. There followed suits and dresses, each outfit a little more upmarket than the last. It was like she couldn't wait to shed her working-class skin. And now she was wearing Chanel, with a slim gold watch on her wrist and a good string of pearls.

The one thing which hadn't changed was the sense of

201

the deal. Or the drive. Benham had expected she would make some money, then settle down and marry an investment banker. But if anything, success had only made her hungrier.

'This is interesting,' she said finally.

His whole face brightened. 'You want me to make an offer?'

Hell, Benham's commission on this one — three per cent of the Rego Park hotel . . . six hundred thousand . . . three per cent . . . *thirty-six thousand dollars*. A fine mist of sweat broke out on his forehead.

'It's really a jewel of a property . . . '

'It's a dump, George. A roach-infested dump.' Rose tapped the papers. 'I'm going to have a look at these.'

'I have more for you — '

'I don't need to see them.' She stood up, and the expensive hose she was wearing slithered against her skin. 'I must go; I'm late for class.'

Rose Fiorello walked out of George Benham's office, leaving nothing behind her but the faint scent of lavender.

He thought he would have traded the thirty-six thousand for five minutes between those long, lean thighs. But who was he kidding? She was so hot, he probably wouldn't last thirty-six seconds.

★　★　★

'Oh! Jacobhhh! Ohhhh!'

Emily Clarkson raked her French-polished nails over Jacob Rothstein's chest as her back arched in orgasm. He felt a surge of pride mingling with the pleasure as he exploded inside her, as if he had just scored a walk-off home run. Emily's breasts jiggled stiffly. They were implants, but Jacob really didn't care about that. He just enjoyed watching another prim and proper Boston Brahmin sobbing with pleasure, her three-hundred-dollar hair cut plastered to her forehead.

'Oh . . . oh . . . ' Emily panted, as he slipped out of her, reaching to take off his condom. She'd said she was on the pill, but Jacob didn't take any chances. His father and uncles were always lecturing the Rothstein boys . . . no glove, no love . . . the family fortune was just too large, they said, for women to resist trying to trap them.

Jacob had no intention of being a parent before his time. Bringing up a child with a woman you didn't love, didn't even like much . . . what a frigging nightmare. No thanks.

'Jacob . . . you're incredible.'

'Thanks, sugar.' He gave her a friendly pat on her ass, which was a touch too skinny. 'You're gorgeous.'

'You think so?' She blushed crimson with pleasure.

Rothstein propped himself up on his elbow. This was the tricky bit, but he was a master at it. How to make it clear to a girl that there was no future in it, but on the other hand, leave them with their self-respect.

Jacob had nothing against Emily. She was a great fuck. She was also a nice girl. Kind to animals, that sort of thing.

But she was as bland as tap-water, and he was a whisky-sour guy.

Besides, Jacob believed every woman could be a great fuck. You just had to work them up the right way. He was an egotist, and loved watching women's bodies leap and arch under his touch, loved feeling them writhe against his chest muscles, loved how they rippled around him when he made them convulse in helpless climax.

'Sure. I've been watching you for months. I remember that blue dress you wore to the polo match in June . . . '

'You noticed,' Emily breathed. She pushed her floppy fringe out of her eyes.

'Of course. I always notice a beautiful woman with an independent spirit.' Jacob gave her a friendly smile. 'I knew we'd get on great. I'd like to see you again, if you're ever free. A gorgeous chick like you will get snapped up by some boyfriend soon . . . '

He could see by the sharp flash of annoyance in her brown eyes that she'd registered this.

'Aren't you gonna be my boyfriend?' Emily asked, in a little-girl voice.

Jacob flinched inwardly. She wasn't marriage material; he employed the double standard: he wanted a modest wife. And anyway, he hated women who pretended to be helpless. They were no challenge, not like . . .

No. He wasn't going to think about her.

'I'm no good to anybody as a boyfriend. I'm not really ready for a relationship, and I don't want to cheat anybody . . . especially a girl who's so pretty she can do better whenever she wants.'

'I guess. When you put it that way,' Emily said uncertainly.

Jacob rubbed her thighs. 'Doesn't mean we can't see each other, though. If you want to of course.'

She felt a little of the heat returning. 'Yeah, I'd like that . . . '

He heard the footsteps a fraction too late. His bedroom door was wide open, and Rose Fiorello was standing in front of it.

'Oh! Excuse me,' Rose stammered. She gently closed his door, and Jake heard her footsteps running away.

Damn it. He grimaced in annoyance.

That was another mistake. Emily was looking at him with that furious, hurt look chicks always got when they realised they weren't the only female he was interested in.

'Maybe *that*'s your girlfriend?'

Her petulant tone was grating.

'She's a study partner.'

Emily got up from the bed, grabbing her clothes as she went.

'Sure. That's what they call them now!'

'It was my fault. I forgot we had to meet for an essay class . . . She came here, I didn't lock the door.'

'Convenient,' Emily hissed.

'Believe what you want,' Jake said neutrally.

Thankfully, she was getting dressed, tugging on her chinos and mules.

'Right, because so many students wear Chanel,' Emily snapped. She picked up her coat and bag and stumbled toward the door. 'Maybe you can give me a call when you finally grow up, Jake.'

He sat there as she slammed the door, muttering curses. Jake breathed out in relief. *Don't hold your breath, baby.*

How could he have forgotten Rose was coming here?

Jake grinned. Woman trouble. His usual.

He slipped out of bed and into the shower. Most student rooms didn't have them, but his father had slipped Columbia such a large donation that Jake Rothstein had whatever he wanted. These rooms had previously belonged to a tenured professor. They had a neatly tiled bathroom and even a small kitchenette area, which he never used because he preferred to eat out.

The shower came in handy, though, when you had as much sex as Rothstein did. Plus, it was a bonus to be able to go running in the mornings and not have to queue to use the communal showers afterwards.

'Why do you even want to room there?' his father had asked.

Jake shrugged. 'Student experience.'

'You have the place on Eighty-fifth Street.' For his last birthday, his father had handed him the deeds to one of his many apartments: a glorious pre-war duplex with views of the river, eighteen-foot ceilings, marble floors, and an obsequious doorman. Fred Rothstein had heard of his son's reputation as a stud from the irate parents of several young debs in his social circle. It was the one thing about his child that really pleased him. He had imagined Jake fucking his brains out in the Upper East Side place. Money like that made women drop their panties at the drop of a hat.

'It's great, Dad. But I want to be like the other students.'

Well, up to a point. Fred Rothstein wasn't having his kid treated like cattle. That was for the poor.

He had compromised on the best student rooms money could buy. Jake didn't fight him. A private bathroom was a necessity.

In his shower, Jake let the water sluice over his chest, soaping himself off briskly. He was tickled. It was good to get rid of Emily. And he liked the idea of Rose Fiorello catching him in bed. Arrogant bitch. He wanted her to see other women with him, to be jealous.

Jake Rothstein was egotistical, but he could usually back it up. Women flung themselves at him. Even the ones who played hard to get eventually wound up squirming underneath him. And after they broke up, he would still get calls.

Jake's private theory was that most guys sucked in bed. Otherwise why would his girls always be ready and willing?

All except Rose Fiorello.

She had started out acting up. Insulting him regularly. Jake had taken it as a mating call. There was a certain type of woman that liked to provoke, to challenge. They wanted reassurance that he was a dominant male.

Jake always gave it to them. He never stood for bullshit from a female.

It was his way or the highway. Jake thought the aggressive types were his favourite. It was a particular pleasure to pin those girls to the bed, to make them explode in ecstatic submission.

But Rose had not followed her stand-offish signals with come-hither ones. Instead, over the last academic year, she had become polite — almost friendly, but not quite. She went out of her way to be helpful, as far as their studies went. She was an indispensable research partner. But it was as though she couldn't bring herself to be really warm.

He wanted her.

Despite the fact that he'd just had Emily, he wanted Rose. It aroused him to think of Rose walking into his bedroom.

But he couldn't do anything about it right now. Jake turned the water to cold, blasting himself. That was better. He couldn't walk into Rose's room with a hard-on. Never let them see you're interested.

Jake dressed himself quickly. She was almost too beautiful. Most girls on campus were somewhat insecure; they always had to have a man, or they'd start talking about how they'd just dumped some poor sucker. It was still considered embarrassing for a chick to be single. Even at the start of the Nineties.

Not for Rose Fiorello, though. She was just too beautiful for it to matter. That slender figure, that fountain of hair, the she-wolf eyes, the high, arrogant cheekbones. Every man wanted her. She didn't need a status symbol.

★ ★ ★

'Rose?'

'Um, yeah.'

She opened the door to his knock. Pink Chanel, Gucci shoes, expensive-looking hose. Completely incongruous in a college setting. Emily had been right. Why was she dressed so smartly?

If you crossed a senator with a supermodel, she'd look like this.

'Come in, Jake.' Rose gave him that smile of hers, the empty one. She was as pleasant and as impersonal as a doctor's receptionist. 'Sorry about earlier.'

He noticed the discreet flash of gold at her wrist.

How the hell did she afford this? A year ago she'd worn jeans and beat-up sneakers. She'd castigated him for being a rich boy.

'I thought . . . the door was open.' The faintest tint of red was on her olive-skinned cheeks.

'My fault. I forgot to lock it.' He grinned at her. 'I was a little distracted.'

Rose refused to let the picture flash back into her mind. Jake Rothstein, with his muscular chest, its smattering of hair, sitting up in bed, those dark-lashed eyes staring at her. And the girl, her skin all sweaty and mottled from sex, squealing, glaring at Rose with jealous hatred. Like Rose wanted her precious stud!

*You're only one in a long line, honey,* she'd thought. Didn't the bimbette know that?

OK, so he had a certain animal charm. She was a realist. She couldn't deny that. He was square-jawed, dark-eyed, and well-built. He had a smattering of hair on his chest, and he was tall and imposing. And he carried himself with total confidence.

She also knew first-hand how intelligent he was. But that was OK. She wanted a worthy adversary.

It would make retribution all the sweeter.

There was a lot wrong with Jake Rothstein. She hated how he treated women. Like toys, playthings. Girls around campus cooed in the bathrooms about his stamina in bed. But so what? Rose was still a virgin, not that she admitted it to anyone. Wasn't sex just friction? It couldn't matter that much.

And he had the best rooms, drove a Ferrari to school, and pretty much paid his exes off. A pair of diamond earrings, or a Mikomoto pearl necklace. Not uncommon for Jake's ex-girlfriends who didn't make a fuss.

The dreadful thing was that women seemed to love this!

Rose despised Jake, and she despised the girls that idolised him. He was nothing but a playboy with brains. And the heir to Rothstein Realty.

They were coming up to the end of their time at college. Rose was beginning to worry. She hadn't been able to bring herself to make friends with Rothstein, and she needed him. He was her entrée to Rothstein Realty.

He was the key to her revenge.

'Doesn't matter.' She smiled softly at him now. 'Let's just get on with it, OK?'

# 23

'Impressive.'

Jake looked at the paper she had presented to him, the neat system for revision, the work on their two theses. Her arguments had been so interesting he had briefly forgotten how much he wanted her.

But now it was done with. Their term papers were due next week.

Rothstein pushed the paper back and regarded Rose Fiorello. For once, she was sitting there awkwardly, her fingers twisting in her lap, as though she didn't know what to do with herself.

'Your work, too,' she said.

'Thanks.' He knew it had been.

'So, I guess this is it for us,' Rose said.

'Not necessarily.' Jake grinned. 'This is it for college. I like that suit, by the way.'

She smoothed down her skirt. 'It's new.'

'If you don't mind my saying so, it looks expensive. Very expensive.' He waited for the rebuke for getting too personal, but she didn't say anything. 'Did you get a job, or win the lottery, or something?'

'Other people in this world are allowed to have money,' Rose snapped. Then she bit her lip and looked away, flushing. 'I — I'm sorry. Yes, I've made some money.'

'You don't have to tell me how, if you don't want to.'

'No! I want to.' She was suddenly eager. He was surprised at how she blew hot and cold. 'I actually bought some property. I own a couple of rental houses.'

'You?'

He regretted it as soon as he'd said it. His expression was one of disbelief. Everyone knew she'd come here without a cent to her name.

'Yes, me,' Rose said, a touch of steel underneath her polite smile.

'You own rental houses. Well, that's the American dream.'

'You're Jake Rothstein of Rothstein Realty, aren't you?' Rose asked.

Jake laid back in his chair and looked her over, slowly.

'So,' he said. 'You did notice me.'

'Hard not to,' Rose almost whispered.

Jake felt a sense of power flood him. Now he knew how his father felt, sometimes. He was more than just another student to Fiorello; he was a player. Instantly his focus shifted, away from history and into the real world. Where he was about to become a senior, stock-holding Vice President in a billion-dollar company that would one day be all his.

Most girls knew about his wealth and his reach by reading the society pages. Rose Fiorello had not come by it that way, he thought. She'd gotten into property, in a tiny way. Maybe she owned a couple of condos, rented them out.

He was impressed. Jake didn't really rate women when it came to business. He instantly saw that Rose must be savvy; she had managed to get financing somehow when she'd been dirt poor. FHA loans, maybe. And she'd made enough to afford a Chanel suit and a gold watch.

That was very nice, he thought. But hardly important.

In his pond, she wasn't even a minnow.

Rothstein knew Rose Fiorello. She was a queen of research, very thorough. He pulled the picture together. She'd made a deal here and there, gotten a taste for it, and started reading up.

And, of course, found out about Rothstein Realty.

'Guilty as charged,' he said.

*Ironic answer.*

'I wondered if . . . if I could ask you for a favour,' Rose said.

It almost came out as a mumble.

Jake grinned.

'You want a job?'

'No.' The wolf-grey eyes regarded him coolly. 'Just some information. To learn, that kind of thing. Maybe study what you do. That is, assuming you actually work there.'

'I've run projects every summer.'

'What kind of projects?'

He shrugged. 'Luxury condos in Westchester, a high-rise in Soho . . . about eighty units in that one.'

'What was your budget?'

What could that possibly matter? This was out of her league. Rothstein was enjoying himself now. Flexing his muscles.

'Over a hundred million. They had a project manager, but he reported to me.'

Rose was quiet for a few seconds. She hated herself for this, but she was getting turned on. Jake Rothstein was handsome, in an obvious sort of way. And he was looking at her like he was a pasha, and she was the latest addition to his harem.

'You were in charge of a nine-figure budget?'

Her hostility tickled him. 'Sugar, I've been running projects since I was sixteen. I supervise architects and contractors. I deal with the unions. I pay off the Mafia.'

'And how do your projects come out?'

He leaned across towards her, so Rose could feel the warmth of his body, see the muscles under his shirt. A pulse of animal lust flooded her belly. She looked down, but she could still sense him in her space, breathe in the masculine tang of him.

'On time. Under budget. And making money,' he said.

Her head was down. Her lips were parted. He thought he could feel the desire rising up out of her skin.

Another guy would have grabbed her head, kissed her.

Jake moved his mouth closer to hers, half an inch, so their lips were almost touching. But not quite.

Her mouth widened just a fraction more.

He had her. He pulled back.

'If you're interested in learning the business, I can get you an internship.'

Rose sat up, confused and embarrassed. Had he been going to kiss her? God, she'd nearly kissed him.

Her body was a traitor. Little tendrils of desire crawled over her skin, hooking into her belly and breasts.

Jake was still talking. 'To be honest, though, I don't know that you'd want it. We get hundreds of applicants. I wouldn't apply that standard to you. But once you were in, you'd have to behave like all the other interns. Otherwise it really wouldn't be fair to them. At work, I have to be professional.'

'I can be professional,' Rose said shortly.

'You'd have to report to my department. You'd work for somebody that works for me.'

'Fine by me,' Rose insisted.

Jacob said, 'You'd have to call me 'sir'.'

He thought he saw a muscle twitch in her face. Yeah, she wouldn't like that. Arrogant, stuck-up beauty that she was. But he'd enjoy it.

Jake made plans to have Rose work near him. He wanted her to see his power, the extent of his slice of the empire. He wanted to make her pant for him.

'I can do that.' Rose dropped her head. 'I — I really would like to learn the business. I'd appreciate it.'

It cost her to have to ask him.

'No problem,' Jake said. 'Give me a number where you can be reached.'

She wrote it down and handed it to him. 'Thank you, Jake.'

'No problem, honey,' he said.

★ ★ ★

Rose seethed all the way back to Tribeca.

She had bought herself a great apartment. A foreclosure in an old industrial building, it wasn't considered the best area. Rose had picked it up for a mere hundred and fifty.

Her place had everything. First, she liked the location. Manhattan prices were rising everywhere. In a few years, she was confident there would be nowhere on the island that was 'unfashionable'. Give it a decade, and even Harlem would be through the roof. Restaurants and diners had started to open up down here, and there were film-makers and models moving into nearby places. This was going nowhere but up.

Second, the old warehouse had space. Lots of it, in a town where a broom cupboard could be let for more than most people could afford. Rose had a loft, with huge industrial windows. The place had an elevator; old and creaky, but it worked. She was on the second-to-top floor, with great views of the Financial District.

Clusters of skyscrapers. She loved it. It made her want to own them all.

Rose had hired the contractors that worked on her house. There was no mystery about renovations, and nobody ever ripped her off. She had sanded the old floors, painted the walls a soft cream, dismantled the fluorescent lights and put in sconces, and added an upper level, where she kept her Queen-size bed and Moroccan rug. The kitchen she spent money on, but a good kitchen and bathroom added value to a place. The

214

look of the place was sleek, modern, very luxurious. Rose decorated everything in soft shades of white, with just a few splashes of colour to break things up: a crystal vase of yellow roses, the red tones of her rug, a candy-striped cushion in royal blue.

It was her haven.

Like everything else, it was an investment too. If she sold it today, she'd clear at least double what she paid for it. Rose had got over the need to nickel-and-dime herself.

She was going to be a real estate mogul. It was time she started treating herself like one.

# 24

'Wanna room? We're all-suite here.'

Rose looked at the receptionist. The girl was about her age. Young, cracking bubble-gum as she talked. She had too much make-up on and smoker's fingernails.

At least she was wearing a uniform. It was an ugly green-striped vest over an olive-coloured shirt. Rose noticed wrinkles and smudges.

She felt contemptuous. Being poor was no excuse for being a slob. Rose had been poor, her mother had been poor. But they had both dressed neatly at all times.

'How much?' she said.

Today she was wearing a pair of old jeans and a clean white Gap T-shirt. No need to call attention to herself. The pearls and the gold watch were in her mini-safe in the apartment.

'Forty dollars. If you'd waited till tomorrow, you could have gotten the weekend special.'

'How much is that?'

'Thirty-five.' The girl blew a pink bubble and popped it.

'Yeah, well. I need a place to stay tonight.'

'Smoking or non-smoking?'

'Non,' said Rose.

'How you gonna pay? If it's cash you can't have a key to the minibar or connect the phone. For that we need a card, OK?'

'Sure,' said Rose. She handed one over.

'Awright,' said the girl. 'Here's the minibar key, sign here.' She pushed over two keys. 'This one is for your room, number sixty-eight on the sixth floor, elevators is over there. Need help with your bags?'

Rose glanced at the leering doorman. 'Um, no thanks.'

'Enjoy your stay,' the girl said automatically, turning back to her magazine.

'Oh,' said Rose, 'I will.'

She took her overnight case to the elevators. There were three of them. The lobby was quite small and somewhat gloomy; it had a bad case of Seventies carpeting. Why had people ever thought orange and brown was a good colour combination? Rose wondered. The walls were white, but covered with that ugly textured paint. Very depressing.

It excited Rose. The windows were large. She imagined the place repainted, smooth-white, with a plain beige carpet, some plants and statuary. Maybe a water feature. They were cheap to run, easy to maintain, and looked fantastic. She glanced at the elevator when it arrived. It was brass.

The sixth floor was more of the same. Hallways were a little narrow; well, you couldn't have everything. She walked to the end of hers and looked out of the grimy window. Residential area, lots of traffic. Not a problem for what she wanted to do. There was a parking lot, that was very important, and some browning grass at the front. It was never going to be Park Avenue.

The key was figuring out what people needed in the price bracket. Clean and safe would sell here. It wouldn't cost a lot to fence the place in with ten-foot-high industrial fencing, and put a guardhouse at the gate.

New York was a dangerous city. Security would sell.

Rose opened up her room and shut the door behind her. The doors were heavy, with double locks, chains, and fish-eye peep-holes. They could stay.

Breathless with anticipation, she glanced around.

Oh, man. This was perfect.

A Queen-size bed was perched on a raised area, about two feet up from the living room. There was a large living area with a kitchenette. Of course, it was filthy; peeling paint, debris in the kitchen, probably infested with roaches. A bluebottle fly was buzzing lazily and hopelessly around the windows, and the bedside table was dusty.

But the fundamentals were there. Seven-fifty in the square footage. A decent-sized bathroom. Big built-in closets, and light from large windows.

Rose picked up the phone by her bed and punched zero.

'Yeah?'

'This room is kind of dusty,' Rose said. 'Got any other ones?'

She heard the receptionist bristle. 'It was cleaned this morning.'

'I think I'd like another room,' Rose said.

'I don't know if I got any.' The girl was hostile now.

'You didn't look all that busy to me. Plus I'd like something bigger.'

'All the rooms are exactly the same size. *Exactly*,' the receptionist snapped. 'Except on the top floor, they're bigger, but they're the honeymoon suites and they cost, like, *hundreds* of dollars. You can have one if you want. Do you want one for *hundreds* of dollars?'

'No, that's OK,' said Rose.

'*Thank* you,' said the girl, with a long-suffering air.

Rose checked the place out. She ran the shower, noted the water pressure. There wasn't much to do.

She had an instinct about property. This was the one. This would make her.

Five minutes later, Rose picked up her overnight case and rode the elevator back downstairs.

'Here.' She handed both keys to the receptionist.

'You can't just change your mind,' the girl said

defensively. She glanced at the doorman to see if he was blaming her for this.

'Your service is dire, your rooms are filthy,' Rose told her. She looked at her name-tag. 'Tracy. Nobody cleaned the kitchen or changed the sheets on my bed. Do you want to be a receptionist for ever?'

Tracy stared at her. 'Excuse me?'

'Because if you don't, you could always go to your boss with some ideas. You know, like cleaning the place up. Or wearing a fresh uniform. That way you might not be going out of business. And you could get a promotion.'

'I'm gonna charge your credit card. You didn't give me any notice.'

'That's fine with me.' Rose gave her a wink. 'It was worth it.'

She turned and walked out, and the receptionist stared after her.

'Weirdo,' she called.

Rose grinned.

★  ★  ★

Rose called George Benham the next day.

'Have you thought more about the hotel? The hospitality industry is up and coming — '

'I'm not interested in the hospitality industry. Can you set up a meeting with the owners?'

There was silence at the end of the phone.

'Maybe you should just make an offer.'

Rose blinked. Since when did George Benham go against anything she said?

'I want to do it in person, George.'

'But . . . but, Miss Fiorello . . . '

She got annoyed. 'I don't pay you to ask questions, George. Just set it up.'

He called back fifteen minutes later. 'You got an

appointment in Park Slope in Brooklyn in half an hour.'

'Half an hour! I can't get myself together that fast. It will have to be — '

'That's the only time he has to see you. If I were you, I'd take it. And Miss Fiorello, make sure to be very, very polite.'

★ ★ ★

She pulled up outside a nondescript brownstone with barely two minutes to spare. The neighbourhood was rough; broken window panes in some of the houses, trash littering the gutters. The address Benham had given her was an island in the street. Its windows were intact, its step was swept clean, and the car parked right in front was a gleaming Cadillac.

There was a restaurant on the lower level, a trattoria. Rose looked around for the door that led up to the rest of the building, but couldn't see it.

Benham had been so mysterious; she didn't want to be late.

Rose pushed open the door to the restaurant. A little bell rang. The place was very clean, but somewhat gloomy; all dark wood panelling. It had tables with red chequerboard cloths and candles in empty Chianti bottles shrouded in straw.

It was half past four. Too late for lunch, too early for dinner. But there were a few men sitting at some of the tables, drinking wine and coffee.

She felt conspicuous.

'Excuse me.' Rose walked up to the barman. 'I'm meant to meet someone in this building, but I can't find the way upstairs . . . '

He didn't look up from the glass he was polishing. 'Who you meeting?'

'Vincent Salerni,' Rose said.

The man's head snapped up. He looked her over, curiously.

'Wait there a second,' he said.

Rose stood at the bar while he lifted the partition and went over to the group of men sitting at the tables. He bent down deferentially and whispered in the ear of one of the men.

They all looked over towards her. Rose heard laughter. Then one of the smaller men shrugged.

The barman straightened up and beckoned her over.

Rose walked across the restaurant. She felt herself straighten and shook out her hair as she went.

'This is Mr Salerni,' he said.

Rose suddenly understood. Adrenaline flushed through her body, prickling on the palms of her hands. She felt herself dew with perspiration. She thanked God it was dark in here.

'You're Rose Fiorello?'

The man's eyes were intense. He was small and wiry, and very frightening. The huge-chested men who sat around him didn't scare her half as much as Vincent Salerni did.

Salerni's eyes swept her slim, young frame, with the usual male interest. In fact all the men were staring at her body in a way that made Rose incredibly self-conscious.

'Yes,' she said. '*Piacere, Don Salerni.*'

'You know me?'

Rose tried to control her racing heart. She forced herself to appear calm.

'No,' she said. 'I worked it out.'

Salerni chuckled. His henchmen chuckled after him.

'You are Italian?'

'Yes, Don Salerni.'

'And you are here on behalf of a husband? A boyfriend?'

The dark, piggish eyes were keen with interest.

221

'No, Don Salerni. For myself, alone. I — I wish to do business with you.'

'So I was told.' He spoke to a lieutenant without moving his head. 'Get the young lady a seat.'

A bull-necked man pulled a seat up at the table for Rose. She sat down, feeling very small, very conspicuous in the crowd of men. Her father would have forbidden her to ever get involved with these people. Her mother would be terrified to see her here.

But Rose had come. It was too late now.

She had to be very, very careful.

Rose lowered her eyes. 'My respects, Don Salerni. I wish to apologise for arriving improperly dressed.'

Salerni gave a surprised grunt of approval.

'I did not want to seem conspicuous at your hotel. And when I told my man to set up an appointment with the owner — '

'Your man?' Salerni laughed.

Rose shrugged, in the way she had seen the men do. 'He wets his beak on my deals.'

Salerni's eyes danced.

'He told me I could not be late. So I had no time to change.'

'You want to buy the hotel?'

'I do. It cannot be of interest to you, Don Salerni. It makes no money . . . '

'I have uses for everything I own. The Rego Park hotel handles a lot of cash.' He was telling her he used it to launder money. 'And it is a convenient place for a man who may not want to be at home.'

A love-nest for Mafiosis and their bits on the side? Rose blinked.

'Pardon me, Don Salerni, but I would not have thought the Rego Park was good enough for the second mode of use.'

'You haven't seen the penthouse suites,' Salerni said mildly. 'Why are you asking these questions? You are a young girl. You cannot do business with us. You have no idea what you are asking.'

'With your permission — ' Rose said. She opened her briefcase and produced a slim file. 'I have been investing since I was eighteen. I own nine buildings, thirty-one units — '

'You?'

'Yes, sir,' Rose said, respectfully.

'Your family is in real estate?'

'No. Just me.'

'Humph.' Salerni glanced over her figures. 'You have done well for yourself.'

'I would like to do a little better. I can make more use of that hotel than you, Don Salerni. I understood the business was on the market, but I don't want the business. I want the building.'

'To do what with it?'

'To convert it to condominiums,' Rose said truthfully. Lies to Salerni could get her dead. 'Of course, I would use your people to do the work. And I can provide you with another cash business as part of the deal.' She thought about it. 'Benham has a Chinese restaurant for sale. Then, as to the matter of the suites, I would, of course, retain one floor for your exclusive use, Don Salerni. Free of charge. Just permit me a month to outfit it to the proper standards.'

Now they were all staring at her.

'How will you cover the cost of the work?'

'I will sell what I own and do a 1028 tax-deferred exchange,' Rose said. 'Of course, I cannot offer you your asking price.' She named a sum that was 30 per cent below Benham's quote.

Salerni laughed uproariously.

'Salud,' he said, when he had finished wiping away tears of laughter. He raised his glass of anisette to Rose. 'You are a brave little girl. You should have been a man.'

'That would have been a waste of all this,' Rose said flirtatiously, tossing her long, dark hair.

He laughed again. 'True, *bellissima*. But you are brave. Still, one does not bargain with Don Vincent Salerni.' The piercing eyes glittered. 'I am not angry.'

*Fortunately for you* hung in the air unspoken.

A fresh mist of perspiration dewed Rose's brow. 'I do not wish to waste your time, sir.'

'Good.' Salerni reached over and laid a claw-like hand on her knee. Rose fought with every ounce of will not to shrink from his touch. Salerni was like an animal; she knew he could smell fear. 'Then you get to walk out of here intact, no?'

'But,' Rose said; her voice sounded very small, but she could not stop herself, 'I can make up the deficit to you by using your firm to do the work. Then, with the profits, I will buy more buildings all over the city. And of course, I will work with Don Salerni's people exclusively.'

He did not reply, and she hurriedly got up to leave.

'Don Salerni, I am twenty-one years old and I already have more than a million dollars. I know this is small stuff to you. But if you will consider doing me this favour, I will be able to repay your generosity in the future.' Her voice was almost a whisper now. 'Many times over.'

One of the goons stood up and folded his muscular arms across his chest. Despite the expensive suit, she could see the hard brawn of his biceps. Butcher's arms.

Rose muttered, 'Goodbye, Don Salerni,' and fled.

★　★　★

Outside, she reached into her bag and pulled out a small linen handkerchief, dabbing the sweat from her brow as she walked to her car. Her heart was beating wildly. Man, she was dumb. Thinking she could negotiate with a scorpion.

Please God, may she not have offended him.

Rose parked the car near her own apartment. She had managed to calm down. She might have annoyed Salerni, but surely she had been as humble as a peasant petitioning a prince. Which in a way, she had been.

It was terrifying, but Rose forced herself to be logical. He wasn't going to hurt her. Not if she did not bother him again, anyway. All she had lost was Rego Park.

And that had been a stretch, anyway. She wasn't even thirty. Who was she to start doing big-time deals? Donald Trump in a skirt? She should go a little slower, buy some more four-families . . .

Rose ran a bath and poured in some L'Occitane lavender bath oils. Great clouds of fragrant steam rose up and filled her room. She peeled off the T-shirt and jeans and stepped into the warm, comforting water.

The phone trilled.

'Damn it,' Rose swore. She jumped out, dripping, grabbed a towel and padded into her living room. 'Yes?'

'I'm looking for a Rose Fiorello,' said a haughty voice.

Rose clenched her fist. Yess! It was Don Salerni, calling her back! He was going to do the deal with her! It was all going to happen!

'It's Rose,' she said.

'This is Ella Brown in Jacob Rothstein's office,' said the voice.

'Hi,' Rose replied, not bothering to keep the disappointment out of her voice.

'We understood you applied for an internship with Rothstein Realty. I'm happy to tell you that your application has been accepted. You'll be starting in the office of Mr Richard White. Arrive at reception at eight-thirty sharp on Monday morning. Interns do not have parking privileges. Smart business dress is required. Any failure to arrive on time or arrival in incorrect attire will result in your termination as an intern with Rothstein Realty. Is this clear?'

Rose trembled with annoyance.

'Perfectly.'

'Good, then we'll see you at eight-thirty on Monday.'

Ella hung up without further pleasantries.

Rose stumbled back into her bath. It was still nice and warm, but she couldn't enjoy it. She lay there wondering if Jake had listened to that conversation. How he must love having her as a supplicant.

Yeah, well. Not for long.

This was the second step towards her vengeance, Rose thought. The first had been to establish herself, get a little money. Now she had to move up to the majors. And learn how to destroy Rothstein at the same time.

Rego Park hadn't come off, but it wouldn't be the only deal in the world. To find deals like that, you needed to be where the action was.

Rothstein Realty.

Rose thought of her father. She needed to call him, to go back to her parents, have dinner, remind herself why she was doing this. So she didn't get distracted by Jacob. A pair of predator's eyes, a square jaw and a well-built chest . . . she couldn't let it stand in her way.

He was an arrogant fuck. She was going to destroy him.

# 25

She wasn't going to be too impressed, Poppy told herself.

She was standing in Joel Stein's office. Summoned by the master. Her little stunt had paid off; it was a classic piece of record industry chutzpah. If she could just get through this interview, he was gonna hire her.

Her music business career was off and running.

'How old are you?'

'Twenty-one,' Poppy said breathlessly. She was standing in Stein's office, trying to keep the huge grin off her face.

He sat there, tapping the Silver Bullet tape against his desk.

'Not at college?'

Poppy grimaced. Mom and Dad had tried to talk her into going to college. Her grades had been outstanding. But she had no intention of wasting three years.

'No. Not my speed. I want to do things.'

'You'll have to start at the bottom.'

'Not as a secretary. I brought you this band — '

'No, not as a secretary. Not as a manager, either.'

'But — '

'You don't know enough to handle an act, honey. You don't know shit about contracts, about deals, about promotion. You may — *may* — have good ears. In which case the sky's the limit. Or this could be a fluke. But in either case, you have to learn. Got it? Good,' he said, without waiting for her answer. 'How's your math?'

'Pretty good,' Poppy muttered, crestfallen.

'You organised?'

'Yes,' she lied.

'Like Green Dragon?'

Poppy glanced up at the huge tour poster for Green Dragon. One of Dream Management's hottest acts. They were crude, rude, and multi-platinum. She'd had a crush on the singer for ever.

'Are you kidding?' Poppy's eyes gleamed. 'Oh, I *love* them. They *rock*. They're *rad* — '

' — and they're on tour with Mission Status. Arenas. We're getting back to the people,' Stein said with a touch of irony. 'I need an assistant tour accountant.'

He picked up the autographed Sid Fernandez baseball that was sitting on his desk and tossed it at her without warning. Poppy had great reflexes; she snapped out her left hand and caught it.

'You're up, rookie,' Stein said.

★ ★ ★

Poppy brought the band in that afternoon. They had washed their hair and put on their stage clothes. They were nervous, but they looked great. Kate thanked Poppy all the way in.

'Poppy, man, how can we ever thank you, we'll be with you for ever, you've just changed our lives . . . You don't know how long we've been plugging . . . '

They stared at Dream's glittering offices with hungry eyes. Stein let Poppy sit in while he sketched out a future plan for the band. Support slots, studio time, the works.

'Go home, get ready for a showcase,' Stein said finally.

The band were all over it.

'Wow, thanks — '

'Thank you so much — '

'We can't believe this — '

'Thank Poppy,' Stein said. 'She's the one that found you.'

They signed management contracts on the spot.

Once they'd left the office, Stein turned to Poppy.

'Got a passport?'

She nodded.

'Good. The tour's in France. You're flying out tomorrow.'

★  ★  ★

Her parents insisted on driving Poppy out to the airport.

'Really, Mom, I'm gonna be OK,' Poppy insisted.

'All those junkies and punks,' her mother twittered.

'Poppy, you just say no. You don't have to do any drugs. Honestly, I can get you a great D-girl job over at Artemis Studios,' her father added.

'Look, I'm not going to do anything. The record business is really clean these days. All water and going to bed early.' Poppy stepped out of the car, hoisting her red cases with her. 'I'll be fine. Honestly. Love you both.' She kissed her parents and hurried into the airport; goodbyes made her cry, and there was always the possibility that her nose had grown out a foot or two . . .

★  ★  ★

'Welcome to Continental,' the stewardess said. '4F? Just over there.'

The flight attendants stared at Poppy. Who was she, a movie star or something? They didn't recognise her. But she was wearing tight-fitting black pants round that tall, slim frame, she had a fountain of glossy raven hair — Poppy had dyed her hair black, and was growing back her natural hair colour — and a black leather jacket.

She looked like she'd just stepped out of a rock video. The Metallica shirt was the last straw. They wanted to serve rich businessmen, not a teenage girl in leather and studs.

'Can I get you some champagne, ma'am?'

'I'm not old enough,' Poppy said sweetly. She didn't want to give them the chance to demand some id. Never mind about the petty humiliations. She was on her way to France.

Poppy settled back into the luxurious leather comfort of her wide seat and reached into her carry-on, pulling out the tour schedule. It was stapled together and printed in black and white, with a drawing of a skeletal dragon. 'Fight or Flight Tour, 1993.' It had plenty of dry-as-dust instructions on making the bus, hotels, venues, and phone numbers for the production office.

Poppy thought it was the most exciting thing she had ever read.

She accepted some freshly squeezed orange juice and leaned back, flicking through the pages. Her stint with Snaggletooth had been nothing more than the occasional van ride to some gig in the LA suburbs. This was completely different. This was the big time.

As the plane lifted off and they pulled away from the city's glorious smog-bound sunset, Poppy felt the plastic laminate around her neck. She couldn't stop smiling.

This was it. Her life as an adventure was finally starting.

This was Paradise.

\* \* \*

'I don't care how you get me there. Just get me there,' Poppy snarled.

The guy looked at her. He had a face as tough and brown as old leather, his cab stank of cigarettes, and his mean little eyes were hostile. He shrugged in that particularly Gallic way.

'Voila, Nancy,' he said.

'I *know* it's Nancy, goddammit.' Poppy was exhausted. The flight had been eleven hours, and even in business class, that sucked. She had practically memorised her tour schedule, watched three bad movies, and got cramp. Now all she wanted was to get to her hotel and go to sleep. What time was it here? She was utterly disorientated.

The bastard cab driver was pretending he didn't understand English. Poppy had forgotten how much the French hated the Americans. He'd taken her to Nancy, but not to her hotel; the guy wanted to drop her in the town square.

'*L'hôtel Reine Catherine*,' Poppy insisted.

He shrugged again.

Poppy pulled out her wallet and produced three hundred-franc notes.

'*Ah oui, La Reine Catherine, je le connais*,' said the driver, his face creasing into a fake smile.

'Yeah, that's what I thought,' Poppy said.

Fuck him. He wasn't getting a tip. She hoped her day was about to start getting better.

★   ★   ★

The Reine Catherine was a soulless block of concrete. It reminded Poppy of a Novotel. Despite the blazing French sun, there was nothing exotic about the place. Coaches were parked in the forecourt, tourists were dragging their wheeled cases inside. The day was very hot. She felt sweaty and disgusting. She wanted to get to her room.

Poppy walked in through the revolving door and up to reception.

'Wait a minute, please,' said the snotty receptionist. He was on a phone call, and it sounded like it was personal. The guy laughed and chatted while Poppy just stood there.

She looked around the lobby. Green and purple industrial carpeting, a plastic ficus tree in a pot, and a little row of leaflets in plastic containers advertising local sights. But there were also lobby chairs and a bar in one corner. A group of loud American guys were sitting on the chairs. They had crew cuts, sun-beaten faces, keys jangling, tell-tale little red strings around their necks that were tucked into their T-shirts.

Road crew.

Two of the guys looked over at Poppy appreciatively. One whistled, the other one said, 'Ooh la la.' Then they all laughed.

The hotel porters and the receptionist said nothing. They had clearly seen it all before. Nobody reproved the men or asked them to stop ogling Poppy.

'Hey, she's in the wrong hotel,' one said.

'No need to tell her that. Maybe they sent her over here on purpose. Added bonus.'

It was clear none of them thought she could speak English.

They all laughed again. The receptionist was still chatting away. Poppy snapped. She leaned over the counter and put her finger on the phone.

He looked up, shocked.

Poppy pulled the laminate out of her shirt.

'Monsieur,' she snarled, 'I'm with Green Dragon. Actually, I'm with Dream Management. I'm a tour accountant and I'm going to be settling the bill at this hotel. So unless you want to make an appointment for me to speak to the manager, I strongly suggest you give me my *fucking* key right now.'

'Oooh,' said the crew guys, chuckling.

Poppy ignored them. The receptionist flushed and hurriedly fished out a little paper wallet with a plastic rectangle tucked inside.

'Mademoiselle, ah *oui*, I see you 'ere, you are on ze

third floor, room 346. Do you want some 'elp with your bag?'

'From this hotel? No,' Poppy snapped. She grabbed the key and stormed off towards the elevators. She had to stand right next to the crew guys.

'What's up, sugar?' one of them cooed.

'Hey, baby, you showed those Frenchies,' said another.

Poppy saw nothing but annoyance and hostility in their faces. She was too tired to think about that now.

'See you guys later,' she muttered.

Mercifully, the doors hissed open. Poppy rode up to her room, slipped the electronic key in the door. The tiny light switched to green. She threw her bag on the floor, tempted to just collapse on to the bed. No, it was more important to get the sweat off her. She staggered into the bathroom, so tired she felt drunk. It had one of those tiny tubs you couldn't stretch out in. Never mind, she'd just take a shower. Poppy thought wryly that if she could stretch out, she might just fall asleep and drown.

She peeled off her clothes and dropped them on the tiled floor. Then she ran the water. The instructions were in French and her shower was only lukewarm. Poppy couldn't be bothered to figure it out. Mechanically she sluiced her body down, lathering it with the cheap soap. Then she reached for a towel; this wasn't America, obviously; the hotel towels were scratchy little white handkerchiefs. Her parents had a bigger towel than this for the dog.

Poppy stumbled into her room. The windows had thick curtains with white chiffon panels floating across them. She didn't even have the energy to pull the curtains closed. Poppy set her alarm for two hours and flopped on to the bed. She was asleep in minutes.

# 26

The taxi dropped her off at the end of the street which led to the arena. It was an open-air gig; kids were parking in a lot, in fields, in streets, and walking down.

'You get out 'ere,' the cabbie said. 'I cannot — '

He gestured at the mass of humanity streaming towards the gates. It was more crowded than rush hour in Tokyo: leather, studs, teased hair everywhere; T-shirts ranging from Slayer to Cinderella, Megadeth to Bon Jovi; naturally, a ton of Green Dragon jackets and shirts. The rock 'n' roll uniform.

Poppy was wearing a black T-shirt, leather jacket and jeans. She figured that was the professional way to go. She had selected her ankle boots, wore no make-up except a slick of concealer to hide the dark circles under her eyes, and had tied her hair back in a severe pony-tail. No time to wash it; thank God for baseball caps. Her laminate was tucked safely inside her bra. Last thing she needed was some deranged fan to snatch it from her.

Her sleep had only taken the slightest edge off her tiredness. Jet lag and the time difference made her feel spaced-out; when she'd woken, for a few seconds she'd had no idea where she was or how she'd got there.

She paid the cab and stepped out. No time for weakness right now. Anyway, the procession of teenagers and twenty-somethings was better than any cup of coffee; it jolted her senses and made her feel alive.

The excitement started to build up as she trudged towards the stadium. Already she could hear the sound of one of the support bands, the cheering of the crowd already inside. She felt slightly dizzy. She had an insane impulse to jump up and down and clap her hands wildly. She was a part of this. She was actually a part of Dream Management.

The box-office loomed in front of her. Gates A — E, F — K . . .

Poppy found a security guard.

'Where's the backstage entrance?'

He looked at her blankly.

She fished the laminate out. *Access All Areas.* Her photo beamed out from under the coiled Green Dragon logo. He examined it with a grunt, then reluctantly pointed to a small iron turnstile to her left. It had four security guards and a posse of groupies, all in high heels, wearing fishnet tights and low-cut tops, standing outside pleading with them.

Poppy marched up to it and flashed her laminate. The surly looks of the guards disappeared; they opened the gate and let Poppy through, forcing back the chicks that tried to slip in after her.

She was standing backstage. Laminate-wearing crew were everywhere. There were tents and signs in English. Catering. Press. Production Office.

Poppy breathed in deeply. She stood still for a second.

She felt absolutely overwhelmed with pure joy.

★   ★   ★

'Hi,' Poppy said.

She had stuck her head in at the production office. People were sitting around wooden tables, on the phone or shouting into walkie-talkies. Nobody paid her any attention.

She said loudly, 'I'm looking for Mike Rich.'

'I'm Mike,' said a man. He wore chinos and a white shirt, a gold Rolex, and a string with several laminates, the Green Dragon one on the top. 'You with Special?'

That was the name of the promoter.

'Nope, I'm here from Dream.' Poppy held out her hand. He didn't take it.

'Fucking Joel. Like I need a fucking kid.' Rich looked her over, unimpressed. 'You're a girl.'

'You're perceptive,' Poppy said.

'I don't like women on the road.'

'Too bad,' Poppy said. 'What do you want me to do? I'm supposed to be your assistant tour accountant.'

Rich handed her some envelopes. 'Go give the band their per diems. And then bring us all coffee.'

Poppy told herself the hostility was to be expected. They always hazed you on the road, right? That was part of rock folklore. She got the coffee first.

'That's great,' one of the men said. 'We could use our own waitress.'

She ignored this. Pick your battles. The vital thing, Poppy told herself, was that she was about to meet the band. Excited, she grabbed the envelopes full of hundred-franc notes and headed off for the tented area signed 'Band Only'. It was set up like an enclosure at some mad garden party. A security guy was outside; even people with laminates couldn't get in here, she knew.

Poppy had Green Dragon posters on her closet door. Blaze, the singer, with his fountain of dirty blond hair, had been one of her first crushes. She also fancied Drake, the bassist. Blaze, Drake, Tony and Mark; four names well known to Jack Daniel's-swilling frat boys and horny teenage girls across America. They had tunes as well as looks; they rocked. And now, now she worked for them.

Poppy forced herself not to grin. She had to make these men take her seriously. It was a man's world. She had to be the ultimate pro.

'You can't come in here,' the guard said. An American; band security.

236

Poppy showed him her laminate. He just shook his head.

'Mike Rich sent me over. I've got something for the band,' Poppy said.

He grinned. 'Another one, huh? Go right in, honey.'

Poppy walked into the enclosure and froze.

Five or six good-looking girls were sitting around with their tops off, leaning over the band. She recognised Blaze at once; he was the one standing up, pants around his ankles, being expertly serviced by a girl whose face she couldn't see.

'What are you waiting for, baby?' Mark said. 'Get 'em out.'

Poppy screamed. Then she turned and fled, through the little corridor of fabric, out to the main backstage area. Her face was the colour of a tomato, her entire body hot with shame.

She stormed back into the production office. The men saw her and started to laugh.

'You fucking asshole,' she spat at Rich.

'You're gonna let her talk to you like that?' said the man who had made the waitress comment. He had a coarse English accent.

'Who the fuck are you?' Poppy snarled.

'Leo Ross. Tour manager,' he said flatly.

'Oh,' Poppy said. That took some of the wind from her sails. The tour manager was God as far as a roadcrew was concerned. He ran the show. However, he was also hired and fired by management, Poppy reminded herself.

'Sugar baby, you gonna cry?' Rich asked. 'I told you, the road is no place for a woman. Why don't you just get on a plane and go home? Save us all a major headache.'

'I'm here because Joel Stein sent me,' Poppy said, forcing herself to be calm.

'And are you gonna ring him and start crying about

237

the big bad boys on the crew?' Ross asked.

'I can handle myself,' Poppy said. 'Of course, I won't guarantee not to spit in Mike's next coffee.'

The other men chuckled at that.

'Why don't you give me something to do? There's got to be at least some grunt work you can't be bothered with,' Poppy said to Mike.

He was still hostile, but she had raised a grin from Ross. He shrugged.

'Might as well let her stay till she fucks up,' Ross said.

'That won't take long,' Rich told him. He looked at Poppy. 'OK, toots. Go find Jacques Remy, he's the promoter. Ask him to give you the latest expenses. Bring them back here. Don't drop anything. Then call the band's hotel. Get the bill for last night. They were complaining. Tony doesn't want to pay an extra five thousand. Take care of it.'

'OK,' Poppy said. That was something to do, at least. She took a breath. 'OK.'

She got out of there before they could screw with her some more.

\* \* \*

She tried to go over the primer that Joel had given her.

'Bands are on a percentage of the net. Tour accountancy is all about verifying gross ticket sales, subtracting promoter costs, then take a percentage of the net. Our percentage is ninety.'

'That's a lot.'

He ignored her. 'You also settle the hotel bills, give out per diems, check band and crew in and out of the hotels . . . '

'Plural?'

Stein smiled faintly at her naivety. 'You think the rock stars sleep with the catering crew? Not exactly. And then you take care of certain expenses. Be creative.'

238

'Like what?' Poppy asked, mystified.

In answer, Stein bent close to his desk, pressed a finger against one nostril, and snorted up an imaginary line of blow.

'I see,' Poppy said faintly.

His eyes narrowed.

'Can you handle this, kid? I don't have time to play nursemaid.'

'No problem,' Poppy had said brightly. 'I'll take care of everything.'

★ ★ ★

She made herself useful. The promoter handed her a sheaf of papers without comment. Poppy delivered them, then got herself a fold-out wooden chair in the production office. Her stapled tour book told her the band were staying at the Hotel Charlemagne.

'*Parlez-vous anglais?*' Poppy tried.

'Certainly, we speak English, madam,' said the woman on the front desk soothingly. Poppy could hear the sound of running water faintly in the background. A fountain. She could tell instantly that this hotel was a classy joint.

She was aware that the men in the room were listening as she spoke.

'I'm with Green Dragon. Dream Management. I'm calling to check on the bill.'

'Hold on, please,' said the woman, a little more coldly.

Poppy was put on hold for a second. An older man came on, and his tone was severe.

'You are responsible for the Green Dragon bill? It comes to fifty-eight thousand francs.'

She did a quick conversion in her head. That was over seven thousand US dollars.

'Furthermore, I'm afraid I must ask you for

immediate payment and for one of your representatives to come back here and remove the luggage from the rooms of these *guests*.' She could almost see his lip curling. 'They have destroyed two rooms, and I can no longer admit them to our property.'

'Can you hold on a second?'

'Very well.'

Poppy hit the hold button. She turned to Mike Rich. 'This is the hotel manager, Mike. He says he wants the band checked out, that he's throwing them out of the hotel, and that the bill is seven thousand dollars . . .'

Rich just stared at her. 'Well, sort it out. You're supposed to be a tour accountant, right? Fix it.'

Poppy picked the line up.

'Monsieur, I will be right over. I will need to see you personally to settle the damages.'

'That is fine, madam.'

Leo Ross walked in. 'We got a problem with the PA. Somebody get over to the band, clear the tarts out. The wives' limo just pulled up.' He glanced at Poppy. 'How you doing, kid?'

'I'm gonna go sort the hotel thing out.'

Ross laughed. 'Oh, are ya? I'm afraid we're gonna have to eat that one.'

'I'll be right back,' Poppy said.

★   ★   ★

It was everything she had expected. The Charlemagne was central, elegant, formal, and, quite obviously, expensive.

Poppy walked into a marble lobby. There was the water feature, a Japanese-style flat fountain mounted against the wall. Gold rails and soft white carpeting were everywhere. She told the receptionist she was there to see the manager.

He materialised. He was about fifty.

240

'If you will follow me, mademoiselle,' he said.

They rode the elevator up to the top floor.

'These are our presidential suites,' the manager said.

He opened the doors and showed them to Poppy, one by one.

They were wrecked. Poppy was actually quite impressed. She hadn't thought this kind of decadence was still out there.

TVs were overturned, wine had been spilt on the carpets, lamps were broken, there was glass everywhere, stains on the walls. The bathrooms stank of vomit. In one particular room, Tony's, she assumed, the TV had been smashed to pieces and the curtains were blackened where somebody had set them on fire.

Poppy looked grave.

'Monsieur,' she said, 'can we talk about this in your office?'

*   *   *

He had a picture of his family on his desk. Poppy studied it as she eased herself into the chair. Two teenage daughters.

She spoke confidently.

'Monsieur' — she read his name tag — 'Souris, I am a lawyer in a firm in Beverly Hills in the United States. We manage a great many clients, including film stars. I know your hotel has a record of hosting many of our clients.' She nodded at a signed headshot of Tom Cruise that was mounted on the wall. 'I would hate for that relationship to be adjusted.'

He swallowed hard. 'But the damage — '

'Yes, the damage is significant. But not seven thousand dollars' worth. How long have you had those televisions? Those curtains? Many years. I am not paying brand new prices for them. Lamps? A few francs. If you present me with that bill, I will pay it, and then I will sue. I guarantee you, Monsieur, that you will spend many more times the amount in legal fees than you gouge from my clients in costs.'

He was staring at her. Poppy ploughed on. 'As you can see, I brought this camera with me to meticulously document everything and prevent false claims. Make no mistake, we will sue for a fraudulent bill.'

'But, my maids will not clean that — '

'If I take them into court and ask them if you have ever asked them to clean up vomit, what will they say?' Poppy smiled. 'Give me their names and I will personally give them such a generous bonus they will be glad to do it.' She made a little gesture at his family photo. 'Monsieur has two lovely daughters. Will they be at the concert this evening?'

He sighed. 'I could not get tickets — '

'I can take care of that.' Poppy beamed at him. 'There is no need for unpleasantness, Monsieur. Two thousand, the band stays, I personally call the Chairman of your company with a glowing report as to how helpful you have been, five hundred to split between the maids, and I will escort your daughters and two of their friends to the concert as guests of the band. Teenage daughters can be hard to get along with, no? Just think, Monsieur, what a hero you will be — both to them and to your boss.'

He smiled back. 'Mademoiselle is very persuasive.'

'I thought you'd see it that way.' Poppy tapped his computer. 'If you'll just put that in writing.'

Back at the stadium, she turned up in a taxi with four ecstatic French girls in the back. Poppy escorted them backstage, stuck them in a generic hospitality area, and then picked her way through the dusk to the production office. Mike Rich wasn't there, but Leo Ross was.

'I fixed it,' Poppy said simply.

Ross grabbed the paper from her and scanned it.

'Well, fuck me,' he said.

Poppy grinned. 'No thanks.'

'Out the way, out the way,' came a man's voice from the crackle of a two-way radio.

'Leo — '

Poppy drew back. Surrounded by ferocious-looking bodyguards the size of bears, Green Dragon had entered the room. The men around them yelled into their radios as though they were the President of the United States. Poppy blushed scarlet.

'Well, look 'oo it is.' Mark's famous English accent. He and the band were staring at Poppy. 'The squawker.'

'What, the band's not good enough for 'er but you are?' Blaze laughed. 'That's a turn-up, innit?'

Leo said calmly, 'Lads, Poppy here works for Joel.'

'Didn't know Joel was that way inclined,' Tony said, to laughter.

'She's your new tour accountant. Gonna help Mike.'

Drake looked sceptical and as though he was about to say something, but Leo ploughed on.

'You know that bit of bovver at the 'otel?'

'Don't go on about that again, mate,' said Tony, but he looked sheepish. 'It was only a few fucking TVs and that.'

'They wanted to charge you five grand.'

'Seven,' said Poppy automatically.

Leo glared at her. 'In pounds, doll.'

They were all Brits, of course. 'Oh yes,' Poppy muttered.

'Lippy little bit, ain't she?' said Blaze.

'I'm not fucking paying five fucking grand, fuck that,' said Tony, getting furious.

'Well, you don't have to, now.' He passed Tony the piece of typed paper. Poppy held her breath as he looked it over; then his face broke into a wide grin.

'That's one thousand pounds.'

'For the whole band, not just you, Tony.'

'How the 'ell did Mike pull that one off, then?'

'Not Mike. Poppy here.'

The band, who had been following this conversation carefully, all lifted their heads and looked at Poppy again. There was silence.

'I hope that's OK, Mr Watson,' Poppy stammered.

'Mr Watson!' said Tony, to laughter. 'You call me Tony, honey. Great job. Nice work.'

'Yeah, well done,' said Drake. The others nodded. Poppy felt as though she'd just won an Olympic gold medal.

'I still want to see your tits, though,' said Mark.

She froze, not sure what to say. But then the guys laughed, and Poppy felt the tension dissipate. Mark slapped her on the back. 'Welcome to the road.'

★   ★   ★

They put her up on stage during the gig. Poppy watched from the wings, in the gloom, staring at the band running around out front and the crew running around out back; how the drum tech crouched behind the riser, periodically fiddling with things, how the lighting guys sat up in the rigging, double-checking the large coloured spotlights. She'd seen stages before, playing the bass.

But nothing like this.

Those had been sweaty, stinky, tiny little dives with a handful of teenagers out front and a tiny, cramped stage with a crapped-out PA. This, this was . . .

Poppy hugged herself. This was heaven.

It was dark outside now. The set was the famous Green Dragon logo. There were more lights than Times Square. The PA was so thick and rich and heavy that the sound was almost 3-D. Out front, the French summer sky was inky black, but the lights from the gig blocked out the stars.

And then there was the crowd.

They stretched out in front of the band almost endlessly, a great throng of humanity. They cheered and screamed so loud you could hear it over the crash of bass and drums and guitar; the electric excitement crackled from the crowd to the stage and back again, so that Poppy gasped and her skin prickled. Lighters were waved, punctuating the blackness, and spotlights swept across them, so she could see the fists thrust in the air, the forest of hands, the wave as sixty thousand kids all fought to get just a step closer to the stage, to the band, to the magic . . .

'This one's called 'Force Ten'!' Blaze yelled.

A roar from the crowd.

Poppy sighed in sheer bliss. Her favourite song.

I'm with the band, she thought. I'm with the band!

# 27

For the first month, Poppy kept her head down.

She learned the basics. Checking expenses, giving out per diems. Mike let her check the band and crew in and out of the hotels. She made coffee, she ran errands, she subtly disappeared when rows of groupies and strippers turned up. Poppy knew at once that that was important, if she wanted to stay on the road. Rock stars liked fucking easy women, and the girls liked to screw the rock stars. Sometimes, to get to a rock star, they would give head to the crew. There was nothing so debased that some chick wouldn't do it; half the guys had albums full of Polaroids to prove it.

As a woman, she had two choices. Be disgusted and quit, or ignore it.

Poppy chose the latter.

There was a double standard. The men on the tour regarded themselves as players but the women as whores. Poppy learned fast that there was no point in bitching about this. Nobody forced these girls to do what they did.

She remembered her own teenage fantasies about sneaking backstage and making wild love to every guy with long hair and a platinum album and shuddered, just a little. But the truth was, rock was all about sex. And drugs. And she still loved it.

Poppy found creative ways to write off the cocaine and poppers and other junk the band liked to use. At least they weren't doing smack, she thought. There was no point pretending the stuff wasn't out there. Some acts were destroyed by it. Not Green Dragon, at least not so far.

The first time she was offered blow on the crew bus

Poppy shook her head.

'No charge, honey,' said the lighting guy, perplexed.

'Not for me,' Poppy said simply.

She had discovered something else. Drinking and drugs didn't offend her, even groupies didn't bother her all that much. But what excited her was the business of music. Taking the flights, organising a big tour, like a marching army fighting battles. She was part of the logistics. Watching an expert crew raise the same stage with mechanical precision in thirty different venues, watching the production office being built like an ants' nest, sorting the problems, climbing into the bus, rocking the house, then ripping it down again. Partying happened after the gig, not before it; a roadie who drank pre-curtain was unceremoniously fired.

Poppy drank it all in. She learned. And she loved it.

The crew tolerated her. Giving out per diems was a good job; people were always happy to see her. Docking a guy for every minute he delayed the crew bus was not so good. But they understood. The tour ran on a schedule, calibrated down to the minute. Joel Stein, the manager, was due to turn up on one of the Spanish dates; he'd review and check everybody's time sheet, make sure they were running on time and under budget. Nobody wanted to run foul of Joel, when he did turn up. So if Poppy had to dock the daily allowance for lateness, the guys didn't even bitch that much.

Poppy also made sure the band would like her. She reduced all their personal hotel bills. They loved that; never underestimate how much rich people like extra money, Poppy thought. She also phoned ahead to warn their security when the wives and girlfriends were on their way in to the stadium. Sometimes a wife would 'surprise' her husband. It was Poppy's job to see he was never so surprised he couldn't get the groupies out in time.

But there was one person who didn't like her at all,

and that was Mike Rich.

Mike made her life a living hell. Poppy didn't say anything about it to Joel. He called in to Production often, and she just told him everything was fine.

The road had its own rules. One of them was that you didn't squeal.

★ ★ ★

'Hey.'

Poppy looked up from her table in the production office. They were in Barcelona tonight, one of the last gigs on this stretch.

Joel Stein had just walked in.

'Hey. I forgot you were coming tonight.'

'Wouldn't miss it,' Stein said. He pulled up a chair, turned it around and straddled it, looking her over. 'You having problems, kid?'

★ ★ ★

'So it's your last gig.'

Poppy nodded. 'Yeah.'

Drake smiled at her. He had a new crew cut which was driving the girls crazy. They were sitting in the band's enclosure backstage, in a field near Milan. Another open-air show.

Poppy was leaving the next day. She didn't smile. She was going to have a chance to get some rest, to do her laundry properly as opposed to washing her panties in the sink with handwash liquid, to report triumphantly back to Joel Stein. And all she felt like doing was crying.

The crew hadn't stopped ragging on her once. There were obscene songs on the bus . . . she knew most of them by heart now. She'd been tossed fully clothed into swimming pools, had eighty pizzas charged to her room, and her butt had been patted and squeezed and generally assaulted. They called her names, 'Miss Priss', 'the Virgin Mary', whatever. And now she felt like crying.

It was pathetic.

Drake saw the redness in Poppy's eyes and grinned.

'Always the way, babe. First tour? Forget it. You think you'll never forget these guys, that they're your brothers in arms, whatever . . . '

Poppy nodded and shook her head to get rid of the nascent tears.

'Yeah, well. One week back at home and you won't even remember their names. Trust me. It'll all be a blur, until the next one.'

'I guess,' Poppy said.

'You can't go on the road, anyway. Not like this. They should find you something else to do.'

Drake was in the band, which meant Poppy had to kiss his ass. He was a client of her boss. But she fought to stop bristling.

'I'm damn good at it,' she said shortly.

He chuckled. 'Prickly little pear.'

'I didn't mean anything by it . . . ' Poppy said, panicking.

'You don't need to worry about me, love. I'm not gonna tell on you. You did fine. But that's not the point.'

'Then what is? That I'm a woman?'

'That you're a gorgeous woman,' Drake said. 'That won't work long-term. Trust me.'

Poppy blushed richly.

'Soundcheck,' said a runner, poking his head into the enclosure.

'Later.' Drake walked out.

Poppy went to the cooler and pulled out a bottle of Evian from the ice. The band liked her enough that she was allowed to pick at the food in their area. Normally that was absolutely off-limits. Being on the road was like a court that followed a king around; the band were royalty, and the others were just servants.

The familiar sounds of soundcheck drifted back from the giant stage. 'One-two. One-two.' Why couldn't roadies find something else to say? There was a definite lack of imagination . . .

The sun beat down on her face. She was leaving tomorrow. Poppy felt a lack of something, as if she had failed in some way.

Not by anything she'd done. She knew her record was very good, for a rookie. The crew accepted her, even if they tormented her, the band was pleased, she'd run her errands with efficiency and even some flair.

But it wasn't enough.

She desperately wanted to go back to Joel Stein in a cloud of glory. To show him why he should give her an act of her own to manage under his umbrella.

The record business was a man's world. Period. If you were a chick, you had to be more than just competent. You had to knock them out.

But what could an assistant tour accountant do, exactly?

She'd had an uneasy feeling about Mike Rich from the start. His hostility couldn't be explained by her mere presence. Poppy knew all about soothing egos, and she'd done everything he asked, promptly and obediently. She even made his goddam coffee, just the way he liked it.

She sat and thought until the first support band was announced. Then she got up, and tucked her laminate into her T-shirt, so nobody could rip it off her, and headed out of the backstage compound into front of house.

★ ★ ★

It was early, but the place was already three-quarters full. This gig had sold out in half an hour when it went

250

on sale four months ago; the promoter told Poppy it had melted a local phone bank. She remembered him rubbing his hands together gleefully.

'*Ch'e fantastico*,' the guy had purred.

Fantastic. Yeah, a bonanza for him.

Poppy stared out at the sea of people. They were crowded into the standing area and filling the seats at the back. They were nodding politely as the first support, a local act, desperately ground out their best tunes in front of a backdrop of plain black drapes, set up to cover Green Dragon's set.

There sure were a lot of them. Queuing up at the food stands, thronging the T-shirt stall, drinking the overpriced, watered-down beer.

A little bell rang in her head. Something wasn't right. What was it?

Something's wrong with this picture, Poppy thought.

Then she found it. A section had been added. The crowd extended to the right of the stage, to the left of the stage. She focused and brought up the seating diagram in her head. No, they hadn't intended opening those seats up. You were at a really bad angle, you couldn't see a thing, and the PA sound would be tinny and off because of the acoustics.

Other bands liked to gouge every dollar from their fans. Not Green Dragon. Not Dream Management. Not her boss.

Poppy's heartbeat accelerated. She marched back inside the backstage compound and threaded her way through the chaos directly to the production office.

Mike Rich was sitting there with the promoter, drinking. He was laughing, too, as though he'd made a big score. Poppy saw there was a wad of notes in an envelope sticking out of his pocket.

Surreptitiously she glanced at the seating diagram on the wall.

Those seats weren't there.

'Hey, Mike.' Poppy kept her tone light and calm. 'Where are the ticket stubs?'

The two men's expressions changed instantly.

'Honey, wha' you wan' stubs for?' the promoter purred. 'All is done auto, the band is gonna get paid, you think I don' pay *Green Dragon*?'

'I just like to be thorough,' Poppy said pleasantly.

'I already counted the ticket stubs,' Mike said shortly. 'Everything matches.'

'That's nice,' Poppy said. 'What's up with the seating at the side of the stage?'

'All accounted for. Not your business. I don't like your tone, missy,' Mike blustered. 'You report to me, so why don't you take that tight little ass of yours and get the fuck out of the office? You're in the way.'

She held her hands up. 'OK, OK. As long as you counted it all, I guess I have nothing to say . . . see you guys later.'

She went to catering to kill half an hour, then came back to the production office. There was a little dusting of coke on the tables where they'd been sitting, Poppy recognised the white powder instantly. Her heart was in her mouth as she dialled the office in LA.

'Dream Management.'

'It's Poppy. Let me speak to Joel.'

'He's in a meeting.'

'Just put me through, Lisa.'

That aggravated sigh at the end of the phone. Poppy didn't give a damn.

'Is this an emergency?' Joel's voice snapped. 'I'm in a meeting with RCA.'

'Mike's ripping you off,' Poppy said succinctly.

A pause. 'Extra seats?'

'Extra sections, I think a kickback.'

'Document it,' Joel Stein said. Then he hung up.

Poppy smiled to herself and reached for a camera. She knew what was about to happen. She was gonna climb the second rung of the ladder, after only her first road trip. Six weeks to a promotion, Poppy thought.

She loved the record business.

# 28

'So,' Ted Elliott said. The super-agent spun slightly on his modern, sleekly ergonomic chair, which perfectly matched his sleekly ergonomic offices. They overlooked the Thames, with vast floor-to-ceiling windows; interior design that looked as though it had come from someone hipper than Terence Conran; a kidney-shaped couch on which an utterly overawed Daisy was perched; a glass coffee table laden with copies of *The Bookseller* and *Publisher's Weekly* and publishers' catalogues; a kilim rug, and a chrome-covered espresso machine.

Daisy thought it was rather incongruous, because Ted Elliott was about her father's age, and as upper-class as they came. He reminded her of Edward Powers, many years down the line. An old-fashioned gentleman. But the thought, for once, did not stab at her heart, because she was too jumpy to think about anything other than getting through this.

★   ★   ★

'Ted Elliott of Elliott & Russell?' Edward had asked, when she'd finally met him in the bar. 'You're not serious, Daisy. But that's fantastic!'

'Is he a big agent?' Daisy had asked nervously, looking around for Edwina.

'She's not here, had to run,' Edward said, answering her unspoken query. 'But as for Elliott, he's the biggest agent in London, bar none. Represents . . . ' and he ticked off a list of gargantuan bestselling authors. 'No romance, though, as far as I'm aware.'

★   ★   ★

254

And now Daisy was here. She'd jumped on the bus to London, and she was actually in an agent's office. A really big, important agent.

Ted Elliott could make her dreams come true. If only he'd take her on.

'Have you had any other interest?' he asked.

Daisy nodded, blushing. It had been a week since the summons to Elliott's office, and three other agencies had written to her asking to see more of her work. It was a great response to the chapter she'd mailed out.

'Curtis Brown, ICM, William Morris,' she mumbled.

His eyes were polite, but rather steely.

'I'll tell you what I am not interested in,' Elliott told her, 'and that is a beauty contest.'

'Right,' Daisy agreed, not sure what he meant.

There was a silence. She had no idea what she was supposed to say.

'So we'll get this out to a few people. I know a couple of editors I think could be right for the material.'

Daisy had no idea what was going on, and the super-agent was pushing back his chair like the meeting was over. She couldn't let it end like this.

'Will you represent me?' she blurted out. Subtle as a brick, but she had to know. This was torture. She had no idea if she was supposed to walk out of here despondent or elated.

'Yes, of course.' He looked at her as though she had just arrived from the planet Mars. 'We'll get contracts out to you tonight. What are you crying for?'

'I'm sorry,' Daisy mumbled, because she wasn't being remotely cool. 'I'm just so happy.'

The older man's face crinkled into a broad smile. 'No need for tears just yet, I imagine. Do you have a job?'

'Yes, I'm a waitress,' Daisy said fiercely, 'and I can't wait to pack it in — '

'Over my dead body.' Now he really did look like her father. 'You have no idea if the book will sell.'

'Oh,' said Daisy, yanked back down to earth. She hated her crappy job in Oxford.

'Never give up a job until you know your future is secure; and that can take years.'

'Oh,' said Daisy gloomily.

'Just go home. We'll call you,' Ted Elliott said, and the meeting was over.

★　★　★

Daisy went back to Oxford and tried to concentrate on her studies. She was six weeks away from her final examinations. After the agency contracts arrived, she signed them, and that was about all that happened. The strange thing was that the lack of news about her manuscript concentrated her mind.

She rented herself a new place — away from Edward Powers. To be around him hurt too much. It was a nasty little dump on the ring-road, modern, with a handkerchief-sized patch of neatly clipped lawn out front boasting a garden gnome showing his workman's bum. She had to share it with a glue-sniffing teenager called Spike, which actually wasn't too bad as he was never home.

But more importantly, the rent was as tiny as her room, and she was out of danger; he was never going to 'drop in' with Edwina here, and she wasn't surrounded, every day, by reminders of him. Daisy told Edward that she needed to buckle down, to get her degree. He understood that, and didn't pressure her into going out for a drink.

'After finals. Quite right,' he said.

Sometimes she wondered if he knew how she felt about him. But she tried not to obsess about it, else she'd go mad.

Daisy went to the library for her course, pulled out books, buried her head in them. It was strange how she was actually starting to find it interesting. Even though there were no calls from London, the very fact that a big agent had signed her gave her a new zest for life, something that had been missing for so long she almost felt drunk.

A sense of achievement. How strange; she looked at herself differently now.

She started to lose more weight, without noticing it. She was too busy to think about eating, and quite often she'd grab a Boots Shapers sandwich for lunch, not because it was low-cal, but just because it was there. And fast. The last few pounds of puppy fat were melting from her thighs. Daisy had to walk a mile each day just to get to and from her nearest bus-stop; the inaccessibility of the nasty suburban house was one reason even she could make the rent. And then she'd be on her feet at night. Waitressing.

As she dropped the weight and started to like herself a little, Daisy found she was making more money. She would make up her face with something cheap such as No. 7, just a dab of foundation and a black eyeliner. And her tips increased dramatically.

Pretty girls made more money. She resented it, but she needed the cash; it didn't hurt to smile, Daisy told herself.

Some of the diners, emboldened by cheap house red, asked her out on dates, but that was a bridge too far.

'I'm taken,' she'd reply, grinning in a friendly way. That was usually good for a fiver.

Daisy met Edward for a last drink, still no Edwina, thank God, and promised to keep in touch.

'You don't think I'd let a famous author slip out of my clutches, do you?' Edward joked.

Daisy laughed gently. 'I suppose not.'

That was a rough night. All she could think about was how much she loved him, but there was absolutely no chance of telling the truth. Even though the girl was not in town, Edward talked about her constantly. He was smitten, and Daisy was history.

She sat her finals, and left Oxford without looking back.

* * *

Daisy was out in the garden, helping her mother pull some bindweed out of the fence. Her parents had managed to find a flat to rent; nice enough, but hardly their old house. It had two bedrooms, was part of an old Victorian schoolhouse, and had its own small patch of garden. Daisy was thankful for that; her mother loved to garden, and she had planted roses and clematis around the trellis fence.

She hoped it would keep them distracted.

Her arrival had been enough for two weeks' worth of conversation. She had lied merrily to them about prospective boyfriends and chatted about her course, her friends; anything to make them feel that her time in Oxford had been nothing but bliss. Her degree had been a good one — she'd got a First. Daisy might have told her mother about Brad, or even Edward, under other circumstances. But her parents needed to hear nothing but good news, so that was what they got. Daisy didn't comment on the silver-grey streaked through her father's hair, or the fact that her mother had lost fifteen pounds and now looked gaunt.

She also didn't tell them about her agent, and her possible book.

'Daisy!' Her father was calling from the kitchen, with a cup of tea in one hand. 'Phone for you. Some chap named Elliott.'

'Daisy!' her mother huffed, because Daisy had trodden on one of her newly planted petunias as she raced for the kitchen. Mrs Markham smiled, watching her daughter go. A reaction like that, it had to be young

258

love. She hoped to heaven the boy was a man of means.

'Thanks, Dad.' Daisy grabbed the receiver, palms sweaty.

'Daisy?' It was Gemma. 'Can you hold?'

'Sure,' she said, breathlessly. They piped the Four Seasons down the line till she thought she was going to scream.

'Hi, Daisy,' said Ted Elliott finally. 'How are you?'

'OK,' she said. Who the hell cared how she was?

'I've sold your book,' he said casually. 'In fact, I've also sold the next one.'

'But I haven't written the next one,' Daisy said, feeling stupid.

'How much did you think these books were going to go for?'

She paused. The important thing was that she was going to be published. New writers got very little, Daisy knew that much. But it would still beat six months of waitressing.

'About two thousand pounds?' Daisy suggested tremulously.

'Ha! I think you'd better sit down,' he said, a touch smugly.

'Ted, just tell me, please!' shouted Daisy, losing it completely. Her father was giving her a concerned stare across the kitchen. He set his cup of tea down on the countertop.

'I've sold this book and a sequel for seventy thousand pounds,' Ted Elliott said.

# 29

The tube pulled into Leicester Square and Daisy got out, electrified with excitement. She was due to meet her publishers for the first time.

Her editor had spoken to her on the phone and said nice things, but Daisy wasn't listening; it all felt like a blur, just a huge blur. Today would make it real.

Not even six months out of college, she had traded a waitress's apron for being a writer. A real writer, with a proper contract.

Daisy felt slightly scared they would think they had made a mistake. She was nobody, really, not Jackie Collins, nor Jeffrey Archer, nor Jilly Cooper. She was going to be a real author, published by the same firm that put out Richard Weston.

She glanced at her watch. It was still only ten. She had fifteen minutes before she was due at her meeting but she hadn't wanted to be late.

'Nothing to be worried about,' Ted Elliott told Daisy. 'They love your writing. Fenella said it had sparkle she hasn't seen for years.'

Fenella Granger, a publishing titan, apparently. Her new editor.

'And they'll all be very glad to meet someone as young and as glamorous as you.'

Daisy burst out laughing.

Her agent crooked an eyebrow. 'What on earth is so funny?'

'Glamorous! Me? Have you taken a good look at me, Ted?'

He steepled his fingers and regarded her. 'I think perhaps the question is have you taken a good look at yourself?' Ted pointed to the gold-framed mirror hanging behind her. 'Check yourself out. Isn't that what the young people say?'

Daisy looked. The girl standing in front of her was beautiful. She hadn't been paying attention to her transformation. She was slim; her clothes were actually hanging off her. Was it possible? Could she have dropped to a size ten? She'd always loved her eyes, but now you could actually see them, as they weren't hidden behind folds of fat. She had real cheekbones — high, aristocratic cheekbones that seemed to go on for ever — and her hair, because she hadn't bothered with it, was tumbling down around her shoulders in a rich, dark and glossy mane. She had full lips that were . . . well, pretty sexy. Her jeans and T-shirt didn't exactly fit, because they were both too big, but the natural curves of her body were still impressive. She had a high, tight butt, full breasts, and she wasn't too skinny, and . . .

'You look amazed,' Ted Elliott said. 'Most girls your age can't keep away from the mirror. My nieces, for example. The only time they get out of the bathroom is to get on the phone.'

'I've never liked mirrors,' Daisy said truthfully. The mirror had been her enemy. Who wanted to be reminded of being a lump?

'Well,' Ted said, losing interest, 'it never hurts to be young and pretty when you're selling something. Perhaps you should go shopping and buy something, um, funky.'

Daisy had taken the advice to heart. She'd popped down to Harvey Nicks — how she'd always longed to say 'popped down to Harvey Nicks' — and bought herself something flattering by Ghost, a cute dress in dusty pink with a matching lace cardigan, wedges from Dior, and a little Kate Spade pink-leather handbag. The price tag almost made her faint, but Daisy told herself it was business.

She wavered between not wanting to count her chickens and a steely determination to make this work. It was so hard not to think of herself as unworthy.

But I am, Daisy told herself, I am worthy. They didn't sign me for fun. They think I can succeed.

She smiled. She was starting to value herself.

★ ★ ★

Artemis Publishing was located on Tottenham Court Road, right in the heart of book country. There were gleaming modern booksellers and mazy little specialist shops, antiquarian dealers and feminist presses up and down the length of the street, mingling with the odd record business building, like the Astoria, EMI publishing, and the instrument sellers on Denmark Street.

She wandered up towards the Royal George pub, ducking into Waterstone's on the way. The rows of pristine books on the shelves, the posters, the tables of bestsellers and new releases . . . she felt as though she was floating. Daisy picked up *Savage Outcome*, the latest Richard Weston thriller. It had big gold letters on the cover, fantastic reviews on the back — quotes from *Company* and *Elle* and the *Daily Mail*. And right there on the spine was the little 'bow' insignia of Artemis Books.

This was going to be her, Daisy thought, and suddenly she felt a wash of sheer joy rush through her. Everything was going to be all right.

★ ★ ★

Artemis Publishing was just what she had imagined. It was housed in a tinted-glass and polished-steel temple, with large potted palm trees under the skylights in the lobby, marble floors, and modern elevators with the cars

262

made out of glass. In the front of the building there were couches, with more of the trade magazines she saw in Ted's offices, phones, and rows of Artemis's latest publications displayed behind glittering glass cabinets under miniature spotlights. The Richard Weston book was in prime position.

'Like it?'

Daisy spun round to find a chic woman at her shoulder. She was beautiful and elegant and wearing something in cream and gold that looked like Chanel.

'Fenella Granger. You must be Daisy Markham.'

'That's right,' Daisy said, 'hello.'

'It's nice to meet you, finally. The entire team is looking forward to saying hi.' Fenella turned and led Daisy to the bank of lifts. 'I hope you're not scared of heights.'

Daisy had never liked heights.

'A bit,' she admitted.

'Don't look so worried.' Fenella grinned disarmingly as the doors hissed shut. 'And don't panic if you forget everyone's names. I've been working here for three years and I still don't remember them all.'

Daisy smiled gratefully at her. She had to try to remember to be businesslike, when actually she wanted to start twirling around and singing like Julie Andrews on the mountain top.

★ ★ ★

Fenella introduced her to a crowd of people. There was Jack Hall, the urbane and charming publisher; there was Sarah Lawrence, an efficient, hip-looking marketing chief; there were people from Art Direction and the Sales Force and Legal Affairs. Daisy smiled at everybody and determined that she would not feel intimidated.

After the glad-handing was over, Fenella took her into

her corner office. It was all windows, with a glorious view of Soho, the black London cabs crawling below them glinting in the summer heat; there was even a haze over the city.

'How did that go?' Daisy asked.

'Great.' Fenella nodded approvingly. 'You look gorgeous, which always helps. They see posters, they see press campaigns. You'll soon learn there's a lot more to being published than just delivering a great book.'

'There is?'

'Sure. After I've edited it, and we pick a cover, we have to start selling you. And the first place to do that is Artemis Publishing.'

Daisy was confused. 'But you've already bought the book.'

'Yes, but without support a book will go nowhere. We publish over fifty titles a month. Not all of them get the attention they deserve. Every editor is fighting inside the company for their own pet projects to get marketing money, sales force attention and so on.' Fenella's beautiful eyes were serious. 'If you publish a book and don't support it, it'll be in the remainder bins before you know where you are. And after one failure it's twice as hard to get people excited about a second book.'

'I see,' Daisy said, and she did. 'I suppose lots of people think that once you sign a deal the bestseller comes automatically.'

'Too many authors,' Fenella said. 'Unfortunately.' She smiled. 'Look, I'm not trying to scare you. We're going to make this happen. You've got the talent, and that's all that counts. Well, along with desire. It's a lot of work. Are you up for it?'

Daisy looked at the neatly stacked bestsellers and framed book covers that hung on Fenella's wall.

'I most certainly am,' she said.

# 30

'So.' Fenella shuffled her notes and looked at Daisy brightly. 'That shouldn't be too hard, now should it?'

They were sitting in the kitchen of Fenella's glorious Cotswolds manor house. There was a gleaming red Aga in the corner, bunches of dried hops and beaten copper pans hanging from the ceiling, and a collection of chipped mugs hanging from nails driven into a beam. It had lead-paned windows and warm stone floors that were cool in the summer heat. Outside, there was a large garden with lavender-lined paths and wild roses climbing riotously up a trellis. Daisy had no idea how Fenella ever got any work done.

'I suppose not,' Daisy responded gloomily. She had just finished hearing all Fenella's editing suggestions for her book, *The Lemon Grove*. There were so many of them she wondered why Artemis had bought the manuscript in the first place.

'Don't look so upset.' Fenella grinned. 'I told you, you've got huge talent and your characters sing, but the plot just needs some tweaking.'

'Tweaking!' Daisy protested. 'You want to get rid of Carl altogether and change the firm from clothes to make-up — '

'If one rival runs a store, clothes isn't different enough. And Carl just isn't likeable enough. He's not necessary. Think about it.'

With a bit of resentment, Daisy considered it. She supposed Fenella might have a point.

'It's going to mean a page-one rewrite, you know.'

'I know. That's where the work part comes in.'

265

Fenella handed her a cup of coffee, stirring in the sugar. 'This is your launch, and we only launch a writer once, so let's get it right.'

Daisy sighed. 'I hear you.'

★ ★ ★

At home, in the rented flat, her parents gave her her own room and let her lock herself away. Daisy would watch her mother in the garden from her small, neat, double-glazed frame as she planted and mowed and began to make something interesting out of the small space. Her parents were motivation enough, even if this hadn't been a dream of hers.

Daisy wanted this book so badly. She wanted to see her name in print, pick her own book up at W.H. Smith's, in the station's Menzies, maybe even see somebody reading it on a bus. She also wanted to get her parents out of this rental situation, but they wouldn't hear a word of it.

'Darling, you only have thirty thousand pounds for this book.'

'Thirty's a lot, and there's forty for the next one.'

'Yes, it's a lot of money for a twenty-two-year-old, but you'll have to make it last. Get yourself a house. Your father and I are going to be fine. He has that new job at the bank.'

'And he gives all his extra money to bloody Lloyd's,' Daisy said resentfully. Her father was far too honest, too damn noble for his own good.

'It's a debt, darling,' said her mother proudly.

Daisy was filled with a mixture of rage and pride whenever she thought about it. She would have expected her father to insist on doing the right thing. But she could not bear to see him do it.

She felt responsible, and the thought was strangely

exhilarating. Daisy knew that opportunity was knocking for her right now.

She was not about to let the moment slip.

★　★　★

She worked furiously. At first there were problems. Daisy turned in some chapters and got worried phone calls from Fenella.

'This isn't working, Daisy. It doesn't have any of the zest I found when I first bought the book.'

Daisy felt fear close a clammy hand around her heart. She couldn't lose this, she just couldn't. What if they said the book was unacceptable and refused to pay her, to publish it? Would she have to go back to waitressing? She felt nausea rise in her throat.

'Let me give you a bit of advice,' Fenella said. 'You're overthinking it. Go out to the bookshop, buy tons of the sort of books you like to read, and curl up with them for a week.'

'A week,' Daisy said horrified. 'I write three thousand words a day, that's going to put me six chapters behind — '

'You need to remind yourself what it is *you* like. Honestly. Trust me on this one.'

Obediently, and still feeling scared, Daisy went into town and found a Books Etc. Now, the gleaming gold-spined rows of blockbusters didn't seem so exciting, they seemed intimidating, mocking.

Resolutely, Daisy marched up to 'Popular Fiction' and pulled out her favourites. If she was going to learn, it might as well be from the masters. *Kane and Abel*. Best trashy novel ever written. *Riders*. Close second. *Lace*. Close third. She piled up her arms with fantastically plotted classics. Judith Krantz's *Scruples*. Sally Beauman's *Destiny*. Penny Vincenzi's *Old Sins*. Hmm, she was actually starting to enjoy herself. Ken

Follett! Pile it on . . . and finally, of course, her personal hero: Richard Weston. Daisy bought *Savage Outcome* with delicious anticipation.

She tumbled her purchases on to the counter in front of a jaded shop assistant, who paused from cracking her gum long enough to blink.

'Bored, are ya?' she demanded. 'Or are ya flying to Australia or something?'

'Or something,' Daisy said sweetly.

There were plenty of places that offered creative writing courses; even universities. But Fenella was right, she could do no better than immerse herself in the kind of stuff she wanted to write. If you read the complete works of one writer, you usually started pastiching them. Especially with people like Jilly Cooper — one had to be careful of that. But Daisy thought this way was safe, just to read the best of the best and let it all sink in. She loved to be whisked away into the hearts of dark rivalries, strong men and gorgeous, cunning women, to read about the LA sun and the Siberian ice and World War Two and Argentinian polo matches . . .

She spent the next two weeks on the living-room couch, reading through one pop fiction legend after another. Her mother kept her supplied with hot tea and packets of Hob-Nobs. When Daisy was finished, she'd put on eight pounds. Ugh. But she was also prepared.

She could hardly wait to start writing again. Whenever she booted up the computer, Daisy got a buzz. And now her fingers were flying across the keyboard.

She faxed the new pages to Fenella and held her breath.

'This is great, Daisy. This is exactly right. Keep it coming.'

Daisy did. She also pulled on a pair of old shorts and started jogging in the mornings. She had no intention of sliding back to the way she had been before. Maybe Edward wasn't in her life, but that wasn't the point.

Daisy had no interest in men right now, not even Edward Powers. She didn't have time to brood and mourn over him. Her career was all that counted. If she wanted romance, she worked it out in the pages of her novel. She didn't care about looking good for men. She cared about looking good for herself.

It was a fun summer.

Everything was coming together. Daisy felt the sense of achievement every day, when she finished her run, when she finally ran the last word-count of the evening. Maybe it wouldn't work, after all, but she knew that she was giving it everything that she had. It might not have been blood, sweat and tears, but it was bloody hard work, and it was the best she could do.

★   ★   ★

'So this is the cover. Or covers,' Tony Morris told her. Tony was the Artemis Art Director, and he was known for being one of the best in London.

'Ahm, very striking,' Daisy said uncertainly.

*The Lemon Grove* had been packaged up like a boiled sweet in two flavours. The book was laid out before her in two covers: neon lime-green and neon hot-pink, both with the title in block silver letters. Daisy loved the silver letters; that was proper blockbuster stuff. But neon green?

'It's meant to be striking.' Tony smirked. 'I know what you're thinking, love, but watch this.' He picked up the two books and balanced them against the bookshelf on the far wall. 'Now take a step back.' He pulled Daisy over to stand by the window. 'See?'

She did. Even with the other books' brightly coloured covers, there was no mistaking *Lemon Grove*. It screamed back at her as though it had been on fire. The two different acid colours were even more obvious when they were contrasted next to each other.

'Ah,' Daisy said, thrilled. 'I'd pick them up.'

'And that's half the sale,' Tony informed her.

# 31

It took Daisy six months of rewrites, and when finally, exhausted, she handed the book in, Fenella told her it wouldn't be published until next year.

'But why?' Daisy asked, disappointed.

Fenella smiled gently at Daisy's gutted face. 'Look, it takes about nine months for copy-editing, type-setting, promotion, proof copies, marketing . . . about the same time as a baby. We'll start planning and writing book two. And publication will be here before you know it.'

★ ★ ★

*The Lemon Grove* was published in July, just in time for the August holiday season. Fenella told Daisy she had written an instant classic; 'the ultimate beach read'.

'Wow, I just hope you're right.'

'I'm always right,' Fenella said with supreme confidence.

And she was. Artemis was excited about the book, and the marketing push got it out there. Tony's neon covers screamed at browsers in chains across the country; there were dump-bins, point-of-sale material, posters, and even ads on buses.

'That won't work by itself,' Fenella warned Daisy when she rang up, thrilled, because she'd seen a bus with her book cover plastered across it. 'It only means the book has a chance. People will see it. After that, the work has to stand by itself. Which it will.'

It didn't take long for the company to know they had a success on their hands. Daisy got her first phone call from Fenella within a month.

'Daisy? It's Fenella.'

'Hi,' said Daisy, desperately trying to appear casual. Her fingers were white-knuckled, gripping the receiver. She was a first novelist. If it didn't go well for her now, her new career, her new life would be stillborn.

'I have good news.'

'OK,' Daisy said, but there were tears in her eyes. She exhaled raggedly.

'You're a hit. Our first printing has completely sold out. We're reprinting right now.'

'That's wonderful,' Daisy said, gleefully.

When she hung up, she danced around the room.

★ ★ ★

A week later, it was Publicity who were calling.

'People are surprised. This kind of novel is supposed to be dead. It's all murder mysteries and financial thrillers out there right now,' Helen Moxie told her. Moxie was the head of the Artemis publicity department, and she was on the phone telling Daisy her publicity schedule. 'They find it strange you're having such success with a romance. So, you have the itinerary?'

'Yes,' Daisy said, feeling a bit fraudulent.

'There'll be a first-class ticket to London waiting for you, and I'll be there half an hour before your first interview, just to make sure things go smoothly, OK? Don't worry, you'll be great.'

'I suppose I don't see what the point is,' Daisy said tremulously. 'I mean, it's a fictional story, what's interesting about talking to the writer?'

'Just think of it as free advertising. See you Thursday.'

On Wednesday afternoon her father drove her to the station. 'We're so proud of you, darling. Doing all the interviews, it's marvellous. You're a big star.'

'I'm not, Dad, shut up,' Daisy said, but the truth was she was excited.

272

'Have fun. See you soon.' Her father kissed her and handed her her little suitcase.

Daisy walked into the station and picked up her first-class train ticket. She didn't think she'd ever travelled first class in her life. The carriage was mostly empty and had slightly wider seats, which were a different colour, and had little tissue things on the top.

Big fat hairy wow, Daisy thought, but she still revelled in it. Why not? Artemis was footing the bill.

When the drinks trolley trundled past Daisy ordered a gin and tonic. To hell with it. This was a celebration.

★   ★   ★

Her hotel was the Halkin, very upscale, with a Japanese décor mingling with funky Jackson Pollock-esque abstract paintings. Not Daisy's cup of tea but, just like the train, that really wasn't the point. The point was her publishers thought she was worth spending the money on.

Fenella had taught her a lot more than good storytelling. She had educated Daisy on the realities of publishing and Daisy knew now that every penny they spent on promotion and publicity showed their commitment to her.

She was being groomed to be the next big thing, and she loved it.

Helen Moxie arrived bang on time the next morning, but Daisy was already waiting for her in the lobby. If her publishers were going to be this helpful, she at least wanted to show willing. It couldn't hurt to be professional.

'Mm, very nice.' Helen took in her outfit: boot-cut black Joseph trousers and a cute little silky top, teamed with Daisy's long, loose hair and a pair of dangling Moroccan silver earrings. 'I wish it was TV and not radio. You look cute. Are you ready?'

273

'Ready as I'll ever be,' Daisy said.

She spent the morning having desultory interviews with bored reporters from the tabloids and the *Evening Standard* who kept asking her about her sex life.

'Your men really like that, Daisy?'

'Into bed-hopping, are ya?'

'Jason's a bit of a strong man, ain't he? You into bondage, then?'

Daisy tried not to get flustered, but she couldn't help it. 'I'm sorry, I don't discuss my private life' didn't seem to cut it.

'Try to be quotable,' hissed Helen. 'Say, 'I read it in *Cosmo*, that's my story and I'm sticking to it.' '

'Right,' Daisy said, trying not to get upset.

After lunch a taxi took her to That Radio Place. They signed in in the lobby, got little laminated badges that said 'Visitor', and then Helen led Daisy up in the elevator to an anonymous warren of corridors that looked and smelled like school. She had the surreal experience of being 'interviewed' down-the-line; Daisy sat in a booth with headphones over her ears and a mike in front of her and nobody else there, while they piped a show from Radio Scotland or Radio Tyneside into her ears and she had to interact with some phantom DJ. She didn't think it was too bad, apart from the watery coffee in the plastic cups, and she had just about recovered from the morning's nastiness when she was taken to Max Radio 96.3 in Camden.

'This is the biggest thing we've been able to get you,' Helen said. 'It's Mutt and Jeff. It's really important. They go out almost nationally, you can get this station in Oxford.'

'I know, I used to listen,' Daisy said, feeling slightly worried.

Mutt and Jeff were 'shock jocks'. The UK's answer to Howard Stern, they had a huge audience, they were always getting bleeped, and they were funny but mercilessly cruel to a lot of their guests.

'I think you can take them on. Just flirt with Jeff. Mutt's gay, so that won't help you any.' Helen took in Daisy's anxious look. 'It's the audience, Daisy. They're such huge publicity. You couldn't pay for it. Just plug the book every chance you get.'

'No problem,' Daisy said, though she thought it might be.

★ ★ ★

'Well fuck me,' Jeff said.

Daisy, with the headphones on, was stuck in the Mutt and Jeff booth. It was decorated with posters of girls with their tits out, presumably not Mutt's choice.

The two radio superstars were small men who had spots and looked mean as hungry ferrets.

'No thanks, mate, not my type,' Mutt giggled in that famous high-pitched squeak.

'She's gorgeous, isn't she? A right bit of totty. Want to pose for the Jeff cam, sugar? I wouldn't mind looking at those jugs all day.'

Daisy wondered if she should get up and walk out, just cut her losses.

'No thanks, Jeff . . . '

'But sex is your thing, ain't it?' Daisy saw with horror that he had *Lemon Grove* open in front of him. He flipped to a pre-marked page and started to read out loud one of her hottest sex scenes. 'Bugger me! Went to Oxford, didn't you?'

'Not the University.'

'Is that what they teach you there? Sex Ed?' He was ignoring her.

'No, for that I tuned into the Mutt and Jeff show,' Daisy said.

He hadn't expected that. 'Faithful listener, were you?'

'Sure. Nobody does puerile sarcasm like you two.

275

Students love that kind of thing.'

'And nobody does sex like Daisy Markham?' needled Jeff.

Well,' said Daisy, 'if everybody buys *The Lemon Grove* they can find that out for themselves.'

'But your book is full of sex. You *gotta* be a sex maniac. I bet you're great in bed. Why do you think you got on this show?'

'Most trashy novels have sex in them,' Daisy said firmly, 'because people do have sex. Not people that look like you two, obviously. But other people.' She leaned closer to her mike. 'I wish you guys out there could see what a couple of skinny pizza-faced bastards these two are. Reading from my book is probably the best sex Jeff's had all year.'

Behind the glass partition she could see Helen Moxie gaping at her in utter horror. Daisy looked defiantly at the DJs, but they didn't seem to mind.

'Ooh,' said Mutt, delighted. 'It's got teeth.'

'Make a lot of money, do ya?' Jeff said. His tone was fractionally less mean now.

'Why don't you find another hot passage and read it out on the air? Then I'll make even more,' Daisy said, grinning.

When the bit went off air for commercials, skinny Jeff reached out and shook her hand.

'Well done,' he said, 'great radio.'

★ ★ ★

The papers were full of it the next morning. Daisy had been just about the only girl ever to take Mutt and Jeff on. The following week, sales of *The Lemon Grove*, which they plugged for three days, doubled.

'Daisy, my love,' said Fenella when she called her with the latest figures, 'I think a star has been born.'

276

# 32

So here she was again.

It was eight-twenty on Monday morning. There was a crisp chill in the air, and New York was bustling with the Fall's back-to-work energy. Business men and women scurried past her in their dark suits, clutching paper cups, with the Greek key design on them, full of steaming coffee; a little warmth and caffeine to kick the day off right. Lots of Brooks Brothers navy and black out today, Rose thought. Ambition in the air.

And plenty of it here, at Rothstein Realty.

She had been sixteen when she came here last, scamming her way in to see William Rothstein. Six years later she had turned twenty-two. But she remembered everything about that day. Was William still in PR, still at extension 1156?

The office buildings had not changed one bit. The sleek granite casing of the midtown skyscraper still glittered in the thin sunlight. Rose took a deep breath and walked into the lobby.

Yes, it was as she remembered. Marble streaked with the palest pink. Receptionists in pearls, oriental rugs. They'd changed the art, but it was the same sort of stuff. Stuff that screamed dollars.

A group of kids her own age were clustered around reception. There were about twelve of them; only one was a girl, a keen-looking chick in a nondescript fawn dress and cardigan. Rose was wearing a Donna Karan navy suit, cut beautifully, with a skirt that sat just above the knee. She had teamed it with a pair of CK pumps, plain gold studs in her ears, neutral make-up, and a leather-strapped watch.

It had been a rookie error to let Jake see her in

Chanel. No need to draw attention to the money she had. Rose didn't want anybody at this place noticing her until she'd got what she wanted.

She walked over to join the others.

'Hi.' Rose smiled at them briskly. 'I'm Rose Fiorello.'

'Bob Flet,' said a short, blond kid. He looked at her disapprovingly. 'You're the last one here.'

'I make it eight-twenty-five,' Rose said.

His disapproval didn't waver. 'Cutting it fine, huh? You better register.'

Rose moved through them and gave her name to the receptionist.

'Just in time, Rose.' No 'Ms Fiorello', Rose noticed. 'You'll be joining the other interns for orientation before proceeding to report to Mrs Thompson in Mr White's office.'

'Thank you,' Rose said dryly.

'I can't believe they hired another broad,' one of the young men said. The crowd laughed, except for the mousy girl, who pretended not to hear them. 'I guess it's quota time, huh?'

'Or maybe I'm better qualified than you?' Rose suggested.

He rolled his eyes. 'I'm summa at Harvard, sweetheart. I don't think so. You're just window-dressing. Real estate, it's like Wall Street. Not a game for chicks.'

'Did you hear Rothstein bought that parcel in Hell's Kitchen?' Bob Flet said to him.

'Yeah. Nice spot, put up a tower with amenities and parking. I'm psyched to be here . . . '

The men all started talking animatedly, ignoring the two young women. Rose turned to the mousy girl.

'So what got you into real estate?' Rose asked.

The girl smiled nervously. 'Oh, I'm not here for the real estate. I'm interning in the human resources department.'

Of course you are, Rose thought. Human Resources was where companies like Rothstein stuck all their women. They let them organise the vacation roster and allocate the parking slots. At the head of Human Resources and sometimes PR they put some girl Vice-President. It looked good in the company report.

Sheer window-dressing.

The male students continued to talk loudly, ostentatiously ignoring Rose. She bit back a smile. They were tossing out technical terms, showing off to each other about how much they knew — 'cap rate', 'multiple listings', 'gross income multipliers' . . .

'Are you going to be in public relations?' the mousy girl asked Rose.

'No. Richard White's office.'

The boys stopped talking.

'You're in Richard White's office?' asked Flet.

'That's what I said.'

'He works right with Jacob Rothstein,' one of the others noted enviously.

Rose blinked. 'So what?'

'So *what*? You don't know about Jacob Rothstein? He's the hottest young executive in real estate.'

'Rookie of the year,' said Flet. The men laughed admiringly.

'Ladies and gentlemen.'

A plump man in a well-cut suit was standing in front of them. There was instant silence.

'Follow me. We will begin your work schedule with a brief orientation.'

The men fell into line. Rose and the other girl walked behind them to the lifts. As the doors hissed open, the boys jumped to get into the car with the Rothstein executive. Rose tried to push forward too, but the mousy girl held her back.

'That car's full. Let's get the next one.'

'But — '

The girl held her arm firmly as Bob Flet punched a button, and the bronze doors shut.

Furiously, Rose shook herself loose. 'What the hell are you doing? What is this, Iraq? You want to walk four paces behind them?'

The young girl paled. 'You can't talk that way in here. I was an intern here last summer, too. It's a very tradition-oriented workplace.'

'You mean it's sexist.'

'I mean that women aren't expected to be forward here. They don't like it. It's for your own good, you know,' she said, lowering her voice. 'Last year there was a girl called Sally in my department, she kept insisting she wanted to be placed in acquisitions instead, so . . . they let her go.'

'Did they indeed.' Rose sighed.

'I know where orientation is, don't worry. You'll soon get the hang of it. It helps if you make them coffee. And, you know, take care to get it just how they like it because they can be very particular,' she added confidentially.

'What's your name?' Rose asked.

'Joan.' She punched the button for the tenth floor.

'Well, Joan. If you regard yourself as inferior to men, then so will they.' Rose winked. 'Just a tip.'

Joan looked cold. 'OK, well. I tried to help you,' she said prissily.

Rose suppressed a laugh.

'This way.' The doors slid open and Joan marched ahead of her down a corridor. They entered a large, sterile room with a projector screen, a long, empty table, and a few chairs lined up in the front.

The male interns were already seated. They had left open two chairs at the very back. Rose slid into one, and almost as soon as she had sat down — Joan's body stiff with dislike beside her — a man entered the room and dimmed the lights, walking up to the projector screen, so that only his corpulent frame was lit up from the machine.

Rose gasped.

It was William Rothstein.

'Shh!' Joan hissed.

'My name is William J. Rothstein, and I am the Senior Director of Public Relations at Rothstein Realty.'

'Good morning, sir,' chorused the young men. 'Honoured, Mr Rothstein,' chirped Joan inaudibly.

Rose said nothing. She knew a little more about the business now. William must really have no talent, she thought, if they'd shoved him into PR. That was a ghetto job. Of course, he 'ran' the division, with a million women reporting to him. Like that busty secretary he'd had when she'd gone to see him.

'You're here today because you're very fortunate. Or very ruthless. Either one works.' Rothstein smiled at his own joke. 'This is one of the most prestigious firms in New York, with a portfolio valued at over a billion dollars. Our yearly turnover is routinely in the hundreds of millions.'

He clicked his fat thumb on a button, and pictures of buildings flashed up. A prestigious hotel, skyscrapers, a row of luxury Brooklyn brownstones.

'You'll be assisting the executives who do deals like this. It is an incredible opportunity to learn, fought for by hundreds of applicants. You won.' Rothstein's eyes narrowed. 'You will be expected to be punctual and to do whatever you are asked to do. You will address your bosses as 'sir', unless told otherwise. Files on your performance will be kept in Human Resources and will determine your future employment here.'

Joan shot Rose a nasty look.

'This is an expansion period for Rothstein. Many of our new deals have proven to be extremely lucrative.'

He clicked up a few more pictures, then stopped on one gleaming skyscraper.

'This deal was one of our most successful in the last five years. After sales were completed, it netted the company twelve million in after-tax profits.'

Rose stared. She recognised the image flickering on the screen. It was her father's old building. In the space where Paul's Famous Deli had been was a nice, corporate little Starbucks.

'Well.' William Rothstein clicked the projector off and turned up the lights. 'Remember that only two of you will wind up hired. Now get to work.'

Rose stood up with the rest, lowering her eyes, just in case he recognised her.

*Get to work, huh? My goddam pleasure.*

★   ★   ★

'Mr White, Rose Fiorello is here.'

The secretary hovered in the doorway of her boss's office. She was nothing like Joan; petite, large-breasted, wearing a skirt that was about an inch too short, platinum-bleached hair, and three coats of mascara. Her name was Mary-Beth and she was from Texas. She regarded Rose as though she were a rattlesnake.

'Oh, yeah. Show her in,' Richard White responded without enthusiasm.

Mary-Beth turned to Rose. 'You can go in,' she said, unnecessarily.

Rose walked through the door and gasped.

White's office was nothing short of spectacular. It had huge floor-to-ceiling walls with breath-taking views of midtown. She could see St Patrick's cathedral on one side, people sitting on the steps eating their packed lunches like little ants, and the Rockefeller Center on the other, the ice-rink glittering in the pale autumn sun like a huge diamond, surrounded by flags. On the two walls that were not made of glass hung huge canvases, modern art; Rose hated abstract art, but it certainly reeked of money. The floor of the office was buttery, soft beige carpeting with a twenty-thousand-dollar Turkish carpet thrown over it, and the desk was carved of mahogany, with a state-of-the-art computer and a phone system that looked like it belonged on the Starship *Enterprise*. Rose recognised the chairs in front of the desk and behind it as being Eames, ergonomic, top-of-the-line.

Sitting in the best chair behind the mahogany desk was Richard White. Rose made an instant assessment. He was young for an office like this; maybe thirty-eight. He had a soft face and manicured hands, a little effeminate, a little cruel. The hazel eyes were set above a smallish nose, a weak jaw and fleshy red lips, a bit rubbery. His well-cut suit hid a body that was not fat, just weak, Rose decided.

She fought back a shudder of revulsion. Gross.

'Come here,' White said. He crooked a polished fingernail, beckoning her over, like a pasha with a slave.

Oh well, he wasn't gay, then, Rose thought. Pity. She fixed a brisk, impersonal smile on her face and walked obediently up to his desk.

'Good morning, Mr White.'

'Good morning, sir,' he corrected her.

Rose swallowed hard, clenching a fist. 'Good morning, sir.'

'You're very lucky to get this assignment, Rosa,' White said.

'It's Rose, sir.'

'It's whatever I say it is — *Rosa*. Why didn't they assign you to Human Resources?'

'I'm interested in real estate.'

White rolled his eyes. 'This is a very serious business. My area of expertise is sales. What do you think sales involves?'

'Selling,' Rose snapped, before she could stop herself.

White's piggish eyes were undressing her. They

travelled with approval over her figure before resting squarely on her tits.

'Ah . . . hah . . . I see why Jake decided to put you with me,' he sniggered. 'What a clown that boy is! Great sense of humour. Sometimes women can be useful in sales . . . conferences, meeting clients . . .'

The phone on his desk buzzed. White pressed the button.

'Is this important?' he hissed.

Suddenly Rose felt a bit sorry for Mary-Beth. This guy must be a nightmare to work for. She knew a bully when she saw one. And yet, Mary-Beth was still guarding her turf. Why did women do this?

She froze.

White was resting one small palm casually on her butt.

Rose twitched away immediately.

White cupped the receiver. 'It's important to play nice,' he said smoothly. 'You want to get ahead, don't you?'

'Yes, sir,' Mary-Beth said nervously. 'Mr Jacob Rothstein is here to see you.'

'Oh well.' White's tone instantly changed from bully to sycophant. 'Show him in at once.'

The door swung open and Jake walked in. White straightened and smiled widely, ignoring Rose, rushing over to him and pumping his hand.

'Good to see you, Jacob, excellent to see you. How are you? Get my memo on the Walker Building leasing? Sixty-five per cent already.'

He was like a dog fawning over its master, Rose thought, but without any of the real affection.

It was freakish. This was Jake, whom she had competed against at college as an equal, Jake, to whom she was so rude, whom she was always challenging. Even though she could destroy this place, it had hurt her to have to pretend to ask him for a favour . . .

And now look. He was treated as a god, or as a prince at the very least. She half expected to watch this miserable little shit in the super-fancy office bow from the waist when Jake walked in.

White preened and scraped, and Jake glanced up over his head at Rose and winked at her.

No, Rose told herself.

A wash of heat licked mercilessly at her lower belly.

Stop that. It's not sexy to watch everyone fawn over him. You shouldn't respond to power like that. This man is your enemy.

'You shouldn't take the trouble to come down here, Jacob. I'll always come up to you, just say the word,' White was gushing.

Jake extricated his hand.

'I see you have an intern with you, Richard.'

'What? Oh, yes.' White's plump face snapped round to Rose, annoyed. 'Get out. Can't you see Mr Rothstein is here? We're going to talk business.'

Rose blushed furiously.

'That's OK. I actually came to see how she was settling in. Rose Fiorello is my special pick for the intern programme. I selected her myself.'

'Fine, thank you,' Rose said.

White stared at her.

She was forced to add, 'sir'.

'Ahhh,' White said, in the tone of a man who sees how it is. Rothstein wanted the chick for himself. He had to back off. 'Rose will be fine, we're happy to have her in the department, Jacob.'

'Good. Show her the ropes, would you, Richard? I want her to get a decent grounding in what we do here. Leasing, sales, all that sort of stuff.' Jacob looked over at Rose. Ah, she was so delicious, in that cute business suit. And she obviously loathed calling him sir. He didn't think he'd ever enjoyed his authority more.

'Um, of course, Jacob. A thorough basis.' White was

aggravated. 'Of course, you're OK with her doing the normal intern stuff? Filing, that sort of thing?'

'Absolutely. She's here on the same basis as the other candidates,' Jake said gravely.

'Fine.' White turned to Rose. 'Go make us a couple of coffees. Black, no sugar. Mary-Beth will show you the kitchen.'

★ ★ ★

Breathe deeply, Rose told herself.

'There you go, sir,' she said sweetly, passing Richard White his coffee.

He was sitting on one of the chairs in front of the desk, chatting with Jake. 'And there you go, sir.'

'Thanks, Rose.' Jake took the coffee, enjoying her bent over him, those splendid breasts near his face, the spectacular wolf-eyes downcast, probably, he thought, so he couldn't see the desire to rip his throat out which was, doubtless, there. Of course, he was only teasing her a little bit. He'd made it clear to White while she was in the kitchen that she was not to be touched. Jake was actually looking forward to seeing what Rose could do.

He wanted to try something radical with this company. He was going to need radical thinkers, to sweep out the dead wood. He thought maybe she could be a part of that.

Jake knew she had great instincts. A little training might be all it took. But he didn't see why he shouldn't tease her a little first.

He wanted Rose Fiorello to ache for him. When she finally came to his bed, she was going to beg him for it.

'Great coffee,' he said, sipping it.

Rose's skin was scarlet.

'Rose, Mary-Beth, my assistant, will show you around,' White said. 'You'll be required to assist with some filing and photocopying.'

'Yes, sir,' Rose said, meekly.

She withdrew from the room, gently closing the door behind her.

' . . . So I got a four-year commitment from Ellison Broadcasting. Inked yesterday — '

'Yeah, I heard.' I know everything that goes on in this company, Jake thought. 'And that's great. Good work, Richard. But I don't want you riding Rose too hard, OK? Don't waste her time with menial work. The odd bit of filing, whatever, but I want her taught. Any problems, call me and I'll handle it.'

'No menial work?' White blinked. He blustered, 'You want me to really let her in on our deals? What is she, something special?'

'Actually, yes.' Jake's eyes narrowed. 'She's a friend of mine. Now you can handle that, can't you, Richard? Or maybe you'd rather not do me this favour, and I'll have her work for me direct?'

'No! No, of course not. That's not it,' White gabbled. 'Delighted to help, Jacob, of course, always ready to be of service . . . '

'Good man,' Jake said. 'Later.'

He walked out. The secretary was standing with Rose, lecturing her on the filing cabinet. The two girls straightened up as he passed them, the secretary falling into a reverential silence.

'See you later, Rose,' Jake said casually.

'Sure, Mr Rothstein,' Rose muttered.

Mary-Beth poked her in the ribs. '*Sir*,' she hissed.

'That's OK,' Jake said magnanimously. 'She can call me Mr Rothstein.'

He walked off down the corridors, chuckling quietly to himself. He didn't see Rose's pale eyes boring furiously into his back.

# 33

It was freezing.

New York was big on everything, and it was especially big on cold. Winter had Manhattan in its grip. There was a fresh sprinkling of snow atop the large grey piles of slush, and black ice and frost glittered over the roads; municipal salting trucks could barely make a dent in it. Chill winds howled down the hard glass canyons of Tribeca, and a late dawn was breaking, weak and miserable, in the east.

Rose Fiorello didn't give a damn.

She tugged on her clothes with a sense of rising excitement. Today she selected another smart, modest outfit; a neatly cut suit that tapered to the knee in charcoal grey with a cream silk shirt, a string of cultured pale grey pearls, and a spritz of Chanel perfume. Classic, classic, classic. She teamed it with Wolford hose and a neat pair of mock-croc pumps. Of course, it was far too cold to go out like this, but Rose had a warm woollen coat that swirled down to the ground, silk-lined and very comfortable, and a thick cashmere scarf and gloves. Most New Yorkers didn't move out of their front doors without a balaclava and ear muffs, but she didn't see why she had to sacrifice style completely, just to be warm: she selected a 1920s flapper-style cloche hat in a matching charcoal felt, and tugged it on. A Hermes handbag was a tiny extravagance; just a little too rich for an intern, but she was confident Richard White would never notice.

'Dick' White, as she thought of him.

He was too egotistical to notice what other people did. Especially women, of course. Mary-Beth flirted with him every day as she slavishly made his coffee; he

288

watched her boobs as she leaned over his desk, obligingly putting them on full display. Rose was sure that Dick was fucking Mary-Beth in a broom cupboard somewhere. Screwing a secretary was a perk of the job for most Rothstein executives, as far as she could see. But Rose was off-limits to White, and therefore useless.

He was useful to her, though, and that was what counted.

Going into Rothstein Realty was a blast. Rose woke up before her alarm every day, she was so excited. Getting dressed, she felt like James Bond suiting up, going down to Q to get his equipment. Because she was a spy in the house of her enemy.

She was like a sponge, soaking it up. Rose had spent the last month photocopying and filing — and making extra copies for herself. Every day the picture got a little clearer for her. At first it was simply how Rothstein worked, how the principles she applied in her tiny mom-and-pop properties translated to corporate tenants, net leases, and millions of dollars. A market valuation approach gave way to more esoteric numbers, to cap rates and replacement costs.

She wished she were in acquisitions. But leasing was good too. Those were the two departments Rothstein was built on: buying skyscrapers, and renting them out.

Rose relished every scrap of knowledge.

Real estate was thrilling. Behind the cold numbers, the filed reports on each transaction, she perceived the adventure; the heart-stopping moments when financing notes were called, unions paid off; and the cold sweat of the billion-dollar landlord as each day a floor of some costly tower stood vacant.

You had to buy right. With these prices, you couldn't afford mistakes. You had to build right. Every 'i' had to be dotted, every 't' crossed; make a zoning error, fail to get a permit, and you were sunk. In reality, this meant bribes. Oh no, wait, she thought, grinning to herself, 'campaign contributions'. Rothstein donated to every-body. Democrats, Republicans, cops, you name it. The price of doing business. And, lastly, you had to lease right.

Manhattan businesses wanted everything for their money. And you had to give it to them, before one of your competitors did.

She was learning leasing. Learning about Rothstein's big clients, the ones they had trouble with, the building spaces that didn't sell. Rose wondered now how to get into Acquisitions. She wanted to get her hands on some of that fiscal data.

She had a nose for these things. The large numbers didn't scare her, they thrilled her. Sometimes gleaning information was more than reading reports; sometimes it was listening to the way executives talked.

And Dick White sounded scared.

Rose tugged her gloves on a little tighter, took one last sip of her steaming cinnamon coffee, and walked out of her door into the early-morning chill, thoroughly looking forward to Monday morning.

★ ★ ★

Ella Brown fixed her wrap-around tie shirt a fraction tighter around her boobs and did that annoying eyelash-batting thing.

Jake almost admired her persistence. She had been after him since the day she was assigned to him. Yeah, it was so like Dad. Send up a personal assistant with the emphasis on personal; huge fake tits, dark hair — his father had noted his penchant for brunettes — long legs, the whole bit, and a crawling, slavish mentality.

Except he'd never liked slavish women. It put him off. Without a challenge, it was just no fun. Sure, he might have thrown her a shot under other circum-stances, but this was work. Women were plentiful; good secretaries less so. And he didn't particularly relish having to fire a woman. She might, he reflected with distaste, cry or something.

He'd canned a bunch of Rothstein executives, but they were all men. Some people had slid over the years; friends of the family, dead weight making loser deals and costing the company money. It was all going to be his one day, and Jake didn't want hangers-on shaving a few million here and there off his bottom line.

His father never objected to Jake canning someone. In fact, he seemed to approve. Ruthlessness was a trait they shared.

So every morning Jake ignored Ella's hopeful routine. Today, however, it was bugging him.

Goddam *leasing*. He wanted to buy, build, let others take care of the details.

It burned him to be stuck down here.

'Got something in your eye, Ella?'

'No, Mr Rothstein.' He didn't go for that 'sir' shit from his assistants. People kissed his ass quite enough; it was boring.

Ella looked crestfallen and Jake felt faintly ashamed of himself. She was just a dumb hick, no need to snap at her.

'OK. Fetch me the Fulton file and a cup of coffee, please.'

'Certainly,' Ella said with a full-wattage smile.

Next time, Jake thought, he was going to insist on an older woman, a married woman, with a moustache and German efficiency.

Oh well. He'd stay here a month, a sop to his father. But after that, he was going back to Acquisitions. Or he was quitting.

There were some advantages to this floor. He could keep an eye on what White was doing; Jake had never really trusted him.

And, of course, he could keep an eye on Rose Fiorello.

★  ★  ★

Rose stood in the file room. Mary-Beth hated this place, but it was one of Rose's favourite spots in Rothstein. A photocopier, no security, and rows and rows of data . . .

She reached up on her toes, on the stepladder, and slid out the 'F's. Follon, Fong, Foxley . . . Fulton was in here somewhere . . .

'Hey.'

The voice was a shock. Rose jumped out of her skin and lost her balance. She grabbed at the shelves, missed, and felt herself teeter backwards into space . . .

'I got you.'

Rose shrieked, but she was OK. A pair of very strong arms were holding her weight like it was nothing.

'Jacob.' Angry, she spat the word out. Her skin had prickled with adrenaline, and there was a fine sheen of perspiration all over it. She felt tendrils of hair sticking to her forehead. 'Goddammit. You scared me. Let me go.'

'You could at least ask nicely,' he said, mildly. He spun her around lightly so she was facing him. Man, was she ever beautiful. Those wolf-eyes stared up at him fiercely, but she was so slight, so female. He enjoyed the feel of the soft breasts brushing against his sleeves, of her futile struggles against his grip. Jake held her a second longer than he should have, just to make the point. Then he let her go. He never let women dictate to him.

'Maybe I should call you 'sir'?'

'Maybe you should.'

Rose tried not to drop her eyes. His stare was so unflinching, so dominant. She didn't want to be attracted to him. And she didn't want to lose.

'For someone who owes me a favour,' he said lightly, 'you sure are angry.'

Then he reached out and traced the angry line of her mouth with his fingertip.

Desire rushed through her groin like an electric shock. Rose pulled back.

'I don't want you to touch me,' she hissed.

'Liar,' Jake said.

He grabbed her by the waist, pulled her to him, and kissed her.

His mouth was on hers, his strong lips crushing her soft, full ones, his teeth raking over them, like he wanted to devour her. Waves of desire for Jake pulsed through her; Rose felt her hands come up, but they didn't push him away; they curled gently against his collar. Traitors. She felt as though time had slowed down, and she was seeing everything through a blood-red mist. Her heart was thudding, crashing against her chest, her palms were sweating.

Oh, fuck. She wanted him so much she ached.

Rose's brain tried to rein her in. It was that small part that let you know you were drunk when you were drunk, not that her control had ever slipped far enough to get drunk. Right now, it was a small voice telling her to get out of Jake's arms.

But she wasn't listening. Her body was lifting to him, almost helplessly, pressing against him, so she knew he could feel the hot blood pooled in her belly, hear her heart racing . . .

Jake took a step back. Almost a step. He was struggling with himself. He wanted to rip her clothes off right there in the file room, but that was no good.

Control yourself, Rothstein thought.

She excited him. Her responses were profound, her mouth was soft and yielding, her pulse was light, fast . . . she was so soft, so slight . . . he wanted to push her down on the floor and take her. But this was work. A public area. For a wild second, Jake considered dragging Rose upstairs to his office, locking the door, and thrusting her over his desk . . .

But no. No. He breathed in, hard, forcing his blood to slow. Not for Rose Fiorello. She was a prize, a quarry, he thought. She was different from the other women. He wanted to take her home to the penthouse, and spend a long time on her total and abject conquest. An entire weekend, making love to her hard, slowly, a hundred different ways, until she lay nestled in his arms, utterly spent and ready to beg him to see her again.

Jake snapped out of that pleasant fantasy and looked at Rose. She was panting, gulping little breaths, fighting to snap out of it. He saw her pupils were slightly dilated, her plump lips parted just a touch.

'You know how long I've been waiting to do that?' he asked.

'I've got some idea,' Rose said. Then, enchantingly, she blushed. He couldn't remember when he'd last seen a woman blush.

'I want to take you out to dinner,' Jake said.

'I'm busy,' Rose said instantly.

He chuckled. 'No, you're not. Or are you about to retreat back into pretending you don't want anything to do with me? It's really not going to fly, you know.'

She hesitated. Goddammit, he was right. If she turned him down now it would look real odd.

'I meant I'm busy tonight . . . maybe later in the week.'

'Friday night.' His dark eyes drilled into her. 'Come over to my place.'

'Great,' Rose said weakly.

Jake reached out and traced the line of her jaw, which almost made her knees buckle. Then he said, 'See you then,' and turned and left her.

Rose steadied herself, leaning against the filing

cabinets. She had to get a grip. It was crazy, getting a crush on a Rothstein. This Rothstein, the crown prince, no less. She was here to crush him, not kiss him.

Never mind. I can lull him into a false sense of security, Rose told herself.

She wanted him. Badly.

Disgusted with herself, Rose strode into the women's bathroom and splashed cold water on her neck.

Her pager buzzed against her side. Rose lifted it out and looked at the number.

It was nothing she recognised. She went into Mary-Beth's office — the coast was clear, she was probably in with Richard White, leaning over his desk, giving him his schedule for the day in that fake, breathy voice. Quickly, Rose lifted Mary-Beth's phone and dialled.

'Yeah?'

'Somebody paged me.'

'Who is this?'

'This is Rose Fiorello. Who is this?' Rose asked, but she already knew. Her heart started to race again, but this time it wasn't desire.

'Don Salerni wants to see you.'

'I can be there after five-thirty — '

'He wants to see you now, chickie.'

'Right.' Rose breathed in sharply. 'Of course. I'll be right there.'

'Hurry up,' the voice said, and hung up on her.

Rose hadn't noticed Richard White's office door opening. Mary-Beth stood there, her face a picture of rage. Rose realised she was still holding the receiver in her hand.

'You aren't allowed to answer my phones!'

'It wasn't an incoming call.'

Mary-Beth's lips tightened with pleasure. 'You mean you were making an *outgoing* call on the company phone lines? Well! That's a dismissal offence for an intern. I'm gonna tell Mr White.'

Rose smiled. 'I wouldn't, if I were you.'

'You're not me.'

'Not unless you want me to go to Jacob Rothstein about it. He asked me out. We're having dinner on Friday night.'

Mary-Beth's face was a picture. Rose had to admit she enjoyed watching the emotions sweep across it. Disbelief, then envy, then fear.

'I — I — might have been a little hasty. I guess it's OK. Actually, it's fine. No hard feelings, Rose?'

'No hard feelings,' Rose replied.

Mary-Beth was still staring at her as though she'd just been told Rose had won the lottery.

'Jacob never asks any of the girls at work out,' she said. 'Oh, my. You're soooo lucky . . . '

'Actually, I think he's the lucky one,' Rose said. 'Will you tell Mr White I was taken sick with a migraine? I'll be back tomorrow.'

'Oh sure thing, Rose, sure thing,' Mary-Beth said deferentially, but she couldn't do a very good job of hiding her rage. *Jacob* the lucky one! Who the hell did this arrogant minx think she was? She glared at Rose's retreating back. It just wasn't fair! She, Mary-Beth, had been making eyes at Jacob for ages, like every other girl around here, and this un-feminine harridan had managed to snag him instead.

Mary-Beth stamped a high-heeled pump. Bitch! Jacob Rothstein must be a weirdo, that was about all there was to it.

Rose's cab deposited her in front of Salerni's brownstone fifteen minutes later. She hoped to heaven that was fast enough. Rose paid the guy, and grabbed a Kleenex out of her purse to wipe her sweating hands.

She hoped they meant her no harm.

Surely they meant her no harm.

It would be crazy of Salerni to do her this way. He

could have had her jumped at any time, if he were really mad. She had no doubt at all that George Benham would have told them whatever they wanted to know. All her personal details.

Her hand trembled on the restaurant doorknob. Maybe she should run.

No point, Rose decided. If they were going to rub her out, they could find her wherever she went. She lifted her head. She was Paul Fiorello's kid, not a coward.

She walked into the restaurant. Yep, same as before. There was Salerni, seated at his table, his goons around him, glasses of wine on the table. This time she didn't go up to the bartender. She marched straight up to him; the conversation at the table died.

'Don Salerni.' Rose gave a slight bow, feeling awkward. At least today she wasn't in a T-shirt and jeans. 'You summoned me.'

'That's right,' he said.

He drew a cigar out of an inner breast pocket and lit it up. Fragrant smoke curled up as he puffed at it, regarding her. Rose felt like an insect under a magnifying glass and wanted to scuttle back to the darkness, away from him.

'I accept your offer,' Salerni said.

'You . . . '

It took her a second to get his meaning. Then a wave of excitement swept across her.

'You're going to let me buy the hotel?'

'Subject to certain conditions, to which you will not object.' That was a statement, not a question.

'Of course,' Rose said, thrilled. 'Thank you, Don Salerni . . . you will be very pleased with the results of this deal, I guarantee it . . . '

'I'm sure I will,' Salerni said. He seemed amused; his men chuckled. 'You made me curious. I want to see for myself just how good you are.'

'Oh, I'm good,' Rose said confidently. 'You won't regret it.'

'Well.' Salerni puffed out smoke at her. 'If I do, you will. Now, sit down — Louis — '

He made the slightest motion with his little finger, and one of the fat-bellied men sprang up and awkwardly pulled out his seat for Rose. Nervously, she thanked him and slid into it as gracefully as she could.

'Tell me about yourself,' Salerni said. He leaned forward. 'I want to know everything. And I do mean everything.'

# 34

Rose went to work early the next morning.

She got up at five. It was pitch black outside her windows, and desperately cold, but she hardly noticed. Rose tugged on her clothes and rushed out of her apartment, forgetting her gloves. The frozen air sent hundreds of tiny daggers into her skin, but she didn't notice. Her heart was pumping blood, like a smuggler walking past customs.

This would be her last week. If she was going to destroy Rothstein, this was it; her last chance.

She had used her internship, studied well. Rose thought she had a wonderful overview of the company structure; she knew their weak spots. They didn't consolidate, and they were overpriced. Sure, the buildings were nice, but so were the competition's.

From what Rose could work out, it was the perks that filled most of these buildings. Dick White and his leasing team were world-class ass-kissers. As long as Rothstein's prices were market-comparable, he could get clients to take leases out by schmoozing the managers. Gifts, hookers, booze . . . probably drugs, she thought . . . everything was supplied. Lunches at Lutece and 21, tins of caviar, a diamond ring for a wife, a high-class call girl.

None of it was listed on the balance sheets, but White wasn't as discreet as he thought.

Now Rose had to get specific.

George Benham had received his phone call at 3 p.m. yesterday, after Salerni had done probing her. He was already rolling over her other properties. She was starting to think of them as chicken feed.

Rose had no doubt. This was it, right here. Everything

she had built up was on the line.

This was her last week at Rothstein. She had to make it count.

Rose stood outside of the revolving doors and pressed the night-time bell. After a few seconds, the security guard appeared. Rose flashed her security pass, and he buzzed her in.

'It's not even six a.m.,' the guy said, looking at her approvingly. His professional caution was mitigated by the fact that the chick had a willowy figure and a great pair of tits. Damn, she looked like a model. He could hardly take his eyes off that tight little cashmere sweater she was wearing. Gawking at the secretaries here was one of his favourite job perks.

Rose pouted. 'I know, but they want me to catch up on some filing . . . you know how it is.'

'Absolutely,' the guard said. 'Just sign in at the desk.'

He wanted to see her butt when she bent over. Great pins, too. Man . . . he wished he were one of those fancy executives. What he wouldn't give for just five minutes.

Rose waggled the tips of her fingers the way the Southern belles did as she jumped into the lift. She wouldn't have any trouble from him.

★   ★   ★

Mary-Beth's area was deserted. Rose passed her desk and tugged at the drawers. They weren't locked. White's office was locked, but this was good enough. Her heart beating wildly, she ran to the photocopier. Rose's hands shook as she fed the papers through the machine. What if Mary-Beth decided to come in early? Or anybody, for that matter? Were there more guards, doing their rounds?

She carefully slotted the papers back together and fitted them back in Mary-Beth's desk drawer. Next up, the filing room.

Rose checked her watch. Ten past six. She had a lot more papers to get through. Better speed this up . . .

★  ★  ★

Mary-Beth watched Rose Fiorello through narrowed lids, artfully done in a wash of green-and-gold shadow.

She couldn't stand her. Look at her, that little cow. Thought she was better than Mary-Beth, better than all the girls here. Her well-cut clothes and minimal make-up felt like a reproach to the Southern girl. She reminded Mary-Beth of her sister Louisa who was always going on about being a 'career girl'. Mary-Beth didn't like Louisa all that much either.

And somehow, this chick had scored a date with Jacob Rothstein!

Jacob. Mary-Beth sighed. She had been concentrating her fire on Richard White, because she knew to pick the easy target. Richard was lousy in bed, though, despite the pretty trinkets he bought for her, and he showed zero signs of moving the relationship forward to the ring stage. But Jacob would have been a much bigger prize! Water-cooler consensus was he didn't soil his own doorstep.

If only she'd known.

Jacob's reputation had reached Rothstein Realty. Some of the girls avidly kept scrapbooks of his appearances in the press; the gorgeous society chicks he was seen out with seemed to change every other week.

Legendary between the sheets, gave awesome jewellery, good-looking, and heir to . . . everything she saw around her.

And he wanted this little workaholic. Why, she was half a dyke! Mary-Beth glared at Rose.

She wondered if there was any way to get back at her . . .

Rose worked tirelessly. She sat in White's office, as usual, taking notes, but excused herself every chance she got. She'd been assigned a little cubicle in front of Mary-Beth's desk, and she sat in there shovelling photocopied documents into the briefcase she'd brought with her.

There were coffee breaks, a lunch hour . . . She snuck off down the hall to the filing room whenever she could. Rose cursed herself for being lazy. She should have done this copying before now, but she hadn't wanted to attract attention, and she'd thought she'd have much longer at Rothstein. Supervising the Rego Park deal was not something she'd be able to do after hours . . .

'Excuse me.'

Rose spun around, flushed with guilt. Shit. She'd been working too feverishly, had gotten careless about checking to see that the coast was clear.

Mary-Beth stood there, her arms folded across her chest, one sky-high heel tapping away furiously.

'I'm just wondering what y'all are doing in here.'

Rose froze for just a second.

'I'm getting some stuff for Jacob Rothstein,' she said.

Mary-Beth sniffed. She didn't believe her for a second, but what could she say? Just in case it was true.

'I'm going to have to report this to Mr White,' she said, and pirouetted away.

Shit. Shit. Rose had over thirty confidential leasing agreements in her briefcase, including names and addresses of some of Rothstein's biggest customers. Hurriedly she snatched up her latest batch of papers and stuffed them into the briefcase.

Then she stood and thought.

Come on, Rose. Come up with something. *Fast.*

She raced back to her cubicle. White's door was open; she could see Mary-Beth in there, gesticulating wildly to

302

her boss. White was looking angry, standing up . . .

Rose went over to Mary-Beth's desk and flipped through the company directory. Rothstein, Rothstein . . . here he was . . .

She punched in his direct number and crossed her fingers.

Please be there. Please be there . . .

'Jacob Rothstein.'

Rose breathed out. 'Jacob, I need your help . . . it's Richard White . . . can you get him off my back?'

'What?'

'I can't explain right now, but I will in a second.'

'Rose, I don't interfere in employee things,' Jake said flatly.

'Jacob . . . '

White was at the door now. He was frowning thunderously at her. 'What the goddam hell are you doing on the company phone, missy?'

'I'm just talking with Jacob,' Rose said sweetly, covering the receiver with one hand.

'With Jacob Rothstein?'

She saw White hesitate.

'Hand me the phone,' he snapped.

'Mr White wants to speak to you, Mr Rothstein,' Rose said demurely.

'Rose . . . ' Jake sighed. 'Put him on. You'd better have a real good explanation for this.'

Rose handed White the phone, and stepped back.

'She was sneaking about in the file room,' White almost bellowed. 'My girl caught her . . . '

Rose flushed a rich, hot red. Her fingers clamped around her briefcase. The executive fell silent.

'She was? Oh, she was.' He glanced murderously at Rose. 'If you say so, Jacob. Sure, I'll send her right up.'

White hung the phone up.

'He wants to see you. And in future, if you need to do something for Mr Rothstein, clear it with me first. We

303

have a chain of command in these offices, Rose. Don't think you can make an end-run around me.'

'Yes, sir,' said Rose meekly. 'Sorry, sir.'

She grabbed her case, and ran to the elevators. So much for seeing out the week; she wouldn't be coming back here.

One down, one to go.

The lift was mercifully empty. As soon as the doors hissed shut, Rose dropped the case, stepped out of her shoes, and ripped off her hose and panties as fast as she could. Fumbling, she stuffed the hose into a pocket of her knee-length, bias-cut skirt, and then dropped the snatch of caramel-coloured lace into the top of her briefcase.

She had just managed to get it closed when the doors hissed open and she almost jumped out of her skin.

Jacob was standing there. And he looked furiously angry.

'Come here.'

Rothstein grabbed her by the arm. His grip was strong, almost painful. He hustled her into his office, past a gloating Ella, and slammed the door.

'I can't have this, Rose. I don't run my office that way. Favouritism.' He passed a hand through his hair, his eyes glinting with fury. 'I don't want people pulling out their influence with me, bullying my employees, especially a senior Vice-President. You may not like him, but he's been here years and he — '

'Jake. I couldn't let him see what I was putting in the briefcase.'

'You shouldn't be putting *anything* in a briefcase. Why do you even need a briefcase for the notes you take . . . ?'

Rose snapped open the brass locks and flashed him a look of the tiny scrap of lace.

Rothstein blinked.

'I was changing in there . . . '

He grinned and looked at her. 'Mmm.' Then he reached into the briefcase and dangled the panties between his thumb and forefinger.

'Jake!' Rose hissed. His office had glass walls. 'Cut that out.'

'You were planning something?'

He pulled her closer to him and ran a hand up her skirt, caressing the bare flesh.

Rose felt his touch as though it were white-hot. She stiffened and pushed him away.

'Not here, OK? I was just going to . . .'

She couldn't think what she had just been going to do. She hadn't expected him to touch her. Now she felt vulnerable and exposed before him. Demeaned. She wanted to run.

'To do what? Flash me?'

'Yes.' Flash him, right. 'I wanted to warm you up for Friday night.'

Jake chuckled. 'You thought that was necessary?'

Rose dug him in the ribs and pointed to Ella, who was sitting at her desk outside Jake's office, staring at them jealously.

'You're making such a big deal, you're kind of causing a scene. I better go back to work. See you on Friday night.'

'Yes, you will,' he said.

She pirouetted on her heel to leave and Jake slapped her lightly, possessively, on the butt.

Rose fled.

As soon as she got into the lift, she punched the button for the next floor down. Rothstein was laid out on one plan; the women's bathrooms — small, cramped affairs — were always in the same place on every floor, in the corridors that stretched to the left of the elevator bank. Terrified that she would trip or catch a gust of wind or something, Rose bolted out of the lift and raced for them.

A secretary saw her and started to shout. 'Hey! What are you doing here?'

Rose knew she looked guilty, and that she wasn't acting like an employee. But that was too bad. She had to pull her panties on. She bolted into the bathrooms and raced into a stall, locking it quickly.

Frantically, she flicked open the briefcase and retrieved her underwear, pulling it on. She wasn't going to bother with the hose. She snapped the case shut, concealing the precious data, and let herself out, walking out into the corridor to find the secretary, a petite redhead with a blouse open one button too low, just reaching it.

'I don't know you. Who are you? Shall I call security?'

'I'm Rose Fiorello, I work in Dick White's office,' Rose said calmly. 'I got off on the wrong floor.'

'Richard White,' the girl said, shocked.

'I think of him as Dick,' Rose replied, enjoying herself. 'I was just seeing Jake Rothstein upstairs, I got off on the wrong floor.'

The girl scowled. Rose saw she had correctly assumed that the gossip bush telegraph had informed everybody about her putative romance with the boss.

'Then why were you running like that?' she demanded.

Rose put her fingertips to her forehead and made a face. 'Sudden wave of nausea. I think it might be morning sickness. See ya.'

She retreated to the elevators and hit the button for the lobby. That would give them something to talk about.

She did like leaving on a high note!

★ ★ ★

Her pulse didn't properly slow until she got home. Rose took the papers out of her briefcase and locked them in her safe. Then she went out to the liquor store along the street and bought herself a bottle of chilled vintage champagne; Veuve Grand Cru. She popped the cork and poured a flute of the icy-cold wine, taking a big gulp, letting the alcohol calm her and the bubbles fizz on her tongue.

Well. This was it.

Rose drained the first glass, then set it down and dialled Rothstein Realty.

'I want to talk to Joan in Human Resources.'

'This is Joan,' came the response after a second. Rose pictured the mousy girl sitting at her desk. This conversation would have to be handled subtly; she wanted to still the alarm bells for as long as possible.

'Joan, this is Rose Fiorello, the intern in Richard White's office?'

'Yes?' came the unenthusiastic reply.

'Joan' — Rose pretended a sob had caught in her throat — 'I'm afraid I'm going to have to resign as an intern. The pressure's too much — I just don't understand a lot of what's going on and I don't think I'm cut out for real estate.'

'Uh-huh. Thought you might.' There was undeniable relish in the other woman's voice. 'I did tell you that this is hard for women, you know.' A note of reproach crept in. 'There were a lot of guys who applied for that intern spot who didn't get it . . . it'll be too late to start anyone new on the programme now.'

'I know. I feel really awful,' Rose whimpered.

Yeah. How terrible that another spoilt frat-house king wasn't gonna get his shot at Rothstein Realty, to learn greed and sexism from the masters. She was all cut up about that.

'You'll need to send in your pass.'

'I'll drop it in the mail today,' Rose whispered contritely. 'Thank you for being so understanding.'

'Yes. Well.' The young woman sniffed. 'You should

have tried Human Resources or PR, Rose. Those are more up your alley. Leasing is very business-oriented.'

'I'll remember that next time,' Rose said solemnly.

She hung up and poured herself another glass of champagne. So what if it was only eleven and she hadn't drunk in years? This was a celebration . . .

She took a bath, got changed into something warm and comfortable, and drank half the champagne before getting totally bored.

Face it. She just wasn't cut out to be a lady of leisure.

★　★　★

Rose drove out to Queens and parked opposite the hotel.

Mmm. The potential. Great access to Manhattan, to Long Island City . . . Rose drew the complex in her mind. Definitely gates; a high, thick wire fence with a guardhouse. That would be much cheaper than wrought iron or brick. She would have to be careful not to over-improve, to keep her costs at a minimum.

The secret to being a wealthy seller was to give buyers what they wanted, and nothing more.

Here, that was going to be a matter of large, cheap apartments with fresh paint and linoleum, security outside, and maybe some new kitchen appliances. Every condo comes with a microwave, Rose thought, and brand-new ovens and freezers. She could get a great discount deal, and it would pay for itself many times over. There would be a luxurious-looking lobby — she'd keep those brass railings — and there were so many apartments that maintenance charges to pay for a doorman and security guard would be minimal.

Then she was going to sell them at fifteen per cent below market value. And just hope it worked.

Otherwise, she'd be in the hole to Salerni for

millions. And the Mob weren't known as the most patient bankers.

Rose shivered, and it wasn't from the cold. She had an urge to start right away. She stepped out of her car and walked into the hotel.

Time warp. It was exactly like the last time she'd been in here, months ago. There was the same air of furtive shabbiness that came with being a pay-by-the-hour joint for hookers and drug dealers and people who couldn't afford anything better. And there was the same gum-cracking receptionist, on the day shifts, no doubt, sitting behind the desk.

Rose dug deep and retrieved the information.

'Hello, Tracy,' she said.

Tracy looked up blankly. Rose could see the little hamster-wheels going round in her mind.

'Oh, it's you,' she said.

'Don't you think you should say 'Good morning'?' Rose asked. ' 'Good morning, ma'am' would be even better.'

Tracy scowled. 'You're just here to make trouble again. I'm gonna have you banned. Jason!' She yelled for the security guard.

'I don't think so. I own the place.'

The girl laughed out loud. 'Yeah, OK. Vincent Salerni owns it. You don't look nuttin' like him.'

'He sold it to me,' Rose said, coolly.

'Sure,' Tracy said, but she sounded a bit nervous. Rose tapped the phone in front of her. 'Give him a call, he'll tell you. Do you want the number?'

The girl paled. 'No. No, ma'am. Wh — what can I get for you?'

Rose grinned.

'A set of skeleton keys,' she said.

# 35

Jacob Rothstein smiled to himself as he dialled Mary-Beth's extension.

'Mr White's office.'

'Mary-Beth.' Rothstein's voice was low, caressing. It was that way with almost all women; he did it automatically. 'This is Jacob.'

'Oh, Mr Rothstein. Yes, sir?'

'Put Rose on, would you?'

'Rose Fiorello?' The breathy, little-girl voice gave way to a snap of triumph. 'Why, sir, I do declare you're behind the times; didn't you know she left?'

'Already? It's only ten a.m.

'No, sir. She *left*. She resigned yesterday.'

'What for?'

'I really don't know, sir. But I can help you with anything you need,' Mary-Beth added hopefully.

'That's OK,' Jacob said.

He hung up and thought for a few moments.

★ ★ ★

Friday night was unseasonably mild; muggy and wet, with none of the crisp iciness Rose was used to. She selected her outfit with care. Something sexy, but not too sexy. This date was going to have to be very carefully played.

She'd let him touch her.

It had been necessary. Rose told herself that. But now what? Now what?

She was nervous.

Rose hadn't thought of men. She'd been way too busy. The fury that had driven her had been all-consuming. At Columbia, she had barely noticed any of the boys that swarmed around the lecture halls leering and whistling.

Except Jacob.

She'd noticed him.

She liked to tell herself it was because he was a Rothstein. Her enemy. The gatekeeper. But she knew that wasn't true. She never had dreams about his uncle William, even though her hatred of that man still burned. I'm Italian, she thought. I can keep a vendetta in my heart for a generation, waiting until I can strike. And it probably would take a lot less time than that.

Jake disturbed her in other ways. Of course, there were those looks. Obvious good looks, she thought disdainfully. The square jaw, the muscles, the dark eyes and hair, the thick black lashes. But that was only the wrapping. A man could have all that, and still be effeminate.

Not Rothstein.

Rose was too smart to dismiss it as the money. True, Jake threw it around. Diamonds for his girlfriends, a Ferrari, the whole bit. Money might give you some confidence, she supposed. But Jake's came from two sources. His womanising and his intelligence.

She was forced to admit that retro and sexist as it might be, she found both attributes attractive.

Rothstein had a mind like a scalpel; cutting and precise. Unlike others she'd met, he didn't cower when faced with her own. He competed with her. He might, he might . . . the thought burned her, but there it was all the same . . . he might actually be brighter than she was. But Rose had a different edge. She was driven in ways he could not imagine. Brains or no brains, she was going to crush him.

And then there was the womanising.

Rose had not been immune to his reputation. All the girls talked about him. Hushed tones, fanning themselves. And the way he looked her over, as though he were peeling the clothes right off her back. He had confidence, arrogance and power, and he took none of her shit, and he was a full-on dominant male and he wasn't even ashamed of it.

God help her, she found that amazingly attractive.

His kiss had made her weak at the knees.

Remember who he is, Rose told herself as she pulled on her dress of pale-green silk, modestly long but clinging in all the right places. Remember the family he comes from.

Rothstein. Rothstein. Rothstein.

★  ★  ★

Jacob had set up his place well. He'd called the caterers; almost a thousand dollars for dinner, but it was money well spent. A magnum of Cristal was chilling in the Tiffany silver ice-bucket by the mahogany table in his dining room; he had dimmed the chandelier and placed candles around the room, lighting up the oil portraits of other people's ancestors his father had bought for him. The pre-war arched windows looked down Fifth towards St Patrick's, with Manhattan glittering in the dark, the neon lights matching the sparkle of the service at his table; champagne flutes in Waterford crystal, napkins of crisp Irish linen, napkin rings and cutlery of silver, and bone-china plates. He had thought about sushi, but that was too risky. Instead, there was a heaped pot of beluga caviar with blinis and chopped egg and delicate bone spoons by Rose's place. That was to be followed by roast pheasant with chestnut sauce and an individual poached pear with ginger ice-cream. Silver bowls crammed with very short-stemmed yellow roses were dotted around the table next to his antique candelabras, and they were matched by vases of roses everywhere, the freshest blooms in a pastel medley of pale pink, white, yellow, blue, and even green; the apartment smelled like a summer meadow in the depths of winter.

He hoped she liked it. Not that dinner was the point, of course, but he wanted to impress her.

The bedroom was also full of flowers. Jacob had considered having the florist strew rose petals across the bed but he decided against it. No point in trying *too* hard.

If last week was any indication, Rose Fiorello was a done deal.

Something about that whole thing had made him uneasy. Not touching her; she had been a fantasy of his since he first laid eyes on her in the lecture hall. Maybe the fact that she had quit.

Was she embarrassed by what she had let him do? Scared because White had shouted at her?

It wasn't Fiorello's way.

During the months she'd been there, he'd heard nothing from her. No ideas, no reports. Jake had half expected something every day; he had thought he might walk in to a folder on his desk containing some neatly typed, earth-shattering idea. Such as how to restructure his company from the ground up, a suggestion for a stock buy-back, or even a project proposal to buy some building or other.

He had always marked her down as that ambitious, and that bright.

And that cold.

Instead, what did he have? An intern who had made no waves until the last day. He knew the secretaries didn't like her. But she was beautiful, so that was to be expected.

She had come upstairs naked under her skirt and flashed him.

The kiss had not surprised Jake. She wanted him, he knew that. Once he had her in his arms, her resistance

313

was always going to crumble. And yeah, she had been hot. But one of the things he'd found most delicious about Rose was how she fought it. What happened to her hot contempt for him, her belligerence? One kiss and now she was ripping off her panties?

It didn't fit.

He was, in fact, disappointed.

Ah, don't be a dumb-ass. You've been wanting to get in there for years, Rothstein told himself. Tonight she was coming over and tonight he was gonna get laid. What the hell was he crying about it for?

The bell rang.

★ ★ ★

'Let me help you with that,' Jacob said.

Rose shrugged off her coat. Expensive, a cashmere blend. He saw that the label was Donna Karan. Underneath she had on a stunning dress in close-fitting silk, a delicate pale green colour that picked out her startling eyes. The girl had curves everywhere, except that narrow waist. Rothstein smiled; he approved.

'Do you like the place?'

Her eyes swept over the fantastic windows, the ornate mouldings, the portraits, the marble mantelpiece, the antique furniture, the view . . .

'I've seen better,' Rose said.

He lifted an eyebrow. 'Where?'

'The Met,' Rose admitted. She grinned.

Jacob was charmed. 'You look beautiful, you know.'

Rose shivered, even though he had a fire crackling in the grate and it was seventy degrees inside. 'I need a drink.'

He poured her some champagne. 'Cristal OK?'

'And there I was thinking you were going to offer me a Thunderbird,' Rose joked.

'The stuff that's three bucks a litre?' He laughed.

Most women were so keen to impress him with their sophistication, as though every date was a casting session and they were auditioning. 'Maybe I should have. Just to make you comfortable.'

She could hardly look at him. He was wearing a tuxedo and black tie. Combined with the muscles, it made him look like James Bond.

Rose wished he would be foul to her. She couldn't find anything to reproach him for, apart from being a Rothstein. Maybe, maybe she should give him a pass . . . some kind of out.

'I think we should talk . . . '

Jake enjoyed her awkwardness.

'Before dinner? It ruins my appetite.' He indicated the dining room. 'Shall we?'

★  ★  ★

'Mmm.' Rose sipped at her champagne, her fourth glass. The meal had been exquisite; his conversation light, about nothing, really, just banter. And Jacob was very good at banter. He deflected any probing comment, he held her gaze until she was forced to drop her eyes, and he ate his meal as though he wasn't nervous, not even slightly.

Goddam confident bastard.

She needed the alcohol. As delicious as everything was, Rose found it hard to eat. She had no appetite. She was torn between wanting Rothstein and loathing him. Every expensive bite was a reminder of how his family had built the wealth to pay for all this.

How many other Paul Fiorellos were out there? Men who didn't have a smart Italian daughter to come and take their revenge for them. Maybe thousands, she thought. And how many women had wanted to get ahead at Rothstein and been fired, shunted aside? In his company discrimination was a way of life.

She also felt defensive. She wanted this. The oak-panelled walls, the furnishings that looked like a page from a Sotheby's catalogue. Her modern apartment in the old factory was nice, and a good investment. But this place would cost twenty times more. Jacob had not earned this. It had been handed to him on a plate, and it wasn't even the best his family had. This was nothing but a pied-à-terre for the Rothstein boys. Rose knew this because the bimbos in the office talked up their wealth, creaming their little lace panties over every unmarried Rothstein in the place.

'Glad you enjoyed it,' Jake said. 'Are you done? I could have got a butler to clear the plates away, but I didn't want us to be disturbed. Just leave it; I have coffee and a digestif in the drawing room.'

Rose nodded and walked into the room next door. Her heart sped up a little. Oh shit. Now she was going to be expected to put out.

'Digestif? I think you're trying to get me drunk.'

Jacob poured an espresso into an exquisite, tiny royal-blue bone china cup from a silver pot and handed it to her.

'Drunk's no fun. I just want you to relax.'

If only you knew, she thought.

'Do you normally make this much of an effort?'

She indicated the flowers, the crystal.

'No. I usually don't have to. Women tend to come to me.' He said this flatly, as though it was a statement of fact. Which Rose knew it was.

'Fortune-hunters,' Rose said, with contempt. The alcohol was starting to work its magic; she felt less small in his presence.

'Yes,' he agreed without rancour. 'We have a lot of money. Most women find that very attractive.'

'It doesn't bother you?'

A shrug. 'That's been the way of the world for as long

316

as it's been spinning. Back when we lived in caves, women sought out the guy with the biggest kills. It's instinctual in a female. Why should I resent it?'

Small red spots of outrage coloured her cheeks.

'Because you should want somebody to want you for yourself.'

'Ah. But this' — he indicated the apartment — '*is* me. I come from a high-achieving family, and I'm going to make more money.'

'It isn't just women. Men hang out with rich women too. And men also hang out with rich men. How many people do you know who hang around your family because of their wealth? There are plenty of male hangers-on too,' Rose said.

'True, up to a point.'

'What do you mean?' Rose demanded. God, he was arrogant!

'I mean that while that is true — men do hang-on, as you put it, and some men try to marry women for money — the vast majority of cases of fortune-hunting are women chasing men. Because society accepts a woman who does not work, but condemns a man for trying to do the same.'

Jacob flipped open the antique cigar box in front of him. 'I usually smoke after dinner, but I won't, if it bothers you?'

'Go right ahead,' Rose said. She wasn't interested in his damn cigar. She went back on the attack. 'You sound like you think less of women.'

He considered it for a second. 'Depends how you define it.'

'How do you define it is the question,' Rose said.

'I think men and women are equal in that they are equal souls before God. But if you are asking me about levels of achievement, then men are clearly superior. The history of the world is the history of men.' He cut the end of the cigar deftly and lit it. 'Modern-day history teaching is a joke, quite frankly. Women's historical studies . . . Marie Curie and whoever else they can dredge up . . . but the odd female achiever here and there cannot wipe out the fact that almost every great advance in every field has been made, built, or discovered by males.'

Rose seethed.

'Because women are physically inferior, and that meant men could control them. The technological age has levelled the playing field.'

'Then today we should see equality. And we don't. Because many women prefer to be kept by their man.'

'Some women regard motherhood as a full-time occupation.'

'Do you?'

Rose shook her head. 'I regard it as a relationship, not a job description.'

Jacob smiled. 'You're one of these 'having it all' types?'

'Yes. I intend to strap my babies on my back and go right back to work. I'll have a playpen in the office. Whatever it takes not to cheat my children or my career.'

'And what employer do you think will allow you to do that?'

Rose shook her head. 'Good office day-care should be mandatory. A happy worker is a productive worker. But I won't be one of those poor women scouring the streets for an understanding employer, because I intend to work for myself.' She glared at him. 'I don't know how you can talk that way.'

'Because, quite simply, I am not afraid of the truth.' Rothstein moved towards her, so their knees were almost touching; Rose half shrank in her chair. 'Not all women are like you.'

'And not all men are like you.'

'Women are not interested in equals. They are

interested in superiors.'

'Then I suppose I shouldn't be interested in you,' Rose snapped.

'You seemed pretty interested last week. When I kissed you.'

'Maybe it was all an act.'

Jacob shook his head. 'Part of it may have been, Rose, but not all of it.'

She felt her skin prickle. *Part of it may have been . . . could she have underestimated him? Had he not bought in to her act?*

'Not all of it,' Rose admitted.

'Why don't we conduct a little field experiment?'

Jacob moved closer to her on the couch, put his two strong hands on her knees, leaned in towards her, and kissed her.

Rose felt the fires start again. They licked along her skin, up her belly, across her breasts, making her light-headed. His mouth on hers was gentle, but relentless; his teeth lightly raking her lips, his tongue probing, not too deep, feeling her lips part and open to him, her head tilt, the stiff aggression in her body release, until all her bones were liquid and she wanted to melt . . .

Jacob loved it. She was a slow conquest, not clawing back at him like he was used to. A girl usually had one hand in his buttons, the other in his hair, if she was that modest. Fiorello was awkward, nervous, old-fashioned. Even inexperienced, he thought. It was startling. And charming.

And sexy. He loved to master women. The longer the seduction, the better he liked it. Sex could sometimes leave Jake feeling empty, a little sordid. He had waited for Rose, and now he was going to have her. It felt all the more delicious.

She'd be very hot. He couldn't wait.

'Stop.'

He felt a small, manicured hand against his chest, pushing him back.

'What?' Rothstein blinked, stunned. 'What the hell is it now?'

'I can't do this,' Rose said.

'You — you *what*? You can't do this? You came up to my office naked. You peeled off those little panties for me right in public.' He knew he was being cruel, but he was frustrated and furious. 'And now you want to be modest, act like a lady? A little late for that, don't you think?'

'You goddam bastard. Nobody could see.'

Jacob got to his feet. 'What are you, some kind of virgin?'

'Yes,' Rose stammered. 'Actually.'

'Bullshit,' Rothstein said coldly.

Rose stood up, walked out to the hall, grabbed her coat and purse, and fled.

# 36

'You like it?' Joel Stein asked.

Poppy looked over her office. It was small, but functional. It even had a window looking out towards the gleaming Mercedes and BMWs that drove down the Sunset Strip, sparkling in the sunlight. Stein had provided her with a computer, a phone, a printer, a fax, and even her own couch, a funky kidney-shaped thing in burgundy velvet.

Poppy grinned. 'I love it.'

Joel handed her a business card. 'And how about this?'

Her heart skipped a beat. It had her name in neat black ink on it, very grown-up, very businesslike: 'Poppy Allen, Dream Management'. Then it had her direct phone and fax number next to the Dream logo, a cloud picked out in embossed gold.

'No job title,' Stein said. 'Nobody has titles here but me.'

'And what's yours?'

'Boss,' he said simply. 'Now listen, toots. You did good. Better than good. Which is why you're not a tour accountant any more. I'm going to see what you can do. I'm giving you a band to handle.'

'Green Dragon?' Poppy asked hopefully.

Stein laughed. 'Yeah, right. What are you, crazy? You get to handle Silver Bullet. You brought them to me, let's see what you can do with them. You'll find people will take your phone calls when you're calling from Dream.'

'OK,' said Poppy. It wasn't a big band, it wasn't even a real band yet. But it was her band. 'OK.'

'There are people who don't like you,' Stein said.

'What? Why?'

'Because they've been working here longer than you have. Years, in some cases. And who still aren't getting a shot like this. Plus, you've got a serious enemy in Mike Rich. And you're going to get others. This business is not for shrinking violets.'

Poppy squared her shoulders and looked her boss in the eye.

'I got in to see you. That shows initiative. I found a great band for you. That shows talent. I survived a road trip. That shows stamina. And I stopped a crooked guy ripping off your client. That shows smarts. I'm in this office because you think I *deserve* to be. And the fact is, you're right.'

'Hmm.' Stein crooked an eyebrow. 'Chutzpah, yet. Let's see if you can back it up with action.'

He made to leave the room. Poppy let him go. She wanted to ask, 'Now what?' but she didn't. She knew that was up to her.

★　★　★

'You're going to manage us?' Kate said.

Poppy sat in her office behind the desk, with the girls on the couch. They looked somewhat underwhelmed. She knew they were disappointed, that they thought Joel Stein would be handling them personally. And now they were right back with Poppy; a kid from a failed band, a kid their own age.

She had to inspire confidence.

'That's correct. Me for Dream Management. The first thing Dream is going to do is get you signed. I have a showcase gig booked in two weeks, girls. Reps from all the major labels will be attending.'

Now they sat up. Poppy watched the band exchange glances.

'What I want you to do is two things: rehearse till you

can perform the songs in your sleep, and get even prettier. Molly,' Poppy turned to the plump brunette, 'you're going on a diet. I know it's sexist and it sucks, but these are men, all men, and they'll be looking at you guys. No White Castle this week. You're strictly on Slim-Fast.'

Molly looked as though she were about to argue the toss, but Poppy ploughed on. 'I've got a stylist booked for tomorrow afternoon. She worked wardrobe on the Green Dragon tour last Fall.'

'Wow, Green Dragon,' Claire muttered.

'Just think of this as a makeover.' Poppy leaned forwards. 'I'm gonna get you guys signed, I'm gonna get you on the radio. I'm gonna make you stars. And all you have to do is listen to me.'

'How long is the showcase going to be?'

'Half an hour. You're only going to do five songs.' Poppy passed them the set list.

'I think we should do everything we've got,' Kate argued.

'No. Just the best stuff. These are your best, wouldn't you agree?' Reluctant nods. 'Then we hit them with this. All killer, no filler.'

★   ★   ★

The next day Poppy called the stylist. She told her it was a personal favour for Joel Stein. She called the record companies and told them this was Joel's hottest new act and she was just able to slip them in before a general submission went out. Then she called the lighting director from the tour and asked him for the name of a friend, and the same for the sound guy . . .

★   ★   ★

It was a buzz. It was even better than the road. Poppy felt as though her phone had been permanently welded to her ear. She lied, she dissembled, she pleaded, she got things done. She didn't sleep all that much. When she finally got to go home at night, she instead went straight out to the broken-down warehouse where the band was rehearsing, and stayed up with them, making sure everything was perfect.

It wasn't just sound. That had to be slick, but so did the moves. Even the way Lisa twirled her drumsticks.

Most every new act was rough, unpolished. Not her babies. Poppy wanted them to be groomed, to look like pros.

'Manicures?' Molly groaned.

'Manicures. Eyebrow waxes. Get your teeth whitened.' Poppy spun her bassist around to look in the mirror. 'You've dropped about eight pounds.'

'My clothes don't fit,' Molly grumbled, but she looked pleased.

'I don't see why we have to do all this work,' Kate said petulantly. 'We'll be playing in the middle of the day. There'll be no atmosphere . . . '

'Actually,' Poppy said quietly, 'I got a pro lighting guy and a sound mixer coming. It'll be dark and you'll be spot-lit, multiple colours, big sound, everything perfect.'

Kate gaped. 'But do you know how much those guys cost?'

'In your case, nothing.' Poppy shrugged. 'I arranged it all.'

'You're incredible,' Lisa said.

'I'm just the manager,' Poppy told them.

The day before the gig, Poppy marched them into the hairdressers.

'You're getting a new look,' she said. 'Lisa, you're going to have brown hair. Kate, you're going blonde. Claire will be a redhead and Molly's going raven-black.'

'But I like being blonde,' Lisa protested.

'Doesn't matter. It's a gimmick. One of each hair colour. Once you're signed, you can go back, if you still want to. The singer is the front woman, she has to be blonde.'

'Sounds great,' Kate purred.

Lisa scowled, but she submitted.

They were beginning to do everything she told them.

★   ★   ★

The day of the gig, Joel was there. Poppy had made sure the little club was packed with executives. She had radio guys there, promoters, local TV stations, even some pony-tailed Armani-wearing suit from MTV.

Silver Bullet came out to dimmed lights, even smoke from the dry ice. Poppy had taken pro headshots of each girl, heavily made up, and had them blown up to gigantic size. They hung around the walls of the club. Spotlights swirled over the excited crowd even before the first note was played.

And then her act burst on to the stage. They wore semi-matched outfits in black and silver PVC, very Barbarella. Their hair colours looked fantastic. Kate's hair was a gleaming fountain of platinum. The lights were bright, amazingly flattering and soft. And then, through a wall of professionally mixed speakers, they started to play.

For twenty minutes they ripped through the set. Just the best songs, performed fast and sleek. When they finally left the stage, hair flying, Kate blew little kisses, waggling her fingers like a cheerleader; Molly shoved her fists in the air like a biker.

Huge applause.

House lights up.

Poppy was surrounded by drooling talent scouts, pressing cards on her, telling her to call them.

She looked over at Joel Stein, standing at the back.

For once in his life being ignored.

He winked at her.

★　★　★

After that it was gravy.

Poppy signed the band to Musica records for an advance of a million dollars. She didn't let them spend more than five grand of it. She rented them an apartment, found them a producer, booked them on tour with Diamondback, one of Dream's mid-size acts. By the time the record was out, Silver Bullet had already been on three magazine covers.

Their first single went in at number 5 in the rock charts, number 15 in the Billboard Hot 100. It broke out on radio like a rash and peaked at number 7.

Silver Bullet were stars. And so was Poppy.

# 37

Poppy was good at it. Better than Joel Stein had expected. Better than *she* had expected.

Nobody wanted to take her seriously, but that, Poppy thought, was their problem. She wasn't gonna tone herself down for anyone.

She was young, and she wasn't going to try to dress old. No red power-suits with gold braiding and shoulder-pads. She wore jeans and Metallica shirts with high, strappy heels; little black dresses that clung to her curves; denim shorts with a Daisy Duke-tied shirt over the top. Poppy liked to wear her hair loose, to go light on make-up and perfume. Most days she wore nothing except sunscreen and a little scent, Hermes perhaps. She didn't need much else.

Several times Poppy got turfed out of offices. MTV told her: 'We don't let fans in the lobby, miss.' Record company receptions called security. Bank managers rolled their eyes.

Not for long.

Poppy was armed. She carried her business card like a weapon. And she had Silver Bullet.

★ ★ ★

'I can't believe it,' Kate said.

'Believe it.' Poppy grinned at her singer. 'The cover of *Rolling Stone.*'

Molly looked as though she wanted to cry. They were in the back of the limo, riding towards the Rosebowl, where Silver Bullet were third on the bill at the Monsters of Rock Festival, behind Skid Row and Guns n' Roses. Her girls looked great; Poppy had worked out a black-and-silver theme for the set, to coincide with the band's name. She'd come up with a new look for them, which would be featured in Jan Wenner's prestigious magazine. Ironically, the once-rebellious *Rolling Stone* was now as establishment as it got.

Gracing the cover was an industry stamp of approval. One that said: 'Made it.'

'I have some more good news for you.' Poppy said. 'Our marketing campaign really worked and 'Hellacious' is going to debut at number one.'

Claire made a strangled sound in the back of her throat.

'I'll take that as approval.'

Poppy felt a small thrill of pride. She liked these kids; she thought of them as 'kids' somehow, even though they had a year or two on her. And she had been instrumental in changing their lives.

A good manager did a little bit of everything. Jill of All Trades. She helped pick the producer, the artwork, the set designer, the tour manager. She supervised how the record company did their job; she breathed down Promotions' back, making sure her girls were all over the radio; she took the calls at 3 a.m. when Molly was drunk and needed bailing out of a holding cell.

And this was the reward: her band in demand, albums flying off the shelves, video on Headbangers' Ball on MTV, fans outside the hotels, great slots on tours. T-shirt sales weren't great; teenage boys wouldn't wear a shirt with the name of a girl band on it, even if they wore leather and studs. But the picture was rosy.

And now they had a number one record.

Poppy tried not to get too cocky. After all, she wasn't *in* the band. It wasn't her music on KNAC. It wasn't her twirling the drumstick, flirting with the front row, posing for sexy shots next to Harley Davidson bikes. Silver Bullet were talented.

But not, said a little voice in her head, *that* talented.

The fact was, talent alone didn't guarantee you big sales — just ask Mott the Hoople. And sometimes you didn't need talent at all. Just ask Milli Vanilli. A Grammy award, and they hadn't sung one note on 'their' record.

You needed a man with a plan. Or a girl.

Like me, Poppy thought.

She looked at the band high-fiving each other. No way could they have done it without her.

⋆ ⋆ ⋆

'We're Silver Bullet!' Kate flung her arms in the air, gave her patented fists-thrust-skyward salute. 'Thank you and goodnight!'

The band bounced offstage to cheering and whooping and a surge towards the lip of the giant festival stage. Poppy watched it with a clinical eye, to check security was on it and no kids were going to get injured. Roadies were there with bottles of water, white fluffy towels, so the girls could mop their sweat off before heading into the shower.

'Poppy.'

There was a hand on her shoulder. Poppy jumped out of her skin.

'Dude, Joel, you scared me.'

'Great gig,' Joel Stein said. He was wearing a gorgeously cut suit and a platinum Rolex that cost about four times her yearly salary. 'My girls are doing fantastic stuff.'

Your girls? Poppy thought, but didn't say it.

'*Rolling Stone* shoot's tomorrow,' Poppy said.

'I know, I spoke to Jan personally. They're going to go with Annie Liebowitz for the shots.'

Poppy nodded, but of course she already knew that. She'd been negotiating this for over a month now.

'I've got some very exciting ideas for the band,' Joel

329

said. 'I'm gonna take a band meeting after they get out of the shower.'

Poppy stared at him. 'You are?'

Silver Bullet was her band. She took the band meetings.

'You can sit in if you like,' Stein said, easily enough.

Poppy debated internally, with the chaos all around her, as crew guys ran on to the stage to rip down the Silver Bullet set and set up for Skid Row. Stein was sending her a clear signal, and she didn't care for it. The best thing would be to suck it up and say nothing. That was clearly what he expected.

'Silver Bullet are my act, Joel. I set up *Rolling Stone*. I've been handling them for a year now. I take the band meetings.'

'Last time I looked, they were a Dream Management act.' Stein's eyes warned her not to go any further. 'You did a great job, Poppy, but the girls — '

The girls, right.

' — are at a stage now where I can be of more use to them than you. They're ready to go to that next level. What I want you to do is to start thinking about our roster, maybe pick another band to work with closely. How about Highway? They need refreshing, you might be just the girl for the job.'

Highway? Fucking Highway? Joel's teen-pop act, his manufactured answer to New Kids on the Block? Highway were two years too old and on the way out. Their fifteen minutes were up.

She smiled briskly. 'I'll think about that, Joel.'

★ ★ ★

Poppy left the gig early. She was too angry to trust herself to stay. Arguing the toss with Joel wouldn't do anything for her, it would just make her look weak. She didn't want the band to see her upset.

She wasn't overly worried. Silver Bullet would be loyal to her, would stick with her. After all, it wasn't Joel, busy with Green Dragon and his other multi-platinum giant acts, that had broken Silver Bullet, and they would know it. If necessary, Poppy thought, she would just lay it on the line with Joel. The group would want her, not him, and the customer is always right.

She tried to think of it as 'just business'. But she was fuming.

Poppy took her new BMW right back to her office. She marched inside, slammed the door and grabbed a yellow pad and a Bic biro. Every crisis hides an opportunity, they said. Very well; Joel was forcing her into something she might have waited on. But no longer.

She wanted a bigger slice of the pie. She wanted to be credited separately on all the albums: not just 'Dream Management' but 'Poppy Allen for Dream Management'. A bigger percentage of the management cut. And no more interference from Joel.

I might be young, Poppy thought, but look at the way I've performed. Silver Bullet love me. He can't say no.

★   ★   ★

'No.'

Stein shook his head. Once. Firmly. 'Anything else, Poppy? I'd love to hear the ideas you have on Highway.'

Poppy struggled not to lose her cool. She was standing in her boss's office. It was a typically mild and gorgeous day in LA, with a cool breeze to temper the sunshine. The fronds of the palm tree outside his window rustled gently.

Inside this office, however, the atmosphere was getting very cold. Very fast.

'You want to come in just when my act — '

331

'Dream's act.'

'I've done all the goddam work, Joel. My act suddenly hits number one, is on *Rolling Stone*, and now all the heavy lifting's been gotten out of the way,' she could not stop the sneer in her voice, '*uber* manager Joel Stein comes in and takes all the glory? No way. That's not fair.'

'That's not fair,' Joel mimicked. 'Listen, kid. I gave you your shot. Don't think you're some magical hotshot who waved her wand over this act. You wouldn't have gotten any place without the name of Dream, without *my* expertise. They weren't taking your calls. They were taking Dream's calls. My company and my reputation broke this act. Now, you did a good job with the tools; I want you to do it again with Highway.'

'You want my advice to Highway? Quit. It's over,' Poppy snapped.

'Defeatist?'

'I don't want to manage bands that suck. I want to manage my own act. The one I found.'

'And I signed.' Joel jabbed a manicured finger at her. 'It's my way or the highway, princess. No pun intended.'

'The band don't even know you. They won't stand for this.'

'On the contrary.' His smile was crocodile-wide. 'I explained my plans for a switch in the day-to-day handling, for me to take them to the next level. And they're all for it.'

'Bullshit,' Poppy almost shouted.

'Now, now, dear.' Joel pushed his phone towards her. 'Don't get your panties in a twist. Call them yourself. You'll see.'

# 38

The 747 began to judder and shake slightly as the wheels lifted off the tarmac.

Poppy settled back in her seat and tried to focus. She was heading to New York for the weekend. She'd told Joel she had urgent family business, but the truth was she just needed to be out of LA. And out of touch.

Betrayal.

Poppy could hear those voices still. Kate's awkward pleasantries: 'Yeah, Joel told us about the new arrangements. Sounds pretty good, like some other band will be lucky enough to have you working with them, Poppy . . . '

'You don't want me working with you?' Poppy demanded.

'Seems like a waste to have you *and* Joel, ya know . . . '

The acid in her stomach had started to seethe. Kate had never wanted Poppy, not really, not from the first moments she'd talked to the act. She'd always wanted Joel, Poppy suddenly realised, with a flash of insight.

Poppy had been second best.

'Do the rest of the band feel that way?'

'Yeah,' Kate mumbled.

'Even Molly? Let me talk to Molly.'

'Sure, hold on.' Poppy heard Kate covering the receiver with her hand, heard muffled girls' voices. Then Kate again, still awkward. 'Um, Molly just stepped out for a second, she can call you back in a little while . . . '

Poppy closed her eyes for a heartbeat. When she opened them, Joel was still there, sitting in front of her, with a look that said 'I told you so.'

'No,' Poppy said, 'no need, hon. I think this will work

out wonderfully for Silver Bullet. Joel will help you guys to the next level.'

A small, thin smile from her boss.

'It's not like you're never gonna see us again, or something, is it?' Kate asked brightly.

'Hmmm,' Poppy said, making a non-committal grunt. 'Later, OK?'

She had hung up, bright spots of colour high on her cheekbones.

Joel Stein chuckled. 'Honey, don't take it so personally. You really are a greenhorn. Bands aren't your friend, they're your client. First lesson.'

'A good one,' Poppy said grimly.

'Second lesson.' Stein waved the piece of paper. 'A couple of successes does not make you Tom Zutaut, sugar. I hired you to be smart and inventive. You've delivered. You're gonna get a bonus. But Dream is my company and I divide up the roster. Always remember that.' He shook his head. 'I'm not looking for a partner, but you keep going like this, you could wind up my number two. And be very well rewarded.'

'I'd like to take a vacation,' Poppy said on impulse. 'I got some family business to deal with . . . '

She'd spun him the story and he'd accepted it. Why not? Poppy thought bitterly. You win a major victory, you can afford to toss the loser a bone.

★   ★   ★

'Ladies and gentlemen, welcome to Continental Airlines flight 41 to JFK'

The man next to her was sarcastically mouthing the words of the tannoy announcement under his breath. He suddenly looked at Poppy.

'Oh, I'm sorry.' It was a rich Southern accent, which slightly surprised her, because the man was so urbane;

wearing a discreet tailored suit, very expensive — probably from Europe — handmade shoes, and a plain gold watch. He was older, with salt-and-pepper hair and blue eyes and a square jaw. Muscular, too; good-looking, Poppy decided, in an ultimate capitalist pig-type way.

The voice sounded as though it belonged to someone with a stetson and cowboy boots. 'It's a bad habit. I can't stand that yapping. Cruising at 35,000 feet — who cares. You know?'

Poppy nodded, smiled at him. 'I'm Poppy Allen.'

'Henry LeClerc.'

The name sounded faintly familiar, but she couldn't place it.

'You looked kind of upset, if you'll pardon the intrusion. Don't like to fly?'

'It's not that. It's business,' Poppy said.

He chuckled. 'Business?'

Poppy frowned. 'Why is that funny?'

'You look too young to be in business,' he said, frankly. 'You look like you should be in college.'

His eyes were dark-blue, very confident.

'I'm flying business class,' Poppy pointed out.

'So do lots of rich kids.'

Arrogant sod, she decided. 'Well, it's not like that. I work in a business with . . . a global reach.'

'Ah,' he said. 'So do I, I suppose.'

Poppy didn't like his tone. 'People think you can't do shit because you're young. But that's bull. Alexander conquered the whole world before he was thirty.'

LeClerc grinned. 'I'm sure I try not to underestimate the young, ma'am.'

'Champagne?'

A flight attendant was hovering, one of the prettier ones. She was made up to the nines, and she was staring at LeClerc with an incredibly submissive air and a brilliant smile. She ignored Poppy.

'I'll take some champagne,' Poppy said. She had paid plenty for this seat.

'How old are you, miss?'

Poppy flushed. 'Twenty-three. OK?'

The woman looked sceptical.

'You can serve this young lady,' LeClerc said softly.

The flight attendant instantly handed Poppy a crystal flute of champagne. 'There you go, ma'am. Sorry for the misunderstanding. And for you, Congressman?'

Poppy blinked.

'I'll just take an orange juice,' he said.

★　★　★

It was a bumpy flight, but Poppy took no notice of it. She felt like she was fighting a rearguard action, trying to get back a little dignity.

'So I'm stuck with a politician,' she remarked when they served the food.

'Afraid so.' He waved away the lunch tray.

'Congressmen don't eat?'

'Not that swill.' LeClerc reached into his carry-on luggage and brought out a small, elegant silver box, monogrammed with his initials. 'I do too much flying. I insist on eating decent food.' He flipped open the box, and Poppy's mouth started to water. Inside was a ripe peach with a heavenly scent, a small tin of Sevruga caviar, some fresh blinis, and a set of sandwiches, very thin brown bread, smoked salmon, and lemon slices.

'Take some. I insist.'

'Absolutely not,' she said, but her mouth was watering.

He opened the tin of caviar, spooned a little on to a blini. 'Open your mouth.'

She did. It was heavenly.

'Tell me about your business problem,' LeClerc said.

So she did. She spilled her guts. But he seemed to be

336

taking her seriously, and he was a congressman. Poppy told herself it was flattering, and not just because he was a good-looking guy old enough to be her father.

'Resign.'

'Resign? But this is one of the biggest management firms around. What am I gonna do, move to New York and work for Q-Prime?'

'Start your own firm.'

'But I don't have any acts,' Poppy objected.

LeClerc shrugged. 'Find some. You did before. Now you're a proven quantity, to some extent. It seems to me that you're always going to be wanting more than a boss will give you. Only one thing for it: start your own firm.'

Poppy considered it. Starting up with Silver Bullet would have been perfect, but she would pretty much have nothing. And she was barely old enough for this champagne. But it wasn't totally unheard of. Ron Lafitte managed Megadeth and he was, like, twenty-five. The thought was terrifying. And somewhat exciting.

'That takes a lot of work, lot of contacts . . . '

'Lot of guts.' LeClerc looked at her. 'Course, y'all can make excuses, take the bonus, manage Headway . . . '

'Highway.'

'Or you can make up your mind now to do what needs to be done.'

'You're very annoying,' Poppy said mutinously.

'So the Democrats are always telling me.' LeClerc inclined his head slightly.

'You're a Republican,' Poppy said, disapprovingly.

'Yes. Low taxes, low spending. Strong defence.'

'Militaristic build-up, no education spending . . . '

'Interested in politics?'

'Not really,' Poppy said. 'But I'm a Democrat. I believe in a woman's right to choose.'

'I believe in a baby's right to life,' he answered, not in the least perturbed.

'Doesn't anything faze you?' Poppy demanded.

LeClerc considered it a moment. 'Losing,' he said. 'That's why I don't do it.'

She felt a small thrill of admiration and interest. Something she hadn't had for a long time, at least it seemed like a long time. Since her last bastard musician. Crazy! LeClerc wasn't her type. He was about fifteen years older than her. And a Southern gentleman. And his hair was a military cut. There was not a rock 'n' roll bone in this guy's body.

'Don't look at me like that,' LeClerc said, softly.

'Like what?' Poppy blushed.

'You know like what, miss.'

'My name's Poppy.'

What the fuck are you doing? LeClerc asked himself. She's a child . . . all right, with those tits and that body, not a child, but come on . . . he was thirty-eight. And in politics. His staff would not like this at all. A leather-jacketed co-ed in a T-shirt with a skull on it.

'So.' He heard himself say it. He couldn't help it. 'Where are you staying in New York?'

★  ★  ★

What the blue hell am I doing? Henry LeClerc asked himself.

At that moment, he was sitting up in bed in a suite at the exclusive and, more importantly, very discreet Victrix hotel in midtown Manhattan. The reddened light of early dawn was spilling through the bay windows; his balcony, fringed in climbing roses, a fragrant spray of blossoming pink, beckoned invitingly; the immaculate Louis XIV-style furniture of the suite was covered in clothes, strewn where they had been ripped off last night; and, nestled in the white silk Pratesi sheets of his incredibly huge and comfortable bed, was a girl. A girl barely old enough to drink. A rock

338

chick, for God's sakes. And the most incredible lay he'd ever had in his life.

LeClerc found the situation disturbing.

Very disturbing.

He hardly wanted to move, because then she'd wake up. The congressman from Louisiana shook his head. Why was this bothering him?

Henry LeClerc was used to women. Even the occasional woman as young as this one. All of them achingly beautiful, too; nothing remarkable about that. LeClerc had had women throw themselves at him since he was thirteen. The only son of an old Bayou family, he had lost his father when he was twelve, which had meant that Henry had grown up master of a crumbling mansion, supporter of his mother, and sole guardian, as his white-gloved, incredibly proper mamma never failed to remind him, of the LeClerc family tradition.

He'd been forced to grow up fast, and that had given him confidence.

White Gables, his family home, was Henry's first love. It didn't die on him like his daddy, and it didn't have a never-to-be-mentioned drinking problem like his mamma. Unfortunately, the house had its own problems. The 'romantically' crumbling façade had plenty of ailments, including termites and rot from the wet, soupy Louisiana air; and while he laboured to fix them, he also had to find a way to pay off the government tax liens which threatened to take away the place his own granddaddy had been born in.

Henry LeClerc hadn't cried about it, whined about it, or even talked about it. He'd just set himself to fixin' it.

The years of struggle formed LeClerc into the most independent young man for miles, and the girls loved it. Even the bureaucrats in Balieu, Louisiana, had to respect the serious, intense young man that turned up in the County Assessor's office with a business plan. He called everybody 'sir', he wore a suit, and he argued persuasively that historic buildings should be cherished by the town of Balieu, not forced into condemnation. He wanted a deal on the tax.

'How old are you, son?' the Assessor asked.

'Fourteen, sir,' LeClerc said.

The older man didn't ask where Henry's daddy was. It was a small town, everybody knew already. Instead, he thought of his own kid, getting high all the time and growing his hair long and listening to the Stones.

He signed the papers. LeClerc kept the house.

He also got interested in the law. He needed money, so he took a job as a paralegal in Balieu. Saving his wages, he invested in the stock market. LeClerc was quiet and savvy. He put himself through law school, graduated, and became the youngest-ever partner in Davies & Polk, New Orleans's largest law firm.

Money had been his drive, his focus. And he'd made a ton of it. LeClerc drove an imported Rolls Royce, wore tailored suits, tipped his hat to ladies in the street; he was a real Southern gentleman, a relic of a bygone age.

Everybody adored him. Men wanted to drink with him — bourbon on the rocks; women wanted to marry him, or, at least, to bed him. But LeClerc had not been easy to catch. He remembered his parents' unhappy marriage from his childhood, and the idea of having somebody else messing with White Gables — it was deeply distasteful. Plus, he wanted a lady. Not a modern, go-getting, money-hungry career chick. Not somebody who'd sleep with him at the drop of a hat.

LeClerc was a big figure in Louisiana. He did pro bono work for the Historical Society; he had personally saved sixteen of the state's beautiful old mansions and estates from disrepair, graffiti, and the death tax, preserving the culture. It had been a very short hop from man-about-town to the Honorable Gentleman from Louisiana. The Republicans had recruited him, and they thought they had a star.

They were talking Senator now. An old, incumbent, yellow-dog Democrat was retiring. They had LeClerc all groomed for the slot.

He wanted it. Senator. Then Governor. Then, who knew how high Henry LeClerc could rise?

But soon the Senator-to-be, they had told him, drawing him aside in various oak-panelled club rooms thick with pungent cigar smoke, would need a wife.

Somebody pretty, feminine, ladylike and inoffensive. Somebody with a manicure and white gloves, like his mamma. A lady who would not smoke, drink, swear, or, obviously, work . . .

Poppy stirred in his bed. Her glorious, heavy breasts, firm and dusky, sprinkled with a sexy dusting of freckles, moved with her silky café-au-lait skin. The tiny gold Star of David she wore round her slender neck glittered in the morning sunlight.

A twenty-something career girl. A *Jewish* girl. And a Democrat.

What the hell had he been thinking? Well, no matter. He'd given her a roll in the hay; that wasn't exactly the same as proposing.

So why did this feel different?

Poppy opened those spectacular, wolf-blue eyes and stared up at him, and Henry LeClerc caught his breath in his throat. Goddammit, she was beautiful.

'Good morning,' he said.

'Isn't it?' Poppy replied.

Oh, shit, Henry, LeClerc thought. You're in trouble now, boy.

# 39

Poppy thought that maybe she had lost it.

Twenty-three was a little young to burn out and go crazy, but here she was, doing things that could have her certified. She had just spent practically an entire weekend in bed with a man she hardly knew, a man way too old for her, too goyishe, too right-wing. And instead of being glad to be rid of him, Poppy felt as though someone had stabbed her through the heart with a knitting needle.

All she could do was think of when she was going to see him again.

Love at first sight? She didn't believe in it. This had to be lust. She had a crush, like a teenager drooling over Axl Rose.

But Henry LeClerc had not called her. She had come home, waited. Expectantly. Then angrily. And finally, with a level of disappointment which shocked her, Poppy had stopped waiting for the call.

I'm getting over it, Poppy told herself firmly.

His rejection made her feel dirty, made her feel as if she had given up something precious, and been tricked for it; the way he'd made her body feel she'd taken for love. But it wasn't. It was no different than drunken sex in a motel with a guitarist. And that pissed her off.

She was gonna make a real effort to forget the jerk.

But business first.

Poppy was at home, in the new house she'd bought for herself, just off West Third Street, near the Beverly Center. It was tiny, set on a little side-street, with a handkerchief-sized garden of manicured green lawn and a fragrant bougainvillea bush, but it was all hers. One good-sized bedroom with a walk-in closet, a bathroom with a sit-down shower and long tub, a small, modern kitchen, and a large living room. The house was Mission-style, and she loved it. It was all hers.

She was standing in the little alcove off the living room which she had set up as a home office. She had a computer, a fax machine, a copier and a phone. The receiver was in her hand; the dial tone was buzzing.

'If you'd like to make a call,' a mechanised voice said, 'please hang up and try again. If — '

Poppy took the advice.

This was hard. Harder than she'd thought it would be. Much harder than the obvious solution it had seemed while she was draped over Congressman LeClerc's hard, muscular body, drinking in the scent of fragrant cigar smoke and the musk of his skin. His advice in New York had sparked something in her. Heady excitement, a longing to get started.

Maybe he wasn't interested in seeing her again. Poppy smarted at the insult. But she also knew that she was going to follow LeClerc's advice. He might be a jerk, but he had at least left her with one thing: this plan.

Her own firm. Her own acts. Her own rules. Poppy didn't want to be a number two woman, one of the myriad loyal female executives that littered Los Angeles, highly paid wage slaves without any real power. The back-up. The lieutenant.

Joel Stein had made it clear he wasn't sharing the limelight with Poppy or anybody.

So why was this so hard?

Poppy knew the answer. Because Joel was right. People hadn't taken *her* calls, they'd taken Dream's calls. And she was twenty-three years old right now. The same age, or younger, as the people she wanted to represent. Joel had sworn she'd be nothing without him, and Poppy was afraid he might be right.

It didn't matter. She didn't have a choice.

Poppy picked up the phone again, and this time she dialled the number.

'Dream Management.'

'Yeah, it's Poppy,' she said. 'Is Joel in?'

★ ★ ★

'You have to understand — '

'I don't have to understand shit,' Stein said, nastily. At least he'd stopped screaming. 'Your stuff is already in the garbage out back, Allen. Just like your career. You know how many goddam ungrateful brats come through the record industry every year, think they know better than the guys who find them, train them? One good year with one of *my* acts and you think you're fucking Yoda. You're just a kid. A stupid kid. Unless you find some mogul to screw, you'll never get another job. Believe me.'

'So, no use in coming to you for a reference then?' Poppy joked, although she was feeling queasy.

'Go fuck yourself,' Joel snarled, and hung up on her.

Poppy replaced the phone. Her hands were shaking. She had once thought how much she'd hate to be on the wrong side of the desk from Joel Stein.

Whatever. Feel the fear and do it anyway.

She called her bank and checked her balance over the phone. Twenty-five thousand, four hundred dollars. Not a whole bunch of money when you needed to start a new business. Plus, she had no college degree, no job she could use to get employed. There was her parents' money, of course, but Poppy wasn't going to touch that.

No, this had to be all her.

She refused to be cowed. Everything would be OK. She even had a name for the new business: Opium, Inc.

It was sinful and rebellious. Just like rock 'n' roll. Poppy loved it. She had gone to a cheap business-card place and picked out her own logo: a stock image of a

344

red poppy, with 'Opium Management' underneath it in blood-red letters, and 'Poppy Allen — President' in black.

She put a few business cards in her wallet and got ready to go to work.

* * *

Man, it was depressing!

Poppy went to club after club, gig after gig. The first thing she needed was an act to manage. But there was nothing out there.

She began to have the sick feeling that Silver Bullet had indeed been a fluke. What a parade of losers! Lipstick-wearing poison clones with thinning hair and thinner songs. Thrash-metal acts who obviously believed that speed and volume were all it took to make it; never mind about a tune. About a hundred Guns n' Roses copy acts; one girl band who managed to get called back for an encore only by flashing their plastic tits at the crowd.

Not one band who had a song she could recall three seconds after they'd stopped playing it.

Poppy started to have a new-found respect for A & R men. Musicians liked to call the industry the enemy, but the enemy was the lack of talent out there. Nobody seemed to get it, that this was all about tunes.

Poppy wanted to shake them all, the junked-out denizens of the Sunset Strip with their rock 'n' roll dreams, and scream, *It's all about the tunes!*

Look at thrash. Only one band had survived out of the entire genre, only one act was still making money: Metallica. And that was because every headbanger in the world knew Metallica's tunes by heart. Sometimes, when that band played, the crowd was so loud singing the songs that the group was almost irrelevant. Slayer, Anthrax and Megadeth would never be able to match that. Ever. All the other bands had three or four hit songs at the most.

Poppy was desperate. She had to do this. It was her joy, her bliss. What she wanted in life. But she couldn't invent talent where none was to be found.

★ ★ ★

She found the answer in a way she had never expected.

'What you fixin' to get, honey?'

Poppy looked at the waitress hungrily. The girl was a Texan, in her late thirties now, but still with the body of a cheerleader and big, teased blonde hair.

She was sitting in a late-night Southern restaurant, a cheap place off Melrose. It served big steaks and lots of chilli; generally, the kind of artery-busting cuisine she liked to stay away from.

But she had come in here just to hear a Southern twang. Poppy was Jonesing on Congressman LeClerc. He wasn't calling, and she'd headed to this place to stew in her memories. Was she nuts? Eating in a dump like this just to remind herself of some salt-and-pepper-haired politician with a fancy suit?

'Barbecue spare ribs,' she said, 'Jack Daniel's and a Diet Coke.'

She handed over her ID; in LA they checked thirty-year-olds.

'Comin' right up, sugar,' the cheerleader said.

Poppy was suddenly starving. She hadn't eaten since a low-fat Yoplait at lunchtime, and that was no kind of fuel for a depressing trip around LA's dank nightspots, listening to band after band and singer after singer that stunk. The burgers and steaks were sizzling in the kitchen, and they smelled good.

She missed LeClerc.

Of course, she wasn't going to call him.

'Here you go, honey.' The girl put what looked like a

bucket of JD and coke in front of Poppy. 'Food'll be right along in just a second now.'

She disappeared, and Poppy took a relaxing sip.

'Good evening, Los Angeles,' said a voice.

Poppy spluttered with dismay. Oh God. A mike was set up in a little stage area right out front. She'd come in here to get away from acts that sucked. Now she was trapped with some diner crooner. She looked around for the waitress, wanting to cancel her order and get the hell out, just go home.

But the girl was nowhere in sight. Poppy drooped visibly. She felt defeated.

'Got a couple new ones for y'all tonight,' the voice said. It was male and husky, with that rich country twang she thought was so sexy. 'My name's Travis Jackson.'

And then he started to sing . . .

' . . . Blue . . . I can't stand the thought, another day . . . '

The song was a lament. His voice was soft, heartbroken, exquisite, like the strings of a bluegrass guitar, or a wail of Patsy Cline. Poppy glanced around, her food and booze forgotten. Couples had stopped eating; women had tears in their eyes. A lot of hand-holding was suddenly going on.

She focused on Travis Jackson. He wore beat-up, faded blue jeans, cowboy boots, a plaid shirt, and a bandanna. The shirt had short sleeves; the boy was muscled, and covered in tattoos. He had a smattering of silky black hair visible at his collar, a square jaw, and five o'clock shadow. Plus a way of looking at women that made them melt inside.

Poppy felt her heart thud.

She was staring at Travis. He locked eyes on her, sang right to her. Gave her a wink.

Poppy felt her heart flutter.

But that was right where she kept her wallet.

She beckoned the waitress over.

'What's his story?'

'Cute, ain't he?' The woman leaned low. 'But honey, trust me — you'll have to take a number and stand in line. We got women come eat here every day just to be in a room with him.' Her blue-lined lids took in Poppy's youth and slim figure in that Azzedine Alaia dress. 'Hmm, but you got a shot, though.'

Poppy scrawled her number on a piece of paper and gave it to the woman in a twenty.

'I really want to speak to him,' she said. 'Like, really. Give him the number, OK?'

'Sure thing, sugar,' said the waitress, eyes widening at the tip.

Poppy threw some more money on the table to cover the bill, then stood up, leaning forwards so Travis would get a good look at her breasts. He continued singing, with that angelic voice, but he'd got a devilish look in his eyes.

Poppy blew him a kiss and headed towards the door. The waitress grabbed her sleeve.

'One thing, honey, lemme warn ya. You're from Cali. You gotta know, these Southern boys . . . they look real good and they sound real good. But they'll break your heart.'

Poppy looked and saw the woman was talking from experience.

'I'll be careful,' she said.

She took one final look at Travis Jackson. But she was thinking about Henry LeClerc.

★   ★   ★

Poppy went home, washed her hair, and carefully selected an outfit. It had to say money and class and record-industry nous. She picked out black Levis, Manolo Blahnik strappy heels, a Green Dragon roadcrew shirt, and an Armani black leather jacket. She made up in neutral tones, designed to make herself look gorgeous and sophisticated, but still young. There would be no point at all in trying to pretend she was something she wasn't.

The phone rang at eleven-thirty. Poppy had no illusions; she was a hot chick, one of the hottest. She'd known he wanted her.

'Who's this?' Poppy asked.

'You know who it is, ma'am.'

Damn, you *are* sexy, Poppy thought. Total confidence; the guy acted like he was the prize here and she was the huntress. Which was truer than he knew.

'Travis,' she said, breathily.

The smile in his voice was almost visible down the phone line. 'Mm-hmm. And what's your name, sugar?'

'Poppy Allen,' Poppy said.

'Now ain't that about right? Cause you're just as pretty as a flower.'

Lord Almighty, Poppy thought, with an adrenaline rush of excitement, the man was perfect. He was a babe, he was talented, he had songs, and he was a pussy hound. And if anything sold records to men and to women, it was a guy that liked to fuck. Indelicate, yeah, but the way it was.

Girls wet their panties for guys who liked women. It was always the bad-boy womaniser they went for. It had been that way since Errol Flynn, or Elvis Presley.

'I'd love to meet you for a cup of coffee,' Poppy said. 'If you have the time.'

'I always have the time for a girl as pretty as you,' Jackson answered. 'Where you at, sugar?'

'Third Street.'

'You know the Rattlesnake Bar?'

'Yeah.' The Rattlesnake was a few blocks away; a dimly lit, cheap-but-charming little bar, decorated in a Southwestern theme. Poppy was duly impressed. The guy probably had a romantic hang-out in every part of town.

'I'll see you there in twenty minutes, honey.'

'Can't wait,' Poppy said truthfully.

★ ★ ★

He was sitting up at the bar when she got there, nursing a beer and looking as masculine as a walking Y chromosome. The beach babes were staring at him, heads together, giggling in their little groups.

Travis stood up and touched the brim of his stetson. Out of the corner of her eye, Poppy saw the girls swooning.

'Jack,' he turned to the guy behind the bar, 'get us a table, would ya?'

'You got it, dude,' the man said, and led them into a booth for two right at the back, nice and secluded.

'Regular?' Poppy asked.

'They know me here,' Travis admitted. He grinned that bone-melting grin. 'Glad you could make it. You're a fine-lookin' young lady. You know that, right?'

Poppy grinned back. 'So I'm told. And you seem to have the votes in from the female contingent.' She stuck her tongue out at a table of long-haired blondes who were fluttering their eyelashes at Travis, and they hastily looked away.

He laughed. 'Cute. You the jealous type, baby?'

'Actually, not at all,' Poppy said. She took a deep breath; she had to be six years younger than this guy. 'I have a proposition for you, and it's not to do with sex.'

'How disappointing,' Travis said.

'I'm interested in your music. I want you to hear me out. My name's Poppy Allen, and I want to manage you.'

He stared at her a second, then burst out laughing.

'Who, sugar? You? You don't look old enough to get a

beer without givin' the waiter a kiss.'

Poppy nodded quickly. 'Hear me out, OK? If you don't want to know, I'll buy you that beer and leave you to your fan club.'

He smiled, but it was just polite. She could see he wanted to call a halt to the conversation. So she ploughed on.

'I found Silver Bullet. You've heard of them?'

'The rock band.'

'That's right. I signed them to Joel Stein at Dream Management. Then I was a tour accountant on the Green Dragon tour, saved that act a bundle.' She opened her purse, pulled out her tour laminates and tossed them to Travis. 'When I got back, they handed me Silver Bullet. The girls didn't even have a label, nothing. I signed them to a record deal, I set up the showcase, I changed their look, I designed the set. Just last month, they hit number one and had the cover of *Rolling Stone*, and Joel Stein, my boss at Dream, told me he was taking over the act.'

'So what did you do?' Jackson asked.

'I quit,' Poppy said simply. 'And I started my own company. I want to manage you.'

'I dunno,' Travis said. 'I ain't a rock act, hon.'

'Doesn't matter. You've got songs. You've got the voice. You play cool. And you're hot enough to fry eggs on.'

His grin turned rueful.

'I wish the record company folks thought like you do.'

'They will,' Poppy said, confidently. 'If you give me a shot. Look, I'll be right upfront — Dream's a big company, and everybody wants to take their calls. And I'm just one person. But people know me. I can get you seen. Sign a six-month contract with me. After that' — she shrugged — 'if you want to split, I won't stop you.'

He took a swig of his beer, thinking about it.

351

'Get you folks something?' said a waitress, brightly.

'Jack and Diet Coke,' Poppy said. Maybe this evening she'd get to finish one.

'Are you two staying for dinner?' the woman asked, perkily.

Travis tipped his beer towards Poppy.

'Yes, ma'am,' he said. 'We are.'

★ ★ ★

'I want to know how long you've been out there,' Poppy asked.

He sighed. 'Try eight years. I guess I'm just a damn fool. Been doin' this since I was a kid. Getting that restaurant gig is about the best job I've ever had. Tips are good, and they feed you for free, and let me use the washroom in the back. They got an old shower there, place was an apartment once, I guess.'

'A shower? Why don't you do that at your place?'

'Honey, my place is the back of my banged-up old Chevy, outside,' Travis said. 'Or whichever lovely lady I happen to be crashin' with that night.'

'Well, the first thing I'll do for you is rent you an apartment. Six months, rent-free to you unless we get a record deal. If you'll sign.'

She held her breath.

'Miss,' Travis Jackson said, 'I'm all out of options. I was gonna sign with you anyway.' He stuck out his hand. 'Partner.'

# 40

'Not interested,' Clayton Roberts said. He pushed back his chair, to indicate the meeting was over.

Poppy didn't move. 'Excuse me? You were all over me when I worked at Dream. Remember? You said anything Silver Bullet needed . . . '

The banker smirked. 'Anything *Silver Bullet* needed, yes. I deal with multi-platinum acts, baby.'

'Ms Allen,' Poppy said, acidly.

He grinned at her lazily. 'Whatever.'

'I have a new act,' Poppy began again. 'Somebody I'm very excited about. I have experience — '

He chuckled. 'You're twenty-three.'

'I still have years of experience. Rock music is a young person's game.'

'Baby,' the banker said, being deliberately insulting, 'you're a fiery young chick, but you're too young for me to write a loan to, and you've got no capital.'

'What are you talking about? I own my own house.'

'Not interested,' Roberts told her.

Poppy finally stood up, defeated. 'You're going to want to do business with me some day, Clayton. And it'll be too late then.'

'Yeah . . . sure, honey.' He opened the door for her. 'Have a nice day.'

Poppy walked out on to the sunlit expanse of Wilshire Boulevard, a red mist of rage seething in front of her eyes. Fuck him. Son of a bitch . . .

Clayton Roberts wasn't the first banker to turn her down, just the most insulting. Just one of the guys who'd liked to press the flesh at record company junkets last year. The music business had its own bankers, guys that looked after the private accounts of rock stars and moguls, managers and promoters. They understood the needs of the industry, the way things worked.

And how they'd all sucked up to Poppy last year, when she was a prized lieutenant at Dream!

And how quickly they'd told her to get lost this week! A real lesson.

Well, no matter, Poppy told herself. She was learning, and she was doing it fast.

She found a cheap studio apartment near her own, in the Park la Brea complex. Only $850 a month, and it came furnished. The complex was a nice one, Travis's rental even came with access to a gym and a pool. That was important; she wanted him to keep lean, keep hot.

He was grateful, but gave Poppy the sense he'd be almost as happy crashing in the Chevy. All Travis was interested in was getting a deal.

Poppy wondered if Joel Stein had made some calls, tried to spike her before she started. Yeah, she thought, as she headed into Starbucks for a bagel and some caffeine, maybe he had.

She needed to think laterally. Take Travis where people could understand his talent, not some place Joel Stein could stop him even getting heard.

LA and New York were the places all the acts got signed, and Nashville for country music acts. However, the A & R men who scouted new talent were bombarded in those cities. They were invited to a million showcases each night, and blew off 99 per cent of them. Unless you were a big manager, like Joel Stein, it took months of pleading to get ten seconds of a junior scout's time.

She did not want to go that route. Travis Jackson was Poppy's first act, and you only got one chance to make a first impression.

Poppy sipped her walnut mocha and pondered. It would come to her. It always did.

★　★　★

'Are you sure this is a good idea? I mean, Chicago?'

Jackson looked warily out of his window seat at the concrete forest of Chicago glittering below him.

'We're almost there,' Poppy said reassuringly.

He snorted. 'Like I care.'

But Poppy could see he was nervous, fidgeting in his seat, checking his watch, his strong hands gripping the armrests whenever there was turbulence.

'I guess you're more comfortable on a horse?'

Travis's face softened. 'God's own mode of transportation, ma'am.'

'You really are a country boy.'

'And this is the city,' Travis said with disdain. 'It looks real grimy and dirty. And nobody big is here, record company wise . . . '

'That's the whole point,' Poppy said.

He raised a brow. 'It's your dime, honey. I hope you ain't throwing it away.'

Poppy thought about the cost of two round trips to Chicago with four nights in a hotel, separate rooms.

She hoped so too.

★　★　★

Poppy set up the showcase at Zadar's. The club was downtown, and it was a rock fixture. Metal-heads loved it; every inch of wall was covered with graffiti. It specialised in punk rock and hardcore thrash metal.

Dispirited A & R scouts were here every night, looking for something, anything, to justify their low-level salaries. They usually stayed for less than one song. That was all it took to establish that yeah, yet another act was up on stage and in the middle of a royal suck-fest. Chicago had even less talent than LA or New York.

Poppy wanted to do what Travis had done to her; shock them out of their complacency.

She called every scout in town.

'Yeah, hi, this is Poppy Allen, calling from LA. I think I met you last year on the Monsters of Rock tour, when I was working with Silver Bullet? No? Maybe when I was on the Green Dragon tour? Well, anyway, I got something for you. Tonight, and tomorrow night, at Zadar's. Limited crowd.'

And the hooked rep would always ask, 'What is it?'

Poppy said mysteriously, 'It's something different. I got Warner's coming, CBS, RCA, Atlantic, shall I put you down?'

'Sure,' they'd answer.

It was a small white lie, the kind they told every day in this business. In New York or LA it might not have worked. In Chicago, they had nothing better to do.

★   ★   ★

Travis performed on a chair, with his guitar plugged in. No lights, no Silver Bullet-style pyrotechnics. Poppy knew he didn't need any of that crap.

Before the end of the set, she was clutching a bunch of business cards.

The second night, the audience was bigger. There were the original scouts, and now their bosses, who had taken the shuttle from New York city. Poppy grinned. The old flies-on-shit principle; they all saw the other big boys there, and now they were fighting for a piece.

She signed Travis Jackson to a three-album deal with Musica Records at twelve midnight on the third night they were in Chicago. When they flew home, Poppy upgraded to first class.

Travis was going to be a star, she told him, and the star treatment started now.

Congressman Henry LeClerc sat at the dinner table and tried to concentrate. His spin doctors were giving him good news, after all; his opponent's numbers were crumbling . . .

'Sixteen points since August, Henry.'

'Nobody likes her stand on defence. She actually said our troops were overpaid.'

'Henry, I think we got her, I really do. Her campaign team's in a real scrabble for funding. They just took a big donation from TexOil, so they must be desperate.'

'Uh-huh,' LeClerc said absently.

He was eating with the Three Stooges, as he liked to term them. Keith Flynn, Jacob Harvey and Tim Greenwood. They ran the polls, they interpreted the numbers, they formulated 'media response'.

Apparently, his campaign for Senate was off to a good start.

But LeClerc wasn't interested. He was thinking about Poppy Allen. He'd been thinking about Poppy Allen for six months.

He didn't understand it.

She had been a great piece of ass. Even sensational. But so what? Lots of women were great in bed. Henry thought that there were no bad lays, only bad lovers. Any woman could be turned into a scratching, moaning animal. It just took the right man to do it.

He was confident, even arrogant — but he could back it up.

LeClerc loved women. He didn't even have a type. He liked short, curvy girls and lean, aristocratic beanpoles. If they were smart and passionate, that was for him. He had even been known to date plain women, because often they turned out to be the hottest between the sheets; sobbing and bucking and clutching.

Best of all was dating a woman that hated him. A

political rival, say. Seducing her, then forcing her into wild and ecstatic submission after hours of careful love-making. LeClerc enjoyed teasing a woman. Most men could not be bothered with foreplay, then wondered why their girls lay there inert as tapioca pudding. He liked to stroke, and kiss, and lick, and pin down with one hand, until they were aching for him.

Poppy had been amazing, but weren't they all amazing? Smart, but he only dated smart women. Beautiful . . . but . . .

He was crazy. Losing it for some tween. Wasn't that what they called the twenty-somethings these days? Teens and tweens.

The most utterly ridiculous thing of all was that when he tried to compare her to his other women, he felt odd. Not right. Like one of his most enjoyable leisure-time pursuits was actually a little seedy.

He wasn't so much thinking of fucking Poppy Allen again as of talking to her. Damn it, she *had* been interesting, when most everybody was boring. She had some kind of life in her little sub-culture. Henry LeClerc liked Mozart; Metallica to him might be from outer space. But he'd enjoyed her passion. Her fire. Her raw ambition.

'You know what would really help, Henry? Port?'

'Yes, thank you,' he said.

They poured the Cockburn's reserve into his small glass.

'A lady. Somebody we can introduce as your wife.'

'Even fiancée would be good.'

'But make sure she's suitable. She has to be suitable, Henry. Nobody with a past.'

LeClerc paused and nodded.

'I hear you.'

But it was no good. He had to meet her again. To talk to her, to see her. It was an obsession. Once he physically saw Poppy, she'd stop being this young goddess, and he could get on with his life again.

'I have to go, gentlemen,' he said.

He would find out a little more about Poppy Allen. Maybe go see her, have one more round.

Just to get her out of his system.

# 41

Six months had changed Daisy's life. Her book was a success. Royalties were pouring in, and Artemis wanted to extend her contract. Ted Elliott renegotiated the advance. Daisy was now earning six figures instead of five.

She decided to do something special with her money.

★ ★ ★

'I've got a present for you,' Daisy said. 'Get in.'

'Darling,' her mother said, 'this is so silly, you don't need to buy us any more presents.'

'Just humour me,' Daisy pleaded.

'All right,' her father said, sighing.

Daisy had made them both wear blindfolds. Her parents got awkwardly into the back of Daisy's new car. It was a gleaming racing-green Bentley, drove as smooth as silk and handled like thistledown.

*The Lemon Grove* had been a runaway bestseller. Daisy was up to nearly a million sales in paperback. Suddenly, she had a fleet of advisers around her: a specialist accountant, a stockbroker, a money manager. She had bought a loft-style modern flat, the penthouse of a new development in Camden; she had a wardrobe full of Joseph and Prada and Armani; she had membership of all the hot clubs in London — the Groucho, Soho House, you name it.

And Daisy loved it. Her whirlwind of promotion, book-signings, and sales conferences had hardly stopped long enough for her to start work on the sequel. Money and success were transforming her life, and it was very sweet.

This morning, though, would be the sweetest moment of all.

Daisy hit the accelerator and drove like Nigel Mansell through the leafy Sussex roads, the narrow, twisting lanes overhung with trees so that light made dappled shadows under the emerald leaves, glowing in the sun. She felt giddy with pleasure. If there was one thing she had wanted to do for her parents this was it.

'How much longer, Daisy?' her father demanded.

She turned the steering wheel and crunched on to the familiar gravel path to the left.

'We're here. Now no touching the blindfold until I get you out of the car.'

Daisy got out, opened the car door, and helped her parents out, standing them in the drive facing the house. Then she walked behind them and pulled off the blindfolds.

'Ta-da,' Daisy announced.

They were standing in front of their old house. Two brand new Mercedes were neatly parked in the garage by the gnarled apple tree; red for her father, silver for her mother.

'I don't understand,' Mrs Markham said unsteadily. But her father did. 'Oh, Daisy,' he murmured, and stumbled against the car.

'I had to pay them an extra ten thou to get out,' Daisy said, 'and they painted the den orange so you'll have to take care of that, but it's all yours. Actually, it's in a family trust, so you couldn't give it away to the bank even if you wanted to.'

Her mother burst into tears.

That, Daisy thought when she got home, had been one of the high points of her life. The toys, the fame, it was all very well, but it was also ephemeral. Doing something nice for her mother and father had meant something.

So why was she suddenly feeling so down?

Her flat was immaculate; the maid came on Wednesdays. Daisy had chosen a colour scheme in oyster-white. She kicked off her shoes and padded across the soft, springy carpet to the cream couch, curling up on it in front of one of her floor-to-ceiling windows with a spectacular view of the London skyline. The last moments of sunset were fading from the sky; dying streaks of orange against a deep-blue background. The serenity of twilight was rather sad, Daisy thought. Her apartment had soundproofing; there was no drone of traffic to disturb her, nothing but the neon street lights and the orange and yellow of the cars on the road below, a constant river of artificial light. A low silver bowl was crammed with the heads of ivory roses, and the air inside her apartment was fragrant with the blossoms.

Daisy's usual routine was to open a bottle of chilled white wine, pour herself a glass, and switch on the Macintosh to do some writing. She was almost done with her chapter plan for *The Orange Blossom*, her next book, but tonight, she wasn't interested.

She wanted to cry. Why? Why was that? Everything in her life was perfect. This was ridiculous.

Daisy picked up her copy of *Hello!* magazine and started to flick through it. Nothing like a series of mindless puff pieces to distract her.

And then there they were, on page two. Not featured, of course, Edward would never have allowed that; just pictured as guests at the wedding of some young earl and the lucky American model about to become his countess.

'Mr and Mrs Edward Powers,' said the caption. Edward, resplendent in a morning suit; had he even put on a little weight, Daisy wondered? But it was Edwina she couldn't take her eyes off.

Daisy had, thank God, been in America when Edward had got married. She had sent him a gift and a card, a lovely set of Pratesi sheets. He'd written to thank her and to invite her up to his house in the country, but Daisy hadn't seen Edward since the day she left Oxford.

More importantly, she still had never seen Edwina, until now. What do you know? Daisy thought dispassionately. The woman's not horsey at all. She's stunning.

Edwina Powers had long blonde hair, an aristocratic nose, blue eyes, and no curves to speak of. She was the epitome of cold, patrician beauty, miles away from Daisy's hot peasant curves. She kind of looked like Gwyneth Paltrow. With the equally skinny Edward, they made an ideal couple.

Daisy breathed in. Her heart had sped up violently. She felt dizzy, almost like a panic attack. She dropped the magazine on to the carpet, and felt a hot tear trickle down her cheek.

Oh God, oh God. She was still in love with him.

★　★　★

She woke early after a sleepless night and stumbled into her bathroom. It was large, like the bathroom in a good hotel, with a snowy marble floor, heated towel rails, a jacuzzi, and plenty of Diptych scented candles ranged around the tub, but that wasn't going to help her achieve serenity this morning.

Daisy needed to see him. Edward. With a wedding ring on. After all, if you were away from someone for a good length of time you started to idealise them. Edward Powers was just on some kind of mental pedestal.

Daisy climbed into her stand-alone shower, lined with blue enamel tiles splashed with gold daisies, a whimsical notion of her designer's. More importantly, the shower had three heads that pummelled and massaged her back. Jets of hot water blasted away her sluggishness, and she washed her hair carefully with John Frieda and soaped herself down with L'Occitane lavender bath and shower gel. After she had swathed herself in fluffy white towels, blasted her hair dry, and pulled on some of her best clothes, she felt a little better, but not much.

For one thing, there were dark circles under her eyes that no amount of Touche Eclat could wipe out; her eyes were bloodshot, and her skin felt dry with stress. But no matter. She still had to see Edward.

Daisy dug out her Wayfarers and put them on. Yeah, much better. She was wearing a long, figure-hugging Katherine Hamnett skirt in dark-blue velvet and a white silk shirt, and she teamed it with a strand of platinum-blue Akoya pearls she'd picked up in Manhattan, light, sheer make-up, and a spritz of Amarige on her wrists.

She was beautiful. More beautiful than Edwina? Probably not. Certainly not so bloody well-bred. Daisy inventoried her outrageous curves: her butt was firm and tight, but it still stuck out there, no question . . . and her breasts, well, at least she was no longer trying to hide them. She had a trim enough waist, her thighs were strong but not stocky, and her arms were toned. Daisy considered her hair and skin critically. Olive-ish, with rich, dark locks . . . And those wolf-blue eyes, hidden away behind the glasses . . .

I wonder, she thought suddenly, who my real parents were.

But she didn't dwell on it. Her real parents lived in Sussex. Still, she bet her birth mother had had good genes . . .

Daisy went to the phone and dialled Edward's home number. It was disconcerting that she still knew it by heart.

A woman answered.

'Hello?'

Daisy's heart hammered. Edwina. Speaking to her,

she struggled to sound calm.

'Hello, is that Edwina?'

'Yes, it is. Who's this?'

'Hi, Edwina, this is Daisy Markham,' Daisy said, smoothly enough. 'I was a friend of Edward's at Oxford.'

'Daisy Markham! Of course. The famous novelist, how exciting. Edward's just in the garden, hang on a mo, I'll get him for you . . . '

There was a pause. Daisy's knuckles were white around the receiver. She thought she could yank it from its socket at any minute. Edwina hadn't been a bitch, or nasty . . .

Daisy was almost faint with jealousy.

'Daisy!' Edward's voice came on the line, warm with pleasure. 'How good to hear from you.'

'It's been a long time,' Daisy agreed. 'I meant to get in touch, but I've been so busy.'

'Of course you have, tremendously exciting. You've done splendidly.'

'I thought perhaps we could meet up for a drink.'

'Love to. When?'

'Today?'

Edward called out, 'Darling . . . ' and she heard him cup the receiver. Then he came back on. 'Wina can't make today, how about tomorrow?'

'I'm leaving on a trip tomorrow,' Daisy lied. 'How about just you, can I see you today? I'd love to catch up.'

There was a pause. She held her breath. Then he came back. 'Three-thirty suit? At the club?'

'Fine.' Daisy was giddy with relief. 'I know it, near Charing Cross. See you there.'

★ ★ ★

The Jugglers was just the sort of thing Daisy associated with Edward Powers. It was gentlemanly, discreet,

365

tucked away, and very, very luxurious. The club was housed inside an old Georgian townhouse in the heart of Covent Garden, with a courtyard full of Rolls Royces and Aston Martins, a guard at a gatehouse, and a splendid wrought-iron fence. There was a blue ceramic plaque outside the front entrance that said Disraeli had once lived in the house. When she stepped into reception, she saw that there was a stone floor and a wooden board on which were the names of members of the club who had died in the Second World War.

'Can I help you, madam?'

A uniformed receptionist smiled impersonally at her. Daisy smiled back. 'I'm meeting a Mr Edward Powers.'

'Ah yes, Mr Powers. Of course, madam. He's waiting for you in the Drawing Room. If you just walk down the corridor it's the third room on the left.'

The Drawing Room was hung with red fabric wallpaper and lined with what looked like original Regency chairs, chaise-longues and sofas. Hung around the walls were solemn oil portraits, all of men, and men in suits, with just one or two women, were sitting around at little tables, drinking, smoking cigars, and talking in a muted hush.

Daisy scanned the place. Yes, there he was. Tall as a long drink of water, as the Americans said, and in his usual three-piece suit. He was occupying an ancient burgundy leather armchair, comfortably broken in by hundreds of similar men, she had no doubt.

Edward saw her and shot to his feet. He came over, smiling broadly, and shook her hand warmly.

'Daisy, splendid to see you, splendid.'

'Hi, Edward,' Daisy said, kissing him on the cheek. Did he blush a bit? Behind the dark glasses she couldn't tell.

'Come and sit down.' He led her back over to the burgundy chair and waited until she had settled in a skinny mahogany chair covered in nineteenth-century gold silk before taking a seat himself.

'Something to drink, madam?'

A waiter had materialised silently. 'A cup of tea would be lovely. Lapsang, if you have it.'

'Of course, madam.'

'It's so good to see you,' Edward said. His eyes flickered over her. 'But you've lost too much weight, Daisy. Any skinnier and you'll go down the plughole next time you have a bath.'

'You can talk,' Daisy said, and felt some of the tension drain out of her. It was just as though she'd last seen him yesterday. She was so relaxed, so comfortable with Edward. She felt that it was fate, and nothing should keep them apart, especially not some inconvenient little marriage . . .

'I'm upset you have to leave. I can't wait for you to meet Wina. You'll love her, she's such a doll.'

'You call her Wina?' Daisy asked numbly.

Pet names! She couldn't bear it.

'Edward and Edwina was a bit much.' Still is, Daisy thought. 'But tell me, how is fame and fortune? Of course, I always knew it was a matter of time,' he added politely.

'Splendid,' Daisy said brightly. 'I do enjoy it. I bought my parents their old house back.'

'But that's wonderful,' Edward said, with genuine enthusiasm and warmth. 'What an amazing thing to be able to do.'

The waiter arrived with her tea and poured it out into a bone-china cup. The whole scene was so civilised, so restrained. Daisy longed to take the delicate vessel and smash it against one of the gloomy portraits and shake Edward by his bony shoulders. Didn't he see? Didn't he see? This *had* to be a mistake, she was sure of it.

'It truly was,' she said. 'But never mind about me. Books and publishing is very boring. Tell me all about you and Wina. You married very quickly, Edward, I was a bit surprised.'

'Well so was I, rather.' He shrugged. 'But once you meet somebody who's the right person, you want to get on with it. I daresay I'd have proposed to you had you given me the slightest encouragement.' He laughed cheerfully.

Daisy started to burn. Her cheeks reddened. 'Well, don't you think people can change? That you shouldn't rush into things? I know I've changed, for one.'

He ignored her implication. Deliberately, or did he just not get it? 'I don't think you've changed a bit, old bean.'

'I have,' Daisy said mulishly.

'Yes, you've got far too thin. But Wina and I just clicked. She likes all the same things, we have similar backgrounds, ambitions, she's a Catholic, and she's a very pretty girl. What she's doing with an old stick like me I have no idea. But we're extremely happy. Newly-weds, I suppose,' he said, charmingly bashful.

'I see,' Daisy said, forcing a smile. 'Well, that's wonderful. What does Wina do?'

'Do? Keeps house for me. Gives the menu to the cook. You know. Ah. You mean work. Well, she doesn't. We're quite well-off, and I prefer having her around, so there's no need for her to work.'

'I never thought of you as trying to keep women down,' Daisy said.

'Good God, nobody could keep Wina down.' The way he talked about her, Daisy thought, it was like he had a smile in his voice. 'If she wanted to do something, I shouldn't give a damn, but she doesn't, and we don't need the cash, so I suppose there's no point.'

'I suppose not,' Daisy was forced to agree. There was a lump in her throat, but she forced it back with a scalding gulp of Lapsang.

Change the subject, change the subject, Daisy

thought. 'And do you see many people from Oxford?'

They talked about nothing for twenty minutes, until Daisy thought she could decently leave.

'Well, lovely to see you again,' Daisy said. She didn't kiss him on the cheek this time, just shook his hand.

'And you. Where are you off to?'

She looked blank, then remembered her excuse. 'Oh, New York. I'm going to do some shopping.'

'Have fun. And you must come down to meet Wina soon. You'll probably have to come down to the country, because she won't be doing too much travelling.'

'Why's that? Is she a country person?' Daisy made herself ask.

'Very much so,' Edward said. 'Rather like me, in fact.'

★   ★   ★

Daisy was proud of herself. She managed to flag down a taxi and make it all the way back to North London, and into her own flat, before she burst into tears.

Edward was happily married. And he would never, never be hers.

But she wouldn't accept it. No way. Hadn't he said he might have proposed to her? Edward had been the one, at Oxford, who had loved her for herself, made her feel like she wasn't just fat Daisy, that she was worth something. Edward had tried to steer her right when Brad got married; Edward had looked after her when she lost her flat; Edward was her protector and her ideal and her destiny . . .

Anything could happen, still! There had to be a way round it. This situation was all wrong!

She couldn't face talking to her editor tomorrow, couldn't face her parents, couldn't face even being in the same country as Edward. The pain was too fresh. Well, she'd told him she was going away, hadn't she?

New York? Why the fuck not, Daisy thought. I *do* work, and I'm rich. Sod it.

She dialled up her travel agent. In ten minutes, she had booked herself on a first-class flight to JFK, leaving at eight the next morning.

# 42

The plane banked and dipped towards Manhattan. Daisy looked out of her window; the city glittered in the warm afternoon sunlight. She had been sitting here for six hours, but it hadn't been a bad flight, and, if anything, she felt energised. It was good to get out of London.

'May I take that for you, ma'am?' said the steward, giving her a warm All-American smile.

Daisy handed over her last crystal split of champagne. 'Sure.' She didn't drink much on flights, because it dried out her skin, but she liked to have a couple of glasses just before landing; a celebration.

'Meeting anybody special?' he asked.

Daisy thought about it. 'Maybe,' she said.

★   ★   ★

It was strange to be here and have no plans. She had booked a suite at the Victrix, supposedly the most glorious hotel in a city which specialised in glorious hotels.

It didn't disappoint. A towering Art Deco building, the hotel commanded a splendid view of Central Park, and when Daisy had checked in, wandering through an exquisite lobby with marble pillars, fountains, and topiary hedges, her bags were already laid out neatly by her four-poster by the time her elevator arrived at the twenty-third floor. She had a set of huge bay windows that overlooked the sun, only now sinking down behind the lush green trees of the park, and looking towards the skyline of upper Manhattan; she had an Aubusson rug, Regency-style furniture, a bath big enough to swim in, a working fireplace, and enough fax machines to run a business empire.

Daisy picked up a ripe, scented nectarine from the complimentary bowl of organic fruit and took a bite. It was delicious, exactly as she had expected.

Well, if she was planning on getting over Edward Powers, this was the place to do it.

Daisy padded into her marble-lined bathroom to shower. The free shampoo was from Bumble & Bumble, the skincare lotions from Clarins. Very nice. It would certainly do to wash away the dust of travelling and set her up for an evening out.

So what if I don't know anybody, Daisy thought defiantly. This was the Nineties. A single girl could go out by herself and not be embarrassed about it. She would call the concierge. In a place like this, they'd have some suggestions.

★　★　★

She knew as soon as she sat down in the bar that every man in the place was looking at her.

All the magazines said that New York was a nightmare; one single man for every five single women, with desperate divorcees and ring-hungry debs all competing for the same small pool of smug commitment-phobes.

Didn't bother Daisy. Her heart had already been broken, so what was the point in guarding it any further? She knew she looked good, and she had her own money. If they like me, great, if they don't, great, Daisy told herself, selecting a stool right in the centre of the bar.

She was at Le Spinasse, an extremely expensive midtown restaurant, decorated like Versailles and almost as costly. Appetisers were twenty bucks here and a glass of wine about the same. Well, fuck it; money was no object on this trip.

Daisy stared defiantly at the crowd of suits eyeing her up. She had blown her hair straight and picked out a simple, elegant sheath dress in platinum-silver silk, to complement her eyes, with a pale grey lace cardigan from Ghost that matched it perfectly, strappy sandals, and a cashmere pale-pink pashmina that was resting in the cloakroom. She had tickets to *Les Miserables* in her velvet evening bag, and she planned to enjoy a cocktail, a light snack, and an evening at the theatre. What did these men think she was? A high-priced hooker, maybe? Some of them probably thought just that.

Well, sod you all, Daisy thought. She smiled warmly at the female bartender. She was starting to feel very anti-men.

'I'll have a Kir royale,' Daisy said, when the girl stopped serving the businessmen in their Rolexes who were standing next to her.

'Certainly, ma'am.' What was it with Americans and their 'ma'am'-ing all the time? It made her feel like the Queen. 'I'll just need to see some ID.'

Daisy blinked at her. ID? Oh, of course, Americans didn't let you drink until you were twenty-one. Ridiculous Puritanism. 'I'm twenty-three,' Daisy said helpfully.

'I'm sure you are, ma'am, but I'll need to see some ID.'

'Like what?'

'Driver's licence, passport.'

Daisy started to flush. People were looking at her now. This was *not* what she had intended when she had planned her rebellious solo evening on the town. The barwoman's eyes were unyielding. Stroppy cow, Daisy thought.

'Look,' she said reasonably, 'I'm not American, so I don't have my driver's licence with me, and my passport is back in the hotel . . . '

'I'm sorry,' the barwoman said, turning away.

Daisy flushed crimson. She couldn't believe it. She was dressed like this and she was about to get thrown out of the bar! Everybody was looking at her. She wanted to tell herself it was just one of those things, but there was a hot flush of total embarrassment. She should get up from the bar stool and walk out, but she was rooted to the spot.

'Katy,' said a low voice next to her.

The barwoman spun round immediately. 'Yes, Mr Soren?'

'This young lady is twenty-three. I can vouch for her.'

Daisy looked at the speaker. He was young, about thirty-five, and tanned, with a muscular torso hidden under a well-cut charcoal grey suit. He had dark-blonde hair, and looked almost Nordic; tall, with something of the Viking about him.

'Of course, Mr Soren.'

He was very attractive, but Daisy didn't want some rich guy's pity. She was utterly humiliated. 'I don't know this man,' she said sharply, and slid off her bar stool.

The girl was waiting, looking at Soren to see what she should do.

'And I don't know you, at least not yet,' Soren said easily, 'but I can vouch for you, because you must be Daisy Markham.'

Daisy stared at him, rooted to the spot.

'Kir royale,' the girl said, 'coming right up, and it's on the house. Sorry for any trouble, ma'am.' She turned nervously towards Soren. 'Mr Soren, sir, I do hope I haven't caused any offence . . . '

Who the hell is this man? Daisy wondered. Did he own the restaurant, or something?

★ ★ ★

His name was Magnus Soren. She had pegged him right; he was from Sweden originally, he told her, but he had been working in New York for ten years and was a naturalised citizen.

'My company works in media. We have broad interests in publishing, films, TV, some magazines. I make it my business to keep up on new trends. You made quite a stir last month. I see reports on things like that. Your photograph was with your bio, and it was . . . quite striking,' he said dryly.

'I can't believe you would remember one photo,' Daisy said. 'Well . . . thank you.'

'You're drinking with me,' he said. 'Quite thanks enough.'

'You haven't asked me what I'm doing here alone,' Daisy said.

'Because it's none of my business.'

Daisy lifted her glass to him. 'You're very smooth. You know that?'

He laughed out loud. 'And you're very funny.'

'I was going to go to the theatre,' Daisy told him, 'after supper, which I wouldn't have stayed for if they wouldn't let me have the Kir royale.'

'And I have just finished a long and boring meeting and was on my way home. What were you going to see?'

'*Les Mis.*'

'But that's so mainstream. You're not a *Les Mis* type of girl. More like *Chicago*. Maybe I can persuade you to change your plans and go there with me?'

'I heard tickets were impossible to get,' Daisy said.

'Nothing's impossible except the Red Sox winning the World Series.' Soren picked up his cell phone. 'Excuse me a second.' He speed-dialled somebody and had a brief conversation, then turned back to her. 'It's done, we have a box.'

Daisy said, 'I'm impressed.'

'Good.' He grinned. 'That's the general idea.'

'What's the name of your company?' she said.

'Soren Enterprises,' he said.

★   ★   ★

They stepped out of the theatre at nine. Daisy had enjoyed herself thoroughly, but she was now exhausted, and felt herself slipping in and out of sleep where she stood.

Soren had somehow magicked up a box for them; they had skipped supper, but they had been plied by waiters with trays of little thin-cut smoked salmon sandwiches on brown bread, chilled champagne in a silver bucket, miniature pizzas, and caviar and blinis.

She had kept her eyes fixed on the show, and Magnus hadn't tried to engage her in conversation. Daisy felt a bit nerve-racked, now she was here; she was on a real, proper date with somebody who had as much juice as Rudy Giuliani, apparently. But she had started to fade by intermission.

'You look like you're all in,' Soren remarked. 'Shall I have my driver take you home?'

'I can manage the second half,' Daisy said. 'Aren't you supposed to be hitting on me now? My defences are low.' She swayed gently as she spoke.

'Ah. No.' He winked at her. 'That's no fun. I only want women saying yes to me when they're in their right minds.'

She was still expecting him to pounce on her when he showed her inside his limousine; a long, sleek black monster that was waiting for them when the crowd poured out of the theatre. But instead, he ordered his chauffeur to take her to the Victrix.

'You'll sleep, you'll feel much better.' He handed Daisy a thick card, with small gold-embossed letters, which she slipped into her purse. 'Normally I wouldn't expect a girl to do the phoning, but if you're up for brunch tomorrow, you let me know. I know a wonderful restaurant.'

'Thanks,' Daisy said sleepily.

The limo pulled up outside the hotel, and Soren helped Daisy out, with the aid of a white-gloved doorman. He kissed her hand.

'See you tomorrow at brunch,' he said.

'Rather sure of yourself, aren't you, Mr Soren?' Daisy asked.

'Yes,' he agreed, getting back into the limo.

Daisy staggered into the elevator, let herself into her room, and only just managed to peel off her clothes before she flopped on to her goose-down coverlet and instantly fell asleep.

★   ★   ★

The next morning, she woke early, when the light began to stream into her windows. For a moment, she didn't remember where she was, and then it all came back to her. The drink . . . Magnus Soren.

Daisy smiled slowly. Goodness, wasn't that romantic? Magnus Soren, huh? She remembered him as being very good-looking and very well-connected. But you couldn't be sure when jet lag was making you see double.

She was chilly. Oh yes, she hadn't even got under the covers last night. She was sprawled naked over her bed. Hell, that meant she hadn't even taken off her make-up. Or brushed her teeth. Ugh. Daisy ran to the bathroom to check on the damage. Thankfully it wasn't too bad; hastily she ran a bath and dug out her tube of Rembrandt, scrubbing herself clean of that dead-parrot feeling.

Once she was washed, blow-dried, and made up, Daisy unpacked. She had a pretty white floral dress from Miu Miu, and she teamed it with a crocodile-strap

Patek Philippe and a pair of white-leather Dior slides. It looked fresh and attractive; Daisy twisted her hair into a French pleat and put on nude Shu Umera lipstick and Shiseido blusher together with white eyeliner to make her look awake. That was sexy, she thought, kind of a Sixties vibe.

Good enough for Magnus Soren? Certainly. Daisy went to her abandoned velvet purse and dug out the card.

Magnus A. Soren, it said. President and Chief Executive Officer, Soren Enterprises.

It was only 7 a.m., but in England it was already noon. Daisy lifted her phone and dialled Ted Elliott's number.

★ ★ ★

'Just for a break, Ted. No, the book's not behind. Tell me something, have you heard of a firm called Soren?' She listened. 'OK, thanks. Just curious. Talk to you when I get home.'

Interesting. Magnus Soren was apparently self-made. He had started with a small film-editing business in Stockholm, taken over a commercials house, and expanded his empire from there. He was regarded as a young Turk; only thirty-seven.

She'd wanted to ask if he was married, but held back. After all, she wasn't about to jump into bed on the rebound. Edward was the one for her, not Magnus Soren. He was altogether too slick, Daisy thought righteously.

Still, it wouldn't do any harm for her to have a boyfriend . . . a rich, powerful boyfriend. Somebody to provide a cover while she thought about what she could do to break up Wina and the man she really loved.

Daisy tapped the business card against her thumb,

then made up her mind. She'd call. It was brunch, and she was hungry.

★  ★  ★

'Soren Enterprises,' said a woman's cool, professional voice.

'Can I speak to Magnus Soren, please?'

'Who's speaking, please? I'll see if I can transfer you,' the woman said, a touch sceptically.

'This is Daisy Markham.'

'Miss Markham,' she said immediately, 'of course, madam, hold on.'

Daisy was flattered. Magnus must have left word that if she called she was to be put right through.

'Daisy,' Magnus said. 'Sleep well?'

'Wonderfully.'

'Glad to hear it. We'll meet at eleven, then. The Beaux Arts, that OK?'

'It's just fine,' Daisy said.

'Perfect, see you then,' Magnus said, hanging up.

Daisy's neatly manicured fist curled against her palm. Was this crazy? She knew, in her heart, that she was still in love with Edward Powers.

She looked at her svelte, curvy, gorgeously groomed reflection, and flashed back to that dreadful night when she, fat Daisy, unpopular Daisy, had waddled out of that bus to the derision of the public schoolboys clustered around it, rating her out of ten. Her palms went clammy, just thinking about it. And who had asked her to dance? Who had saved her? Edward.

Surely *that* was her destiny. The man who had found her attractive when she was a fat, ugly duckling.

Daisy sometimes felt like a fraud. She'd been so used to rejection, it was in her blood. Writing had saved her, but not from these sneaking feelings of inadequacy. No wonder she came back to Edward, he'd been there for her when nobody else was.

And surely he'd loved her at Oxford.

But now he was married to somebody else.

She had to at least *try* to stop obsessing over him. Magnus Soren was dynamic and gorgeous. Maybe she could make a go of it with him. She tried not to think, 'But I doubt it.'

★ ★ ★

The Beaux Arts restaurant was a little jewel of a place on the Upper East Side, with a sunken courtyard garden and wrought-iron tables. Magnus was waiting for her when she got there.

'You're just as beautiful in daylight,' he said, standing up and kissing Daisy on the cheek. 'Remarkable.'

Daisy smiled at him. She had been thinking the same thing. He really was ridiculously attractive. His eyes were a light-green flecked with hazel, and the blondness of his hair was countered by the broad shoulders, the strong chest, and the set, square jaw. He didn't wear any jewellery, like many American guys; no tie-pins or diamond pinky rings. And no wedding band.

'So what do you recommend?'

'Everything.' He waved the menu. 'They do great health food, if that's what you're into. Fruit salads, egg-white omelettes with herbs and capers.'

'I suppose I should,' Daisy said.

'You should eat whatever you normally eat, because whatever you've been doing to that body, it's working.'

Daisy blushed. 'I thought you weren't going to hit on me?'

'Of course I'm going to hit on you.' He smiled wolfishly. 'It's morning, you've had a chance to regroup. It's now open season.'

'Well.' She laughed. 'I'm glad you warned me.'

'I'll have the bacon fried to a crisp, grilled tomatoes

380

on toast, fresh orange juice, cinnamon coffee,' Soren rattled off to the waiter.

Daisy's mouth watered. 'Same.'

'My kind of girl.' The waiter brought them a pitcher of freshly squeezed juice, and Soren poured glasses for them both and raised one to her. 'My kind of girl. Now tell me all the things I don't know from reading your sales figures. You have brothers and sisters?'

'No. I'm an only child. In fact, I was adopted,' Daisy said.

She instantly wondered why she'd said it. That was private, something she never brought up.

'How interesting.' He studied her face. 'Of course, nobody could hide that from you. Those incredible eyes. Do you have any contact with your birth parents?'

'No, why should I?' Daisy said. 'They never had any contact with me.'

'Of course,' he said, politely, moving on.

'No, it's OK.' Daisy could see he had stopped himself talking. 'I'm not going to be offended, what were you going to say?'

'My father was adopted. He was always angry about it.'

'I never give it a thought, really,' Daisy said.

'Eventually he found out that my grandparents had smuggled him out of the Jewish ghetto. They had both been killed in the Holocaust. It gave him a kind of peace when he found out they'd originally loved him.'

Daisy was taken aback. 'That's . . . that's an amazing story.'

Soren shook his head. 'I didn't mean to lay the heavy stuff on you until at least dinner tonight,' he said.

'So we're having dinner?' Daisy enquired.

'Of course. You don't have anything better to do, and

if you do, you'll cancel it.'

She shook her head.

'You're a very arrogant man,' she pronounced.

'Possibly.' Magnus Soren smiled at her. 'But I believe in giving destiny a helping hand.'

# 43

Daisy spent an incredible weekend with Magnus Soren. He was everything she thought of as American, everything she thought of as New York; big, brash, unashamedly extravagant.

The word 'subtle' was obviously not in his vocabulary. He picked Daisy up in different limousines; took her on a chopper ride for Sunday lunch at his estate in Dutchess County, where his cook served up a meal worthy of Les Quatres Saisons; he tried to buy her a necklace of Mikimoto pearls the size of marbles; he insisted on picking up the bill for everything, including her ridiculously expensive hotel.

'You're too much. It's all too much,' Daisy complained. 'Magnus, really. You're making my head spin.'

'But that's where you're wrong. It's really not enough. You aren't letting me spoil you properly.'

'I don't want to be spoiled,' Daisy said.

'That's a character flaw. You have to conquer it.'

They were sitting on the balcony of his farmhouse in Dutchess, sipping mint juleps. It was sunset, and Daisy was staying over before her flight in the morning. Magnus had provided her with her own room. She loved this house; it was old, for an American house, anyway, dating from the eighteenth century, with some modern additions. Magnus had filled the place with antiques, many of them Swedish, and it felt rustic — very, very luxurious, but rustic. He had stables and horses, fields full of clover, and, endearingly enough, two mongrel dogs imaginatively named Brown and Yellow. Brown was part-terrier, and Yellow was part-Lab and all enthusiasm. The dogs bounded on to the deck, almost knocking over the original Quaker table their drinks were resting on.

'If I ever had a burglar they'd lick him to death,' Magnus said, scratching Brown behind his ears.

'Would you ever have one?'

'Not up here. People don't bother locking up their cars.'

Daisy sighed. 'Gorgeous, but I suppose that's what you get when you live hours and hours from the city.'

'It's only twenty minutes by chopper,' Magnus explained reasonably.

Daisy sipped at her mint julep. It was delicious. 'Magnus, you are disgustingly rich and you have an insane amount of toys.'

'Yup.' He grinned. 'Isn't it great? All you have to do is buy and sell companies and then one day you wake up and you have all this.' He waved. 'Of course, it would be nice to have someone to share it with.'

'I hear you have someone to share it with every week.'

'Well, you can't expect me to be lonely and bored, can you?'

Daisy laughed. 'At least you're honest about it.'

He looked her over. It was a stripping, assessing look. Daisy felt some heat between her thighs. She put down the mint julep. Now was not the time to weaken. Magnus wasn't the one for her; she didn't want to end this weekend in his bed, when her heart belonged to Edward Powers.

'Look, Magnus . . . I'm not going to sleep with you.'

'How disappointing,' he said, easily enough. 'Or it would be, if you meant it.'

Daisy bristled. 'I *do* mean it.'

'No. You mean you're not going to sleep with me this weekend. But you are, in fact, going to sleep with me. I want you and I mean to have you.'

He said this with such seriousness that Daisy didn't know where to look.

'And I don't just mean to have you in my bed. Although that will be a good start.'

'Are you about to tell me you think we should get married?' Daisy scoffed. 'Come on, Magnus. You're young, you're single, you're rich and powerful.'

'You forgot handsome.'

'You've already admitted you play the field,' she said, ignoring the last remark. Handsome, was he ever. 'And I don't intend to be one of those girls who drape themselves over the arm of some billionaire — '

'I'm not a billionaire. At least not yet. Maybe next year if the Raton deal goes through — '

'And then gets dumped for a newer model or something. I'm not interested in your money. I have my own. It may not be this much, but it's more than enough for me. And I'm also not interested in being, what do you call them — '

'Trophy wives, arm candy,' Magnus said helpfully.

'Yes. Exactly.' Daisy had the uncomfortable feeling that Magnus was laughing at her, even if he wasn't doing it out loud.

'I have a career. I write romance novels. I'm good at it, I sell well — '

'Yes, I remember the marketing reports.'

'And I intend to continue doing it. Work is very important for the soul, even when you don't need to work.'

'I agree completely. I don't need to work.'

'So, you know you'd be better off with somebody different.'

'If you'll be so good as to allow me to pick out my women myself,' Magnus said. 'I tend to do the best job in that regard.'

Daisy looked at him. He had been nothing but a perfect gentleman. Showing off wasn't a crime, and he was sexy and he made her laugh.

'Look, Magnus. You're very nice, but I think I should

be honest with you.' She sighed. 'I'm in love with someone else.'

'I don't care,' he said, calmly. 'Eventually, you won't be.'

★　★　★

Daisy flew back to London first class; the only part of her trip she'd wound up paying for. Maybe just as well, she thought, as she accepted a chilled glass of freshly squeezed orange juice. She had to be careful; her money was great, but it wasn't like Magnus Soren's. Next time she felt miserable and needed a break, she should go somewhere cheaper, like Rome.

She was decidedly better for the long weekend, she thought. Her ego had needed a boost, and Magnus had been perfect. And she'd been honest with him, she hadn't used him, even though the temptation to do so had been strong. She'd told him straight out there was somebody else, somebody she was tied to through destiny and fate. He could not overcome those odds.

But he'd said he still wanted to see her. Well, she couldn't object to that. He knew that she wasn't going to be Mrs Magnus Soren.

Daisy found herself hoping that he *would* call. Soren was a lot of fun.

★　★　★

When she got home it was pitch-black. She paid the taxi, then went into her building to see if she'd had any post.

'No letters,' Enriquez, the receptionist, said. 'But something come for you, something very nice. Hold on a sec.'

He reached behind his desk and pulled out a gigantic

bouquet of dark-red roses, almost as big as Daisy.

'Wow,' Daisy breathed.

'I count them.' He winked. 'Six dozen. Very nice. Who they from?'

Daisy didn't bother to open the card. 'Magnus Soren,' she said.

'Who's he?'

'Just a friend.'

'Some friend,' Enriquez said. 'Goodnight, Miss.'

★   ★   ★

Magnus waited until lunchtime to call her.

'Thanks for the roses, they were beautiful.'

'Six dozen roses are not as beautiful as one Daisy,' Magnus said gallantly.

Daisy groaned. 'That's terrible. Stick to Brown and Yellow.'

'You're the wordsmith, no?'

'Thanks for calling. I really had a good time with you,' Daisy said.

'Don't make it sound so final. I'm going to be in London next week. I'll be seeing you then.'

'Magnus — '

'Gotta go,' he said, hanging up.

Daisy shook her head. He was stubborn, that was for sure. But after all, he wouldn't have got to be so successful so young without being bull-headed. She didn't mind; but she hated to see him waste his time like this.

She went to her computer, switched it on, and started to write. The words tumbled out of her; it was a Zen-like experience, the flow she got when she was really cooking. For a while, she could forget about Edward and Magnus and lose herself in the world of her new book, where everything worked out the way she designed it. But in the back of her mind, the thought simmered below her consciousness: it was time to come back to England, back to reality, and start thinking seriously about Edward Powers, and how to make him see he had made the wrong decision . . .

# 44

'Get me the files on Rose Fiorello,' Jacob said.

'Files?'

Ella was hovering in the doorway, nervously. Jacob had strode in to the office, flung his coat on his chair, and started to bark orders. She had never seen him like this. Angry. It made her want to run away.

'Yes. Personnel, whatever we have. Do a search. Talk to Dick White's office. I want complete results on Fiorello. Whatever she sat in on, whatever she did.'

'Is something wrong, sir?'

'I don't know.' Jacob was grim-faced. 'But I'm going to find out.'

★　★　★

The winter winds whipped down across Queens. The mild snap was over; it was back to normal, New York weather at its most unforgiving. Rose stood shivering in her boots at the construction site. Nothing could keep the bone-chilling cold from her skin; not the luxurious cashmere cloak, the fur muffler, the soft pashmina, or the supple black leather gloves. Inside her Jimmy Choo boots, her toes were frozen.

She didn't think she'd ever been this happy.

'No time to waste.'

Rose had selected her construction firm after diligent research. Paul Igorsky was the foreman.

'I want this job done in four months.'

'That's almost impossible.'

'Nothing's impossible, Mr Igorsky. The skeleton of the building is going to stay intact. You're just constructing a fence and a gatehouse, and doing some minor cosmetic work. Your firm has a good record.'

Igorsky, in his fifties, looked askance at the young woman. How could this tootsie possibly know what she was doing?

'That's because we build quality, Miss Fiorello. You want this place real nice, it's gonna take some time.'

'Yes. Four months. There'll be a bonus in it for you when you complete on an early schedule.'

He sighed. Save me from amateurs.

'Everybody offers our firm an early-completion bonus. That's just standard practice. But four months — '

'I'm not talking about the firm, I'm talking about you,' Rose said. 'Look out of the window.'

He glanced outside his office and saw a sleek red Ferrari parked in the lot. The very sight of it made him drool.

'I'll see what I can do.'

'I thought so,' Rose said.

Now the trucks were parked in the lot. Already the dumpsters out front were full of debris; acres of run-down carpet and broken fixtures. Workers poured in and out of the front door like little ants. Electricians for the re-wiring, painters, guys to strip the floors. She loved it. She almost wanted to grab a sander herself, and rush in there and get that ugly black glue blasted off one of her precious hard-wood floors.

But she had better things to do. Rose got back into her car and drove home to Manhattan. She could stay there all day, but if you rest on your laurels, Rose thought, they become funeral wreaths.

★   ★   ★

'These are the results, Mr Rothstein,' Ella said. She leaned over his desk, giving him the undone-button special. This was her big chance!

But, aggravatingly, Jake didn't even notice her.

'Here are the projects Rose sat in on. And here's her entire file.'

Jake flipped through it. 'What's this?'

'Oh, that's some other Fiorello. I just ran the name through the company records to be extra-sure. The IT manager gave it to me every time the name 'Fiorello' appeared. I guess that's some other person . . . '

'Thank you. That will be all,' Jake said.

He stared at the memo in front of him for a long time, an icy chill running down his spine that had nothing to do with the soft snowflakes tumbling outside his windows.

Then he picked up the phone and dialled his father's extension.

'Dad, hi, it's me. I think we may have a problem.'

★ ★ ★

'Sure, I remember her.'

William Rothstein sat in his brother's office, his fleshy body almost completely filling the leather armchair he was wedged into. Fred Rothstein was looking mildly aggravated; William's nephew Jacob was dark-faced.

Lot of fuss about nothing. Jacob was a kid, way too keen. Worrying about everything. William knew his nephew held him in contempt; he really didn't care. Spoilt brats thought they were too good for the men who had brought home the bacon.

'You shoulda seen her, Fred. Great piece of ass.'

'There's plenty of cooch in this town.'

'I know, but this one . . . ' — William's tongue snaked out and moistened his fleshy lips — ' . . . young, real young, like sixteen. Looked like a model, but with tits, nice little ass, too. Would have done anything to save her father's shitty lease. I got mad because she tried blackmail.'

'You should have banged her. We could have gone a little higher.'

Jacob struggled with himself. He wanted to tell his father to stop talking that way about Rose. But she was, after all, an enemy.

'I should have.' William shrugged. 'Ah well. She was gonna be difficult, threatening to go to the press. Too much trouble for a piece of pussy, you know?'

'So what did you do?' Jacob asked shortly.

'Whadda ya think? Sent her away with a flea in her ear. And we ran her father out of his lease without a payment.' William blew a smoke ring out of the cigar he was puffing on. 'He should have settled.'

'Fricking tenants. Always think we're gonna hold up a multi-million-dollar project, build it around their crappy flower stalls and coffee shops.' Fred nodded at his brother. 'I'd have done the same thing.'

'I think she's been nursing this for her entire life. That's why she was so cold to me in school. And why she got the intern post. I think she was trying to copy our data.'

A shadow of concern flitted over Fred Rothstein's face, but only for a second.

'Sounds like it. But, son, who gives a shit? What can she do? She's some little twenty-something piece of cooze. Next time you want to bang some broad, don't bring her into the company, though. Got it?'

'Yes sir,' Jacob said.

Fred rather enjoyed watching his kid squirm. Mr Know-it-all junior hotshot caught with his pants down.

'She can't do anything to us, Jakey. We don't worry about women unless they're filing paternity suits. Her dad was a loser.' He shrugged. 'Not my problem.'

Jacob stood. 'I'm going to check on what she's doing.'

'You worry too much,' Fred Rothstein said. 'Go get yourself laid.'

Jacob wasn't convinced. He went back to his desk and buzzed Ella.

'Yes, sir.'

'Get someone to pull the property records. MLS listings, whatever you have. I want to know what Rose Fiorello owns and where. Have someone get back to me within half an hour.'

'Yes, sir.'

When the answer came back, Jacob listened intently. He didn't like what he heard.

*How could I have been so stupid?*

★ ★ ★

His personal limo took him to Rego Park. It took the driver a few minutes to find it on the map; this was not the kind of place that Rothsteins usually asked to be taken to.

Jake got out and looked at the shabby, run-down building. A swarm of workmen were all over the site, digging, measuring, carting off. There were more workmen there than he ever usually saw on Rothstein projects. Something else; the site was a hive of activity. Nobody was sitting down chewing sandwiches or swigging from hot thermos flasks. These guys were actually working.

It only took him a few seconds to find the foreman.

'You're working for Rose Fiorello?'

'Who's asking?' said the guy.

'My name's Jacob Rothstein. I'm a friend of hers.'

'Then she can tell you her business, can't she? You got a pass, fella? This is private property.'

Jake grinned. 'That's OK. I'm leaving.'

He went back to the warm, heated comfort of his Lincoln Town Car and opened up the file on Rose.

She lived down in Tribeca. He gave the driver the address.

★ ★ ★

She was sitting at her kitchen table with a large yellow legal pad and a biro. Empires had been built on far less than this. Ten versions of ad copy were crossed out with thick black marks. She was determined to get the pitch exactly right.

Her doorbell buzzed.

'Yes?'

'It's Jacob Rothstein.'

Rose wondered what to do. She buzzed him up, then ran to open the safe and locked her ad copy inside it with the Rothstein papers. He'd never find it. She kept the mobile phone in her hand, just in case he tried anything stupid. Jacob wasn't violent, Rose knew that. But the rap on the door still found her jumpy.

'Come in — '

He looked gorgeous in that dark suit. But from the ice in his eyes and the thunderous scowl of his brows, Rose knew at once that he knew.

'Rego Park, huh?'

'You've been to my site,' Rose said, trying not to seem surprised.

'And why not? You've been through my papers. Nice touch with the panties. That was really slutty. A good distraction.'

'This isn't your fight,' said Rose after a second.

Jacob laughed. 'Oh, really? Let me tell you something, Fiorello. I came here to give you a warning. Rothstein is my company. Mess with it, you mess with me.'

'This is between your father and me — '

'My father. My uncle William. Oh, don't look so surprised, you think you're the only one that can do

394

some digging? I know about your father, about the deli, about that stunt you pulled in high school. And I know you've been nursing some stupid idea of vengeance all these years. I'm warning you not to push it, Rose. You've been treated well.'

'Like my dad was? Forced out of his lawful lease?'

'He was offered good money. More than good.'

'Fifty doesn't buy you a new career.'

'He chose to turn his nose up at that money, and your blackmail didn't cut it. Blame yourself if you must; don't blame us.'

'My father,' said Rose, drawing herself up, her voice turning to steel, 'had a legal lease. He didn't *want* money. He wanted to keep his lease. Your family had no right to do what they did. And as for me being treated well, your company is a bunch of assholes. If you take my advice, you'll keep out of it.'

'I have no intention of allowing you or anyone else to threaten my inheritance. Take on Rothstein Realty, and you take on me.'

'So be it.'

Jacob bowed slightly. 'Goodnight, Rose. I'll see you around.'

He let himself out.

*Yes, you will*, she thought.

⋆   ⋆   ⋆

The aggravating thing was that she couldn't start with Rothstein Realty. They were too big for her to attack right now.

First, it was a question of getting established. But Rose didn't wait. She finally decided on ad copy she was proud of, and ran the spots the next day.

'*Own your own piece of the American dream. Condominiums in easy reach of the city. Security, doorman, brand new kitchens. Huge 1 Bdrms*

*— marble lobby, mint. Hurry, won't last.'*

Rose added the number of George Benham's office. She put the ads in the *Times,* the *News,* the *Post,* and the *Village Voice.*

She didn't have to wait long.

'Miss Fiorello.' George Benham's voice was the whine that she remembered. 'You're going to have to get me a new line. This one is ringing all day with Rego Park applicants ... I can't do any other business.'

'As of now, George, you don't have any other business. Do you?'

Rose waited while the answer came tremulously down the line. 'I — I guess not, Miss Fiorello.'

'Tell the applicants there'll be a show apartment ready in two weeks. Get their details and run credit checks. I want pre-approved buyers only.'

'Yes, Miss Fiorello.'

'And it's not going to be called the Rego Park,' Rose said on impulse. 'I'm changing the name ... '

*Fiorello.* Little Flower.

'Call it the Flower of Queens Apartments.'

'Flower of Queens. Yes, ma'am.'

Rose scribbled a note to herself. The next morning she called the architect. A new detail was added in to the building; a rose, picked out in red marble, was worked into the stone above the entrance way.

Her signature.

★  ★  ★

Rose heard no more from Jacob Rothstein. Thank heavens, right? She was relieved about it.

She went out to visit her parents in the comfortable house she had bought for them. Daniella was older, stooped; her hair was silvered all the way through. Her father was lumbering around the house.

'I get bad gout.' He kissed her. 'Great to see you, honey.'

Rose was shocked; she didn't go home enough. She determined to get them a maid, and a home nurse for her father.

'So, how you been doing? Got yourself a nice young man?'

Daniella Fiorello put an extra dollop of penne vodka on Rose's plate. Her baby was skin and bones, even if she did look good.

'No, but I got myself a hotel.' Rose was all excited; it tugged at Paul's heart. His little girl had always been that way, so full of enthusiasm for life.

'You got a job in the hotel business?'

He tried to hide his disappointment. He had thought, after the scholarship and all, that Rose could do a little better than that.

'No, Daddy. I bought a hotel. I own it.'

'A hotel? I don't understand.'

'Mom, I sold what I own, I bought a place out in Rego Park, and I traded it all in for a hotel.'

'Rego Park's a bad area,' said Daniella faintly.

'I'll take you out to see the show apartments next month. People are already calling up. You're gonna love them.'

★ ★ ★

Rose kept her word. As soon as the first apartments were done, she had her parents picked up in a limousine and taken out to the site.

'Look. This is the gatehouse, see? Everybody will have to give their name. I'm putting on a twenty-four-hour guard, and this fence. It's twelve feet high. Total security. Do you like the rose, Daddy? I'm calling it the Flower of Queens. After our name. Your name.' She was thrilled, full of life, animated and happy. Daniella didn't dare ask her daughter if she had found a man to share it with. 'Come through here, come through — '

'Morning, Miss Fiorello,' the foreman said.

Paul blinked. He couldn't believe what he was seeing. The man treated his daughter with such deference, even though she was still half a kid.

'Hi,' Rose said, paying no attention. 'See? All the condos will be like this . . . the new tiles, the new stove and refrigerator, everything brand new, almost perfect, fitted carpet, and the maintenance is really low . . . '

'The mortgage on this place must be huge.'

'It is.' Rose laughed at the look on her father's face. 'Oh, don't worry, Dad. I got the whole place half sold already, and it won't be finished for months. I bet you I can have it one hundred per cent sold by the day the workers are done.'

He believed her.

'I'm so proud of you, honey.'

'I did it all for you, Dad,' she said.

Her father kissed her and hugged her and Rose felt a pure happiness that had not come over her for years.

★ ★ ★

She treated her parents to dinner at Bernie's Steakhouse, her father's old haunt. Rose wanted it to be Lutece or the River Café, but she knew her folks would hate those fancy places. Paul Fiorello's idea of luxury was a big steak cooked just right. Her parents wanted to go over just how far she'd come. Rose let them talk. When her cab dropped them home, she had the feeling it had all been worth it.

She was woken from her sleep at 3 a.m.

Her mother was crying so hard Rose could hardly make out the words, but she didn't really need to. She just knew. And it blew her world into pieces.

Her father had had a heart attack. He was dead.

For the first time in years, Rose completely neglected her work. She moved in with her mother for a whole month, enough time to get her settled, get her over the initial shock of grief.

'He had a great life, Mom.'

Rose said it automatically. She hoped things like this would comfort her mother more than they comforted her, which was not at all.

'Oh, he did, he did. He was so proud of you. You were the apple of his eye. Bored everyone stupid about you.'

'I hope he liked this house.'

'He adored it.' Daniella sighed heavily.

'What's wrong, Mom? What is it?' Rose rushed to her mother, but she waved her off.

'Oh, hell, it's nothing. Just that — '

'Go on.'

'He was so fond of that stupid deli. I wish he'd never lost that deli.' And Rose's hands curled into fists, which she did not let her mother see.

★ ★ ★

Rose arranged for her mother's sister to come up from Florida to live with her. Once that was all settled, she went back to George Benham's office. He fell over himself in his eagerness to greet her. To kiss my ass, Rose thought.

'The Flower of Queens is all sold up. We have a waiting list. Maybe I should put up the prices . . . '

'No,' Rose said. 'They get exactly what they paid for.'

'You've made a hell of a lot of money. Two million dollars. Two million! I can hardly believe it.'

'Two million's nothing. I want to buy a skyscraper.'

Benham laughed. Rose regarded him with icy fury.

'Do that again, George, and you're fired.'

'I — I'm sorry, Miss Fiorello. It's just that the property market is in a bit of a slump, tenants are hard to get . . . banks don't like to lend . . . '

'I know that,' Rose said. She thought of Rothstein Realty and their tenants. 'It's a perfect time to invest, George. You think I should buy when the market is hot, and sell when it's weak?'

'No, but — '

'There are no buts. Get me a building. Something owned by a motivated seller.'

'I'll see what I can do,' Benham said eagerly.

★ ★ ★

He came back to her within a week with a selection of properties.

'Overpriced.'

'Too many violations. I don't want the City down my back for ten years.'

'Too small.'

Benham turned away, fearful he had disappointed his boss.

'What's this one? I like this one.'

Rose had pulled out a picture of a rather seedy-looking skyscraper, sixty storeys high, made of brick, and overlooking the river.

'That's on the wrong side of Manhattan, in Alphabet City.'

'Close to transport?'

Benham nodded. 'Right by the subway.'

'And the seller?'

'He's in trouble, but you know, this a commercial property, and it's a broken-down dump . . . the banks hate the area, because it's not the nicest. You'll find it very hard to get a note.'

'Hard doesn't matter,' Rose said. 'The only thing that

matters is impossible. Which this isn't. Get me in to see the seller.'

She had that glazed look in her eyes. Benham dived for his files. He didn't know what she was thinking and didn't care to find out.

Rose wasn't seeing the seedy skyscraper. She was seeing the first nail in Rothstein Realty's coffin. Time to send those boys a message.

She was going to say it with Flowers.

# 45

'Here it is.' Poppy opened the door. 'Home sweet home.'

Dani looked the space over. 'Yeah, it's great.'

Dani West was her new assistant. She was thirty-one and tired of her dead-end job at RCA, typing for promotion grunts. They called it 'Record Cemetery of America' because it had no acts.

When she had read the small-print ad in *Billboard* asking for an assistant in a management start-up, Dani hadn't really been interested. At least RCA paid benefits. But then she'd seen that it was for Opium Management. And she had jumped.

★   ★   ★

There were ten other girls in Poppy Allen's living room when Dani turned up to apply, and Dani asked, flat out, when her turn came, how many Poppy had seen.

'Would you believe? Over twenty,' the younger girl said.

'Yes, I would believe it. But you shouldn't hire them. You should hire me.'

Poppy Allen had leaned back in her rattan armchair and smiled slightly. She had a magnetism about her. Dani began to understand just why Poppy was the flavour of the month, mentioned in *HITS* magazine's gossip column every week, and why she was already looking after three hot acts.

Travis Jackson. A bona fide star, Travis's first, hastily recorded album had gone gold, then platinum. Screaming girls all over the country attested to his New Country-idol status.

Matrix and Wrecking Ball. Two heavy metal groups, 'hair bands' as they called them — long-haired boys with a taste for spandex, girls, and making money. Both had been poached by Poppy from previous management, and she had already booked them on bigger tours and supervised new videos that were getting play on MTV. Both bands loved their young, hot-chick manager, who was as hard and canny as any grizzled old veteran.

To Dani, Poppy was a rising star herself. The public had its idols: Def Leppard, Guns n' Roses, Madonna, New Kids on the Block. You name it. But the record business had its own stars. Giants, moguls who wheeled and dealed and controlled millions of dollars, the fate of labels, of stadiums, of radio networks. Dani's heroes weren't Michael Jackson or Prince; they were David Geffen, Mutt Lange, Quincy Jones, Peter Mensch, Cliff Burnstein, Bill Graham and Michael Krebs. Women to look up to were in short supply. Who was there, really? Lisa Anderson in London? Sharon Osbourne? Rowena Gordon at Musica Records, for sure.

And Poppy Allen? Well, not yet. One star and two hot newcomers didn't make her Q-Prime. But Poppy was making waves.

Dani was tired of going nowhere fast. She wanted to make waves too.

'And why should I hire you, exactly?' Poppy Allen asked her.

Fuck it, Dani thought.

'Because I have experience. Eight years of it. Because I'm so bored and frustrated at RCA that I'm ripping my hair out. Because I want to work, and most of them just want to get to meet Travis Jackson so they can fuck him.' Her interviewer grinned. 'And because I'm not someone who's gonna be jealous of you because you're twenty-three and skinny as hell and you're making it. I'm not gonna give you a hard time when you ask me to get you coffee. And because I want to impress you so you promote me.'

'The job doesn't pay that much,' Poppy Allen said.

'I don't give a shit,' Dani said, adding hastily, 'Ms Allen.'

Poppy looked at the other woman. She was dumpy, wearing way too much black, and she had glasses with hip black frames, kind of a New York vibe, and she was older than the other candidates by a lot.

'You're hired,' she said.

★ ★ ★

Dani was intense. And that was what Poppy was looking for.

Right now, however, she knew Dani was faking it. Her fixed smile as she looked round Opium's new home masked a kind of horrified glare. Poppy smiled.

'You're thinking it's not very fancy.'

'Fancy? I've seen fancier crack dens,' Dani said. 'Man! Are you shitting me?'

They were standing in a former warehouse in a back street off Vine. The place had huge, grimy windows festooned with spiders' webs, a couple of abandoned orange crates used for packing, cigarette butts and broken glass on the gloomy floor, and a rank smell of old stale sweat and urine.

'Who the fuck is the landlord?' Dani demanded. 'You should sue, Ms Allen.'

'It's Poppy. You always swear like that?'

'Army brat,' Dani said succinctly.

Poppy liked her more and more. 'Do me a favour. Just don't say 'fuck' when record company presidents call up. They're old fat farts and we don't wanna be responsible for any heart attacks.'

'You got it, Ms Allen. But you really need to cancel this lease.'

404

'It's Poppy, and there is no lease.'

'We're going to run the office month to month?'

'No. There's no lease because there's no landlord. I own the joint. Got it for sixty thousand bucks.'

'Wow.'

Poppy looked at her assistant, who seemed to be literally biting her cheeks in order to keep silent.

'You have to be polite to the record company, not to me. What were you thinking?'

'That you only paid fifty-nine thousand, nine hundred and ninety dollars too much.'

Poppy laughed.

'Listen, lesson one, OK? The first rule of being in business is to keep the costs down. Hire only the staff you need, and limit expenses. Especially management. Now I own the building, there's not going to be a rent, except what I charge myself for the tax deduction. And this place is going to be the fanciest joint in LA when we're done.' She grabbed Dani's plump shoulders and gestured. 'Big windows, once we've cleaned them. Lots of light. Lots of space, too. Ample electrical points, and there's a bathroom over there, shower and everything. We'll buy some lamps, some couches and desks from a discounter's . . . you'll see, it'll be awesome.'

'But there're only two of us,' Dani protested.

'Right now there's only two of us.' Poppy winked. 'Wait and see. This is gonna be huge.'

Dani believed her.

'Here.' Poppy tossed her the phone. 'First job: call an industrial cleaner and get them over here. This place stinks.'

★   ★   ★

It took two weeks for them to get Opium Management the way they wanted it. But when they were finished, it was spectacular. The whole building was painted a dark red, and on the black door they hand-painted a giant poppy, hot-looking, with its cluster of dark seeds at the centre. The warehouse was disinfected and swept, and Poppy laid cheap, functional linoleum over the ground, but it was chocolate-brown, and it looked kind of designer under their cream-coloured furniture. Poppy invested about fifteen thousand more to bring the building up to date; it wiped out her early commissions from Travis's first tour, but so what? She got cheap partitions of glass, telephones, two fax machines, computers, everything. Cream couches with chocolate brown throws and a modern kitchenette completed the place.

Dani loved it. 'It looks like that apartment on *The Real World*. But it's still too big.'

Poppy winked. 'Nope. I rented half the space out already, to an indie production company and a fashion designer. We're gonna give the Opium Building a reputation. Hot and happening. Like the company.'

Dani wanted to scoff. The Opium Building! Poppy Allen was an egomaniac!

But a little voice inside her head told her that this wasn't true; that Poppy was a genius.

She was awfully glad to have this job.

★   ★   ★

Dani found her first month at Opium indescribably thrilling. Poppy's energy was contagious. She worked so hard and so passionately, it was tiring just watching her.

Poppy was working the phones every day. Dani's call sheet looked like it belonged to President Bush. There were record companies, tour promoters, press guys, radio, TV, MTV, Nashville, you name it. She also took calls from wives, mistresses, and groupies.

'Kind of sleazy, isn't it?'

'Just remember, we're not here to run our acts'

personal lives. Their morality is their business.' Poppy shook her head. 'Just deliver the messages. Look, Dani. I'm a woman, and these boys are all . . . well . . . boys. Last thing they want is me spoiling the party.'

Dani got the message. Travis, Matrix and Wrecking Ball got theirs.

They started out with Travis's platinum album hanging in pride of place in Poppy's office. By the end of the month, Travis had three more, Matrix's gold record had turned platinum, and Poppy even hung Wrecking Ball's first silver disc up over Dani's kidney-shaped desk.

'That should be in your office,' Dani said.

Poppy shook her head. 'You're part of this now.' She grabbed the copy of *Billboard* that lay open by Dani's phone and flicked to the Hot 200, picking up a pencil.

'Exactly what are you looking for?' Dani asked.

'Targets,' Poppy said. 'Targets.'

# 46

'Any messages?'

Poppy stood in front of the receptionist at the Four Seasons, New Orleans, and swayed gently, like a willow sapling in a strong wind. She was running on bare fumes; her gas had drained out about six hours ago.

It was the penultimate stop on the Travis Jackson tour. They had called it 'Bluejeans Bluegrass', and every stop had been a sell-out. Poppy had had to deal with more problems than Napoleon on his march into the Russian winter. There was an ineffective tour manager, a girl, whom she'd fired and who was now threatening to sue for sexism; there were two paternity suits from sweet young things not famed for the strength of their knicker elastic, as the English longhairs used to say; there were promoters who tried to rip her off, thinking she was as green as they came; there were predatory scouts from the really big agencies, offering her protégé the moon; there were even roadies who demanded she blow them to stay backstage, because they were local help who thought she was just another eager groupie. That was right before they got fired, but it still left Poppy feeling weakened.

Travis was loyal, thankfully. She wondered if her presence on tour had tempted Savannah, the threesome of cute blonde sisters she'd booked as support. They were being managed by their father, and he was grossly incompetent. Poppy wanted them. She thought they were close; by the time they hit Dallas, she thought they'd be asking her if she had room in her stable for more.

Dallas. Oh man. Another 6 a.m. start. Sometimes Poppy thought it was hardly worth going to bed. But right now, she couldn't see straight.

'Actually, yes, ma'am.'

Poppy held out a manicured hand. Please let it not be somebody needing to be bailed out.

She was handed a piece of paper. It said, 'If you're interested, I'm in 201. Enjoyed the show. H.L.'

The tiredness was suddenly gone from her brain, like somebody had brushed away thick cobwebs from a pane of glass. She grabbed her key and headed for the elevators.

★ ★ ★

Henry LeClerc. That was a blast from the past, Poppy told herself. It had been over a year since New York . . .

Over a year. Damn. She actually hadn't had sex for a year. Hadn't even really thought about it, she'd been so busy.

*That's not true*, said a small, persistent voice in her head. *You thought about it plenty. But you wanted Henry, and you were too goddam proud to call him.*

And now he was here. The Honorable Gentleman from Louisiana. Paying her a visit when she came to his hometown.

Poppy punched the second-floor button. When the elevator doors hissed open, she hesitated until they slid shut on her again. Then, feeling utterly miserable, she hit eight.

Her room was small, unexciting. Travis had the penthouse suite, of course. One thing Poppy had learned from the masters was that acts noticed everything you did. Your room was charged to their promo bill, after all, and if managers indulged themselves with ensuite jacuzzis and room-service caviar, they noticed, and they didn't like it.

Her bed was a twin, she had a nice bathroom, and a

view of the wall of the next-door building. There was a basket of fruit; this was the Four Seasons, after all. There were also three dozen red roses.

Poppy picked them up. The card just said 'Henry'.

She dropped them in the wastebasket and headed for the shower.

★ ★ ★

Water sluiced over her, washing the grime and dirt of the night away. The best deodorant, the most fragrant Hermes perfume, nothing could stop the clinging smell of sweat, beer, and cigarettes from clinging to Poppy's tailored Armani jeans and little black silk tees. She used Origins Mint wash, it made her feel clean, and always washed and conditioned her hair with custom-blended shampoos and conditioners from Vidal Sassoon.

Tonight her ritual did nothing for her. Her exhausted mind was racing. She wanted him so badly she felt she could faint.

But he'd turned up, after no calls, no letters, no contact. For a motherfucking booty call. Poppy had spent a year trying not to think about Henry LeClerc, and now here he was, with an arrogant note with his room number on it and some shitty roses. Like that made everything OK.

I'm not going to call him, Poppy thought. I'm not. I'm not.

She suddenly felt more tired than she had ever felt before. Bone-weary. Her career was blossoming, and she loved it; but her love life . . . that rock musician who'd dumped her after a sleazy motel fuck, that boring record company executive, a couple of others who hadn't lasted a month. And now Henry. She had thought there was a psychic connection, but he hadn't even bothered to ring her.

Poppy ached for him. But she knew that if she called

him she'd be no better than the girls who waited for Travis, buzzing like flies around the backstage door and most of them just as dirty. Yeah, it was a double standard: Travis and his back-up band screwed everything that moved, and that was expected; even the roadies got laid. But she knew what the men thought of those chicks.

Whores. Sluts. At best, forgettable recreation for an hour or two.

Was that what Henry LeClerc thought of her? The naïve twenty-something, falling for the sophisticated older man? The JAP from LA bowled over by all that slick Southern charm? Maybe he thought she'd be flattered that he was here, that she'd at least remembered who he was.

How could she forget?

Her skin still recalled every second. She felt her nipples tighten, betraying her, her groin stir, as though feathers had brushed across it.

Poppy gazed longingly at the phone.

Then she climbed into bed and went to sleep.

★   ★   ★

When she woke up, the nasty buzzing of the phone had her feet on the floor and her covers tossed back in two seconds. On the road, you responded to phones like Pavlov's dog to a bell. Poppy hastily dressed and zipped up her small, compact case. Everything was done in less than twenty minutes, including a quick shower.

She was ready before the rest of the crew. Poppy preferred to stay in control that way. She was calling Dani on her cell as she ran downstairs; often that was faster than waiting for a lift.

When she reached the front desk Poppy handed her key over, then quickly scanned the pigeon-holes behind reception. 201 was right there.

'I see Henry LeClerc checked out,' she said, her heart thudding.

'That's right, ma'am.' The suit behind the desk glanced at his computer. 'The Congressman checked out at ten past seven.'

Poppy nodded. 'Did he leave me any message?'

She received a bright, professional smile. 'No, ma'am. Nothing.'

★  ★  ★

Henry LeClerc sat in his limousine and brushed it off. Well, what had he expected, really? The girl was flighty. Just a girl. And yet . . .

LeClerc had been at the Dixie Arena and had watched the Travis Jackson concert from the private box he usually took at sports games. He had been forced to listen to it, too, as it seeped through both the glass and his earplugs. He thought the kid had a nice voice, even if New Country was not his thing. Mostly, he had been impressed. Not as a fan, but as a businessman.

LeClerc recognised the electric sexuality Travis Jackson presented as he crooned to the front rows. It was a rougher version of his own. He grinned as ferocious teenage girls ripped the singer's shirt off, then scowled when he thought of Poppy Allen. What if she and Travis were sleeping together? Two young people, stuck on the road? The thought of the muscled, tanned Jackson, fifteen years younger than himself, anywhere near Poppy Allen made LeClerc's teeth clench.

But what had puzzled him was the pride he felt. One of the perks of being Henry LeClerc was information, sometimes an overload of it. He had found out what the intense young woman had done in this twelve months; and he thought he should have been surprised, but found instead that he had expected it.

And he knew he had to see her again.

412

It took one more phone call to find out the name of the hotel, and the false handles the Travis Jackson party was booked under. He got a room, even though the place was full. He sent roses, he waited.

And she wasn't interested.

He even asked in the morning if his message had been delivered. It had; no reply.

So, she was probably jumping Travis Jackson. She hadn't exactly been shy where he himself was concerned, LeClerc thought savagely. Who knew how many guys had ploughed that field since? Forget her.

The trouble was that he couldn't.

He punched a direct-dial button on his cell phone.

'Congressman LeClerc's office.'

'Katie.'

'Sir,' his assistant said warmly. She was twenty-two, with a big rack and a big crush on him.

'Find out where the Travis Jackson concert tour is playing next and get me a backstage pass,' LeClerc said. 'Do it through the venue. I don't want the act to know.'

There was a pause at this bizarre request.

'Uh, sir — '

'Just do it,' LeClerc said.

He wanted her. He was going to have her. It really was, LeClerc thought, just that simple.

# 47

'Oh, Mr Jackson,' the blonde breathed. 'That was, like, such a great show.'

Poppy watched from a corner of the room, bored. Travis was having a great time, as per usual; tonight her star act would be levelling the city of Dallas to its foundations. It was the last night of the tour. All bets were off.

The last night for 'Bluegrass Bluejeans'. Not the last night for her, however. She had a weekend off, then she was due in Stockholm, Sweden, for her hair bands.

The thought made her dizzy. She needed some help.

'Would you give me your autograph?' the blonde asked sweetly.

'Sure, baby,' Travis said, grinning. 'Where?'

'Right here,' the chick said, pulling apart her jacket to reveal pneumatic tits crammed into a black-lace bra.

'Mmm,' Travis said, pulling out his magic marker while the other cheerleader types hurried to unbutton their shirts.

Poppy looked away. She had to call RCA tonight. They wanted to discuss Savannah. They were torn she was taking over; a good manager helped an act succeed, but it also meant no more rip-offs . . .

'Good evening, Ms Allen,' said a voice.

She jumped out of her skin. She would know that voice anywhere.

'Aren't you even going to say hello?'

Poppy glanced up, hating herself for blushing. Her heart started to race; her palms dewed with sweat. There he was. Henry LeClerc.

LeClerc had made no concessions to his surroundings, Poppy noted with pleasure. He wore an immaculately tailored charcoal suit in light wool, Royal Ascot cufflinks, and a steel Rolex. Decadence raged around him; the bassist was ripping the bras off some of the more willing groupies, and the girls were squealing and giggling; and he didn't even seem to notice.

'What are you doing here?' she asked.

'Looking for you,' he said frankly. 'And my eardrums won't stand much more Dixie pumped through giant electronic amplifiers.'

'I don't really have anything to say to you,' Poppy muttered.

'That's not true.' He gave her an easy smile. 'Let's go out to dinner.'

Poppy hesitated, glancing at her star who was reaching for some of the semi-nude girls.

'Isn't this usually your cue to depart?' LeClerc asked wryly.

She couldn't help but crack a very small smile.

'Possibly,' Poppy admitted.

A screaming groupie, fleeing a roadie who was shaking beer at her, fled towards them and crashed into him, pressing her slightly saggy tits into his waistcoat.

Henry drew back a step, politely.

'Why, excuse me, ma'am,' he said.

Poppy laughed softly. She couldn't help it. 'OK, you win. Let's get out of here.'

★　★　★

LeClerc had a limo waiting.

'Government issue?'

'You must be joking, sugar. You think I want all of Washington to know I'm following Travis Jackson around the country?'

'Heaven forbid they might think you were hip.'

They pulled up outside an expensive-looking French place on X Street. It didn't even have an awning; there was a small, very discreet brass plate outside the Georgian frontage of what appeared to be an elegant town house, and a liveried doorman, who tipped his hat to Poppy as he opened the door.

'How do you know I'm gonna like this? You didn't even ask me what food I like. And places like this usually have a dress code,' Poppy hissed.

'Everybody likes the food here; and there's no dress code for my guests,' LeClerc replied coolly.

The maître d'hôtel, suave in black tie, glided up to them.

'Good evening, Congressman, good evening, madam. May I have someone take your jacket, madam?' A flunky materialised and removed Poppy's black leather Slayer jacket as though it were the finest sable. 'Your usual table, Congressman?'

Henry shook his head. 'Somewhere a little quieter, Henri.'

'Certainly, sir.' He led them into a corner booth at the back of the room, shadowed by an overhanging awning of ivory silk and gold thread. There was a low, round Baccarat crystal bowl crammed with yellow roses and white lilies, silver cutlery, and beeswax candles in gold containers.

'Take a seat,' Henry said.

'Excuse me, Congressman.' Another waiter had materialised, this time with a magnum of Cristal champagne in an ice bucket.

'Did you order that?' Poppy asked.

'Compliments of the house, madam.'

She glanced at LeClerc. It was a pricey compliment, even for a place like this. Poppy wondered just how much juice this guy had.

'What do you like?' LeClerc asked. 'The Chateaubriand is good here. Everything's pretty much good here.'

'I'll take the cheese soufflé,' Poppy said. 'I'm a vegetarian.'

He grinned, which infuriated her. 'Since when?'

'Last week,' said Poppy, mutinously.

'I'll have the Chateaubriand. Rare enough to walk off the plate.'

'Very good, sir.'

The waiter melted silently back into the restaurant.

'You own a dog, don't you?'

Poppy nodded.

'If you're going to become one of those LA whackos that force their mutts to eat vegetarian dog food, I'm going to have to call Animal Welfare.'

'He eats Purina,' Poppy said. 'Those cans stink and they're diseased horse anyway.'

'Fair enough.' LeClerc expertly cracked the champagne and poured a split into her long crystal flute. 'They know not to bother us too much here. I can't stand talking while some guy in a penguin suit hovers over me all the time, pouring out my wine for me.'

'Does that work well with all the other women you bring here?' Poppy asked acidly.

'Why, yes, ma'am.' He was infuriatingly unruffled. 'It sure does.'

'You never called me,' Poppy said, coldly. 'And then you finally deign to show up, the great Washington mover and shaker, and you think a note and some flowers will make it all OK? You think that buying me a fancy dinner will get the stupid young bimbo to jump in the sack with you again? I only went with you not to make a scene. Understand right now, I'm never fucking you again.'

She smiled crisply at him and took a hit of the icy champagne, which was as cold as her pale-blue eyes. Adrenaline was surging through Poppy. She wanted to let this cool bastard know she wasn't buying it.

The profanity, lobbed into his white-gloved, prim and proper little world, pleased her. A touch of the hard

417

rock rebel. Let his Southern gentlemanliness deal with *that*.

'Now ain't that some kind of a pity,' LeClerc said easily. Poppy tried not to focus on his square jaw and salt-and-pepper hair and dark, hypnotic lashes. 'Because the way I recall it, you were outstanding. We were outstanding.'

Poppy breathed in sharply.

'I'm an outstanding lay?' she snapped.

'Yep.' He stared right into her eyes. 'Actually, breathtaking might be a better way of putting it. I'm sorry if what you wanted to hear was that you were about as exciting as an exit poll for a State Senator's primary. But that's not why I'm here now.'

'I can't have been *that* exciting,' Poppy said. 'You didn't exactly wear out AT & T after New York.'

'Because you're all wrong.' LeClerc gestured; his hand was rough, unmanicured. 'You're crude and rude and dangerous to know. You're young enough to be my daughter.'

'And old enough to make those decisions for myself.'

He inclined his head, acknowledging her point. 'You're a goddam spitfire. You know the girls I see, mostly? They're beautiful and elegant and great in bed — '

'Yeah, thanks, that's fascinating, but — '

'But,' he went on, ignoring her, 'they're . . . *boring*. They do whatever I say. They don't want to work. They have no dreams, except maybe a large rock on their left hand and the life of a Washington hostess. I can tame a girl like that in three seconds.' His eyes travelled lazily over Poppy's body, making her nipples harden in the little black T-shirt. 'And that's no fun.'

'I'm more than just your fun,' Poppy snapped. 'You're not the great prize you seem to think you are, Mr LeClerc. I'm really not that interested in you.'

'You were interested enough to listen to my advice.'

418

LeClerc lifted his crystal flute to her. 'I've followed your career.'

'But never called.'

'Because there was no point. You were young, vibrant, in another universe. You're not suited to be my wife. You're a liberal Democrat, you're against everything I stand for, you're not even interested in politics, and I couldn't care less about the high-decibel noise pollution you and your industry inflict on the innocent citizens of America. Like I said, you and me — it's crazy. So I forgot about you.'

'Then why are we here?' Poppy asked.

'Because I didn't. Forget, that is. I tried to. But you were always there.'

Her heart was thudding. 'I bet you had other women . . .'

'Crowds of 'em,' LeClerc agreed shamelessly. 'But they didn't help much, not being you.'

'So what's your suggestion?' Poppy asked.

'That you become mine.' His eyes locked on to hers, holding them in place. 'There's really no point in fighting it, Poppy.'

She countered, but her voice was trembling. 'So you're saying you believe in destiny?' she attempted to sneer.

'I'm saying I intend to make my own.'

419

# 48

At first they kept it quiet. It wasn't that hard. Poppy flew all over the country; sneaking off to Washington, New York, or New Orleans wasn't that hard. LeClerc arranged fundraisers on the West Coast; his handlers loved the big-money crowds in LA, Reagan Republicans, and the opera buffs in San Francisco, with its monied élites. Even Democrats paid to see him; he was charismatic, he performed well on TV. He was a star.

Poppy was tormented with longing. It felt exciting, thrilling, but it was so heady she was afraid she might lose her senses. LeClerc's touch on her skin was electric, masterful. When he mounted her, she was so overcome with lust she sometimes forgot where she was, the time, the day; she blocked out everything except his strong hands, his handsome, slightly cruel mouth, his relentless plunging into her.

It was intense.

And then it was over.

He'd get up, sneak back to his room, taking service elevators to avoid reporters, or he'd grab a cab and head to some airport or other. They beeped each other with codes; Poppy sometimes felt she was in a spy novel.

It wasn't enough. Every crashing, sweating, biting orgasm, every erotic phone call, every bunch of exotic flowers or anonymous trinket from Cartier just made her want him more. Poppy sometimes ached for Henry LeClerc so badly she missed him while he was still inside her.

She felt as though she were managing her acts on autopilot. The business was growing; she hired more people, gave Dani more responsibility, and tried to concentrate. But she wasn't focused, and she hated that.

All she could seem to think of was LeClerc and what he meant to her.

It took her six months to put a finger on her dissatisfaction. She should have known, really. What did she want? What she always wanted. More.

★   ★   ★

'So what's up next week?' Poppy asked.

She flipped over on to her stomach on the bed and kicked the Manolos off her feet. There was a call sheet next to her which was lying wholly neglected. She was in Interlaken, Switzerland, lying on a pristine sage-green coverlet in a Holiday Inn. Her room had a great little balcony and a glorious view of the snow-capped mountains. More importantly, it had a phone, and a connection to Henry LeClerc.

His rough voice grunted. 'LA, actually. So I can see you. Meeting the Mayor about some subway project. Going to another fundraiser, giving some barnstormer speeches. What else do I ever do?'

'Write legislation?'

'Not in an election year.' He laughed. 'I wish that's what politicians did.'

'I want to go with you,' Poppy said suddenly.

'Go with me to the dinner?'

'Why the hell not?' Poppy said fiercely.

'You know why not, sugar. How do you think a group of Social Registry snobs are going to react when I turn up with Janis Joplin on my arm?'

'I don't know. But we're gonna have to find out.'

'After the election.'

Poppy bit on her lower lip. 'Henry, no. After the Senate, you'll be running for Governor. Or God knows what. And there'll always be a reason not to introduce me, to tuck me out of sight. And I'm not settling for that.'

'But you'll hate wearing long dresses, and pearls, and nodding at what I say.'

'I would if I was gonna do that.' Poppy sighed. 'I have to be me, and you have to not be ashamed of me. Because I'm not going to be your secret woman you love and keep in the background. I just can't do the little woman thing.'

LeClerc paused.

'Maybe they'll respect my honesty,' he said.

'Isn't it rather that *you'll* respect your honesty?' Poppy asked. She felt warm, salty tears trickle down her cheeks, and was very glad he couldn't see her. Because she knew this was the way it had to be. She loved LeClerc too much to be just another notch on the bedpost, or a political mistress kept out of sight while he married some other, more suitable woman . . .

If he was truly a man, he would not prostitute his soul for votes. And Poppy trembled on the brink, because she was so afraid that he would weaken, would betray her.

There was a pause.

'You're right.' She could almost see those broad shoulders shrugging. 'It's just one more thing about me they're gonna have to accept.' He chuckled. 'This should be fun.'

★  ★  ★

The limousine purred smoothly through the flood of traffic in downtown LA, moving towards the Pierre. Henry sat in the back with Poppy and a tight-faced Simon Harvey, his campaign manager, who kept giving her little rictus grins, as though twisting his facial muscles up around the mouth would make his hostility to Poppy seem less evident. She thought it just made him look like he had a nervous tic.

She had waited in the drawing room of Henry's

gigantic suite in the Bel Air while the row raged on. Simon and his coterie of political hacks and spin doctors had smiled briskly at her, shut the door, and gone to work on Henry. At first the noise had been muted, then it had raged into a full-on screaming match.

'You have to be fucking shitting me, Congressman!' Simon had screamed at one point.

Poppy allowed herself a little smirk. Maybe she shouldn't have worn that cut-off Iron Maiden shirt with the black leather cowboy boots and sprayed-on jeans, but they were in the privacy of their hotel room. Henry liked her; Simon didn't matter.

She hadn't been able to resist putting a glass to the wall.

'Politicans are always trying to pretend they are what they're not. We never drink, we don't gamble, we never inhaled . . . we're not gay, we don't cheat, we have perfect voting records.' Her man's voice had been firm, like a parent not about to brook arguments. 'I'm different. The public is entitled to my service, but that's it. They're not entitled to choose whom I go to bed with.'

'Go to bed with her all you want. Fuck her all you want. But — '

'Careful, Simon.' LeClerc's voice had a warning in it that made Poppy shiver. Brooding menace; she was glad she wasn't Simon Harvey. 'You're speaking about the woman I'm in love with.'

'Henry!' It was a despairing wail. 'The girl manages heavy-metal bands and she's hardly out of diapers!'

'She's a self-made millionaire. Isn't that what the Republican party stands for? Pulling yourself up by your bootstraps? And as for her age, the lady is over twenty-one. That's all you need to know.'

At that point Poppy had put down the glass and fled into the bathroom. She didn't want the spin doctors to emerge and see her crying.

Tonight was going to be the acid test. Poppy had spent an entire day picking her outfit. She had selected a long Armani dress in pale grey silk, teamed with a chiffon shawl and platinum-silver pearls at her throat and dangling from her ears. She carried a Judith Lieber clutch and wore her black hair up in a chignon; her perfume was Chanel No. 19, her hose were Wolford, her shoes Dior kitten heels. Her make-up was neutral, just a tinted moisturiser and a slick of blusher and smoky-grey eyeshadow.

She looked hot, and elegant; ladylike, but her age. Henry was in a beautifully cut tuxedo with plain gold cuffs. He was gorgeous; her heart melted just to look at the close-cropped salt-and-pepper hair. And he had a confidence about him that was breathtaking. Just like she had on the concert stage; this was his world, his scene.

He was in total control. Not even slightly nervous.

'There might be some press when we arrive,' Simon Harvey said, licking his lips and looking shiftily at Poppy. 'Maybe you'd better — '

'Step out with me,' Henry said flatly.

'Right.' Harvey nodded. 'Yup. Right.'

The car glided noiselessly to a stop outside the hotel. There was a red carpet laid out for them, paparazzi crammed behind the golden ropes, flashbulbs already popping, bursting about them. It was almost like when she took Travis to the Country Music Awards in Nashville, Poppy thought, trying to stem the tide of panic which was suddenly rising in her.

'Congressman,' Simon Harvey implored one last time, 'are you absolutely *sure* about this strategy?'

'It's not a strategy, Simon.' LeClerc offered an arm to Poppy, who took it delicately, as the chauffeur opened the door and the flashbulbs exploded in an artificial starburst. 'It's my life.'

Then he led her out on to the red carpet.

# 49

Daisy looked at the map. Was she on the right road? B237, half a mile down from the Queen Adelaide . . . yes, there was a wonky signpost, endearingly dusty and crooked on its grassy mound. Ashton Under Wychwood. OK, she *was* headed in the right direction. Heptonstall House should be right around here . . .

Yes, here it was. A couple of glorious mature oaks flanked a broad gravel drive. Daisy took a deep breath, turned the steering wheel, and drove on to Edward Powers's property.

Her love. Married to someone else.

As the Bentley crunched along the gravel, she glanced in the mirror to make absolutely sure she looked OK. Not that there was much chance she didn't. Daisy had taken almost three hours getting ready this morning. She had to strike just the right balance between beautiful and casual, between looking sexy as hell and looking like she really hadn't tried *that* hard.

In the end, she had gone for a tousled look, suitable for country pleasures such as . . . well . . . hay-baling, riding tractors, or whatever they did out here. Daisy had picked a red-checked cotton shirt that was well-cut and highlighted her figure, and a dark-blue pair of jeans with Doc Martens. She had teamed this with some dangly silver and turquoise earrings, loose flowing curls, and a smoky-grey eye shadow, with rosy blusher and just a touch of lip gloss on her full pout. The effect was gratifyingly attractive. All she needed now was some straw to dangle out of the corner of her mouth, and she'd be set.

She could no longer put off Edward's invitation to come and meet Wina. No, she had to face her rival head-on. See whom Edward had taken instead of her.

His words from the Jugglers Club kept ringing in Daisy's ears.

'I'd have proposed to you had you given me the slightest encouragement.'

Timing. Bloody timing. Daisy pulled up in front of a gorgeous house, an Elizabethan manor, not too large, but stunning, with clematis in full bloom trained up the side of it, and lead-paned windows, and wonderful gardens with what looked like a mature apple orchard off to one side. She got out, grabbing her Chanel quilted purse, and fixed a warm smile on to her face.

She hadn't given him any encouragement. True enough, but that could be fixed.

She was here to put things right.

* * *

'Daisy!'

The old front door opened, and three dogs came bouncing out: a chocolate Lab, a wiry Jack Russell, and a rather slow fawn pug, who was very fat and waddled a bit. Daisy petted them all, and waved to Edward, who was standing in the doorway with his wife.

Wina was wearing some beautifully cut black slacks and a little matching cardigan, with a string of black pearls. She looked exactly as she had done in *Hello!*; she was tall, noble-looking, slender, a bit sexless, Daisy thought.

She was smiling gently at Daisy while Edward looked overjoyed to see her and was beckoning her in.

'Hi, hi, Edward.' Daisy walked into their mud-room, which was lined with Wellington boots and caked-over iron scrapers. 'And this is Wina! Finally.' The other woman kissed her on the cheek, and Daisy noted jealously that she smelled of baby powder. Of course, nothing so plebian as perfume for Mrs Perfect here, she

426

couldn't help thinking. 'Congratulations, Wina!' she said brightly. 'I'm so sorry I missed the wedding.'

'Me too, but come and have a cup of tea,' Wina invited Daisy. Her voice was light and perfectly modulated, very upper class. Swiss finishing school probably, Daisy thought, feeling middle class and small.

'That would be wonderful.'

'And then I can show you the house.' Wina was leading the way through an oak-panelled hall into the kitchen. She seemed very at ease, in command. 'I know you've never seen the place. Edward told me. It's truly a lovely house.'

Did he indeed? 'I can see that it is,' Daisy agreed. She smiled sideways at Edward, and he winked at her, making her heart flip over slowly in her chest.

★   ★   ★

The big country kitchen reminded Daisy of Fenella's place. There was the Aga, of course, and Wina obviously had a thing for dried flowers, as she had artful little bouquets hanging everywhere. Daisy refrained from asking about them. She really didn't care if Wina was talented at arts and crafts.

'Do you cook? It's a terrific kitchen.'

'Oh no,' Wina said. 'We have Mrs Allsop, who comes in in the mornings and makes up the meals. I couldn't live without her.'

'Of course, Edward told me you had a cook. Like my boyfriend,' Daisy added pointedly.

'Your boyfriend?' Edward grabbed the teapot from Wina. 'You mustn't lift that, darling, it's heavy.'

'For goodness' sake, Edward, I'm not even showing.'

'Daisy, you sly thing. You never mentioned a boyfriend. Who's the lucky chap?'

'Magnus Soren. He's from New York.'

'Not *the* Magnus Soren?' Edward said.

'Yes,' Daisy said innocently. 'Do you know him?'

'I should think so,' Wina said, enthusiastically. 'Edward sees him at parties sometimes, don't you, darling? He's always on the London social scene. He jet-sets. I thought he was dating that Russian model?'

'Obviously not any more,' Edward said. 'Well done, Daisy, he's a good man. And a fortunate one,' he added with a little bow.

Daisy saw his hand unconsciously brushing over his wife's, stroking it. The tender intimacy of the gesture broke her heart.

'I saw him in London last week. He's flying me out to New York in a fortnight; I said I needed two weeks at least to get on with my writing.' She looked at Edward out of the corner of one eye.

He was frowning. Frowning!

That was wonderful, Daisy thought. He was jealous. Now all she had to do was foster that feeling.

★   ★   ★

Wina showed Daisy around the house, which reminded her of the little jewel of a flat in Oxford: plenty of beat-up furniture, well-used antique chairs, original William Morris wallpaper. Daisy was glad of it; the tour gave her something to do, and she could confine her conversation to saying, 'Oh, how lovely,' and other such banalities.

'It's old, but we like it,' Wina said.

'Mmm, lovely,' Daisy agreed. She glanced at Edward. 'Magnus is quite serious with me. I think he wants me to have his baby.'

Edward looked shocked. 'What? How long have you been going out with him? Has he proposed?'

'Not yet, Edward, but don't be so bourgeois,' Daisy said airily.

Edward scowled darkly and Daisy's mood lifted.

428

'Tell me all about work, Edward,' Daisy said. Ugh. How much longer did she have to stay here? She could have lunch, then make her escape.

It couldn't be too soon. Daisy's mind was ticking around, like a hamster on a wheel, trying to find ways to get Edward out of this domestic-goddess mindset he had fallen into.

Think, Daisy, she said to herself. Think.

★ ★ ★

After a fairly stilted lunch, Wina hugged Daisy goodbye.

'I'll walk you out,' said Edward, taking her arm. Daisy shrugged, to hide her pleasure. 'OK,' she said.

At her car, Edward squeezed her arm and looked deeply into her eyes.

'Listen, this Magnus Soren chap. Don't take things too seriously, Daisy. I don't think he's right for you.'

A thrill of satisfaction coursed through her, but she gently shook her arm free and slid into the driver's seat.

'If he isn't, Edward, then . . . who is?' Daisy asked lightly, and she started up the car and drove away.

# 50

The summer rolled on into autumn. Daisy divided her time between writing her new book, dating Magnus Soren, and placing friendly calls to Edward. She refused to allow Magnus to spend too much money on her. She also refused to go to bed with him.

Edward thought they were inseparable; Daisy made sure she always brought up his name. Finally, one Monday in September, the call she had been waiting for arrived.

'Look, old thing . . . ' Daisy beamed with pleasure as she held the receiver; she loved it when Edward used his pet name for her. She could hear his hesitancy and awkwardness at the end of the line. 'Ah. Hmm. I need to see you.'

'Oh, you and Wina are going to be in town?'

'Not Wina. Just me.' Another pause. 'Daisy, we need to talk, just you and I. Will you see me?'

A burst of exhilaration rushed through her, but she was careful to keep any hint of it out of her voice. 'Don't be silly, Edward, I always have time for an old friend.'

'How about next Tuesday night?'

'Magnus is in town, so I'll be having dinner with him.'

His tone darkened. 'And when does Mr Soren leave town?'

'Monday evening,' Daisy said.

'Then Tuesday. For lunch. Can you come to my townhouse? I would rather talk to you absolutely privately.'

'That will be fine,' Daisy said coolly. 'Shall we say one o'clock?'

It was hard to concentrate. She had a week before Magnus was due to arrive, and she knew better than to call Edward. Let him simmer, let him stew. She had to appear disinterested.

Daisy exercised, slept well, and wore no make-up except a tinted moisturiser with sunscreen for a week. She wanted her skin to be perfect; no way was she taking the chance of too much foundation leading to a disastrous spot or something. As far as it was possible, she distracted herself. Work was going wonderfully. Her book was taking shape, gradually, like clay moulded on a potter's wheel; her characters were starting to surprise her, to want to do things that hadn't been in her synopsis. That kind of thing was a blast.

If her nerves over Edward got to be too much, she opened and answered some fan mail. The girls and women who wrote to her always cheered her up. What Daisy was doing wasn't rocket science, it wasn't a cure for hepatitis, but in some small way she was making people happy.

Mostly, however, she thought about Edward. Daisy made valiant efforts to distract herself, but they didn't really work. She had never actually had to say anything to him. And now there was no need.

Edward would say it all himself. She'd have him back, the first man to love her just as she was, to want her when she was fat, unpopular Daisy Markham, the girl who got bullied at school . . .

Daisy shook her head. Never mind about that. First, she had to find some tactful way to get rid of Magnus Soren. He'd been kind, and handsome, and funny, and smart . . . He deserved a gentle let-down.

She was there to meet Magnus when the Concorde arrived at Heathrow on Monday morning.

'Hi.'

Soren kissed her on the cheek. He was wearing a black suit with a matching overcoat, a gold Rolex, and plain cuffs, and carrying a smart navy leather briefcase.

'I didn't expect to see you here.'

'I thought you deserved a welcome,' Daisy said.

Magnus beckoned to his chauffeur, who escorted them out to the waiting car, a sleek Rolls-Royce.

'What, no limousine?' asked Daisy, once they were settled in the back of the car and the partition had been rolled up.

Magnus shook his head. 'When in Rome, baby.' His green eyes looked curiously at her. 'Are you being particularly supportive today? Because of the meeting?'

'What meeting?'

He sighed. 'The Retson meeting. I take it you don't read the *Financial Times*.'

'Not usually,' Daisy said.

'I have an important set of meetings this week. Soren Enterprises is attempting a hostile takeover of the Retson Group. If we get it,' he shrugged, 'we're on a different plane. Of course, their board of directors opposes it bitterly.'

'Why?'

'Because they don't want to get fired,' Magnus said.

'And you'd fire them?'

'I sure would. They're all mid-fifties, and they're stuck in the management philosophy of the Seventies. We can do better. And we will.'

Daisy found the way he spoke about it rather exciting.

'You look like you're spoiling for a fight.'

He chuckled. 'I am. I love it. Back in the old days, men used to conquer countries to get their aggressions out. Now warfare is corporate. I am convinced you get many of the same thrills, with a lot less pain.'

'Unless you are a fired member of the board of directors.'

Soren looked unrepentant. 'They all have golden

432

parachutes, for far more than they're worth.'

The car pulled smoothly and quietly between the lanes of traffic.

'So you didn't come over just to see me?' Daisy pouted.

He looked surprised. 'Daisy, I've never come over just to see you. I always mix business and pleasure. I don't have time to do anything else.'

'Oh . . .'

'And anyway,' he added, 'you and I, darling, are going to have to have what you Limeys call a chat.'

'How boooring,' Daisy sighed. A chat. She hoped he wasn't about to declare his love for her. Or dump her.

'Let's say tonight, at dinner. We'll meet somewhere near you. You can leave a message with my assistant.'

★   ★   ★

Daisy spent the day in the Dorchester spa, getting a massage, a manipedi, and her hair and make-up done. She couldn't concentrate on work, and she was feeling unsettled. In which case, she thought, the best thing to do was to look stunning.

A chat. Magnus Soren wanted to have a chat with her. Daisy didn't like the sound of that one bit. She liked having him around, she thought sleepily as her flesh was kneaded in a dimmed room to the sound of Tibetan wind-chimes on the CD player. Magnus was handsome, and fun. Business wasn't Daisy's thing, but she enjoyed seeing her date rip lesser men and companies to shreds. Like a tiger. Magnus was quite a bit older than Daisy, but for a businessman he was young, a babe in arms. And very masculine. She approved thoroughly of the muscled body and the brash cockiness. He'd earned it, hadn't he?

Daisy thought, with a stab of guilt, that Magnus Soren had been her perfect cover story.

Of course, she hadn't slept with him. That would be too much like cheating on Edward. Even though she was with Magnus, not Edward . . . It had never been about sex with Edward, she had never found him physically attractive, just mentally so.

Magnus, now. Magnus was *hot*. But Daisy was a romantic. Sex had to be more than just satisfying some bodily urge, didn't it? She would rather be Mrs Edward Powers than have the best sex ever with Magnus.

I'm just not a sexual person, Daisy thought. She'd slept with Brad, and so she wasn't a virgin. But the way she remembered it it had hardly been worth the effort of undressing . . .

★ ★ ★

Magnus met her at seven at the Café Des Artistes. Daisy had chosen a feminine dress, all floaty chiffon and appliqué roses, and matched it with a chic little Chanel cardigan in pale green that played up her olive skin, newly blow-dried raven hair, and beautiful face, perfectly made-up.

Magnus grinned when he saw her and kissed her hand.

'Do you like it?' Daisy asked flirtatiously, twirling around.

'To be honest? Not really.'

Her face fell.

'You're so beautiful normally,' Soren said. 'To me, you look best in a white T-shirt and jeans. All that make-up just obscures your skin. It's like gilding the lily.'

'I suppose I should find that flattering,' Daisy said.

'I don't bother with make-up myself.'

'Very funny.'

They ordered some caviar as an appetiser, then moved on to the hen lobsters. Soren ordered

434

champagne; Perrier-Jouet.

'Not Cristal?'

'It's hideously overrated. And overpriced.'

'I thought money was no object to you.'

'It's not; I just don't enjoy being ripped off.' Soren looked at her. Daisy was startled by the expression in his eyes. 'And so, my beauty, it's time for us to find out what the goddam hell is the matter with you.'

★　★　★

'I don't know what you're talking about,' Daisy said, taking a fortifying sip of champagne. It was cold, and it gave her Dutch courage. She didn't want to have this conversation; Soren was making her squirm.

'Why am I always attracted to problem women?' he sighed.

'You date models,' Daisy scoffed.

'Beautiful women have problems too. Take you, for example. You're frigid.'

Daisy started. 'What?'

'You heard me.'

'Just because I don't want to sleep with you, I'm frigid?'

'You do want to sleep with me,' Magnus said confidently. 'But you aren't admitting it to yourself. We've been seeing each other for months. We've had a good time.'

'Yes.'

'And you find me attractive.' He looked at her. 'Don't bother to deny it, Daisy.'

'I do, yes,' she said, slowly. 'Very attractive. But I'm not ready to sleep with you, Magnus.'

'What? You're waiting for a ring?'

'Maybe,' she said, tilting her chin upwards.

His gaze moved over her skin, undressing her, his eyes

focusing disturbingly on her breasts. 'If that were true, I'd respect it.'

'Don't lie,' Daisy said, taking another big slug of her champagne. 'Men need sex, you'd never stand for that.'

'If I need sex so badly, why am I sitting here with you?'

'You could have another girl in New York,' Daisy said mulishly.

'I could,' he agreed. 'But I don't. If I did, I would hardly need to hide it from you. I'd just leave you.'

'You wouldn't wait until we got married,' Daisy insisted.

'I'd just marry you.' Magnus shrugged. 'Problem solved.'

'It's not that simple.'

'Actually, it is. You'll find most things in life are simple.' His gaze narrowed. 'You are one person who tends to over-complicate them. That's always a mistake, Daisy.'

'I don't need you telling me how to live my life,' Daisy hissed.

'Tell me about my rival,' Magnus said, reaching across the table and refilling her glass.

That surprised her. Daisy had told him there was someone else in the beginning, when they were at the farm in Dutchess County, but Magnus had never mentioned it again, and neither had she. Daisy had assumed he'd forgotten all about it.

'That's . . . private,' she said.

'Is he married? Oh, don't look so surprised. I'm not as dumb as you must think I am. If he were single, you'd be with him, you wouldn't be sitting here with me.' Magnus shook his head. 'Saving yourself for a married man who doesn't want you. How counter-productive.'

'How the hell do you know he doesn't want me?' Daisy said, tears blinking under her lashes. She gripped her champagne flute forlornly.

'I told you, dear. Things are simple. If he wanted you, he would have got a divorce, and he'd be with you.'

'Well.' Magnus discreetly passed her a handkerchief, and Daisy angrily dabbed the tears away from her eyes. 'You're wrong, as it happens. He *does* want me. And he will be getting a divorce.'

She pushed her plate away. Magnus reached into his pocket, took out a sheaf of fifties, and threw some down on the table.

'I'll take you home,' he said.

★  ★  ★

When Magnus's car pulled up outside Daisy's building, she felt a stab of remorse.

'Look, I'm sorry how things — '

'Don't be. And don't look so unhappy. I firmly believe in following your destiny. However, *my* destiny is not to be another man's place-holder.'

Daisy went upstairs to her apartment and watched the long black car steal away through the traffic. There was an ache in her heart. But that was natural, right? It had been an enjoyable friendship, until he had started talking about her relationship with Edward.

She went into the bathroom to wash off the careful make-up job he hadn't liked. Oh well. Maybe he'd call her tomorrow and they'd still be friends. She knew he was in town for a week.

★  ★  ★

He didn't call. Not the next day, nor the next. Daisy found herself looking at the calendar, wondering if he would call from the airport.

Nothing. Her phone didn't ring. Daisy told herself it really didn't matter. After all, the important thing was that she was going to see Edward.

She spent the weekend in a fervour of excitement. Finally, she was going to be reunited with him.

# 51

When Tuesday morning came, Daisy remembered Magnus's advice. She wore no make-up at all, just Clarins day cream and a spritz of rosewater, and she chose a relaxed pair of Joseph navy slacks with a simple cream silk shirt and pearls.

When she arrived at Edward's London townhouse, a beautiful Georgian place in Kensington, Daisy wasn't even nervous. She felt strangely calm. There would be nobody here but herself and Edward.

She rang the bell.

'Daisy.' Edward appeared in one of his trademark dark suits. 'Come in, won't you?'

She smiled warmly at him and walked into the house. Typical Edward: paintings, faded carpet, beautiful dark woods everywhere.

'I ordered lunch delivered from a restaurant,' Edward said, showing her into the dining room, which was laid out beautifully for two. 'I hope you don't object to risotto?'

'Not at all.' Daisy sat down, feeling his lack of comfort and slightly enjoying it. She felt powerfully in control.

Edward uncorked the wine; Château Lafite, Daisy saw, wasted on her, but still, a nice gesture.

'Are you hungry?' he asked, pouring her a glass, then sitting down in the carved chair at the head of the table.

'Not really.' Daisy sipped the wine and took a small forkful of risotto. 'I mean, it's delicious, but this lunch really isn't about food, is it?'

His face shadowed. 'No.'

'You wanted to talk to me about Magnus Soren,' Daisy said.

Edward's pale, drawn cheeks actually flushed slightly. 'Ahhm. Yes. I hope you don't think it's too presumptuous, but I really think you're making a mistake.'

'And why is that?' Daisy asked triumphantly.

'Because the man's a playboy. He's ruthless, he has a string of girls. Pretty girls . . . none as pretty as you, of course . . .'

Edward's gallantry was making him tongue-tied. He ploughed on. 'Ahm, and you said you were thinking about having a child with him. But the man's a bounder. He's suggesting this and he hasn't even proposed. You and any child you might have would be very dear to me, and you would both deserve better than that. I really can't stand to see you throw yourself away like this.'

'I'm very dear to you? How dear?'

'Very dear,' Edward said. 'I'm surprised you can even ask the question. After all our years of friendship.'

She waited, but he didn't go on.

'Just friendship?' she prompted.

'What?' Edward said, blinking owlishly.

'For goodness' sake, Edward. Why did you call me here except to tell me you love me? It's not as if I haven't always known it. You loved me back when I was fat.' Unexpectedly, she started to cry at this, but she went on, even with tears trickling down her cheeks. 'You always waited for me. And marrying Wina, you did it too fast, you made a mistake, and now you want to put it right. I know it's difficult.' He sat stock-still, staring at her. Daisy put a manicured hand gently over Edward's bony one. 'But now is the time, or you'll be trapped for ever.'

Her words broke the spell. Edward snatched his hand away, spluttering.

'But — but that's not it at all. My God, how could you have got it so wrong?'

He was a dull red now, the tips of his ears livid with blood.

'What . . . what do you mean?' Daisy stammered.

'I love Wina. Do you think I would invite you here to — to — ' He looked outraged. 'You think I think so little of my wife . . . that I would . . . that I . . . '

Edward pushed back his chair and stood up. He took a deep breath; he was devastatingly, cuttingly formal.

'I'm sorry, but I'm going to have to ask you to leave.'

Daisy didn't move. She couldn't. She felt sick and dizzy, and as though she were going to faint.

'But Edward! Didn't you love me at Oxford?'

'Yes. Then,' he said, his tone clipped and icy. 'Then. When you did not return my feelings I moved on. Something I would advise you to do.'

Daisy stood up. The tears of emotion had become wrenching sobs. She was almost hysterical. Edward looked to right and left, huntedly. Some part of her brain knew that he would not throw her, tear-drenched and gulping, into the street.

'Calm down,' he said, 'for pity's sake.' His face softened. 'I'll get you some kitchen towel.'

'Th — thank you,' she wept.

Edward came back with some sheets of kitchen towel. 'Here. Now look, Daisy.' He ran a thin hand through his hair. 'You must have been interested in me because I liked you when you were . . . heavier. But the point is, you were worth liking then and you're worth liking now. You always made things so hard on yourself. You've always been interested in the wrong sort, or people you couldn't have. I think perhaps,' he said, looking very relieved, because Daisy's sobs had subsided to miserable snuffles, 'perhaps you don't think you deserve to be loved. At any rate, think about it. About yourself.'

He waited by the door, and she stumbled into the corridor.

441

'But can I call you? Can we talk about this?' Daisy said plaintively.

'No,' said Edward gently. 'I'm afraid we can't. I think it would be best if I didn't see you at all for some time.'

His words were soft, but they had the impact of an oncoming train. Daisy managed a nod and stepped out into the street, with its merciless sunlight, and people looking at her red eyes.

She heard Edward Powers shut the door firmly behind her.

★   ★   ★

Daisy never remembered how she got herself home. She knew she must have cried the whole way. It felt as though her heart had been ripped out of her chest while she was still breathing.

Somehow she found herself back in her flat. It was the middle of the afternoon, sun streaming through the windows; her maid had been round, and the place smelled faintly of disinfectant mixed with fresh flowers.

Daisy went into the bathroom to blow her nose. She was a mess, red-eyed, tear-stained. She looked haggard and drawn, despite her good night's sleep and a month's pampering.

A broken heart could do that to you.

She sat on her bed and stared into space until the sun went down over North London, and twilight blue calmed her down. She felt detached from her body; no appetite, no interest in anything. But she forced herself to go and take a bath.

The warmth of the water revived Daisy just a little. She couldn't pretend to herself any more that Edward Powers would ever be hers. Her timing had been off, totally off . . .

Through the bathroom door she hadn't bothered to shut she saw the vase of pink roses, the colour of

442

sugared almonds, she'd bought when the last flowers Magnus had sent had died. Magnus. Now she'd never see him again either.

Magnus had told her she was frigid. That she was over-complicating things.

Frigid? She just wasn't that interested in sex. Like most people, probably.

Then Edward had given her that psychiatry crap.

Why did men want to run her life? She didn't want advice. She just wanted love, Daisy thought.

But something was nagging at her. A sneaking suspicion that Edward might have, in some tiny way, a point.

No question she had messed things up and kept messing them up. Her love life was about as successful as English cricket.

Maybe it was all about Daisy, all about how she saw herself. Daisy went to the bathroom mirror and tried to look past the heartbreak pallor and the bloodshot eyes. Yes, she knew she was beautiful. And if not conventionally clever, well, so what? She had done wonders with her life — she was young, and successful, and she'd looked after her parents . . .

The first faint tinge of shame started to creep into her thoughts. It was no good trying to cheer herself up with what a great person she was. She'd just tried to take a married man away from his wife. Edward had told her she had a problem with self-esteem; Magnus Soren had told her to grow up.

Daisy mulled this over. She had pushed Edward away when he was suitable, pushed Magnus away when *he* was suitable. And made a bee-line, always, for those men who were guaranteed to reject her.

For a few seconds she considered therapy, then rejected it. Fuck that, Daisy thought, I'm English. I don't go for all that hand-holding inner child bollocks —

The phrase stopped her train of thought. Inner child. Weren't you supposed to repeat childhood patterns over and over?

But her childhood had been mostly happy, hadn't it? She'd had great parents who loved her. So why had she eaten herself into unpopularity, making sure, with her shyness and her weight, that the other kids at school would be mean to her, would — yeah — would reject her?

The answer came to her, so surprising and so instantly clear that Daisy, nude, felt weak-kneed and flopped down on to her bed.

She had been rejected before any of these had rejected her.

By her parents. Her first, biological parents.

★   ★   ★

After a sleepless night, Daisy woke and dressed. The first call she made was to her parents. Her real ones, Daisy reminded herself.

Her mother picked up on the first ring.

'Hello, Mum.'

'Hello, darling . . . '

'Mum, I need to ask you something.' Daisy was hesitant; was this going to be incredibly hurtful for her mother?

'Is something wrong, darling? Are you hurt? Sick?'

'No.' She must have sounded worse than she thought. 'Nothing to be worried about. But look, Mum, I'm curious about the adoption. My adoption.'

There was an exhalation at the end of the phone.

'It's nothing about you and Dad. You are my real parents, my only parents.' Daisy heard herself gabbling. 'You know I love you — '

'Of course I know that, darling,' said her mother,

sounding reassuringly disapproving over this unre-strained display of emotion.

'But, you know, I'm curious. I'd like to find out more about it.'

'Well, we always knew you'd ask eventually,' her mother said. 'And I wish I could be more help, darling, I really do. But your adoption was one of those ones where they don't give out any information. Confidentiality.'

Daisy persisted. 'But didn't you ask? Medical records, anything like that? Didn't you insist?'

Mrs Markham laughed. 'Oh, darling, we'd been trying to adopt for years. You have no idea what it's like. When they said they had a beautiful baby girl we took you, no questions asked. If you had been sick, well.' The shrug in the voice. 'We'd just have looked after you. We fell in love with you the moment we saw you.'

Daisy's eyes teared over, but she brushed them away. 'Darling Mum,' she said.

'Darling you.'

'Do you remember the name of the agency?'

'Of course. I have all those details in a file upstairs. Hold on a second, my angel.'

Her mother came back a few moments later. 'They were called InterAdopt, and they were in London.' She gave Daisy the phone number and an address on Tottenham Court Road. 'But bear in mind it was twenty-five years ago, so they may have moved.'

'Don't worry,' Daisy said. 'I'll find them.'

★ ★ ★

It proved easier said than done.

A year passed. Daisy worked on her next book, and continued her search, in between rounds of publicity, booksellers' conferences, and the other minutiae of life as a successful author. It was very frustrating, not to be able to find much out. But phoning and writing and contacting search agencies at least kept her mind off Magnus Soren, and distracted her from her regrets.

The agency had moved out of its premises years ago. It took her six months to find that they had gone out of business, another six months to get even small snippets of information from the public records. In the meantime, Daisy licked her wounds and worked it all out on paper; she was kinder to her characters than luck had been to her.

She even dated, but that was desultory. Her dates never lasted more than four outings, at most. She found she couldn't bear to have men touch her.

Daisy was getting obsessed with finding out about her birth parents. She believed in her heart that she had had a revelation, that she would never be able to move on unless she discovered why they had given her up. Hadn't wanted her.

★   ★   ★

*The Orange Blossom* was published to sizzling reviews and even bigger sales than her first book. Daisy's business manager invested her money and did well, making her returns at almost 14 per cent.

She was rich, and getting richer. She even got stopped on the street a couple of times. Magazines wanted to interview her, talk shows wanted her as a guest. She was young, successful, outrageously good-looking. Daisy was coy about her love life — 'What love life?' — and that just made the press more interested. She did not enjoy the attention. It took away from one of her greatest pleasures in being a writer — anonymity; being lost in her made-up world, at least until the books came out and she could see people reading them on the Tube. Now *that* gave her a buzz.

But this time she thought that maybe she could use it.

Her search was getting nowhere. Every little piece of information led to a dead end.

Daisy made a decision. She was going to go public, and maybe that would lead to the truth.

★   ★   ★

'I was adopted,' Daisy said to Susie Quant.

Susie was the perky host of *Sitting with Susie*, a daytime chat show which had a pretty high rating. It was on Channel 4 and followed *Oprah*, and her publicist thought appearing on it was a coup.

'Give them something juicy,' she had said.

Daisy had decided to do just that. Susie's heavily mascara-ed eyes widened. Daisy could see her thinking, 'Great TV.' 'Were you really?' she purred.

Daisy looked right at the camera. 'I was. The agency was called InterAdopt, and it seems to have disappeared off the face of the earth. If any of my readers have any news, I'd be grateful if they could contact me . . . '

She heard the sharp hiss in the audience, the intake of breath. Well, that should be good for a paragraph in *OK!*. Daisy hated bringing such private matters out in the open, but she was frustrated, and she needed help.

Who knew? Maybe this would work.

# 52

The Lincoln Town Car purred to a halt and the chauffeur got out, walked around to the back, and opened the door. He stood to attention, but noticed, out of the corner of his eye, those long, lean legs as they slid out of the luxurious buttery leather interior of the car. He always did; gams like that were hard to miss.

Rose Fiorello was wearing a chocolate-brown woollen Donna Karan dress with cream buttons and trim, long sleeves, and matching cream leather gloves. Her wonderful legs were encased in brown lambswool hose, tapering down to a pair of knee-high Jimmy Choo zip-up boots. A second later, her warm, protective cashmere coat fell about her.

His boss was as glamorous as a movie star, the driver thought. All the other guys in the service envied him this assignment and pumped him for info. A sweet little thing like that . . . she had to have some rich sugar daddy, no? They talked in hushed tones about Vincent Salerni, the mob boss and Ms Fiorello's patron. He *had* to be in the back of the car sometimes, right? Taking a little 'tribute'? But he had, sadly, nothing to report. Fiorello was hot stuff OK, but she lived like a nun. A very rich, very busy nun. And she took no crap. He'd heard her chewing out men on the in-car phone and he was glad not to be on the other end of the line.

Rose Fiorello was, he had concluded, very beautiful, very rich, and very pissed off. Like, all the time. She had fired the last four drivers for occasionally being late — she was like that, she demanded respect. Even the slightest deviation from *rispetatto* and you got fired. The woman was like Genghis Khan in a cute little short skirt.

Maybe she was gay, but she never had any girlfriends in the back of that limo. As far as he could work out, the boss didn't have time for them. She visited her mom once a week, and that was the extent of her social life.

Not for the first time, he reflected that it was a shame.

'When will you be wanting to be picked up, Ms Fiorello?' he asked, touching his cap deferentially.

Rose didn't look at him. 'I'm not sure, Bernie. I'll beep you.'

'Very good, ma'am,' he said, getting back into the car.

She was staring at the building and she had *that look* on her face. Sometimes, Bernie thought, it seemed like the only thing Rose Fiorello cared about was goddam buildings. Houses, apartment blocks, run-down brownstones; bricks and mortar rather than flesh and blood.

She was obsessed. He put the car into gear, thinking that she needed a good fucking. What a pity he wasn't gonna be the one to give it to her . . .

★   ★   ★

'How many floors?' Rose asked.

The realtor was a nervous little man, somewhat rat-like. He had a pair of black-framed glasses which he kept pushing back up the bridge of his nose. He had heard of the newly legendary Rose Fiorello, and told all the sellers in the office that he was about to take her for a ride.

It wasn't working out like that. She had an aggravating willingness to walk away from the deal. That fact was stopping him from bullying her the way he wanted to.

'Eighteen,' he said. 'That's a great size, Rose.'

'I don't recall asking you to call me by my first name, Mr Robinson.'

'Uhm, right. Miss Fiorello.'

449

'And the top six floors are nothing but a shell. It would have to be completely restored, assuming the building's structurally sound. Which I'm not.'

'We could check that out for you.'

'No bank is gonna mortgage on this dump,' Rose said decisively. 'Which means hard money. Your price is going to squeeze my profit margins.'

'Yes, but think of the opportunities . . . Prime Manhattan real estate . . . '

'Alphabet City,' Rose sneered, making it sound like it wasn't worth living in. 'Do you think this place will rent to the highest class? You got needles in the parks round here, a homeless shelter two blocks over, and graffiti on the walls.'

'There's opportunity in East Manhattan, Miss Fiorello, with Mayor Giuliani in charge . . . '

'Back taxes on this place alone are almost two hundred grand just to clear the title,' Rose said.

He wavered. 'Like I said, the upside is huge, ma'am.'

Rose looked up. Rust was everywhere, debris, and rats. 'Let's get out into the street before the building falls on our heads.'

She made it sound so shitty he was actually glad to follow her.

'What we have here is the potential for a large, bright apartment building with space for a garden and landscaping,' he said unconvincingly.

'What you have here, Mr Robinson, is an unsafe abandoned structure which is being used as a flop house and crack den, in a seedy part of Manhattan, which no bank can lend on and which has been on the market for over eighteen months, because your price is insane.'

'So you don't want it,' he said, crumpling a little. 'We have some other, better buildings.'

'I want it,' Rose said. 'I never said I didn't want it.'

'But you — '

'I don't want it at your insane price. I'll give you three quarters of a million, not including the taxes, which brings it to almost a full mill.'

'The price is three million dollars and that's — '

'Unacceptable. Look, Mr Robinson. You've had this dog on your books for longer than a year. What does that say to some guy looking to list his house? Benkman Martin has inventory that doesn't shift because they can't shift it. I know you've had buyers that have fallen through. And why? Because they're not liquid. Not serious. Now, I can move fast. I have the money and you know my reputation.'

He wavered.

'In a month, you can have this thing closed, and you know what they'll say in the office? 'John Robinson knows how to cut his losses and move out the crap. He got rid of that dog on Avenue A the first day he showed it.''

Robinson blinked. 'How — how did you know this is my first day of showing this property?'

Rose Fiorello looked him dead in the eye and said, 'I'm connected.'

She was in with Salerni. He'd heard that. Suddenly John Robinson just wanted to get back behind his nice cushy desk. And it *was* a dog, and it *had* just sat there for over a year . . .

'I'll have to do a lot of talking to convince the seller.'

'Try telling him that my sources tell me City Hall's about to file a lawsuit on his ass for owning a crack den.'

'I don't know . . . '

Rose reached inside her warm cashmere coat and took out a white paper envelope. She opened it slightly to let Robinson see what was inside: a sheaf of green notes.

'Hundreds,' she said. 'A hundred of them. That's ten

thousand dollars. Get me a signed contract in a week, and it's yours.'

★ ★ ★

'You may be able to do something with this one,' Greg Filkes said. He slid the manila file across the mahogany desk, expectantly.

Jacob Rothstein picked it up, slid the photographs and sheets out of it, and grinned. 'Good job, Filkes.'

'Thank you, sir.'

'That'll be all for now,' he added, disappointing the junior executive, who had been hoping for a round of back-slapping congratulations from the boss's son. But he got up and left the office quietly, closing the door. Doubtless he'd get a bonus, or something . . .

Everybody knew the crown prince was in deep shit because he'd brought his little girlfriend into the company and she'd stolen some data. Now he was looking to crush her, presumably to get back in Daddy's good graces. Filkes had found his master something that would help, and he expected to be in favour with both father and son.

Because this was a little quarrel, but so what? The Rothsteins were a family, and they'd get over that. It was what every suit in the building expected.

Greg Filkes was wrong, though.

Jacob Rothstein stared at the details for twenty minutes, taking them in. Nice choice, Rose, he mused, admiring her taste. She really did have a flair for real estate and under normal circumstances he thought she would have gone far.

But these were not normal circumstances. She had Jacob Rothstein on her tail.

★ ★ ★

452

Jacob made sure everything was in order before he made his move. He hired a new lawyer, not one who was in the pocket of his family, and had him check out his legal status. He was disappointed, but not all that surprised, to find that most of his wealth wasn't his at all; it belonged to a family trust, and without his parents' say-so, Jacob couldn't touch it. The Manhattan apartment and contents belonged to him, though. He had two hundred and twelve thousand in a current account, of which one hundred was last year's bonus, and his new lawyer told him crisply he'd most likely have to pay it back.

That left him a car, an apartment, and a hundred grand, after he'd paid off the lawyer. Rothstein felt a few butterflies, but resolutely ignored them. A hundred grand wasn't much in the Big Apple; maintenance and taxes on his place were two thousand a month just by themselves. Figure in fine wines, food, the necessity of a decent suit, parking, dry cleaning; he wasn't even sure if it would last him three months.

And yet Jacob had had no doubts about what he was going to do.

For the last two weeks he had been quietly tying up every loose end in his department, assigning more work to his underlings, and getting his files in order for a successor. And this morning he was all done.

He picked out a thick brown padded envelope, addressed it to his apartment, and filled it with everything he had on Rose Fiorello. Then Jacob personally dropped it in the company mail-chute, and after that was done, went outside to his secretary.

'Buzz my father for me, would you please, Ella.'

'Yes, Mr Rothstein,' she said breathily. 'Are you going up to see him?'

'That's right.'

'Come back soon,' she said, batting her eyelashes at him. She never saw him again.

'Don't be such a spoiled brat, Jake,' his father said, angrily. 'I have an eleven o'clock and I don't need this bullshit.'

'Take the eleven o'clock, Dad. I'm not gonna change my mind.'

'Of course you are. You're just throwing a temper tantrum.'

'No.' Jacob shook his head. He faced his father across the desk; he had not sat down, and Fred Rothstein wasn't about to get up. 'I'm outta here, Dad. I just wanted to tell you myself.'

'Is that about that skinny wop bitch? For fuck's sake! I can get some girls that look just like her sent round to your apartment, you can bang 'em and get over this crap.'

Jacob winced. His father's vulgarity jarred on him. 'It's nothing to do with her,' he said, not entirely truthfully.

Fred's face darkened. 'So you're about to run off with my company secrets and hook up with her, are you? Betraying me for some piece of second-rate pussy?'

'I'd never do that. Never.' Now he was being convincing. 'I would never help anybody to hurt the firm.'

'Then what is it, you goddam idiot?'

He gritted his teeth. 'Dad. I don't like how we work here. I don't like the fact that we have to screw tenants out of leases, instead of negotiating — '

'That's great; my boy, the pussy-whipped liberal.'

'I don't like the accounting, and I especially don't like being bounced off Acquisitions.'

Fred spread his hands. 'So, we'll talk about that. Don't be so freaking melodramatic.'

'It's too late for that. I realised it the second you had me moved. I just don't want to take orders any more.'

He held up a hand to forestall his father. 'Yeah, I know I run the division. But I need my independence. I just don't like answering to anybody, and I intend to run my own firm my own way.'

'*Your* own firm? You're just a greenhorn, Jacob. Barely out of college . . . '

'Young doesn't mean incompetent, Dad.' Jacob stepped forward and laid his formal letter of resignation on his father's desk.

Fred Rothstein stared at his son. The freaking moron was actually serious.

'You'll have to give back — '

'My bonus. I know. I already wired it back. And the cottage in the Hamptons, and that Ferrari you leased for me. I know, Dad. I know exactly what I'm worth.'

'How?'

'I hired a lawyer. I've thought this through.'

'Open your briefcase!' Fred Rothstein screamed. 'How do I know you're not trying to sneak out of here with our documents like that wop bitch?'

Jacob smiled inwardly and popped the lock to his briefcase. 'Here.' He showed his father; the Coach red-leather case was empty apart from a gold Mont Blanc pen. 'That's mine; Grandma gave it to me, remember?'

'You goddam ungrateful bastard,' Fred Rothstein snarled. 'Get the fuck out of my office.'

'I'll see you for dinner this weekend — '

'I don't *think* so,' Fred Rothstein said. 'You're banned from the house until you give up this craziness and come back to work for me.'

'I'm never coming back to work here unless I have total voting control of the stock,' Jacob said flatly.

Fred blinked. 'You hafta be shitting me.'

Jacob sighed. 'Elegantly put, Dad. But no.'

He left his father sitting there spluttering with rage,

walked out to the executive elevator, and rode it down to the lobby.

★ ★ ★

His flat was a welcome sight, when he got home. It was going to double as an office, for the time being. He had no place else he could use.

Jacob had set aside a small corner of his library, installing a desk, a computer and a modem. He had his subscription to MLS set up, and he had a thick sheaf of realtor files. He also had a one-page list of bank contacts.

It was a bit of a stretch. A privileged young man, working only for Daddy's company, suddenly deciding he wanted to strike out on his own. Easy to applaud, but not so easy to underwrite. And yet Jacob was confident.

The stock market was soaring. It was a good time to own Fifth Avenue property outright. He didn't want to sell — too much Capital Gains Tax. No, the best thing would be to mortgage the property up to the hilt. The gains were the proceeds of a loan, and thus they were both tax-free and tax-deductible. Jacob had looked at some similar spaces and calculated, conservatively, that this one would fetch five million. He would take out four and keep a million in equity as a cushion. That would be the seed-money; that, he could take to a bank. They would need more than his track record as part of a huge corporation, packaged up with a cute smile.

Jacob smiled to himself. Sure, it was a huge gamble, but he felt light, almost carefree. He sat down at the little desk that constituted the sum total of the assets of the JRoth Corporation, picked up his one-page list, and made his first phone call.

★ ★ ★

A week later Jacob Rothstein took stock. The results had been mixed. He'd got his mortgage, and that was great, but the banks seemed unimpressed.

'You don't really have any assets, Mr Rothstein. Now, if you'd like to talk to an investment specialist about letting us manage your money . . . '

It was the same old song everywhere.

'Three million dollars is hardly chopped liver,' Jacob responded, struggling to keep his temper in check.

'That's true, but it's also hardly enough to buy a building in Manhattan. Not on the scale you are discussing.' There would be a limp hand extended across the desk. 'Please call us when we can help you with something.'

Jacob shrugged. 'I wouldn't wait by the phone.'

There was no getting around it, he was going to have to play it a little less safe than his instincts told him to. If he couldn't get a construction loan or an industrial mortgage, he was going to have to acquire an asset.

It wasn't as though he hadn't done it before.

Jacob sat at his desk and looked at the other file, the Rose Fiorello one. He had intended to pursue Rose. Maybe not in quite this way, but it would serve. He found it actually kind of amusing that she was doing all his work for him. The building was a gem, if you knew the right builders, and she was in with Salerni's mob; but he didn't run the only crew in Brooklyn. He knew what she'd want to do; gate the entrance, put up a guard, make clean, functional apartments out of them, and wait for the neighbourhood to gentrify . . .

She'd be paying cash, but he knew how Rose worked. She was the queen of the low-ball sellers, and she talked them into it by moving super-fast. She had her hard money guys lined up. On the other hand, he, Jacob, had four million dollars sitting in a money-market account. Rose might be able to move in a month. But he could move today.

Jacob had a frisson of pleasure at the thought. He lifted the phone and dialled Benkman Martin.

'Hi,' he said. 'I'd like to speak to John Robinson about his property on Avenue A. It's urgent.'

# 53

Rose's day started out pretty normally.

Her alarm woke her at 6 a.m., and she instantly swung her bare feet out of bed and walked to the kitchen, where she put on some cinnamon coffee before heading to the shower. She was a morning person, and relished every second of her alone time before work started. It was as close as she came to a personal life, unless you counted those Sunday lunches with her mother. Rose washed her hair with shampoo from Bumble and Bumble, blasted it dry with an industrial-strength dryer that took less than five minutes, and patted her face with Crème de la Mer moisturising cream; it was two hundred dollars a pot, but it left her skin feeling as plump as a sixteen-year-old's. Then she pulled on her big white towelling robe and sat in her kitchen, sipping coffee and watching the sun come up over lower Manhattan. It was her daily routine, and she loved it.

Next, she took the lift to the lobby to pick up her morning papers. Rose read the *Wall Street Journal* and the London *Financial Times*, as well as *The Economist* weekly. She retrieved her steaming mug of fragrant coffee and shook out the *Financial Times* and saw her own face staring back at her.

Rose blinked, panicked. What was this? Some exposé of her links to Salerni? The last thing she needed right now was the Feds sniffing around her. Or some Rothstein smear? Was he filing some lawsuit for the documentation she'd got away with?

She set her mug down and picked up the paper, looking at it more closely.

'Daisy Markham,' the caption read, 'best-selling

British novelist, signs copies of her latest release *The Orange Blossom* at Barnes & Noble yesterday.'

Rose scrutinised the picture. Sometimes people just looked a bit like you. But no, this was her face.

Am I going insane? she thought. She took the paper into the bathroom, folded it into a square, and held it up against her reflection in the mirror. The girl in the paper had salmon-coloured skin, courtesy of the *Financial Times*'s pink pages, but apart from that minor detail they could have been the same person.

This is a sick joke, Rose thought. But the image gazed back at her with a wry smile that she recognised as her own.

Who the hell is responsible for this? And where did they get that picture of me? But of course, it wasn't of her, she reflected, she had never sat behind a table of books, signing them. So it had to be a digital photo, enhanced until some author looked like her . . .

. . . twin.

Rose's heart started to pound. She felt dizzy and sick. The paper slipped out of her hand on to the floor, and she went to the phone and dialled her mother's number. It was way too early for her mom to be up, but Rose didn't care. She had to speak to her now.

The phone rang and rang and then, finally, she heard her mother's voice, groggy from sleep.

'Hello?'

'Mom?'

Her mother reacted instantly to the tone of Rose's voice, her own tone becoming alert and panicky right away. 'What is it, honey? Are you OK? Have you been in an accident?'

'No,' she said, struggling to breathe normally. 'I'm fine. Mom, I was adopted, right?'

'You know you were.'

'In the hospital . . . was there another baby?'

'What do you mean, Rose?'

'Like a twin, a twin sister. And maybe you only took me?'

'Rose!' Daniella Fiorello sounded shocked. 'You think I would have split up sisters? And not told you about it? No, you were the only one, there were other babies, not many, but there you were and they told us you were next on the list to be adopted, and anyway, once we'd seen you and held you in our arms, Daddy and I wanted only you, darling.'

'Oh,' Rose said. She was so confused, she had no idea what to think.

'Why are you asking me this so early in the morning?'

'I — I saw somebody I thought looked like me.'

Her mother laughed that warm, rich laugh of hers, and Rose instantly felt a little better. 'It must have been a trick of the light, honey; you're so beautiful nobody could ever look like you.'

That was her mom; so proud and maternal. Rose felt her world regaining a touch of normality. 'Thanks, Mom.'

'OK, hon. Call me if you want anything or you want to talk about it.'

'OK,' Rose agreed, hanging up.

She hesitated, then called Fiona, her newly hired assistant. Fiona knew enough to be up at this time of the morning. She answered her cell phone immediately.

'Rose Fiorello's office.'

'This is Rose.'

'Good morning, Miss Fiorello. Do you want to go over your schedule for the day?'

'No. I want you to cancel today's appointments,' Rose said.

There was a pause. 'Are you sick, Miss Fiorello?'

'I'm fine,' Rose said shortly. 'I just have something I need to take care of. See to it, please.'

'Very well, ma'am,' Fiona said. 'Have a good day.'

Rose noticed the shock in Fiona's voice. Was it *that*

461

unusual for her to take a day off? She supposed it was
. . . maybe her mother was right, that she worked too
hard. But what other way was there to live?

She looked at her wall clock. It was now almost 7
a.m. OK, that left two and a half hours before the
nearest bookstore opened.

Rose went to her walk-in closet. What to do with
all that spare time? She supposed she'd just take
extra care getting dressed today. She didn't believe in
*doppelgängers*; she was going to get to the bottom of
this.

* * *

John Robinson moistened his lips.

'It's not that I'm not interested, Mr Rothstein,' he
said carefully. 'It's just that your timetable is
unrealistic . . . '

'I'm prepared to outbid your other offer by 20 per
cent,' Rothstein said. 'Did she make mention of a bonus
to you?'

Greed flickered in the realtor's eyes. 'As a matter of
fact — '

'How much?' Jacob asked.

'Ten thousand.'

'I'll give you thirty,' he said simply. 'Everybody wins
here.'

'Except the rival bidder.'

'Well, that's what she gets for trying to low-ball
Benkman Martin, right?' Jacob smiled at him, man to
man. 'She can be a little disrespectful, no? That's no
way to succeed in business.'

'You're right,' Robinson said, meanly. He remembered Rose Fiorello's beauty and cold manner. Bitch.
'She just lost the deal.'

'You get me that contract by close of business
today, and they get a better price and you get thirty

thou. You also get the gratitude of the only son of Fred Rothstein,' Jacob said smoothly.

He nodded eagerly. 'But of course, Mr Rothstein. Let me get on it right away.'

★ ★ ★

Rose was waiting outside the doors of Barnes & Noble on Fifth Avenue when the staff opened them up, impatiently tapping her feet.

'Good morning, miss,' the staffer said as she entered the large store. 'Is there anything special you were looking for?'

'Yes. A book by a girl called Daisy Markham,' Rose said.

'Oh, great choice. She's taken the fiction world by storm, we can hardly keep the new one in stock. Here you go . . . ' He picked up a glossy hardcover off the Bestsellers table and handed it to Rose. 'Are you a big fan? I just adored *The Lemon Grove* . . . '

Rose was already walking away from him towards the checkout counter, but she stopped. 'I'll take one of those too.'

'Certainly, miss,' he responded, thinking that she was a weirdo. A beautiful weirdo, in a pretty pink Chanel suit, but a weirdo all the same. Quickly he fished out a copy of the book from the paperback bestseller rack. 'Anything else? We have some excellent reads in the same vein, I highly recommend the latest Jenny Colgan novel . . . '

But he was talking to her departing back. Rose was already at the counter, paying with a couple of bills and walking right out while the cashier shouted at her not to forget her change.

★ ★ ★

Rose found a Starbucks, ordered a latte, and sat at a table staring at the picture on the back of the book until the latte got cold and a waitress came over to ask her if she was OK. Then she got up, left, and caught a cab back to her apartment downtown.

There was no denying it. This girl was her double. They had to be twins. Rose also knew her mom wouldn't lie to her. Her mind churned over the possibilities. What if the orphanage had already found a parent for the first baby, and then not told her parents there was another? But this girl was English, and her agency had been right here in New York.

She had to find out what had happened. And she had to meet Daisy Markham. Rose wasn't sure why she felt this way. What could a blood sister mean to her, after all? They hadn't shared a goddam thing, except parents who hadn't given a shit about them. Her only family was her mother, not some rent-a-womb she'd happened to gestate in, Rose thought bitterly.

Still. She had to see Daisy Markham. She could easily have the ultra-efficient Fiona arrange something, but for now, as she sorted out her emotions, Rose didn't want that.

This was something she had to deal with herself.

# 54

It was raining in New York. Dirty, sleety rain poured from a grey-white sky, solid cloud without even a flash of blue. A cold wind blustered through the immense stone forest of Manhattan's skyscrapers, picking up plastic bags and styrofoam coffee cups. It was January, and the freezing heart of winter.

Daisy Markham didn't care. She had been inundated by helpful suggestions from her readers. That made her feel loved and wanted, but it wasn't all that much use. The only thing worth following up was an anonymous note telling her to look into Janus Investigators in the United States.

She had, and now she was here.

Daisy walked down Fifth Avenue, warmly wrapped in her Burberry coat and cashmere sweater-dress in navy blue from Donna Karan, together with her waterproof thigh-high Gucci boots. She looked great, and she felt alive and revitalised. Never mind the weather. She was in New York, and she had things to do.

Janus was the successor to the mighty Kroll Security, the doyen of investigative companies, an outfit that made the CIA look like the Keystone Cops. However, Kroll was reputable, perhaps a little too reputable. Daisy was tired of looking.

She wanted to find her birth parents. Now.

★  ★  ★

The offices were not really what she had imagined. She was down at Twenty-Third Street, near the glorious, weird-shaped Flatiron building that looked like it had been squeezed between two giant crushers until it lay as

465

flat as a cartoon character picking himself up from a cliff fall. Janus was housed in a low-slung office building, only forty storeys high, lined with industrial carpet and fichus plants in red pots. Not much evidence of money, despite their incredible fees, but Daisy supposed that was part of the whole 'discretion' thing.

She noted that the offices all had their doors closed. Nothing was open-plan, she thought as a secretary led her through to the meeting room. No cubicle layouts. No way, she realised, for anybody to hear anybody else's conversation . . .

'I know what you're thinking.' Doug Berkshire, the middle-aged guy with the nice suit, thick glasses and a limp handshake who was dealing with her case, grinned, a bit smugly she thought. 'The walls are all soundproofed. We take internal security very seriously here.'

'I didn't have to pass any security to get up to your lobby,' Daisy pointed out.

The grin did not evaporate. 'That's because we've already had *you* checked out. Just a precaution, you understand.'

'I want to find my birth parents,' she said, disliking him and at the same time deciding that he was the perfect man for the job.

'Yes. So you said.' He spread his hands. 'They made quite a job of covering their tracks . . . but nothing we can't crack.'

'Can you guarantee that?'

'No guarantees. A hundred thousand dollars, fifty per cent in advance. No refunds.'

Daisy blinked. '*How* much?'

Berkshire's eyes gleamed greedily behind the glasses. 'You can afford it, Ms Markham, and that's the price.'

'How would you know what I can afford?'

'You have twenty-six accounts around the world,' Berkshire said softly, 'and your current cleared balance at your account in Barclays, Sloane Square, at 9 a.m. local time this morning was four hundred and fifty-nine thousand, eight hundred and seventy-two pounds and six pennies.'

Daisy sat there for thirty seconds staring at him.

'Actually it was eight hundred and sixty-four . . . '

Berkshire shook his head. 'They added the interest this morning.'

'You son of a bitch,' Daisy said, with grudging admiration. 'You're hired.'

★ ★ ★

She was in her hotel room thirty minutes later. Daisy had chosen the Paramount; it was chic, hip, near Times Square and possessed of New York's best-looking bell boys.

But it didn't excite her. Mission accomplished with Janus, she was now wondering what to do with herself.

Daisy caught herself staring at the phone. Don't do it, Daisy, she told herself. Just don't call him.

Magnus Soren. Playboy. New billionaire, or so *Forbes* informed her.

She'd been boyfriend-less for the last year. The odd date, but nothing that lasted beyond a month. Daisy had been reconciled with Edward, but now she saw him as nothing more than a friend. She'd had the slow, creeping realisation that both the men in her life had been right. About everything. And she, the professional romantic, she had been all wrong, all the time.

There was a *reason* Daisy hadn't gone with Edward back when she'd had the chance. *She just wasn't attracted to him.* It was a profound truth, and she'd known it in her heart. Brad had been just attraction, Edward just friendship. With both men, she had been willing to settle for half of what she truly wanted. Courting that childhood rejection again and again, not willing to give her own heart what it needed.

Daisy smiled ruefully. She had treated her millions of readers better than she'd treated herself.

Magnus, she had liked. And wanted. And . . . dumped.

Smart move, kiddo, she told herself.

Well, he hadn't spent his days pining away. His big deal had gone through, and now he was famous, and a big target for every would-be trophy wife in the world. Even if she'd wanted to forget him, she couldn't. He was in Nigel Dempster's column, he was in *The Tatler*, he was in *Harper's*, in *Vogue* . . . and *Hello!* and *OK!* couldn't get enough of him.

I still have his number, Daisy told herself. I could call him.

Her fingers were itching to do it. No! Why look pathetic? What would she say, I just wanted to look you up . . . ?

Daisy suddenly shook herself. She wasn't supposed to repeat the old patterns, to tell herself she wasn't good enough. What the hell! If he didn't want to talk to her he'd blow her off. And if he does blow me off, I'll survive, Daisy thought. It's not like I haven't had practice.

★ ★ ★

'Soren Enterprises.'

'Magnus Soren, please.'

'One second.' A pause, then the voice of a PA, somebody new, Daisy thought. 'Mr Soren's office.'

'Is he about, please? It's Daisy Markham calling.'

'What company are you with, ma'am?'

'I'm a friend,' Daisy said firmly.

'I see.' The woman had all the personality of an ATM. 'Can you spell your name for me, please?' Daisy did so. 'And this is regarding?'

'I told you that I'm his friend,' Daisy said. She was

starting to feel sweaty and anxious.

'Mr Soren has a lot of 'friends',' the woman said, openly hostile now. 'It's company policy to ask what the matter is regarding.'

'It's regarding Daisy Markham,' Daisy snapped. 'Just give him the goddam message!'

She slammed the phone down and buried her face in her hands. Ugh. Ugh. Oh well, at least she'd had the balls to call . . .

Daisy went into her small, sleekly designed urban bathroom and started to run a hot bath with some Origins ginger bath cream. It was a sexy scent and at least taking a bath would mean she wasn't watching the receiver. Magnus probably wasn't in town anyway. Tonight she would go to the movies, or the theatre maybe . . .

The phone rang.

Daisy dived for it.

'Daisy Markham,' she said, trying to make it come out normal-sounding and not too much like a squeak.

'Magnus Soren. What a genius you do have for pissing off my secretaries, Daisy.'

'Let me turn the water off — I was just getting ready for a bath . . . '

'Don't stop undressing on my account,' Soren said.

'Hold on.' She put the phone down on her bed. I must manage this, Daisy thought, I must control the situation . . .

She rushed to turn off the water then grab the phone again.

'Where are you staying?'

'The Paramount.'

'Room?'

'206. Listen, Magnus, I thought maybe we could catch up, you know, see a — '

'I'm coming right over,' Soren said, and she was listening to a dial tone.

469

Daisy spent the next ten minutes frantically tarting herself up; she cleaned her teeth, smoothed Clarins Beauty Flash Balm over her face, reapplied her make-up, brushed her long, wild raven hair smooth, and changed her dress. The navy wool was great, but the last thing she wanted was to be all nervous and sweaty. She chose a long gown in white crêpe with a zipper and a matching cashmere cardigan for when she was outside; it was un-crushable in a suitcase and played up the olive tones in her skin, and her incredible curves, while still being modest.

It was vital to make a good impression. Daisy wanted to be poised, light-hearted, absolutely in control. A total contrast to the crying wreck he'd seen when he left her last. She reached for her suede 'travel jewellery' case . . . that was the latest thing in London; rich girls had their real baubles, and then they had a second set of elegant little pieces that they could travel with and not have to worry *too* much about the insurance premiums. Toys for girls. Daisy had some pretty cultured pearls, Akoyas, golden in colour, that softened the crisp white of the dress. She put them on, and dabbed perfume on her wrists and the cleft of her breasts. Never put scent next to pearls . . . she chose Hermes' 64 Rue Faubourg, her latest favourite, a little slice of summer in the grey heart of winter . . .

Daisy checked herself out in the mirror. Very elegant, she thought. That would do.

The doorbell buzzed.

She opened it up. Magnus Soren was standing there in a dark suit, a contrast to his blond hair and light eyes. He was muscular enough for it to have had to be specially cut, she thought.

He looked stunning. Daisy fought back a blush. She felt her nipples tauten under the dress and thanked God she had on a padded bra.

'Come in,' she said coolly. 'It's so good to see you.'

Soren said nothing. He entered the room and shut the door, and just stood there looking at her.

'I'm in town for a quick visit,' Daisy said lightly, 'and I thought it would be nice to catch up with an old friend. How have you been?'

She leaned forward and kissed the air at the side of both his cheeks, a perfect social air-kiss, distant and ladylike.

Magnus Soren put his arms around the small of her back and effortlessly tipped her off her feet and into them. Then, as Daisy gasped with surprise, he bent his head towards her, and as her lips parted slightly, involuntarily, he crushed them with his, his tongue probing her mouth, his teeth playing with her plump lips . . .

★   ★   ★

Daisy had never felt anything like it. Soren's hands were on her, all over her body, possessively, masterfully. He unzipped her dress, letting it pool around her ankles in a fluttering cloud of white froth, leaving her tight, toned body in her Manolos and La Perla.

'Magnus . . . '

'Shhh,' he said, breathing it against her neck, cupping her breasts under the bra . . .

Daisy felt as though her belly had turned hot and liquid. She felt as though she could hardly think. His kisses set her skin on fire. Soren pulled her towards the bed, and she didn't struggle with him.

★   ★   ★

'Do you like it? Don't bother with the case. Jenkins will take care of it.'

'Very good, sir,' the chauffeur said, whisking away Daisy's Louis Vuitton. After Magnus had finished making love to her, in a marathon, exhausting session that had lasted through the afternoon into the evening, he had insisted he help her pack and that she check out.

'You'll be staying with me.'

Daisy kissed him, feeling oddly shy. 'Are you sure we should do that?'

'Why wouldn't I be?' He looked surprised. 'You're my woman, Daisy.'

Now they were standing in front of an exquisite Greenwich village apartment building. It had scroll-worked iron gates that were sliding apart to receive the car, and gargoyles peeking out of the corners of its Art Deco walls.

'Very nice,' she said approvingly. 'Which flat is yours?'

Soren grinned. 'All of them. The whole thing. It's a townhouse. Come on, I'll show you around.'

He led her inside and gave her the grand tour. It was stunning, as expected, but Daisy was surprised to find that among the interior-designed rooms, picked out in cool blond Scandinavian woods and buttery marble, Soren had a vogue for plants and waters; he had built a Roman-style atrium in the centre of his house, with a courtyard open to the sky, a fountain, and a mossy rock garden; there were mature trees in the back, cherry and apple, and sprays of climbing roses over the walls that shielded him from his neighbours. Soren had built his own conservatory on the upper levels, crammed with scented, wild tropical plants; ferns, lilies, terracotta tiles underfoot.

'This is magnificent,' Daisy said.

'Winter garden.' Soren shrugged. 'When I was a boy in Sweden we got used to making the most of winter. Candles everywhere, for natural light. Here in New York, one does not need light; I want greenery. And if I can't get to the country, I bring the country to me. I

472

need plants around me all the time, or I get depressed.'

Daisy felt her heart crunch with love. 'I can't see you getting depressed.'

He winked at her. 'That's because I don't, darling.' He waved at the greenery. 'I take precautions. Come and have a drink.'

Soren led her downstairs to the drawing room, which had soft carpeting and a huge crackling fire blazing in the grate. Daisy's heart pulsed with a moment of pure joy. The cold, nasty Manhattan winter outside these walls seemed a million miles away. She was with Magnus, and she had finally made a stride towards finding her family . . .

Soren opened a cabinet with a full bar's worth of liquor and wines and pulled out a champagne bottle covered with flowers.

'Perrier-Jouet. My favourite,' Daisy said, as he popped the cork and poured the fizzing, golden liquid into two flutes.

'I know.' His light eyes held hers, and she blushed, conscious of what he had done to her body earlier that day. 'I've read your press.'

'I've read yours.'

Magnus smiled. 'That's a great way for two people to keep up with each other, no? In newsprint.'

'You could have called me.'

'Ditto.' He regarded her. 'I told you before, I wasn't going to play second fiddle to some married man, or anybody else.'

'That's over now.'

'So we'll get married,' Magnus said matter-of-factly. 'I don't want you to be another meaningless girlfriend. The sooner the better.'

Daisy laughed. 'Oh yeah, just like that! We'll just get married. Wooh-hooh.'

'I told you before, but you didn't listen then.'

'Magnus,' Daisy said, taking her champagne flute and

sipping it, 'be sensible, for heaven's sake. It's not like I haven't seen you in the magazines with a different girl each week.'

'I was single,' he said unrepentantly. 'Now I'm not. You're the one for me. Look around you.' He nodded at his incredible house, the art on the walls, the vines in the courtyard. 'I'm the kind of man who knows what he wants. I have not come this far by second-guessing my instinct. Why waste time? Dance around, date a little? We've done that. What is the point?'

My God, he's serious, Daisy thought, starting to feel nervous and exposed. 'I'm not like you, I need some time to think about it,' she said.

'Think about it all you want,' he said, 'but it's inevitable.'

# 55

'I'm sorry,' the girl on the other end of the phone said brightly, 'but we can't pass messages on to our authors.'

'Then give me the name of her agent.'

'We can't do that either, I'm sorry. Daisy Markham is a very popular writer, so if you want to, you can send fan mail to her care of this address, and we do forward that on to her representatives. But please do bear in mind that she may be too busy to answer this sort of thing, because she gets so much mail.'

'Look. It says on this dust jacket that Daisy Markham was adopted and that she was seeking information about her family.'

'Oh, are you another long-lost relative?'

Rose flushed. 'Yes I am, actually, I'm her sister.'

'Well, that's only the third one this morning . . . '

'Put me through to her editor,' Rose snapped, losing it. The phone clicked in her ear, and she was listening to a dial tone.

'Goddam it!' she shrieked, slamming the receiver back into its cradle. It had taken Rose two hours just to find a person at Andrews Publishing, Daisy Markham's US publisher, who would take her phone call. It had seemed pretty easy, with all the names listed in the acknowledgements, but Daisy's editor's assistant would not put Rose through, and the same went for the heads of Marketing and Publicity and Foreign Rights. At last, Rose had spoken to that junior cow of a publicity assistant, and now she'd hung up on her.

She paced up and down her apartment. Fuck it, who was Daisy Markham anyway? Some author Rose had never even heard of. Of course, she admitted to herself, that might be because she never read any books. But the woman was hardly Madonna. What did she need with all this protection?

Rose picked up *Orange Blossom* and looked again at her own face, staring back at her in black and white with her own smile . . .

Of course! She didn't need to pass a message on to get to Daisy Markham. She *was* Daisy Markham.

★   ★   ★

Andrews Publishing was housed in a gleaming black skyscraper on Madison Avenue, where it rented a full four floors. Rose knew that Daisy Markham's editor was in, because her assistant had refused to put her on the phone, rather than saying she was out. Rose strode into the lobby, smiled at the security guard, and picked up the pen to sign in the visitors' book.

'Which company, ma'am?'

'Andrews,' Rose said, speaking softly and attempting a British accent. 'My name's Daisy Markham and I'm here to see Julia Fine, my editor in America.'

'What time is your appointment?'

'Oh, I don't have one. Tell Julia I just dropped in to see her.'

'OK, wait there please.' The uniformed guard picked up a phone and dialled an extension. He spoke low, and then turned back to her.

'She says to go right up. You know what floor she's on, right?'

'Yes, the sixteenth.'

'Her office is on the fifteenth.'

Rose snapped her fingers. 'I always get that wrong.' She gave the security guard a dazzling smile, and he blushed and said nothing more.

The elevator was fast and modern and whisked her up to the fifteenth floor in a matter of seconds. Despite her outward poise, Rose was nervous as she exited into the Andrews lobby. Her voice, after all — that would be different. And what about Daisy's style? Rose was wearing pink Chanel with a matching quilted handbag and a string of nine-millimetre Mikimoto pearls, but maybe this Daisy was a jeans-and-T-shirt chick . . .

Don't over-think it, Rose; you're here, so do it.

She walked up to the front desk as confidently as she could. The girl there gave her a strange look, but then smiled.

'I'm here to — '

'Yes, Julia's coming right out,' said the receptionist, smiling. 'It's a surprise to see you here after yesterday . . . But great, obviously, I mean it's great . . . '

She was stumbling over her words and seemed anxious, Rose noted; this Daisy woman must be a big cheese in this place. Best not to say anything at all, so her voice didn't give her away. Rose just beamed at the woman, gestured to the couch and sat down on it.

Just a minute later, a tall brunette in something very chic and very black, with a mop of styled white hair, came bursting out of the frosted glass doors that led into the publisher's offices. She held out her hands to Rose.

'Daisy! Darling, what a pleasant surprise. I hadn't expected you back so soon. And so glamorous too, all dressed up, you look like Princess Diana today . . . '

Rose stood up and let Julia Fine get close, real close; close enough to hug her and air-kiss both sides of her cheeks.

'So come on, let me take you inside. What's the reason for dropping by? Not that we don't always love to see you . . . '

Rose took a step back and looked Julia Fine right in the face. 'I'm not Daisy Markham.'

Julia blinked. 'What are you talking about, and what is that accent?'

Rose pulled out her purse, extracted her driver's

licence, and handed it over. 'As I've been trying to tell your staff all morning on the phone, I am Daisy Markham's sister. I must be. We're identical. I know she's looking for her family; well, you just call her up and tell her you found it.'

'Oh my God,' Julia Fine said, looking from the plastic licence to Rose and back again. 'Oh my God.'

★   ★   ★

By 3 p.m., Jacob Rothstein was a million and thirty thousand dollars poorer, and the owner of a burnt-out shell of a building in Alphabet City. He signed the papers, and the seller's attorney told him it was the fastest closing he'd ever been involved in.

'Good luck, sir,' he said, shaking his hand. Jacob smiled. He knew that a man who could just write a cheque for a million bucks was the kind of man lawyers liked to get to know.

'If there's anything else I can help you with, Mr Rothstein, anything at all,' oozed John Robinson with an oily grin. Jacob suppressed his distaste.

'There is, actually.'

'Name it,' Robinson begged.

'You can give me Rose Fiorello's number.'

★   ★   ★

'I'm afraid she's not in,' her assistant said. 'She's taking the day off.'

'Is she indeed? That's not the Rose I know,' Jacob said.

'Any message, sir?' the assistant asked, pleasantly enough.

'Yes. Tell her Jacob Rothstein called. My number is 555–2092.'

The slight pause at the end of the line told him the

478

assistant recognised the name.

'Certainly, sir,' she said, still pleasant-sounding. He admired Rose's choice in employees; this woman was staying out of it. 'Will she know what it's regarding, or should I tell her?'

'I can confidently guarantee she will have no idea what it's regarding,' Jacob said, 'but she will want to know about it, nonetheless.'

'Thank you, sir. Have a good day,' the girl said.

'Thanks,' Rothstein said, and hung up.

He waited for Rose to call him back, but the call did not come in the next five minutes, as he had expected, nor even in the next two hours. So she was playing games, huh? Let her, Rothstein thought. He made calls to contractors, soliciting bids for the work he needed done. There was plenty of planning and work to take his mind off Fiorello. When she discovered what had happened, she'd call him soon enough.

⋆   ⋆   ⋆

Daisy didn't understand at first, when Julia Fine called her, sounding hysterical.

'Julia, just calm down, OK? Calm down.'

'Daisy. I have your sister here. You have to come over to the office. Or should I send her to Mr Soren's?'

'Magnus Soren?' asked Rose, sitting in Julia's corner office. The Daisy woman was involved with Magnus, was she? He was a very rich man, Magnus Soren. She hoped her new sister wasn't a gold-digger . . .

Julia ignored her and continued to speak urgently into the receiver.

'Daisy, you must come now. I am not joking, she looks so like you I thought she *was* you.'

'Julia,' Daisy said patiently, 'I don't have a sister. I'm an only child. I was adopted as an only child. I know that much.'

'But — '

'Give me the phone,' Rose said. The Julia woman gave her a death stare, but Rose was unimpressed. She held out her hand and imperiously crooked her fingers. 'I said give me the goddam phone. That's my sister, you know it and I know it.'

'Daisy,' Julia Fine muttered, 'she insists on talking to you . . .'

Rose snatched the receiver from her.

'Is this Daisy Markham?'

'Who's this?' Daisy asked angrily. 'Whoever you are, I have no idea how you got to my editor, but this is not a joke to me.'

'Nor to me. My name is Rose Fiorello. I own apartment buildings in New York. I was adopted also, and you are identical to me.'

'Identical, how?'

'Identical, as in twins. I saw your picture on the front page of the *Financial Times* this morning. You had my face. I bought your book, there's no doubt.' Rose spoke so matter-of-factly that Daisy found herself listening to her. And . . . she sounded familiar. Very familiar. Under that New York accent . . .

'Your publishers wouldn't take my call, so I showed up here and said I was you.'

'Very resourceful,' Daisy said faintly.

'And your woman here, Ms Fine, thought I was you. She called me 'Daisy'. She thought you were playing a joke on her.' Rose punched a button and put the call on speaker. 'Tell her, Ms Fine.'

'It's true, Daisy, it's true,' said Julia Fine breathlessly. 'I wouldn't joke . . .'

'Send her over here,' Daisy whispered. 'I want to see her.'

# 56

Poppy smiled fixedly at the cheering crowd. The band was playing 'Columbia, the Gem of the Ocean' as Henry stepped up on to the podium, smiling and waving. If she had been his wife, Poppy would now be walking next to him. But as it was, she was only the fiancée, and a controversial one at that. Henry's spin doctors had stuck her up here on the podium, standing behind his chief of staff, and blending into the background as she smiled and clapped.

She looked at the man she loved and wondered what their future together was.

As the cheering subsided, Poppy sat down on her uncomfortable folding chair with the others as Henry began to give his speech — the same one he gave on every stop of the campaign. Poppy could recite it the way she could recite one of Travis Jackson's numbers. Just like Travis, though, Henry could make it sound fresh; he was the rebel Republican, the darling of the South who didn't hide a womanising past or a fairly radical social agenda. Even the unpopular parts of his platform he laid out there, daring folks not to vote for him. Poppy mouthed the words along with him —

'My opponents have said I'm anti-choice.' Big cheer. 'They've also told you that I'm soft on crime, because I oppose the death penalty, and I want gun control.' Tremendous booing, even from LeClerc supporters. This part she liked, because it always made Henry's staff so uncomfortable. 'Well, guess what, Lafayette, Louisiana? Here's one politician who's gonna tell you the truth. I want gun control, and I want an end to the death penalty, and I know those are two things almost none of y'all agree with — '

Cue the standard roar of angry agreement, and Henry lifted his manicured hand in that practised gesture, and said, 'Yes, y'all, and if I could make those two things happen I'd do it in a second. But you want to know the truth? Those laws will never pass, not in my lifetime, not in Louisiana and not in America, whether I like it or not. So it shouldn't stop you from voting for me. You have your pick of guys in suits who are gonna tell you everything you want to hear. I'm a conviction politician. I tell you my convictions and let you make your own minds up. Now, what do we agree on, Lafayette? Stuff that I *can* do something about. Tourism. Taxes. Jobs . . . '

' . . . a strong defence,' Poppy mouthed, 'reforming our welfare laws, educating our kids . . . stuff you can see my track record on . . . '

Now he had them listening, rapt, eating from the palm of his hand. The rock star parallel was pretty close, Poppy thought. Henry played the crowd better than any lead singer.

His strategy had worked, too. LeClerc had come from last to first in the Louisiana Senate race with the revolutionary strategy of telling the truth about what he believed. The polls had shown him with a credible eight-point lead over his nearest rival.

Of course, that was until last week.

Poppy looked down at her outfit. It was very conservative, a concession of love for Henry. She was wearing a short-sleeved, full-length feminine sun dress with daisies all over it; an LA Jew's stab at being the pretty l'il Southern Belle. She also wore white gloves and a delicate face-framing straw hat. Anything to make things a little better for him.

Because last week, Poppy had become the problem.

Henry's skirt-chasing ways had been well publicised, but they had only endeared him to the Louisiana voting public. In fact, with Clinton's charm and Bush's integrity, he had seemed unstoppable. And yet something had put a spoke in the wheel.

The press, failing to find anything damaging in LeClerc's past, had started to investigate his girlfriend. And they had stumbled on a goldmine.

The scandals were delicious, and they just kept on coming. First, the catty, anti-semitic little comments . . . Poppy was a JAP, a Jewish American princess, that was enough to drop Henry a full point by itself down here. And they were not married, but it looked like they might be. (Thank God nobody knew they were engaged yet, Poppy thought.) Next, she wasn't from Louisiana, wasn't even from the South. No, she was the daughter of a slick LA lawyer. And more. Each day brought another screaming headline, another gossip column revelation. Poppy was way too young for their Congressman . . . the older women voters hated that. And finally, perfectly for the Democrats, there were Poppy's unorthodox politics, and her job.

Poppy was against whatever Henry was for. She was pro-choice, and she believed in the death penalty for murder, and she wanted to be able to carry guns; she was an environmental nut and she wanted to relax the rules on welfare . . .

The Republicans hated it. Sometimes, as she walked on to a platform with Henry, she heard them mutter, 'Commie Jew bitch.' The Democrats, her party, didn't hesitate to use her against Henry. Their candidate paraded his white-bread wife and simpering golden-ringleted daughter everywhere.

And then the Menace scandal had come out.

It was the first main fight she'd had with Henry since he'd agreed to take her on campaign, and it had shocked Poppy. She'd been used to having Henry back her up against his staffers, but not this time.

Her latest heavy metal act, Menace, were a hot-selling brand of rap/rock fusion, a sort of heavy-metal hip-hop that urban radio loved and Top 40 played to death, albeit with the swear words bleeped out. Sometimes that was half the song. Menace had a classic bad-boy reputation, trashing everything that wasn't nailed down to a hotel floor, fucking everything that was female and moved within groping range. That was so normal in rock 'n' roll that the group hadn't made headlines outside of *Spin* and *Rolling Stone* until last week.

Their latest release had gone straight in at number one on the Billboard charts. So far so good, except that this single was different. No station would play it, not even BET; it was called 'Spit the Pigs', and it was, well, it was an anti-cop song. It promised various different fates to any cop caught without back-up in the vicinity of Menace (though Poppy knew the band was a bunch of cowards), and all of these fates were very graphic and very unpleasant.

Menace accused the LAPD of being pimps, drug dealers, racists, thugs and killers, and they had some suggestions for their fans as to what to do about it. The chorus of the song was the pièce de résistance, a speed-rapped one hundred ways to kill police officers.

And some enterprising journalist in New Orleans had found out that Poppy managed this band, this enemy to law and order, and yet Congressman Henry LeClerc was still dating her — and might be going to marry her!

Henry's staffers had insisted that she terminate her relationship with Menace.

'Absolutely not,' Poppy said. 'It's just macho posturing, and they're a hot band.'

'Hot? They're burning away Henry's chances,' Don Rickles snarled.

Poppy turned to Henry. 'Darling, this isn't your problem. You just tell them you don't control me or my bands. If you don't approve, say so.'

'The point is that you approve, Poppy,' Henry said softly.

She'd coloured. 'I don't approve or disapprove, my function isn't to tell an act how to write songs. I believe in the First Amendment. Menace has freedom of speech.'

'Sure they do, but they can't demand that you be associated with it.'

Poppy had blinked at him. 'You want me to make this statement? Cut one of my best-selling bands loose?'

'Yes, I do.'

'Well, I won't,' Poppy said mulishly. 'No way in hell. Don't bother asking me again.'

Rickles said smoothly, 'Let's wait until after Lafayette to discuss this, OK?'

And so Poppy found herself here, listening to Henry, smiling sweetly at the press who wanted to destroy him, and wondering if this would be the last time she would ever do this.

No, stop it, she warned herself sternly, as the tears threatened to spring up. Ruining his comeback rally was not the way to go. She would talk it over with him when they got back to the hotel.

There would be plenty of time for tears then.

★  ★  ★

The car pulled up at the airport kerb. Poppy was in the front seat, because Henry was driving her himself. There was no way she wanted some chauffeur to take her; Poppy hated strangers to see her cry; and Henry had wanted to do it.

The fight had lasted into the early hours of the morning. Poppy was exhausted now, as well as weepy, but more than her tiredness was the ache in her heart, and the nasty feeling that she might not see Henry again.

'At least you have no ring to give back to me,' he said flatly, not wanting her to get out of the car and leave him, but also not prepared to buckle.

Poppy wanted to say, 'Because you kept the engagement quiet, because you didn't get me a ring,' but instead just said, 'Don't be like that.'

'What? After all we've meant to each other?' LeClerc said cynically.

'Haven't we?' Poppy asked, fresh tears coming despite herself.

LeClerc looked at her and wanted to brush them away. But he knew if he weakened now he might start crying himself, and he was a man, and that was unacceptable. Maybe it was OK for therapy-boys from Los Angeles, but not for a guy from the Bayou.

'I obviously don't mean as much to you as your career does, Poppy.'

'It's a free-speech issue,' she half-shouted.

'Bullshit.' He shook his head. 'It's a spoilt brat issue. I have never tried to smother you, or make you the little woman, or stop you working. But you putting these scum before me . . . ' He shrugged. 'I'm not a caring, sharing New Man, sugar. If that's what you want, you need to look elsewhere.'

'You *do* want to ruin my career,' Poppy said furiously.

'Well,' LeClerc said, reaching across her and opening the door, 'you've done your damnedest to ruin mine. I'm not interested in being your house-husband. The offer was for you to be my wife.'

'You're a sexist pig, Henry LeClerc,' Poppy snarled, getting out and grabbing her carry-on case.

He grinned for a second, and it tugged sharply at her heartstrings; that old, sexy, confident grin of his!

'So I've been told.'

'Go fuck yourself,' Poppy snapped.

He touched his forehead. 'You have a good day, ma'am,' LeClerc said, closing the door and driving away from the kerb in a screech of rubber.

Arrogant, self-centred son of a bitch! Poppy thought,

striding into the terminal with such fury on her face that the Skycap luggage handlers didn't even bother approaching her. There'd be no tips there, that was for sure.

Well, *screw* Henry LeClerc and his slow hands and fast Southern ways. It had been a crazy idea from the start, Poppy thought. She was far too young for him, and too urban, and she was a career girl and he just thought she should stay home and bake cookies.

Time to get out of Louisiana. High time, Poppy told herself.

She marched furiously up to the Continental ticket counter and flashed her platinum OnePass card.

'What time is the next flight to New York?'

'Twenty minutes, ma'am.'

'Great. I just have carry-on,' Poppy said, 'so get me on it.'

★ ★ ★

She seethed for the entire flight, and no glasses of champagne or soft first-class seats did anything to help her mood. Henry wasn't worth obsessing over, Poppy told herself, but it didn't stop her from doing just that.

Well, she thought when the captain announced the descent and they started to bank and turn above Manhattan, never mind. She had things to do in town. Meetings with Sony, Menace's record company, for one thing. Poppy would review the sales, see how her controversial First Amendment poster-boys were doing. Because that was what it was about, she told herself self-righteously. She was a champion of free speech and a warrior against censorship.

And she would pamper herself. No more of the conservative, dull little outfits she'd been shoehorned into on the campaign trail. No, she was looking forward to wearing some cool-ass black leather pants and a tight little cashmere top, and spiky ankle-boots. It'd be freezing in New York in winter, but that wouldn't stop Poppy from being stylish. That was what the record industry expected of her, and it was time to show everybody that she was more than some smiling and waving political girlfriend.

Poppy Allen and Henry LeClerc. Oil and water. What the hell had she been thinking?

★   ★   ★

Poppy arrived in New York, checked into the Victrix, and went about her business. She called the recording studio where Menace was laying down its new tracks; she set up appointments at RCA, Sony and Musica for some of her other acts; and she called Travis Jackson.

'Hey, baby,' Travis said. But he had that whiny tone she'd come to dread lately whenever she called him up. 'I'm not happy . . . did you see all the play that Shania Twain is getting . . . why can't I have Mutt Lange produce my shit, Poppy . . . '

'Shania is married to Mutt,' Poppy said patiently, 'and he's a little busy with her career right now. Your sales are amazing, Travis.'

'I want Mutt,' he said, insisting on the famously reclusive super-producer, 'or maybe Michael Kravis, can you get me Michael Kravis . . . ?'

When she was done with the litany of complaints from a guy that had just gone sextuple-platinum, she called her hair bands. More whining. Poppy was soothing, but she felt sick of it, sick of them. A manager now was half a babysitter, which she'd never signed up to be. Her acts these days wanted Poppy to bail them out of jail, to find kennels for their pets, and to hear their incessant moaning that somebody else was doing better than they were . . . which was always management's fault, never the band's fault . . .

As she prepared to catch a cab downtown to visit Menace in the studio — they were at a high-rent place in Soho, and it was a good job they were selling to pay these bills — Poppy thought that her client roster suddenly reminded her of Silver Bullet. Was there *ever* an act that blamed a drop in fortunes on themselves? No way. It was always the record label, the manager, the touring crew. Never that their songwriting skills had dropped off, or they needed to lose a few pounds or play some gigs more passionately.

Poppy climbed into her cab, tipped the doorman five bucks, and gave the driver the address of the studio.

I'm too young to be sick and tired of these guys, she thought. If I feel like this now, how will I react when I'm forty?

# 57

'Well, look who it is,' said Tyrone, leering at her. 'What's up, sweetness?'

'Hey, guys,' Poppy said easily, dropping her Prada purse and sliding into the producer's booth beside Jake Ritter, who was working the controls.

Menace raised hands to her. A few of the guys smiled, really just baring their teeth. Two of them didn't even look up.

'Got any blow?' Keith said.

'Not on me,' Poppy replied, unfazed. 'Sorry.'

He looked at her as though she were less than useless. Poppy pressed on; she had always believed you didn't have to be best buddies with your clients. Menace had hired her on their lawyer's recommendation. They just expected her to make them money, and that was fine with Poppy.

'What are ya here for, then?' Tyrone demanded.

'Hmmm, let me see. What *am* I here for? Oh yeah, to hear the new shit. You boys are carving up the charts right now, programmers want some more.'

That got their attention. They started high-fiving each other, grinning and whooping. Good sales were always welcome news, whether you were in hip-hop or country.

'Lay that shit on her, Jake,' Reese told him.

The producer hesitated, looking at Poppy. 'Maybe we should . . . '

'Fuck that. Just play it for the bitch,' Tyrone said.

Poppy stiffened. She wasn't going to let this guy call her a bitch. But before she could call him on it, Jake Ritter had sighed . . . why sighed, their productions were usually spot on . . . and started to play the new track.

490

Poppy listened. And then her mouth dropped open.

'*No means no / Ain't my show / the bitch was crying but she wanted to go / Got her on the floor, make her beg for more / When I'm done Reese runs the back-door / The boys queue up / While she lays down / Street ho runs a train . . .*'

Poppy reached across Ritter and pressed a button to stop the filthy sound from polluting her airspace. She looked at her act, sickened.

'What the fuck is this?'

'Fuck you talkin' bout, *bitch*?' Tyrone asked angrily. 'Nobody asked y'all for critical judgement, fuckin' Tipper Gore.'

'This song is about gang-rape. You're talking about gang-raping a woman.'

'So what? It's rap.'

'Song say she axin' for it,' Reese said, and laughed unpleasantly, which they all thought was highly amusing.

Poppy felt her cheeks burning red. 'You can't write that kind of dirt.'

'We can do whatever we like,' said Tyrone. 'This is black culture, no cracker gonna tell me what I can and can't do.'

Poppy stood up. 'Screw you, Tyrone. Like hell that's black culture. I work with black people and this *crap* isn't their culture. This is slob culture, gang culture, scumbag culture. If it's culture at all. I just call it trash.'

'You know? You weren't upset when we wrote a song about killin' a cop. That you don' mind, huh? But rape bugs you, lady? Killin' is OK, but rape . . . ' He whistled through his teeth. 'Maybe y'all had some experience, maybe it hit home . . . '

'You fucking gross disgusting bunch of animals,' Poppy said, 'find yourselves another manager.'

'Bitch, you fired!' Tyrone screamed at her departing back.

Poppy got outside. She was so overcome she had to walk six blocks gasping for air before she felt she could even hail a cab. It was so sick that they thought that was entertainment. Sicker still that she'd ever had anything to do with them. And sickest, sickest of all was that Tyrone, that evil fuck, had a point.

She was a hypocrite. Rape threatened her, like every woman, and of course she wasn't gonna work with a band that promoted it. But she'd been happy to work with an act that wrote songs about how to kill cops . . .

How could Menace have thought she'd stand to work on that 'song'? Well, maybe because she'd worked on the last one.

Poppy flagged down an approaching cab, jumped in, and let it take her to the Victrix, where she stumbled into the elevator, making it back to her room on auto-pilot. Dear God, she thought.

Henry had been right. Absolutely right. Of course it wasn't a free-speech issue; if it were, she'd have been willing to promote the current piece of filth. And she wasn't. No, the real issue had been that she'd resented doing anything for him. Henry had never asked her to give up her job; but she, Poppy, had asked him to pretty much give up his.

No politician could be elected with a spouse who condoned cop-killing.

LeClerc had called her a spoilt brat. And maybe she had been, maybe she'd gone and thrown away the best thing in her life over a dumb temper tantrum.

Poppy sat down heavily on the bed. It was eleven, too late to call him, and he'd most likely be at a campaign dinner anyway, raising money. She felt sick, stupid and tired. It wasn't just Menace either. Even Travis was bothering her. She suddenly felt a wash of nausea come over her, as though she just couldn't be damn well bothered to hold hands and wipe noses for one more second. She was tired of being mother-hen, scapegoat, lawyer and guru all at one go.

But this *was* her career. If she didn't do this, what would she do?

Poppy peeled her clothes off and headed for the shower. She was too tired to answer that question right now. She'd sleep on it, wake up and call Henry, apologise to him . . . things would be much better in the morning.

It didn't quite work out like that.

★   ★   ★

Poppy woke groggily when her wake-up call came through at eight. The first thing she did was call the Executive Vice-President at Sony to announce that Menace was no longer an Opium act, effective immediately, and that she was cancelling her meeting. The rest of it she'd figure out later. She left messages on the office machine in LA, dictating a statement for *Billboard* and *Variety*. It was short and harsh: *Poppy Allen of Opium Management announces she is severing her managerial relationship with Menace. Due to the nature of the act's lyrics Ms Allen no longer wishes to have anything to do with them.* Yeah, that was a little better than the regular industry platitudes about 'parting of the ways' or 'musical differences'. Let them know what she really thought.

That made her feel a bit better. And then she picked up her morning papers. Poppy had subscriptions to *Variety*, *Billboard*, and *The Economist*, but when she was in hotels, she settled for *USA Today*, the *Wall Street Journal*, and the *Financial Times*. She almost didn't bother with the *FT* this morning, but decided to skim through it, out of habit. Poppy shook out the pink pages over her steaming cinnamon coffee and toasted bagel, flipped over to the features section, and felt her entire universe crumble around her.

493

Her face was staring up at her. Poppy jumped out of her skin, sending her coffee cup crashing to the floor, delicious cinnamon-brewed Colombian now nothing more than an ugly stain on the pristine white carpet. But she barely moved. She simply stared, rooted to the spot.

At first she'd thought she was having a drugs flashback or something, even though she'd only really done the odd joint, and not even that any more. But once Poppy had done most of the same things that Rose had done . . . once she'd stared at the picture, examined it from all angles, and then walked into the nearest bookstore to buy a copy of the book, she was still mystified.

She was the daughter of the Allens of Beverly Hills. This was just some freakish coincidence, something you saw on *Ripley's Believe it or Not*. Wasn't it?

Poppy cancelled her meetings for the day and called her parents at nine-forty-five, a quarter to seven on the West Coast.

'Poppy? You know what time it is?' Marcia Allen asked crossly. 'I need my beauty sleep, young lady . . . '

'Mom,' Poppy said, now suddenly, ridiculously nervous, 'this is going to sound like a very strange question. A real weird question . . . '

And then she heard her mother's sharp intake of breath, as though she'd been waiting for this moment for her entire life, and Poppy instinctively knew that Marcia Allen knew what she was about to ask, and she also knew what the answer was, but she asked the question all the same.

'Mom,' Poppy whispered, 'was I adopted?'

# 58

Daisy waited with Soren, unable to concentrate or to think until the bell finally rang. Magnus offered her a drink — 'To calm you' — but Daisy refused; she wanted to be able to think straight.

This was one of the most important moments of her life, assuming it wasn't some elaborate joke, but why would Julia play one on her? Could she really be that cruel? Or that stupid? Daisy couldn't prevent the thoughts running through her head, but on one level, the calm heart of her, she knew they weren't true.

It would have been impossible to fake the emotion in Julia's voice. So Daisy paced and fretted and finally, when the buzzer rang, she raced to the door as though she were still the fat kid in school when the last bell rang.

Magnus walked behind her, hanging back a fraction, but keeping close.

Daisy wrenched open the door, looked at Rose, and then stumbled back, gasping. She felt dizzy and short of breath.

'Are you OK?' Soren said, catching her. He looked at the replica of Daisy standing in front of him; she, too, was looking very pale, steadying herself against the doorway. 'Are *you* OK?' He moved forward and shook the Daisy-replica girl's hand. 'My name is Magnus Soren,' he said calmly, and the need for social politeness snapped Rose to herself.

'I'm Rose Fiorello,' she said.

'So it's true,' Daisy said. 'You're my twin sister. I don't know how this could have happened.'

'Won't you come in, Ms Fiorello?' Magnus said politely.

Rose looked up at the magnificent Village townhouse. It looked like something that one of the Rothsteins would own; in fact, from what she knew of Magnus Soren, he was probably even richer than they were. She glanced curiously at her sister, wondering if they shared a genetic trait for going for rich, ruthless bastards.

'Thank you, Mr Soren,' she said, just as courteously.

'Oh, for fuck's sake,' said Daisy, 'all things considered, don't you think we should be on first-name terms?'

* * *

This time Daisy did accept a glass of Chardonnay, and so did Rose. Magnus discreetly left them to it in the drawing room, telling Daisy to call him if she needed him.

'I was adopted in New York,' Rose said. 'You?'

'London. When do you celebrate your birthday?'

'June the twenty-eighth. You?'

'May the twelfth.' For a second Daisy was perplexed, then she laughed. 'Oh. Duh. I mean, that's the day I was adopted.'

'Me too,' Rose said, smiling for the first time.

'The agency that adopted me out was in London, though. And they disappeared, no record.'

'Same with me.' Rose shrugged. 'It's all very mysterious. I feel very weird right now. I mean, I hardly know you, and you have my face.'

'I think you'll find you have *my* face,' Daisy said crisply, and Rose cracked a tiny smile.

'You're looking for your parents?'

'Yes.' Daisy leaned forward, all eagerness. 'Do you have any information about them, where they came from, why they split us up?'

Rose shook her head. 'And I guess we're not all that alike, Daisy, because I couldn't care less. My father is dead, and my mother lives here in the city, and whatever those people did, and whoever they are, matters about as much to me as if my mother had conceived me through a sperm donor. I already asked my mother about it, but she had no records, and the agency disappeared. And, you know, it never bothered me.'

Daisy said simply, 'I want to lay the past to rest.'

'I think we do that by building a future,' Rose said.

'I want to know why they rejected me. Or if they did.'

'I think that last part is pretty clear.'

'Without information, we won't know what happened. What if our mother was raped, and couldn't care for us? What if our father died and our mother was destitute?'

Rose considered this for a second, then dismissed it. 'It can hardly make a difference now. If I were you, I'd give it up.'

'You're not me,' Daisy said, slightly resenting her off-handness. How could Rose not want details?

Rose grinned. 'To look at us, you'd never know that.'

Daisy smiled back. At least she had some family now, if this tall beauty would think about that. 'I never realised how pretty I was until today.'

Rose laughed. 'Yeah, it's better than a mirror. But I think I'd sound better with one of those English accents.'

'They're overrated.' Daisy looked out to the kitchen, where Magnus was waiting. 'I think American accents are hot, myself.'

'You have to tell me about him later.'

'I'd like to. I hope you don't think we shouldn't get to know each other,' Daisy blurted out. 'Whatever our blood parents did, I wasn't a part of it.'

Rose sighed. 'I don't see why we can't be friends, but sisters . . .'

'We *are* sisters,' Daisy insisted.

'Biologically. I had a whole childhood without you.'

'Yes, but that wasn't my fault.'

Rose thought about it. 'Look, I don't know if you're going to want to get involved with me. I'm a workaholic, I live for my career, I don't have a boyfriend, I think of my mom as my real family and I can't tell you that you'll ever be on the same level to me. I don't want to hurt you, but you should hear the truth.'

'Are you at least willing to get to know me? We can take it from there, afterwards.'

Rose shrugged. She had no social life at all. No real friends. She suddenly envied Daisy her handsome boyfriend, and her probably full life. She, Rose, was a little lonely now and then. Why not admit it? It wouldn't hurt to be friends with this girl . . .

'Sure.' She smiled. 'Why not?'

Daisy beamed, and it was as though her whole face lit up. 'Magnus!' she yelled. 'Come back in here, would you, and bring the bottle?'

\* \* \*

Poppy called the publisher of Daisy Markham's book.

'Hi,' she said, nervously. 'I think I'm her sister.'

'Hold on, please,' said a woman. There was a pause, then, 'Julia Fine's office.'

'Julia Fine is Daisy Markham's editor, right? I know this sounds crazy, but I think I'm her sister.'

'Yes, of course, Ms Fiorello, right? That's OK,' said the assistant, mystifyingly, and put her on hold again. A second later, another female voice came on the line.

'This is Julia Fine,' she said. 'Rose, I'm glad you called. How did it go with Daisy?'

'What?' said Poppy, utterly confused. 'My name's not Rose. It's Poppy, Poppy Allen. What's going on here?'

'There was some confusion. Another woman turned

up here earlier today claiming to be Daisy Markham's sister.'

'That's impossible,' Poppy said. 'This is all some kind of a joke. How did you get that photograph of me? And why did you put it on the back of the book cover?'

Julia Fine paused. 'I'm not calling Daisy until I check this out for myself.'

'You can call any record company in America,' Poppy said coldly, 'or you can come over to the hotel and meet me in the lobby by the check-in desk.'

Once she heard the woman was supposedly staying at the Victrix Hotel, Julia doubted it was a prank; pranksters couldn't afford that kind of dough.

'And how will I recognise you?' Julia Fine demanded.

'I'll be the one whose picture you stole for the back of your book,' Poppy told her.

'Daisy Markham is a real person,' Julia assured her. 'Were you adopted, by any chance?'

Poppy pressed her fingers to her temple. 'Just get here, Ms Fine, would you, please?'

★ ★ ★

Julia Fine took one look at Poppy and burst out laughing.

'Something's funny?' Poppy said, furiously.

'I'm sorry. Nerves,' the editor said. 'But how many of you can there be? Are you clones?'

She handed Poppy a sheaf of bios and press releases on Daisy. 'I have nothing for the other sister, though.'

'What are you *talking* about?' Poppy demanded. She was aggressive, because she was starting to feel frightened. The woman whose picture she was holding was her identical twin.

'I don't think you'll believe me if I told you.'

'Try me.'

'You have two identical sisters. Daisy, and a woman named Rose Fiorello.'

'You were right the first time, I don't believe you,' Poppy snapped.

Julia looked at her. 'Miss. If you'll let me, I'll take you to see your sisters. I believe they are still together right now.'

★ ★ ★

'Here,' Magnus Soren said to Poppy. 'Have some wine. It's helping your sisters.'

'I don't know if they are my sisters,' Poppy muttered. 'I suppose a DNA test . . . '

'Just look at them, Ms Allen,' Magnus said.

Rose snorted. 'This is too much. I don't like it. This morning I was an only child, now I'm part of a litter.'

'You think *I* like it? Who gave you permission to steal my face?' Poppy snapped. 'This morning I knew who my parents were. Who *I* was. Now I'm adopted. I have no idea what's going on. And there could be God knows how many more of us. Maybe that Julia woman was right and we are all clones and there are twenty more of me out there.' She took a huge gulp of wine. 'This is a fucking surreal nightmare as far as I'm concerned.'

'I know this is hardly my place, but if I may, I'd like to suggest something,' Magnus said quietly.

Poppy stopped glaring at Rose and Daisy and looked at him. 'Go ahead. Any small ounce of sanity you can bring to the proceedings, I, for one, would welcome.'

'Me too,' Rose agreed.

'It's been my experience that everything has an explanation. You just don't know what it is yet. You shouldn't let the shock of the moment blind you to that.'

'If you have an explanation, let's hear it,' Daisy pleaded. 'When I met my family I wanted it to be a happy moment and now everybody's all freaked out and mad at me.'

'I'm not mad at you,' Poppy said, relenting slightly. 'It's not your fault, I guess.'

'Well, first of all, you're not clones, because that *is* impossible. You're triplets. Identical triplets.'

'And how do you know we're not quads or quins?' Rose demanded.

'I don't,' he agreed mildly, 'but I'm working on probabilities here, and triplets are rare enough. Most quads don't make it, and the odds of being a triplet vastly outweigh the odds of being from a bigger litter, as Rose puts it.'

'Go on,' Rose said.

'Furthermore, as you are all sisters, and you were all adopted in different places by different agencies, and you were all named after flowers *before* you were even adopted . . . It's not that hard to see a pattern. Especially when you consider that all three agencies apparently disappeared without trace. I'd say this conclusively proves that something odd happened.'

All three women, his Daisy and her doubles, were leaning forward on the edge of their seats, wearing identical, fascinated expressions. Genetics, he thought. Pretty powerful.

'But what? What?' Daisy pleaded.

'That I don't know,' Magnus said. 'But somebody never wanted this moment to happen. Somebody, or somebodies, took care to see you guys never met. Whether for good motives or bad, I have no idea.'

Daisy frowned. 'I'm going to call Janus and report all this.'

'That's a positive idea,' Magnus said. 'They're real pros, let them do the digging.'

'Who are Janus?' Rose asked, and Daisy filled her in.

★　★　★

They stayed talking until late into the night. Soren listened, intensely interested; the three women seemed relieved that their lives had followed such different paths.

'If you'd gone into real estate I don't think I could have handled it,' Rose said. She felt freaked out enough that there were two identical images of herself in this room; the differences in their careers, in their attitudes, were incredibly reassuring to her. She was distinct, she was still Rose, not a carbon copy, where everything had been predetermined in the womb.

'I hate business,' Daisy reassured her. 'You read much?'

'*Fortune*,' Rose said.

'*Billboard*,' Poppy added.

'I know one way you three are all alike,' Soren said. 'You're all highly successful in your fields. Prominent.'

The girls looked at each other and smiled. 'True enough,' Rose said. 'I don't know if we'll ever get to the bottom of this, but I really don't think you should stress about it too much. You could go mad trying to figure out stuff that happened over twenty-five years ago. We know each other now.' She shrugged. 'My two cents is that we should get on with our lives.'

'Easier said than done,' Poppy said. 'But I guess you're right. I have, well, I have some stuff on my plate right now.'

'I just don't want to lose you both,' Daisy said. 'We'll all go home and never see each other, just the odd transatlantic trip . . . ' Her face fell.

Soren grinned. 'Daisy, what are you talking about? You're staying here.'

'I can't stay here for ever, I have a book to write.'

'You can write wherever you can plug in a lap-top. And I have plenty of sockets.'

'I have an apartment in London . . . '

'Hang on to it, it'll be our pied-à-terre.'

'And my parents . . . '

'We can get them a place here, or they can fly over for visits. It's only a five-hour flight.'

'They're my family.'

'Yes, and so are your sisters. And so am I,' Soren told her. 'Enough games. This is your home.'

★   ★   ★

Magnus served champagne and coffee and juice while the three girls continued talking. He couldn't stop staring at them, but that was only human. He felt an amazing sense of contentment to see Daisy so happy; his prize, whom he had won only after years of pursuit, and whatever came of this, it would give her answers and make her happier in the long run. Magnus had long held the idea that Daisy's rejection of him was down to her lack of self-esteem, down to some idea she had managed to give herself that her birth-parents had rejected her, when she had no idea what the facts were. Even though her two sisters, mirror images of herself, were sitting with her, he found he had no interest in them whatsoever. His girl sounded completely different — they all did; and the other two weren't *Daisy*, weren't the woman he'd fallen so deeply in love with, so fast.

He could hardly wait for the other two women to leave, and when they said their goodbyes at midnight, and Daisy had shown them out, with hugs and kisses on the cheek, he closed the door and looked at her.

'Well?' he said.

Daisy just shook her head. 'It seems like a dream. I would never have believed it unless I'd seen it for myself.'

'Maybe you can get some answers now.'

'Maybe. At least I know my sisters are out there.'

Magnus bent his head to her and kissed her, very gently, very lightly on the mouth, his lips just brushing

503

across hers, his hand holding her in the small of her back. Her lips parted and her eyes were glittering; he felt the warmth of her body and the way it arched in towards him.

'I don't want to just be your boyfriend any more,' he said. 'It's not enough, just not good enough. It feels wrong to me that you can walk around without the world knowing you're mine.'

She tensed, not daring to speak.

'I want you to marry me,' Magnus said. 'As soon as possible.'

# 59

Rose arrived back in her apartment with a sense of gratitude that the surroundings were familiar. There was the *Financial Times* with Daisy's picture inside; she smoothed it out and put it away in a cupboard. She wasn't going to throw it away, but she also had had enough of staring at somebody wearing her face, as Poppy Allen had put it.

She checked her messages. Three from Mom, all worried. Well, it was too late to ring her now; Rose would call first thing in the morning. And one from her assistant Fiona.

'Ms Fiorello, Mr Jacob Rothstein called you and asked you to call him. He didn't want to say what it was concerning, but I got the impression he thought it was important.' She left a number.

Rose passed a hand through her hair. Jacob Rothstein? Why would he be calling her?

Very well, she'd leave him a message. Rose considered not replying at all, but that was impractical. Rose knew herself, knew perfectly well the charge she got from speaking to Jacob. Even when she was fighting with him.

I'll just leave a message for the arrogant son of a bitch, she thought.

She dialled the number, but he answered on the third ring.

'Jacob,' he said.

'You called?' Rose asked.

'It's late. I wasn't expecting to hear from you tonight.'

'Oh, did I disturb your beauty sleep?' Rose snapped. 'What's this about? If you want those papers back, you're gonna need a subpoena.'

'I think we should meet,' he said, and there was that lazy, sexy confidence in his tone that she couldn't help responding to. Her nipples tightened under the prim and proper Chanel.

It had been so long; he was the last one to even touch her.

*Stop that*, she told herself.

'I have no intention of coming over to your apartment, Jacob. There's nothing between us.'

'Well, we both know that's a crock,' he said, 'but I wasn't inviting you over to my apartment. How about Carducci's? It's a late-night bistro in the Village, great food, open till three.'

Rose suddenly felt a stab of hunger. She'd done so much talking at Daisy Markham's pad that she hadn't eaten a thing since breakfast.

'And why would I want to do that?'

'Because you'll want to congratulate me,' Jacob said. 'I left Rothstein Realty. And I'm the proud owner of a new building.'

'What's that got to do with me?'

'It's in Alphabet City,' he said.

It took a second for it to sink in, then Rose's grip on the receiver tightened. 'Son of a bitch,' she hissed.

'Don't bring my mother into it,' Jacob said, grinning as he pictured her rage. 'It would be in your best interest to meet me, Rose. We need to sort a few things out.'

Rose slammed down the receiver.

She only paused to freshen her make-up; Rose would never permit anybody to see her mad without looking gorgeous, and especially not Jacob. She reapplied her lipstick and her neutral Shu Umera eyeshadow, and spritzed a cloud of Hermes' 64 Rue Faubourg, walking into it, so that the scent hung on her, but not oppressively so. *Damn* him! He'd bought her building, her prize? How the hell had he pulled that one off? Rage blew away the cobwebs of her fatigue, and angrily she selected the most important jewels she owned, a stunning pair of canary-diamond earrings with South Sea pearl drops, and a matching canary-and-white-diamond necklace; that was sixty thousand dollars' worth of rocks, *wholesale*, she thought furiously. Rose was dressing to show that bastard how successful she was. He would never beat her. Never. Even if he'd just stolen her new, prize-flagship building from under her nose.

She would be safe, because she would take her own car tonight, drive herself. It was late enough that there would be street parking, even in the Village. Otherwise, she could never have risked wearing rocks like this on the street.

Rose inspected herself in the full-length mirror. Pink Chanel, high-heeled pumps, diamonds and pearls, a Prada purse; yeah, she looked like a million dollars. He could eat his heart out.

She strode out of her apartment, locked the door, and went downstairs to pick up her Porsche. Her emotions were churning. Rage mingled with a kind of relief; battles with the Rothstein family, at least, were something she was used to. Jacob Rothstein wanted a fight? Fine. He was gonna get one.

★   ★   ★

'Rose.' Jacob stood politely. 'Good evening.'

'Let's dispense with the pleasantries, shall we?' Rose said.

Carducci's was three-quarters full, and she could see why. It had no competition locally at this hour, and it was a little gem, tucked away inside a Village brownstone on a typically tree-lined street, with an old-fashioned awning, and torches burning outside. The icy cold of the winter night melted as soon as you stepped through the door; there was a piano playing quiet ragtime jazz, a blazing fire, oak-panelled walls, a crowded bar, and waiters who all looked to be over fifty and highly confident.

Candles were on every table, but no fancy crystal or silverware; it was a real Italian steakhouse. The scent of sizzling steaks and roasted vegetables filled the place and Rose's stomach growled loudly.

'Hmm,' Rothstein said, grinning, 'doesn't quite go with this sophisticated get-up you're wearing.'

Rose sat down. Damn it. Her stupid stomach. She tried to look dignified. 'I want to get this over with as quickly as possible.'

'What, with no time for a meal? I think you need to eat something, at least. They have the most delicious breads here. Foccaccia with rosemary and salt . . . '

'Goddam you,' Rose said, sliding into the dark wood banquette opposite him and reaching into the bread basket. She tore off a piece and devoured it. It was absolutely delicious.

A waiter materialised.

'We'll take a bottle of the house Chianti,' Jacob said, 'and I'll have the Porterhouse.'

'Filet mignon,' said Rose, surrendering to her need to eat. 'So you stole my building?'

Jacob looked at her steadily. 'I bought it on the open market.'

'You only bought it because I wanted it,' she retorted.

He considered it. 'Not *only*. It's also a great deal. I admire your taste and perception. Renovations and some security, changing neighbourhood, I'm looking to make a couple mill on it. It's going to be the foundation of the JRoth Corporation.'

'JRoth? Original.'

'You're too beautiful to be sarcastic; it doesn't suit you. I intend to make that building the cornerstone of my company. Unlike you, I'll only be investing in the

City. Profit margins are greater there. I think there are some unexplored pockets of Manhattan due for a rise.'

'Like where?'

That grin again. 'That would be telling.'

Rose said, 'So, you summoned me here to rub it in my face and tell me I now have two enemies instead of one?'

'Not exactly.' He took a sip of his wine; it was rich, earthy and good. Rothstein thought she looked absolutely stunning. Her anger was as fiery and lovely on her as the diamonds that glittered dramatically around her neck and earlobes. 'It was a warning shot that I fired across your bows.'

'Oooh,' Rose said, widening her wolf-blue eyes, 'I'm scared.'

He ignored that. 'You never got over what happened to your father.'

'Don't even mention my father's name,' Rose said, colouring angrily.

'But I have to. Look, my family aren't saints.'

'Your family are greedy, evil scumbags who made a fortune from ruining other people's lives. My father wasn't the only one.'

Rothstein shrugged. 'I didn't like what I was seeing at the family company, and I walked out. But you must understand something, Rose. Whatever my father's faults, *he's still my father*. I know you are on some lifelong quest to destroy him, and I'm telling you I'm not going to let it happen.'

'I don't have a quarrel with you, Jacob. Just stay out of it.'

'You're not listening to me,' he said quietly, 'and that's a mistake, Rose. I will not let you harm my father. You have to let go of the hatred. It's consuming you. I think you've been hanging around Don Salerni too long. You're nursing this vendetta like you were Italian yourself.'

'I *am* Italian. Fiorello, remember.'

He shrugged. 'I meant by birth. Just look at you.'

She let that pass for a second. 'And then, what justice for my father, who's dead? What justice for all the other tenants your slimy uncle William and your grasping father screwed over? Who compensates all the women that tried to work there and were fired or sexually harassed by the boss? All the harm that Rothstein Realty did, you think I'm going to just let that go?'

'Yes, I do.'

'Then you're *crazy*,' Rose said, tearing off more bread.

'No. I just know what the alternative is. I build up JRoth Corp for a few years, let our shareholders see the profits I can make. Prove myself outside of the family arena. And then I go to an investment bank, and I take over Rothstein Realty.'

'You take it over?' Rose said. 'Just like that, huh? You've lost it, Jacob.'

'Have I? You studied those figures you stole. You know how precarious the empire is. Profits are down, vacancies are up, there's some creative accounting going on.'

'Yes,' she agreed, her eyes glittering. 'I'm not in a position to take advantage of it. Yet.'

'But you want to wait ten more years, nursing your hatred . . . come on, Rose. There's a better way. When I take over, you will get justice. And I will protect my father from being ruined. Because I know if I let you go unchecked, you could ruin him, eventually.'

'And how exactly am I going to get this justice?'

'First, you will see him dispossessed of the company. It'll be a humiliation. But it needs to be done. Second, when I'm in charge, things will change. I will go back through the files and see to it that everybody he ripped off is compensated.'

Rose snorted. 'Everybody, yeah, right.'

'I'm deadly serious,' Rothstein said flatly. 'And I'll hire people according to merit.'

'Women?'

He nodded.

'African-Americans?'

'Even Italians,' Rothstein said, grinning. 'Look, it's good business. If I'm paying a salary I want to be able to hire the best. Sometimes even a dumb brunette with a fine rack like yourself can have an idea or two.'

Rose struggled with herself, trying not to grin. She lost the battle.

'And you really think you can pull this off?'

'I know I can. Because I'm going to have the two best property execs in New York working on it. I bet we can own Rothstein within three to four years.'

'We?' Rose asked.

He lifted his glass to her. 'Of course we. Is there some other, better, property guy in the City that I don't know about?'

Rose's mouth dropped open. 'You want to be my partner?'

'You could do worse. I'm pretty good at it too. I bought that place in Alphabet City.'

Rose shook her head. 'Jacob . . . '

'Here you are, sir, madam,' said the waiter, laying down two vast plates of succulent beef, with spinach and roast potatoes and crisp green beans.

'Why don't you eat on it,' Rothstein said. 'You'll be in a better mood on a full stomach.'

She was starving. 'OK,' she agreed.

Rothstein took a mouthful of steak and washed it down with the red wine. 'Let's not talk about business. Let's talk about something else.'

'Like what?'

He grinned. 'Tell me about your day.'

Rose stared at him, then burst into a peal of laughter.

'What's funny?' he asked. 'I didn't think I was being *that* witty.'

'My day,' she said.

'Something happen?'

'Man,' Rose said. 'You think this conversation was a bombshell to me? Not today. Not after what just happened to me.' She shook her head. 'You have no idea.'

'So tell me. I've got all night.'

★ ★ ★

They ate, Rothstein waiting impatiently while Rose broke off from talking to eat some more food — she demolished everything on her plate, which he enjoyed watching, but not when he was so gripped by her story. He asked her a couple of times if she was joking, but she denied it, and he could see she was telling the truth.

'So what do you think it means?' he asked eventually, when she was done.

'I have no idea. It *means* I have two blood-sisters, and they want me to get to know them, which is fine. But family isn't like powdered coffee — just add genes and acquaintance, instant sisterhood.'

He was thoughtful. 'Look, what are you doing after this?'

'Going the hell home and going to bed,' Rose said.

'Come back with me,' Jacob said. 'I don't think you should be by yourself tonight.'

# 60

Rose couldn't believe she had let herself be persuaded.

It was late, very late. She may have stayed up later than this before, but this had certainly been the longest day of her life, and she was spending the rest of it at Jacob Rothstein's place?

Maybe exhaustion had weakened her will, she thought, as she parked the Porsche in his underground, gated garage.

Just remember one thing: you're *not* gonna go to bed with him, she warned herself. Absolutely, 100 per cent *not*.

'Hey.' Rothstein was standing over her, having courteously opened her door and helped her out. 'Just remember one thing, Fiorello, I'm not going to go to bed with you. Sorry. It takes more than a good steak and a glass of wine to buy my affection.'

Rose laughed.

'Curses, foiled again,' she said.

'Let's go upstairs and talk about this,' he said. 'I have a private elevator right here.'

Rose dutifully followed him. 'I don't know why I'm here, Jacob.'

'Because you wanted to be with me.'

She ignored that. 'I don't even have a toothbrush or a nightgown.'

'I keep a package of guest toiletries. I have a spare bedroom with its own bathroom. And don't sleep in any clothes on my account.'

Rose looked at him.

'I guess I may have a spare pair of silk pyjamas that I keep for ladies,' Rothstein admitted.

'Well, aren't you smooth.'

'I'm not a monk.'

'Then I wouldn't have expected all that stuff. Wouldn't your female guests typically be spending the night in the main bedroom, sans pyjamas?'

Rothstein grinned at her. 'Makes them feel safe to know they have another option, which relaxes them, and then . . . ' He spread his hands.

'Machiavelli,' she said.

He bowed, acknowledging the compliment. 'I tend to go with whatever works. Unfortunately you know that strategy, so now I'll have to come up with another one.'

The elevator, an old-fashioned fantasy in carved brass, burgundy leather and smoky mirrors, hissed smoothly to a stop. Rose's stomach felt as though it had been left several floors below, but she wasn't sure if that was from the ride or from being this close to Jacob.

Male company. She just wasn't used to it.

Of course, he was a little more than plain male company. That strong chest in the well-cut suit, that square jaw, the dark, close-cropped hair, the thick black lashes. Rose's phantom stomach, wherever it might be, squirmed with desire. But she looked away and stepped out of the elevator car.

Now was not the time. Her defences were way, way down.

⋆   ⋆   ⋆

Jacob was as good as his word. He showed her into the opulent guest bedroom, with its marble-and-gold ensuite bathroom and a little balcony that double windows opened on to, with a fabulous view of Fifth and the spire of St Patrick's a few blocks up. He laid out the silk pyjamas, the electric toothbrush, some Rembrandt, a pre-packed case of Molton Brown shampoos and conditioners, Floris bath essences, L'Occitane shower gel, a pair of Moroccan slippers

514

embroidered with gold thread, and, finally, an incredibly inviting, enveloping, warm robe in the softest white cashmere.

'If you want to get changed, I make a mean hot chocolate.'

Rose was impressed, but still suspicious. 'And are you gonna be decent when I come out?'

'I'm more than decent, baby,' he said, 'but you aren't getting to find that out tonight.'

She surrendered, closed her door, and got changed. It felt good to peel off her clothes and take a quick shower with some of that exquisitely scented lavender gel. His towels were white and fluffy, and she dried off, pulled on the pyjamas, the slippers and the robe, and emerged to find Jacob in a pair of karate pants and a T-shirt.

'You're a black belt?'

'Third Dan,' he said, 'so you can feel quite safe.'

He handed her a steaming mug of frothy hot chocolate. She took a sip; it was delicious.

Jacob paused. He had something to say to Rose, and wasn't sure if he should. But she deserved to hear it.

'Look, I'm not trying to freak you out or anything — '

Rose smiled. 'I think I'm already about as freaked out as I could possibly be, so a little more is not going to make much difference.'

'Then don't you think it's a little odd that two identical triplet sisters of yours turn up in New York, today?'

'Well, of course it's odd. It's practically unbelievable, except for the fact that it did happen, and I was there.'

'I don't believe in coincidences,' Jacob said.

'Sometimes they do happen. Somebody wins the lottery almost every week, and the odds against it for that particular guy are fourteen million to one, but he still wins.'

'Do you play the lottery?'

'No.'

'Why not?'

'Bad odds,' Rose said, laughing.

'Exactly. Now, I'm assuming that these two women actually are your sisters.'

'What other possibility is there?'

'Elaborate plastic surgery, I suppose, but I can't see any motivation for that. They both seem very successful and well-known in their fields.'

'Yes.'

'And I agree with Magnus Soren. Somebody evidently intended that you three girls should not meet.'

Rose nodded. 'But that's all in the past, now.'

Jacob shrugged. 'I'm surprised.'

'At what?'

'That you would let this go. After all, you pursued my father for hounding your father out of his lease. But you're willing to let the person who split you up from your sisters get away with it?'

Rose paused. 'I hadn't thought of it like that.'

His words struck her in the heart. She felt pale, and unusually weak, and flopped into one of Jacob's antique chairs.

Concern crossed his face. 'Hey, I shouldn't have said anything. It's too much for you to take in, all at once.'

'No, it's OK. You're right.' Rose looked up at him. 'You sound like you care about me.'

'Of course I care about you,' he said simply. 'You're my woman.'

She felt an instant flood of desire.

Rose leaned over. Her plump lips were slightly parted, she felt hot and weak with longing. She kissed him full on the lips, sliding her tongue in between his teeth, feeling his momentary hesitation, and then his strong arms around her as he pulled her close to him, his rough fingertips sliding in amongst the cashmere and silk to find her breast, cupping it with his hand, stroking and teasing until she was almost maddened . . .

'We can't,' Rothstein said. He pushed her away, and ran a hand through his hair. He was sweating with wanting her.

'We can do whatever we want,' Rose said, 'we're over twenty-one.'

'I can't take advantage of you like this. Not today. Of all days.'

'God*dammit*, Rothstein.'

'Sorry,' he said, unrepentantly. 'When you're in your right mind. I've waited for you too long to take you like this.'

# 61

Poppy decided that she didn't want to talk to Henry right away. She had some things to do first.

She took a flight back to LA, went straight to her offices, and called Dani in.

'What's up?' her right-hand woman said. She could tell right away, by Poppy's face, that it was something serious. 'I don't think you should sweat it about Menace, by the way. You made the right decision. We should have dumped them long ago.'

'Don't you sometimes wish we could dump them all?' Poppy asked.

Dani laughed. 'Yeah! The very next time I take a call from a groupie threatening a paternity suit, or a long-haired stoner rock star bitching about the green M & Ms somebody didn't pick out of his rider . . . '

'I want to get rid of the whole thing, Dani,' Poppy said seriously. 'I mean it. Menace were the worst, but I can't take the hand-holding any more. Even Travis is bitching all the time now.'

Dani blinked. 'But Poppy, management is what we do. What else would we do?' She looked panicked. 'I know they can be selfish jerks, but I *love* the record business. This is my life, and I don't want to give it up. Is this something Henry wants?'

Poppy sighed. 'Not at all. He was right, I was being a bit of a spoiled bitch.'

'You? Never.'

'Cow,' Poppy said, grinning. 'I love the record business too, but I don't think management is right for me.'

'Not right? Opium is, like, the *hottest* new firm, you manage all kinds of different acts, you got record companies begging you to take on their baby bands, I even had some classical guy call me and ask me to take a look at his new violinist . . . '

'Oh yeah?' Poppy asked, momentarily distracted. 'Was it another 'This-chick-plays-the-violin-and-she's-really-hot-so-let's-do-a-rebel-classical-album-where-she-comes-out-of-the-sea-holding-her-Stradivarius-and-wearing-nothing-but-a-G-string type deal?'

Dani laughed. 'Pretty much. The twist was that this was a boy, really buff, looks like he belongs in NSync.'

'Oy vey,' Poppy said. 'I hate those acts. Ugh.'

Dani chuckled. 'But you don't mean it about folding Opium.'

'I mean it about getting out of the management business. I think we can expand.'

'What do you mean?' Dani asked warily. 'You're famous for being a manager. If you switch you'd have to start from the bottom.'

'Didn't stop David Geffen, or Cliff Burnstein or Peter Mensch, or . . . '

'OK, OK,' Dani said, 'so what, then?'

Poppy leaned across the desk and smiled at her. 'How does our own record label sound?'

★ ★ ★

Poppy refused to stay more than a day in Los Angeles. She told Dani to start winding up Opium Management without her, drawing up lists of who would stay and who would go. Everybody got generous severance pay, enough to cushion the blow. But she didn't want to deal with the moans of her former employees, or the sudden panicked wail of acts who realised they were going to lose their manager, the young woman who had nursed them to stardom. She took the time out to call Travis Jackson personally, but that was it.

Travis was surprisingly reasonable, reverting to the

cool young guy he'd been when they first met.

'So you're switching from the side of the angels, huh, baby? Gonna work for The Man?'

'Or The Woman,' Poppy said, responding to his teasing. 'I got some names of people I think would be great for you to go with.'

'They won't be you,' he said, sighing. 'But I guess this was inevitable.'

'Why's that?'

'A girl like you can't really work for somebody else, not even for rock stars,' he said, and Poppy thought it was one of the biggest compliments she'd ever been paid.

'So what now?' Travis asked.

Poppy thought of Henry LeClerc, the next Senator from Louisiana, if she had anything to do with it.

'I have a little personal business to take care of,' she said.

⋆   ⋆   ⋆

She hopped on a flight to New Orleans, where the Congressman was holed up, starting the laborious task of pulling his ratings back out of the drain that Poppy's image had plunged them into. Flicking through the papers in her first-class seat, Poppy noted that his poll ratings had gone up two points since the news had broken that she'd left him, or he'd left her. But Henry was refusing to comment on it. A gentleman doesn't kiss and tell, she guessed.

Poppy rang Don Rickles, his chief of staff, from her SkyPhone. The call was about forty dollars a minute, but it was worth it.

'It's Poppy. I want to see him.'

'Can't you just leave him alone? You come back, you'll ruin everything we've worked for,' the aide hissed at her.

'Actually, no I won't; and you know you can't keep me from him, so don't even try,' Poppy said.

He sighed deeply, and told her to hold. In a minute, Henry's voice was on — polite, guarded; it pulled at her heartstrings.

'Can I help you, Poppy?'

'You sure can. I fired Menace.'

'That's good, but — '

'In fact I fired all my acts. I quit. Look, you were right. When can I see you?'

'Any time you like, sugar,' he said, and she could hear the ear-splitting grin in his voice on the crackly satellite phone. 'Any time. I've missed you.'

'I've missed you too,' she said, 'and I have so much to tell you, you're just not gonna believe it.'

★ ★ ★

Daisy spent the morning with Janus, updating them on everything. Their investigators met her at the utilitarian offices, listening and taking notes, but not doing much talking.

'Well? Don't you think this changes everything?' Daisy asked.

Doug Berkshire smiled thinly. 'We had just put together the files on your sisters. We were about to present them, but it seems you got there first.' He sighed. 'However, we haven't been able to discover anything at all about your parents. Nothing that matters.'

'If you know something, I want you to tell me now,' Daisy pleaded.

'I will certainly give you our files, but we have discovered nothing except that the adoption agencies were dummies, fly-by-night shops that disappeared once each daughter had been adopted. We can't find anybody involved with them. Your case,' and he pushed his glasses up on the bridge of his nose, 'has some well-covered tracks in it. The only mistake that was made seems to have been that the three sisters were allowed to live.'

'At least tell me if there are any more sisters out there.'

'No. Three.' He nodded. 'Three girls.'

'Well,' Daisy said, slightly disappointed, 'I suppose that's enough news to be getting on with.'

'There won't be any more news,' he said flatly. 'I'm afraid we've done all we can here.'

★ ★ ★

Rose woke up, not sure where she was. A very comfortable bed, with silk sheets, and the sunlight streaming in through the windows. Really *streaming* in . . . it was late, she thought groggily; she never got up this late. Automatically, she swung her feet out of bed, but instead of meeting her hardwood floors, they touched soft, warm, thick carpet . . .

She rubbed her eyes. She was in Jacob Rothstein's bed.

His *spare* bed.

The previous day, and night, came flooding back to her.

Maybe Jacob wasn't here, maybe he'd gone to work. She felt instantly self-conscious, embarrassed. She had been panting after him last night like a bitch in heat, and he'd said no, and he'd said he wanted to wait until — now.

'Good morning.'

Jacob's head appeared around the door, and Rose jumped out of her skin. She gathered the white cashmere robe hastily to her, protectively.

'How did I know you wouldn't feel the same way this

morning?' he said. 'You act like a goddam virgin, Rose, you know that?'

'Actually,' Rose said with dignity, 'I *am* a virgin.'

He stared at her. 'Get out. I thought you were joking, before. And still nobody?'

'Not that it's any of your business, but no.'

'Hmm.' Rothstein ran a hand through his hair. 'That's kind of romantic, when you think about it. Weird, but you always were weird.'

'You're weird,' Rose retorted, childishly.

'I'm not gonna be the one to change it.'

'Nobody asked you to,' Rose said, surprised at how disappointed and rejected that made her feel.

'At least not right now.'

'What the hell are you talking about, Rothstein?'

'You. Me. I told you, you're my woman.' He came over and sat on the side of the bed. 'Yesterday I proposed a business partnership.'

'Yes, you did, and I haven't made my mind up about it yet . . . '

'Sure you have,' he said confidently. 'You'd love to take over Rothstein Realty with me.'

She had to admit it. The thought of her sitting behind William Rothstein's desk was delicious. Putting right everything that bastard had done wrong.

'Possibly,' she agreed.

'So let's just go a little further.'

'You're talking about marriage.'

'That's the ultimate partnership, toots.'

'You're talking about me marrying a *Rothstein*,' she explained. 'I hate the Rothsteins.'

'You don't hate me. You've been in love with me from the first moment you saw me.'

Rose grinned. 'You are a cocky son of a bitch, you know that?'

He kissed her. 'Well, you know what they say about birds of a feather . . . '

# 62

Poppy made her peace with Henry. It wasn't difficult. A formal welcome for the cameras, a quick statement to the press about Henry LeClerc's ideals and how she fully supported them, and then Henry tugged her out of the media glare and back to his hotel room, and the formal pecks on the cheek gave way to passionate kisses, kisses that tore at the mouth the same way his hands tore off her clothes, and her fingers pulled off his pants. They tumbled on top of the bedding, hot mouths and skin and hands and limbs meshing together in a frenzy of lovemaking.

'A record label. I think that's a great idea.'

'Suitable for a Senator's wife?'

'For this Senator's wife.' Henry looked down at his bride-to-be, her lips parted in anticipation. 'But please, no more hip-hop.'

Poppy scowled. 'There's gonna be plenty of hip-hop. Just none like Menace.'

'Deal,' Henry said. And made love to her again.

★   ★   ★

'Daisy? This is Rose.'

Daisy beamed into the receiver. 'Hey, you. I didn't think I was going to hear back from you so soon.'

'It was something of a shock. Listen, I'd like to come over and talk to you,' Rose said.

'Be my guest!' Daisy exclaimed. She felt teary. 'I'm so glad we're talking. After yesterday, I need some good news.'

'Why, what happened yesterday? Are you OK?'

'I'm fine.' Daisy sighed. 'It's just that I thought I had

something with Janus, my investigation agency, but they've hit a blank.'

There was a pause at the other end of the line.

'I'll see you in ten minutes, OK?' Rose said.

★ ★ ★

When she arrived at Magnus Soren's house, Rose felt a strange sense of lightness. She had had a night to sleep on the strangest thing that had ever happened to her, and though she was still shocked, she was more accepting of it. Hers had been an extraordinary young life. She thought she could cope with one more curveball.

Last night with Jacob had resolved some things she'd been battling over. Her loathing of William and Fred Rothstein had warred with her love for Jacob, a love she'd tried and failed to suppress. Now she had an opportunity to seek justice, but to do it at his side. If she couldn't ruin Fred Rothstein, removing him would do.

Rose pressed the bell. Before she got ready to strike the last item off her to-do list, she allowed herself a second's delicious fantasy. She, Rose Fiorello, sitting behind Fred Rothstein's desk. Running his company. And wearing his son's ring . . .

Perfect revenge. Her father would have been proud.

A maid came to the door. 'This way, ma'am.'

★ ★ ★

Rose was ushered in to Magnus Soren's gorgeous living room again, where Daisy enveloped her in a bone-crushing hug. 'I'm so glad you're here.'

Rose scrutinised the familiar features. 'Me too,' she said.

Daisy caught the tone.

'Something wrong?'

'No. Let's sit down.'

'Would you like some tea?'

'Nasty Limey habit, but I'll take some coffee, if you've got any.'

The maid disappeared to the kitchen before Daisy could make the request. 'So tell me,' Daisy pleaded. 'I know you're hatching something; I get that look myself.'

'I was thinking, maybe you're right about finding our birth parents. Just to allay the curiosity.'

Her sister sighed. 'I really don't think it can be done. I've been trying for a year, and even Janus, who were very bullish at first, say they've come up with a blank.'

'From what I've heard of them, that seems unlikely,' Rose said.

Daisy blinked. 'You're suggesting they just pocketed my money and didn't bother to do any work?'

Rose shook her head. 'Far more likely, they were scared off. They haven't been on this case long enough to make a determination like that.'

Daisy was silent for a few moments.

'I think I can find out for sure,' Rose said. 'But it would mean getting your hands a little dirty, so we should probably get Poppy to sign off on it, too, before we started.'

'What exactly are you talking about?'

The coffee arrived, and the maid poured it into a couple of wafer-thin bone china cups, disappearing as discreetly as she had materialised.

Rose sipped the fragrant brew, making sure she was gone from earshot before she leaned forward and half-whispered to her sister, 'Do you know who Don Vincent Salerni is?'

★　★　★

Poppy was drawing up wedding plans when Rose called. Running a record company was one thing; getting married was a whole new nightmare. She had to calm her mother down, but Marcia eventually accepted that having a Congressman, soon to be Senator, as a son-in-law was *some* compensation for her daughter marrying a gentile . . .

Poppy had tried, as gently as possible, to break the news of her two sisters to her parents. After they had lowered their hands from their mouths, they were insistent that Rose and Daisy come to visit. Poppy winced.

'Don't you think we all need a little time to adjust?'

'Adjust? What's to adjust?' her father demanded. 'If I can adjust to all your long-haired druggies, Poppy, they can adjust to the family . . . '

When Rose called, Poppy and her mother, who was utterly determined not to be cheated of her role as Planner-in-Chief, were going over swatches of brides-maids' fabric.

'This is a very good colour, strong,' Marcia said approvingly.

Poppy sighed. 'I can't ask Dani to wear tomato-red. She'll look like an actual tomato.'

'So she should drop some weight,' Marcia insisted.

'Mom — '

'Poppy! Phone!'

'Thank heaven,' Poppy muttered, racing downstairs.

'Hey, it's Rose. Sorry to bother you at home.'

'Don't be. Wedding preparations.' Poppy grimaced. 'Ugh. Las Vegas and an Elvis impersonator looks pretty good right now.'

Rose chuckled. 'You too, huh? It's spreading like a virus. We're all getting married.'

'What, you too? Who?'

'Jacob Rothstein.'

'I thought you hated the Rothsteins.'

'Oh, I do. It's a long story. But this isn't about that. Daisy and I were thinking of finding our birth-parents.

There's something off about how we were adopted, and I can't let it rest without finding out what, exactly.'

Poppy paused. 'I appreciate how you feel, but it's no go. Daisy already told me. If Janus came up blank, hiring anyone else would just be a waste of time. They're the best.'

'I have another option,' Rose said, and told her.

★ ★ ★

Her sisters had little faith in Rose's plan, but they agreed to go along with it. Rose wasn't concerned. The other two girls came from different worlds; they had no idea what a man like Don Vincent Salerni was capable of.

She made an appointment to go and see him. Don Salerni received Rose in the penthouse suite at the Rego Park complex, Rose's first and still most-beloved big real estate deal. She had spared no expense in fitting it out; the walls had been ripped down and replaced with Armorlite, UV treated and three inches thick, that glittered like the glass it impersonated and gave Salerni exquisite views over Queens — along with protection from snipers' bullets. If any would dare. The floors were marble, and the ceiling painted in a faux-Italian mural, a pastoral scene. Rose had had the taps and shower head plated with gold, she had installed central air, a garbage chute, the best appliances on the market — everything the modern mob boss could desire. And Salerni had obviously been pleased, because he had kept out of her hair.

More than that. Rose Fiorello had one of the best-run construction sites in the business. Her workers were never late and they never slacked off. The very association with Salerni was enough to get her that respect.

Rose had not had many dealings with Salerni. She had not chosen to get involved with him in the first place; but there was no getting away from it, when he owned the hotel. Still, she knew her father would have disapproved violently. Salerni was an extortionist, a murderer.

And yet she was still here.

Rose wilfully pushed her doubts aside. Jacob was right. She wanted answers. And this was the only way she knew how to get them.

'Don Salerni,' she murmured, pressing his hand. She had to force herself not to bend and kiss it. This guy wasn't the Pope.

'Rose. Sit.' He waved her to a chair, his narrow eyes scanning her, checking her out. She was modestly dressed in a business suit from Donna Karan, a cream silk shirt and a string of pearls, and somehow his glance made her feel as dirty as if she were in a stripper's tassels and G-string.

'Thank you,' she said.

'To what do I owe the pleasure? My personal charms have finally gotten to you?'

Rose swallowed, hard. She'd rather die than let this guy touch her. 'They would have, Don Salerni,' she said carefully, 'but I've recently gotten engaged.'

He chuckled. 'No need to flinch, kid.'

She blushed.

'*Auguri*,' he said. 'Is it an Italian, like you?'

'No. A Jew.'

He frowned, so she moved on, quickly. 'Don Salerni. I have a problem. I wondered if I could seek your help.'

The narrow eyes danced. 'Finally. I was wondering how long it would take you. Trouble with the Rothstein boy in Alphabet City?'

Rose paled. 'No. No! I am engaged to Jacob Rothstein.'

For the first time, Salerni looked wrong-footed. He

blinked, then he burst out laughing. 'Crazy girl!'

'It is about my parents. My real ones,' Rose said. 'I want to find them.'

'You hardly need me for that.'

'It's a little more complicated than usual. If I could explain . . . '

★  ★  ★

Salerni listened intently. Rose was a little put off by how much he seemed to be enjoying her story. He did not interrupt, and neither did he answer his phone, which buzzed quietly at intervals.

'I was thinking it was odd, a firm like Janus, just up and quitting like that.'

Salerni nodded. 'Yes. Well, we can start with the fact that you are Italian.'

'We don't know that.'

'I knew it from the second I saw you, *bellissima*.'

'Possibly,' Rose said, smiling slightly. She bore the name Fiorello, it would be nice to be Italian. And it might explain her desire to be avenged . . .

Salerni smiled thinly. 'Despite what you read in the papers, we still have some reach. Especially in the old country, though things are going to hell down there . . . They even have women running some crews.' He grimaced.

Rose didn't dare say a word. She knew that half of Italy was under Mafia control, especially Sicily and the poor south. She'd done a little research into international real estate, and the harsh climate and earthquake potential weren't all that dampened property values in what was, after all, a G8 nation; nobody wanted to live in a town or village controlled by the Cosa Nostra.

'I can make a few calls,' Salerni said finally. 'Do you a favour. *Perche no?*'

'*Grazie*,' Rose murmured, 'Don Salerni.' She swallowed, hard.

His sharp eyes picked up on it immediately. 'There is something else?'

Rose struggled with her courage. 'Yes. This is to involve my sisters. Don Salerni, they are not of our world . . . I know, when someone receives a favour from a Don, that person is in his debt. But I tell you fairly, you cannot have a hold over my sisters and me. I will never submit to it, and I will not do anything illegal . . . '

'So you refuse to be the mule for the sixty kilos I wanted to get through Newark next month?' Salerni asked, then chuckled at Rose's shocked face. 'Ah, *bellissima*, you never would make a soldier. You are a *woman*. What would I do with you?'

Rose felt bizarrely annoyed that Salerni said he couldn't use her. She could be a fine Mafiosi if she wanted to be . . .

'You have balls,' Salerni said. 'I like you. For you, that's enough.' He waved at the apartment. 'And you keep this place good.'

Rose blessed the day she had decided to outfit Salerni's penthouse with the best of everything and present it to him free of charge.

He flicked his hand, indicating her audience was at an end. 'I'll see what I can do,' Salerni said, and Rose withdrew.

# 63

When she got the call almost a month later, Rose decided her sisters had to be in on it. Poppy flew in from LA, delighted to be away from wedding planning for a little while, and Daisy flew over from England, where she had been staying with her parents. Rose was surprised to discover how much she liked seeing the other two girls. She hugged them, and meant the hug. It was almost like family, she thought to herself with a grin. Maybe Daisy was right; maybe in the end, blood would out, after all.

The other two cooed over the apartment, from which Jacob had tactfully absented himself, and perched on the elegant couch while Rose served up some cinnamon coffee.

'Don Salerni will be here soon. Now, I want you guys to — '

'Wait. What did you say? He'll be *here*? I thought we were just getting an update.'

'He wants to see you two in person. Curiosity factor, I guess.'

Poppy shuddered. 'Man. I don't know . . . some murdering thug . . . '

Rose paled. 'Hey, you don't know if he murdered anybody. Not for sure. And we need him, at least if we want to figure out what happened to our birth parents.'

'Which we do,' Daisy said firmly. 'It's the piece that's missing in my life, Poppy. We should be nice to him.'

'OK, OK,' Poppy said, spreading her hands. 'If he gets results . . . ' She shrugged.

'You need to be very respectful to him,' Rose said. Then, catching the look on her sister's face, she added, 'And if you can't do that, at least keep quiet.'

Poppy grinned. 'Fair enough.'

The buzzer sounded. Rose picked up the handset.

'Speak of the *diablo*,' Poppy muttered, and Daisy kicked her in the shins.

'Sure,' Rose said to the doorman, shooting a warning look at Poppy. 'Send him right up.'

★ ★ ★

Rose had the door open when Salerni arrived, and she ushered him through it into her fiancé's apartment.

'Acceptable,' he said, glancing around.

'Don Salerni, may I present my sisters — Daisy Markham and Poppy Allen.'

Salerni stared. '*Porca miseria!* It's like a three-way mirror.' His thin tongue slid fractionally out of his mouth, and moistened his narrow lips, appreciatively.

Rose saw Poppy start to grimace. 'Sit down, please sit down,' she said, blocking Salerni's view. 'Can I bring you anything? Mineral water, coffee?'

Salerni pointed at the cut-crystal decanter. 'Scotch on the rocks.'

Daisy couldn't stop her eyebrow lifting; it was 9 a.m.

'Story like this, my pretty, needs a little something,' Salerni told her, and instantly Daisy was all ears.

'You know something, um, *Don* Salerni.'

'You could say that,' Salerni replied. He waited until Rose had presented him with a tumbler full of golden liquid and clinking ice cubes, took a pull of it, and started to speak. He was a quiet-voiced man, and that somehow made him more menacing. Even Poppy felt herself fascinated, half-hypnotised. He had that kind of presence.

'First, so you two girls know' — Poppy bristled at 'girls', but Salerni ignored her — 'I do a little business with your sister. She asks me for a favour . . . ' — he spread his hands, as Poppy had done earlier — 'a *padrone* doesn't refuse a client. So I made a few calls. You,' he nodded at Daisy, 'went to Janus. Smart move, but somebody had told them to back off. Which intrigued me, when I found out it was true. The guy on your case had somebody ring his house and leave an answermachine message.'

'What was it?' Daisy asked.

'A gun being fired six times,' Salerni told her. 'Same message was left at all the guy's places: his country house, even the secret apartment he rents under another name where he stashes his girlfriends. He decided you could go fuck yourselves; he wasn't getting involved. So I got a copy of his files.' His eyes warned them not to ask how; none of them did. 'Guy hadn't got far but he'd gotten a couple leads. This man involved with the adoption agency in London died in prison, convicted as an accessory to murder. The murder was related to the Frederici crew, that's a small crew out of Naples, died out. So I asked around some old guys who used to do business with that crew. About three girls got adopted. They didn't know much, but we kept asking around, legit sources too. Finally came up with something. Three babies were abandoned at the door of a monastery in Abruzzo, and they were snatched up for adoption by the Fredericis. Unusual — a family getting involved in anything like that. But the Frederici woman the monks gave the girls to didn't raise them.'

'Did you ask her what she did with them?'

'She's dead.'

'What do the monastery records say?'

'Monastery got destroyed in an earthquake.'

'God *damn* it,' Daisy said, her fists clenched in frustration.

'No need for language like that,' Salerni said mildly.

'Excuse me,' Daisy said, a little frightened.

He enjoyed that look in her eye. 'My guys think the woman lied to the monks. She never wanted to raise the kids, and her crew placed them abroad, split them up. Question is, why bother? Now the Fredericis were never a big crew, never a big family. I think whoever picked 'em was smart, because they don't arouse much interest. Kept to themselves, not big producers,' his lip curled in contempt, 'nothing but local shit. They would have got paid nice to bother with this, send someone abroad.'

'The man who died in jail . . . whom did he kill?'

'Very good,' Salerni said, winking at Poppy. 'He was found guilty of killing a Mrs Harrison.'

Daisy recognised the name. 'The woman who fronted the agency I was adopted from, who then disappeared.'

'Right. She went to Blackpool and was shot. The Frederici guy got caught.'

'So.' Rose was working it out in her head. 'Someone pays the Fredericis to take us from the monastery, and then send us abroad. They hire people to make fake adoption agencies and then to make sure nobody talks, they kill those people. Except that one of their crew got caught, died in prison. He was the only link back.'

'Exactly.'

'Then the question is, who hired the Fredericis, and why?'

Salerni took over. 'I found the whole thing intriguing, at this point. I had my people keep hammering. Why . . . you must have mattered to someone. A lotta trouble, just over three anonymous girls. And there aren't a whole bunch of triplets born, least not before they made up those fertility drugs. It got easier after I knew the date.'

All three girls looked interested.

'About seventy-two,' Salerni informed them. 'They may have put false ages on you at the three agencies. Anyway, you could have been peasant kids, but not likely . . . why would anybody go to such trouble over peasants? I thought maybe you were daughters of some family, maybe smuggled out to stop a vendetta. But you were all girls. Nobody bothers when it's girls.' He grinned at Poppy's outraged face. 'That's the truth, toots. Nobody thinks a girl will come after them.'

'Don't they,' Rose said softly.

Salerni looked approving at her tone, and nodded. 'So I assumed you were born in a hospital. We checked records. There were only four sets of all-girl triplets recorded that year. One set was premature, died early. Two other sets are still living, but they are accounted for. The last set also died.'

Daisy was disappointed. 'So no hospital records . . . '

'I didn't say that. The premature babies I wrote off, because they died in the hospital. But the last set died in a fire. Their bodies were never found.' He shook his head. 'I didn't buy that; did some checking. These were rich girls, very rich. Their father was Count Luigi Parigi, and right before the fire, he died in a shooting accident. His skull was found in the woods, years later; they identified it by dental records. If you believe that.'

'Parigi,' Daisy said. 'I think I saw that name before, in *Hello!*. But it wasn't a count, it was a prince.'

Salerni nodded. 'The Prince was first cousin to the Count. Still is. Your cousin.'

Rose felt her heart start to race. Her palms were sweating. 'How can you be so sure? How can you know that?'

'It's simple,' Salerni said, mildly, but with complete assurance. 'Who stands to benefit from the hit? That's the one that does it. This Roberto was working for his cousin. He's the elder branch, but they got all the money. Anyhow . . . when the Count has children, he leaves his company to them. But if the Count, and then his wife and daughters, all die in a tragic 'accident' . . . ' He shrugged again. 'The Prince inherited everything.'

'But how much can it have been? He was a prince, wasn't he wealthy? Why go to the trouble?'

'It was worth it,' Salerni assured them. 'The firm was worth billions. *Your* billions.' He lifted his glass to them. '*Salud . . . Contesse.*'

'This is crazy,' Poppy muttered, but Daisy was bright-eyed. 'Can you prove it?' she said eagerly.

'Absolutely not,' Salerni said. 'You can try, but it'll never happen; trail's too cold.'

'We'll see about that,' Rose said, softly.

# 64

Rome was everything Rose had ever imagined. She sat with Daisy and Poppy in the back of their hired limousine, resting her head against the tinted windows, exhausted after the long Al Italia flight. The girls had sat together in first class, sipping champagne and discussing everything except the reason they were here. None of them wanted to talk about it, in case they were overheard; who knew where a man like Roberto Parigi had his spies?

Rose had quietly read some back issues of *Business Week*, *Forbes*, and *The Economist* which covered the Parigi billions. She felt the anger simmer and seethe in her belly with each passing page. She now felt almost as exhausted by her emotions as she was by the flight.

But this was Rome; and Poppy and Daisy were ooh-ing and aah-ing with each sight which slipped by their windows; there was the Circus Maximus, and the great ruined palace on the Palatine hill; and the pyramid of Caius Cestius, white and gleaming, incongruous in the Roman city; and lastly, the great curve of the Colosseum and the pillars and arches of the great Roman Forum. Rose couldn't help but look; she felt a strong pull, a real sense of being home.

Because she *was* an Italian. And so had her father been.

Before they got on the flight, Daisy had insisted they find out everything about their birth parents. A Nexxis search had revealed old photographs from the late Sixties: a handsome father, on a yacht at Cannes, with his wife, a gypsy. 'A gypsy!' Poppy had exclaimed, her eyes wide with shock. 'And look . . . Look!' She pointed at the eyes, distorted by the pixels of the computer screen, but still unmistakable. Wolf-white, with flecks of silver, shocking in the aristocratic, haughty olive-skinned face. Daisy clutched at her, and all three women felt first the moment of communion, then sadness, and then, lastly, rage.

'We're our mother's daughters,' Daisy muttered, 'that's for sure.'

Rose said nothing. She turned instead to pictures of Roberto Parigi, and there were plenty, because he was still alive. Unlike her parents. And he was waiting for them.

'Loves the high life,' Poppy said, furiously. Parigi was pictured everywhere, consorting with Eurotrash, minor princelings from Monaco and Lichtenstein, attending film premieres, opera house openings. He had never married, but was photographed with an interchangeable selection of young blonde bimbos. He also did not work, but simply hired the best people to do the work for him.

'He's prospered,' Daisy said, grimly.

'Up to now,' Rose answered. 'But maybe he knows we're coming. When Janus started digging, that sent up a red flag, enough to warn them off. He knows you, at least, are looking.'

'Then we should move fast,' Poppy said.

Rose grinned and extracted three first-class tickets from the inside pocket of her jacket. 'We leave first thing tomorrow. Let's go get this jerk before he decides to come and get us.'

They had all made phone calls, cleared a couple of weeks. Nobody wanted to do anything else. They couldn't think of weddings right now, or record companies or books.

They had seen the fire in their mother's eyes. And the face of the man who had put it out.

The sleek black car wound its way through the narrow streets of Rome, over cobbled roads and through passageways of buildings of ochre-coloured stone, covered in clematis and ivy, past little sidewalk trattorias where tourists sat outside, sipping their drinks; and finally pulled to a halt at the top of the Spanish Steps, disturbing a cloud of pigeons.

'This the hotel?' Poppy said, stepping out, her eyes hidden behind huge Sophia Loren-style sunglasses.

Rose nodded, tipping the chauffeur some lire as he removed their Louis Vuitton bags and handed them to a bell-hop. 'The Hassler. You'll like it. It's the best hotel in Rome, so Don Salerni says, and he should know.'

They checked in and were shown to their suite. An opulent living room, with fantastic views towards the great dome of St Peter's, led out to a marble-and-gold bathroom the size of Rose's old apartment in Hell's Kitchen, and there were two gorgeous bedrooms, one with a king-size canopy bed, the other with two twin beds each draped in chiffon. There were cut-crystal vases everywhere, crammed with roses, and a bowl of fruit, as well as a silver ice-bucket on a stand containing a magnum of Cristal.

'Very nice.' Poppy yawned. 'I'll take the single room.'

'As long as I can have the bathroom first,' Daisy said, deftly slipping past Rose and locking herself in.

'Bitch,' Poppy cursed. 'I need a shower.'

'You're going last,' Rose grinned, 'since you dived on the single room. I bet Daisy snores, too.'

Poppy yawned and reached for a peach. She took a bite; it was delicious, golden-fleshed and rich and juicy.

'I could get used to this fast,' she said.

'Don't get too used to it,' Rose said. 'Tomorrow, we go to work.'

*  *  *

The next day dawned bright and clear. The girls showered, and took a room-service breakfast on the

540

terrace overlooking the Spanish Steps; they sipped freshly squeezed juices and nibbled at croissants, and downed thick, bitter black Roman coffee. Except for Poppy.

'I don't care how the Romans do it,' she said. 'I want bagels and cream cheese. I don't work on an empty stomach.'

When the waiter had disappeared, Rose spread out the map of Italy she'd brought with her. 'We can hire a car and drive out there. There's a palazzo, we should see that, and also Don Salerni said the accident happened at a hunting lodge in the hills. I want to go there.'

'Who knows if it's still there? They probably built over it.'

'If it's where our parents died, I want to see it,' said Rose, and Daisy nodded.

★ ★ ★

They found the hunting lodge first, or, rather, the site of it. Rose parked their little rented Fiat outside a café in the village of Spolina, a thriving hamlet with a post office, a shop, and two restaurants, both bustling. It had been a long drive out of the city, and the sisters were happy to sit in the shade and drink cool water, then follow it with a wonderful, light young Chianti served from an earthenware flagon.

'Can we see a menu?' Rose asked.

The old woman serving them shook her head. 'No menu, signorina. Today, Tuesday. Stew. *Lepre*.'

'Rabbit,' Rose told the others. 'That's fine,' she said, and the woman bustled back inside and brought them three bowls of something hot and black. Poppy took a sip gingerly, then her face blossomed into a wreath of smiles. 'That is incredible,' she said. 'That might be the best thing I ever tasted.'

Daisy tore into it and so did Rose. They were both

starving, not having had the benefit of the bagels and cream cheese, and the stew was a revelation: tender, strong-flavoured rabbit, bits of unidentified herbs floating around, slow-cooked beans and lentils.

'I never tasted anything so good, not in any of the fancy restaurants Magnus takes me to,' Daisy said.

Rose didn't reply; they were too busy guzzling the food. The black-clad old woman smiled toothlessly and murmured encouraging things in Italian. She seemed delighted when they all asked for another bowl, and when that was finished, she brought out three glasses full of shaved ice, flavoured with real lemon.

'Forget the Hassler,' Poppy said, 'I'm never leaving, I'm moving in here.'

While Daisy licked every last drop from her spoon, Rose asked the old woman in halting Italian about the hunting lodge. She crossed herself, and bent down to Rose, and whispered in her ear. Rose threw a generous amount of money on the table and stood up.

'She said that road leads up there, into the hills. Nothing was ever built there, because the locals regarded the place as cursed; the gypsy woman died there. She said it was a terrible fire, and the three little girls were killed. People still remember it here.'

'Let's go,' Poppy suggested.

★ ★ ★

They walked for half an hour, sweating in the boiling noonday heat, up the white road covered with pebbles, little more than a dirt track. It was uncomfortable, but none of them complained. They sipped at bottles of water, all three feeling the sense of darkness and foreboding that loomed over them despite the bright sunshine and clear sky.

Finally, the summit was reached.

'My God,' Rose breathed. 'My God.'

There was no mistaking it. Someone had done a pretty good job all those years ago; nothing grew on the ground where the lodge had been. It was black and lifeless, a stark shadow in the midst of the green woods which sprung up all around it.

'I don't know if it's my imagination,' Daisy muttered, 'but I feel — I just feel sick.'

All three stared at the dark earth.

'Nothing natural started this fire,' Poppy said flatly. 'I didn't know what to think, but now I do. I truly believe it. He murdered our parents.'

She walked forward, slowly, tracing the outline of the lodge, foot by foot, encircling it. Poppy's heart was racing, but she felt calm, resolute. Her mind flickered back to her parents' comfortable house in LA, to MTV and bar mitzvah parties, and learning to drive, and her whole wealthy suburban life; and meanwhile, the other parents who had given her life in the first place, half a world away, had died here, been killed here.

Poppy felt something. She felt as though she were two people, that the old world, here, now, was calling her, her parents were calling out to her. She felt that they had loved her. Tears started to roll down her cheeks. She had, after all, survived, and been saved. Her parents must have done that. And now she was back here, to give them something. Justice.

★   ★   ★

Daisy saw Poppy crying; so did Rose. Neither of them said anything. Daisy felt her heart expand in gratitude, gratitude at last to be standing here, to know the truth. She felt distressed, and still nauseous, thinking of a deliberate fire, of her mother burned beyond recognition. But underneath it there was a sense of gratitude. Because at last she knew that she had not been rejected. She had been rescued. Her parents had saved her life;

her parents had loved her. She pictured her wild, glamorous mother, the woman in those faded magazine photographs, picking Daisy up and swinging her around, taking her to the beach, her baby hand in her mother's slim fingers. Normal mother-type things, that she would have done, if anybody had given her a chance.

Daisy said a quiet prayer for her birth-parents. They had not had that chance, but they had made sure she got one. She looked at Rose and Poppy. She now had her sisters, despite the evil man who had tried to take them from her. Her parents' memory would not be blotted out. After all, they were a family, and that was what she would take away from this.

Two sisters. Family. Which he would never be able to destroy.

★  ★  ★

Rose stared at the scorched earth while Poppy walked around it, weeping, and she felt something connect in her heart, like a circle snapping together. She had always thought of herself as Italian, because her father was, and for her, this felt natural; a homecoming. She wondered what her mother would have wanted. Blood revenge? What would her father have wanted? She had it within herself, at this moment, to be eaten alive with a desire for vengeance. But she knew, even examining this desolate spot where Roberto Parigi had tried to steal her father's life, his family, his inheritance, that her parents would not have wanted that. Rose thought that maybe there was a spark of Roberto in her. She was from the same gene pool, after all. But he had been consumed by anger and desire for revenge. His desire, true, was groundless, it had been sheer envy; and Rose's was not. But she was not about to go down the path Roberto had trodden.

She would have her revenge. Revenge that would please her parents, though; no more blood, because she was better than him.

She was Luigi and Mozel's daughter.

Abruptly, she turned away. She didn't want to look at the site any more. 'Let's go to the Palazzo di Parigi, and see if the Principe is at home. We have some business with him.'

Rose and Poppy started to walk back down the hill. Daisy, with tears glittering in her eyes, kissed her fingertips and placed them against the ground.

Saying goodbye.

# 65

'What do we have today?'

Principe Roberto di Parigi turned to his private secretary. It was his usual morning question, delivered in the flawless upper-class accent he took such care to preserve. Roberto never allowed one word of dialect, or the merest hint of a regional tone, to creep into his perfectly modulated Italian.

Signor Grucci, his assistant, was a small, thin man, with an obsequious manner. He was used to taking abuse from his master. He hated Parigi, but didn't really care as he was so well paid. The Prince liked to be surrounded by toadies and hangers-on, and he paid enough to ensure he always got the respect he thought he deserved.

'Tea in the morning at the Eden with Mademoiselle Fleuri,' he intoned, 'then after that, Principe, you have a meeting with Signor Oliverio from the company, and you have lunch at the Palazzo Barberini with the art commission to discuss the winter ball . . . '

Roberto waved a languid hand. It was hot, and he was a lazy man. He enjoyed sitting on the boards of the important social bodies in Rome; this orchestra, that art gallery; he was a big fish in a small pond, respected and courted, and, most importantly, his name and the name of his house was lionised. But today, Roberto only wanted to see the French model, Elaine Fleuri, with whom he might have some anonymous and selfish sex. Girls like her were little better than high-priced hookers, Roberto thought contemptuously; but he made them submit to his private doctor before taking up with them for a month or so, then dismissing them with some pearls or a pair of diamond earrings. He always had a thug call them afterwards to let them know that their mouths should stay as tightly closed as their legs had been wide open. The carrot and the stick.

'I think cancel all but Mlle Fleuri — I shall read today,' he replied, 'and we can pack for the Palazzo this evening.'

'Very good, Principe,' Signor Grucci responded. 'Can I bring you anything further?'

Roberto shook his head. 'You may go.'

'Yes, Principe,' Grucci said, retiring with a little bow.

Weasel, Roberto thought. But he enjoyed the little bows, and the repeated use of his title. He sighed with satisfaction. He would take his coffee on the roof garden, along with his pills, and prepare for the expert attentions of Elaine. And later on, maybe take a nap . . .

It was good to be in Rome, rich, respected, admired, his family honour quite restored. Roberto had avoided children, and now he thought with satisfaction that no young brat of his could come along and disgrace the name of Parigi which he had so carefully restored. He would leave the Palazzo to the state, and donate his shares to the Church, and leave behind the legend of the last of the Parigis, a true nobleman who shunned work, and ordered the world to his will, instead of the other way around.

He felt perfectly happy. He had achieved everything his heart had ever desired.

★ ★ ★

The Palazzo was on the outskirts of the town. They saw it from the car before they parked, the ancient silhouette rising into the clear sky, looking almost alive and organic. It was huge and imposing, and they craned their necks to look before they parked the car a few streets away and got out.

'Well,' Rose said, 'it's a long way from Hell's Kitchen.'

'And the Home Counties,' Daisy added.

Poppy just stared. None of them could believe that something so old and so noble had belonged to their ancestors.

'You know, this is his,' Rose said. 'This is actually his. He was from the older branch.'

'The older branch,' Poppy snorted.

'I know it sounds ridiculous . . . but that's Europe, and titles. And it's our family too,' Rose said defensively.

'If he doesn't have any children, we would inherit it,' Daisy pointed out.

'Only the eldest,' Rose said, 'but who knows who that is?'

'I don't mind sharing,' Poppy said, her eyes drinking in the beauty of it. She was suddenly consumed with curiosity. 'This is our family seat, huh? Is that what they call it?'

'Yup,' Daisy said.

'I want to go inside.' Poppy turned eagerly to the other two. 'I want to see it. Think we can get in?'

★ ★ ★

They walked around the outside of the Palazzo's grounds, staring up at the Florentine-style walls; Renaissance brick, gorgeously restored, with balconies and turrets and a walled garden, and everywhere a coat of arms which bore a rearing gryphon clawing its way across the shield.

'What is that?' Poppy asked.

'His coat of arms,' Rose said, and corrected herself. '*Our* coat of arms.'

'Place looks locked up,' Daisy said.

Rose walked up to the locked double doors of wood in the middle of the wall and pressed the bell there.

There was a moment's silence, then the sound of footfalls across cobbles as somebody walked to the gate.

She turned to her sisters. 'Just let me handle this, OK?'

The door creaked open. 'Yes?'

Rose batted her eyelids. 'We're here to see Principe Roberto Parigi.'

'The Principe is in Rome,' said the man, a thick-necked security guard type, in perfect English.

Rose pouted. 'I was sure he told us to meet him here. He's going to be very disappointed if we're not waiting for him.'

The guard's dark eyes swept up and down Rose's body, and he grinned.

'Special order? Americans? I suppose you should come in.'

Covered by the noise of the creaking gate as it swung open, Daisy hissed, 'He thinks we're hookers!'

Poppy smirked. 'Ssh, Rose has something here. That dirty old bastard.'

They fixed wide smiles on their faces as the gate swung open, and revealed the guard plus another. Both of them carried submachine guns slung over their shoulders. Daisy blanched, and Rose squeezed her hand.

'A *very* special order,' Rose said, waving her hand at her sisters.

The guard and his pudgy companion took in the three of them, then started to cackle.

'Sisters! Triplets! He's a lucky son of a bitch, that one,' the pudgy guy said, in Italian.

Rose smiled at them both. 'I believe we are supposed to wait in the main hall?'

They were showed inside the Palazzo. 'Stay here — I will check with his staff,' the guard said shortly. Rose waited until he had walked up a flight of stairs, then beckoned to the others. 'Let's go.'

549

They walked quickly though the ancient halls, examining the drawing room, the corridors, the dining hall with its huge fireplace, the portraits, and tapestries, all the while their mouths open, drinking it in. Rose thought it was the loveliest building she had ever seen. That it belonged to the man who had murdered her parents made her feel physically ill; her stomach churned, and she had to sit down.

But not for long. She was resting on an antique carved bench when the guard returned, his eyes colder.

'They never heard of this order. Are you sure it was here?'

'Maybe it was the place in Rome.' Rose sighed. 'Oh well, guess we'll drive down there.'

'You know the address?' the guard asked, his eyes narrowed in suspicion.

Rose had done her research. 'Of course, baby. *Appartamento Cinque, Numero Ottanto, Corso Vittorio Emmanuele Due.*' She rattled it off from memory. 'It's the penthouse.'

He grunted. 'Very well.' He lifted the gun and gestured to them to get out. They moved fast, and headed back to the car.

Poppy groaned. 'Another long drive.'

'You don't want to take a break now, do you?' asked Rose.

'Absolutely not. That goon had a submachine gun, means the guy is pretty serious. He'll probably call Roberto. We should get there before he has time to figure out what to do with us.'

Poppy put the car in gear and sped off screeching down the road, burning rubber; it was Italy, so nobody noticed.

'You know we can't prove anything,' Daisy said, as Poppy took a hairpin bend at lightning speed. 'What if he just laughs at us and says we're crazy?'

'We'll work something out,' Poppy said. 'Maybe Rose

550

just makes another call to Salerni.'

Daisy blinked. 'What, like violence? We don't want to use any violence . . . '

'Speak for yourself,' Poppy retorted.

'Hold on.' Rose jumped in to prevent the fight from starting. 'There's no need for that. We don't want to be like he was. Plus, I don't want to go to jail. Or get myself into a vendetta.'

'So we just let him get away with this?' Poppy demanded.

'Absolutely not,' Rose said. 'But there are other ways to go about it.'

'And what, exactly, are you going to do?' asked Poppy, turning on to the *autostrada* and gunning the accelerator.

'Ruin him,' Rose said simply, 'and destroy all he holds dear. And we won't need to shed one drop of blood to do it.'

'This, I gotta hear,' Poppy replied.

# 66

'I hope that was acceptable, Roberto,' the girl murmured. He looked at her, the Pratesi satin sheets pooling around his scrawny torso, a hideous contrast to her healthy young figure with its smooth, peachy skin. He scowled, and she dropped her eyes.

'I mean, Prince Roberto,' she said. I hate him, she thought, but he was good for a couple of grand if she played the game the way he liked it, and she wanted to stay in her rent-free apartment and keep her chauffeur.

'That's better,' he corrected her. He never let sluts like this one call him by his first name. 'And you were just about acceptable. I find you are getting rather dull. Do better next time.'

'Of course, Prince Roberto,' she said, dropping her eyes to hide the fury in them, and gathering up her clothes. She would dress quickly and then leave. The bathroom and comforts of the suite were not for her. Roberto liked to be alone after sex, to gloat, and the women who serviced him usually couldn't wait to leave his presence.

In this, as in everything else, his quirks were tolerated.

After the model had gone, Roberto Parigi lingered and smoked one of his Cuban cigars. He also took a glass of dessert wine and a biscotti. It was a favoured ritual, one his cousin Luigi had once told him *he* employed; the sensuality of love-making followed by the sensuality of a good smoke, and decent wine. For Roberto, the years of cigars had been a faint reminder of his sweetest victory. He had, in a mockery of his cousin and the gypsy witch, withdrawn to his room after his public show of grief at the funeral, and smoked his cousin's cigar, and drunk his wine.

It tasted very sweet.

Today, as he was sipping his *vino santo*, Roberto missed the message that was delivered to his penthouse suite. It was taken from the fax machine by Signor Grucci, who did not look at it — because he dared not interfere with Roberto's plans. Roberto dressed without any knowledge of it, and quitted the hotel. His driver and limo were waiting to take him back to Corso Vittorio Emmanuele.

Roberto had no clue that anything unusual was about to happen. To him it was just another day.

★ ★ ★

Poppy found a parking spot. It wasn't legal, but so what — they'd get fined, like any other Roman motorist. That was hardly important. If they towed the car, she didn't care about that either. The important thing was getting to Roberto's place in time.

Poppy stepped out, and groaned as the blood rushed back into her legs. They were standing outside Number 80 — a sleek, modern-fronted building in the middle of all the ancient houses, Renaissance churches and palaces. She looked at her sisters.

'Ready, girls?'

Daisy reached out, took Poppy's hand and squeezed it, then took Rose by the hand, and squeezed it too.

Rose found her eyes misted over and when she spoke, they were thick with tears.

'You know, it almost doesn't matter what we do with him. Because for the first time, I feel like I've found my sisters.'

Daisy smiled. 'Me too. But it does matter, Rose. Let's go get this bastard, OK?'

★ ★ ★

'But I don't understand,' Signor Grucci said, politely. He looked at the three women, perplexed. They were certainly Parigi's type; incredibly good-look-ing, even if slightly older than he was used to, and exotic. Obviously triplet sisters. Well, it was just like his boss to go one better than the traditional male fantasy of twins. But hadn't Parigi just finished with the French whore?

He hesitated. His caution did battle with his natural cowardice. Parigi did not like other men messing with his whores. If they were insulted, or dismissed, he had to be the one to do it. No member of staff was permitted to be rude to a woman until Roberto was through with her.

'I do. They told us at the Palazzo about the mix-up and that we should come here,' Rose said firmly. She affected a Texan twang. 'The fee's pretty big, Mister, an' he had us flown in real special-like, on the Concorde to London and then down here on the Gulfstream IV. I don't think we should skip it. But if *you* say so, 'cause our house will be invoicing the john . . . '

Grucci blanched. 'Don't refer to the Prince in that manner.'

'Whatever,' Rose said nonchalantly. 'Come on, girls, let's split.'

'No! Wait!' Grucci mopped his brow. Damn whores! What should he do? Flown here on Concorde and the Gulfstream; that was indeed the company plane, they had four of the jets. He ran the numbers in his head. That was some cab ride Roberto had paid for, and presumably he'd want to see the merchandise. Triplets; that *was* unusual. He leered slightly at them, and checked his Rolex.

'The Prince should be back soon,' he said. 'You may wait here in the corridor.'

★ ★ ★

The girls didn't have to wait long, which was probably just as well. Daisy was nervous and jittery; Poppy squeezed her hand, trying to calm her pulse, not wanting her to blow their cover. Poppy herself didn't know quite what she felt. Anger, expectation, curiosity, loathing, nerves . . . everything seethed together in her stomach, but she took that expensive private school education and put it to its first real use. She kept her face a mask, and glanced at Rose. Rose's eyes glittered like a cobra's, and Poppy felt glad *she* wasn't Prince Roberto Parigi.

'He's here.' The oily little man was back. 'You go into the living room, go.' He shepherded them inside. Roberto enjoyed the company of these women, but didn't like to have anyone else interact with them. Like all johns, he felt a mixture of contempt and shame. Roberto was inured to his own immorality, his conscience had been utterly ignored for years; but his sense of his own rank was very much alive.

It didn't do for him to be openly seeing whores, as opposed to gold-diggers; so Signor Grucci was in the habit of pretending he had not noticed them arrive.

'Good morning, Principe,' he murmured, 'I believe the doorman mentioned you had some visitors waiting; I didn't see them.'

That was the normal, socially acceptable code for 'hookers in the area'.

Roberto blinked. He had not called for anyone to be sent over. A mix-up at one of the discreet, exclusive brothels he sometimes used? He had Elaine; he had not placed any calls for a month, at least . . .

Still; he didn't wish to deal with this while Grucci was present.

'That will be all,' he said.

'Yes, of course, Principe,' said Grucci, bowing slightly and withdrawing. Great; he'd get an early lunch hour.

As soon as the penthouse elevator door hissed shut

behind Grucci, Roberto opened the gilt-laden double doors that led to his sitting room, to dismiss the sluts with a flea in their ear; he didn't like mistakes, especially when he'd just been with Elaine, and had no use for more . . .

There were three young women sitting, together, on the end of his couch. He blinked; they were beauties, for sure, with long, flowing black hair, glossy fountains of it; slender, with light olive skin and high, angular cheekbones. Truly stunning, his favourite type of woman. And, he noted, as he stared with surprise, all exactly the same. Identical triplets.

His first thought was approval of whichever madam had sent them round. If he did not want them now, he could use them later. He took a step forward, and all three girls stood up.

'I didn't order you,' he said, in Italian.

Rose answered. She had spent all last night thinking about exactly what she was going to say.

'You are Prince Roberto Parigi,' she said. 'I am Contessa Rose Parigi. This is Contessa Daisy Parigi. This is Contessa Poppy Parigi. You killed our father, Conte Luigi, and our mother, Contessa Mozel. We have found you. We know everything. And we have come for revenge.'

At first Roberto thought he was dreaming, or that the French whore had slipped some hallucinogen into his wine.

And then he saw their eyes.

His heart started to pound and thud, and he felt dizzy. He staggered into a chair.

His skin went ash-grey.

'Did you think we would never ask questions?' Daisy demanded.

A small glint of hope crept into Roberto's eyes. 'I know you did! Yes. I know you asked questions. And you came back with *nothing*. You can prove nothing!'

Rose smiled. 'We are Mozel's daughters. Do you know what happened to us, after you tried to bury us? But yes, of course you know; you had to get that report after you scared off Janus.'

He had, and he had hated it. Rage and fear washed over him.

'You got lucky,' he said.

'No. We earned everything we have,' Rose said. 'And you stole everything you have. We are here to get it back. Every last cent. And to make sure you end your days disgraced, and in jail. Do you know what will happen, Roberto? You have no children, and you won't get any, now. You'll die disgraced, and we'll inherit everything — the company, the palace, the title.'

'The title?' he spluttered. 'Gypsy brats, that witch's brats . . . '

Rose put her face close to his. Though smaller and slighter, she seemed to tower over him.

'Yes,' she hissed. 'Gypsy girls will be the Princesses of the Parigi. I will have a portrait of my mother painted, and hang it in the hall of your — *our* — ancestral home. And maybe trace my other relatives, my mother's relatives . . . seeing as you hate gypsies so much. Think of them, living in the Palazzo, and enjoying all you hold dear . . . '

'What a good idea, Rose,' said Daisy. 'Filling that dusty old pile with gypsy children . . . '

Roberto gasped. His eyes narrowed with pure hatred, and then fear. He clutched at his chest, gasped again, and then slumped to the floor.

The girls looked at him.

Rose was the first to move. She flipped over the scrawny, lanky body, and straddled his chest. She pushed down violently, breathing into his mouth and doing CPR. Daisy was already on the phone to the doorman, downstairs; he could summon an ambulance. While Rose kept pumping, Poppy broke the spell that had come over her and found the bathroom, and the medicine cabinet. She pulled out the bottles until she found aspirin, then violently unscrewed the top, sending pills everywhere. As she raced back into the living room, she saw Roberto was back, breathing raggedly, and spluttering.

'Aspirin?' Rose said.

Poppy nodded.

'Give it here.' Rose took the tablet, crushed it between strong fingers, and shoved it down Roberto's throat. He swallowed, reflexively, gasping for air. The doors were flung open, and the building's doorman burst in.

'He had a heart attack,' Daisy said.

'I call ambulance.'

'You know CPR?' Rose asked. She mimed pushing down on the chest. The doorman nodded, and she looked down at Roberto. His colour was off, but he was breathing steadily, and staring at them with eyes that were little pin-pricks of hatred and terror.

'He'll be OK,' Rose said. 'Let's get out of here.' She spoke to the doorman in her own, halting Italian.

'My name is Contessa Rose Parigi,' she said. 'Look after my cousin Roberto. We have not finished our business with him.'

Then she stared down at Roberto.

'You're not getting off that easily,' she said. 'Get ready, Roberto. Because we'll see you in court. But ruining your reputation? That starts right now. We're going back to our hotel, and we're going to start giving interviews. And I think you'll find the press will be fascinated. Because, after all — '

Daisy smiled, and finished her sister's thought.

'It's *such* a good story,' she said.

# Epilogue

Daisy was right; the press loved the story, and not just in Italy. It ran worldwide. It was juicy: a prince, a gypsy, a scandal, billions of dollars . . . The girls presented their evidence, and handed out pictures of themselves next to pictures of Contessa Mozel.

'Maybe he'll shoot himself,' Poppy said.

Rose shook her head. 'He's a bully, and a coward. He wouldn't have the guts.'

Roberto Parigi was utterly disgraced. He hired lawyers, but nobody gave him a chance. Society in Rome wouldn't receive him, while the three sisters were fêted. The girls milked it for all it was worth; they announced themselves as Contessas Rose, Daisy and Poppy, and they were accepted as such. Roberto's lawyers threatened with libel any magazine that called them by their titles, but nobody was listening. The glossies told him to prove it; the whole world knew that the court case would end with the Prince in jail, and the girls as billionairesses. The story made the Gucci family intrigues look dull. It was broadcast everywhere, and Roberto's girlfriends couldn't wait to come forward with their tales of his poor performance in bed, his cruelty and egomania.

The case was sealed when an old servant of Luigi's came forward. She had a locket containing a lock of Mozel's hair, and a letter from Luigi, signed, to prove it. The three sisters took DNA tests; they matched. Roberto di Parigi, who had buried three small empty coffins, was arrested for murder. But the girls did not comment on that. Justice would take its course, and he was beneath them.

They flew home after six weeks. Being aristocrats and

559

instant celebrities was all very well, but they had to prepare for running the family company, and for other, more important things; such as weddings.

'Do you realise you'll be richer than me?' Magnus Soren asked Daisy.

'Do you care?' she responded.

'Not particularly,' he said. 'And anyway, you won't be for long.'

'You're a competitive, type-A bastard, Magnus,' Daisy smiled.

'That's me,' he admitted, kissing her lightly on the lips.

★  ★  ★

Poppy was the first to get married. She had two weddings, one Jewish, one Episcopalian. The Episcopalian one was small and discreet. The Jewish one had five hundred guests, and lasted almost twenty-four hours. Daisy and Rose were her bridesmaids.

'How long's the honeymoon, Senator?' Daisy teased her new brother-in-law, Henry LeClerc, who was celebrating his recent win in the polls.

'A month, I hope,' Poppy groaned. 'He said it was a surprise, but I need to recover.'

Henry looked sheepish and drew Daisy aside. 'It's a weekend in Paris,' he said. 'We both have to get back to work.'

'Ugh,' Poppy grunted. 'I heard that.'

'You know it's true,' Henry said, a little pleadingly. 'Come on now, sugar.'

'As long as we can stay in the George Cinque,' Poppy said.

'The horse-drawn carriage, the trip to the *Folies Bergère*, walking along the left bank . . . ' Henry said, temptingly.

Poppy's grimace blossomed into a smile. 'Sounds

perfect. I hate time off, anyway.'

'Me too,' Henry said, kissing her on the lips.

★   ★   ★

Rose went back home to her mother, and brought Jacob with her. Mrs Fiorello doted on him. They set the wedding for the Fall, in St Joseph's, in the Bronx. Already thrilled that there were two duplicate Roses out there, that her Rose had found some more family, Mrs Fiorello went into transports of fresh joy over Jacob Rothstein. Her daughter was successful, and rich, and had finally got herself a life outside her job. She had more family than just Daniella, and even more crucially, she was going to be a wife . . .

'Such a nice boy, such a handsome boy,' she said, tweaking Jacob's cheek. 'Now, you won't be trying to move in with my Rose before her wedding day?'

'Mom,' Rose protested, colouring violently.

Jacob smothered a grin. 'No, ma'am. I waited this long for her, what's a little bit more?'

'Such a good boy, oh, he's adorable, Rose,' Mrs Fiorello said, hugging Jacob violently. 'And tell me, your parents, Jacob, are they coming to the wedding? Mr and Mrs Rothstein? When do I get to meet them?'

Rose and Jacob exchanged glances; Jacob winked at her.

'Uh, Mom,' Rose said. 'That's something Jacob and I are gonna deal with later.'

And she smiled.

561

*Other titles published by*
*The House of Ulverscroft:*

## THE ADVENTURES OF FLASH JACKSON

### William Kowalski

Haley Bombauer (a.k.a. Flash Jackon) confronts the summer of her seventeenth year with glorious anticipation. She envisions herself roaming the surrounding hillsides and forests on her beloved horse. But when she falls through the rotted roof of the barn, she is consigned to spending the summer in a thigh-high cast, stuck at home. The year that follows will transform Haley's life, for it gives her peculiar grandmother the chance to pass along some of the mystical arts that only she remembers. As Haley comes to realise who her grandmother is, she is transformed — from tomboy scamp to extraordinary, powerful woman.

# A KEPT WOMAN

## Louise Bagshawe

Diana Foxton is the toast of New York: she is rich, British and beautiful. Recently married to the head of a publishing empire, she fills her days with lunches, interior decorating and clothes shopping. But when she discovers that her husband is having an affair, her glamorous bubble is burst. On her own for the first time, without money or qualifications, she takes the only job she can get. As Diana gets her priorities right, she finds that there are more important things in life than pashminas, manicures and charity balls — like passion, ambition and revenge . . .

# DEADLY EMBRACE

## Jackie Collins

Prequel and sequel to 'Lethal Seduction'. The beautiful, street-smart journalist Madison Castelli is distraught after finding out her father has been hiding secrets from her all her life, and is possibly involved with the mob. She flies from New York to L.A. to spend time with her best friend Natalie De Barge, a gorgeous black radio personality. Within hours, they find themselves in a restaurant hold-up, where they are held in a life or death situation by masked gunmen. Meanwhile, Michael Castelli, Madison's illegally handsome father, is being accused of two murders, and flees to Las Vegas. He is determined to find the people who set him up, and exact his revenge. And what Michael Castelli wants, he gets . . .

# NASHVILLE

## Pat Booth

When illness ends LeAnne Carson's life, her daughter, Savanna, sets out to be what LeAnne always wanted to be: a country music star. She heads for Nashville, Tennessee, where she plays in rundown bars and slips tapes to stars like the legendary Dwight Deacon. When producer Aron Wallis chances on her, he knows that he has found a star in the making — and also someone he could love. But when he plays Savanna's tape to his record company bosses, their reaction is one of horror. For the song is the same as the one that Deacon has now recorded and claimed as his own. And anyone who dares disagree with Deacon will never work in country music again . . .